# Mary Musgrove

## Queen of Savannah

# Mary  Musgrove

## Queen of Savannah

## Frances Patton Statham

Bocage Books

For Tim

# Mary Musgrove

## Queen of Savannah

# Chapter 1

The woman sat on the wide porch of the island plantation house and waited for the miracle of dawn to unfold, a ritual that she had observed for the past week. As the sky lightened, shapes distorted by the gray mists that surrounded the lush barrier isle gradually began to attach themselves to tree, marsh, and grass. Then, from the sea the sun slowly emerged, persuasive, demanding.

In the distance the sudden nickering of a marsh tacky, bastard descendant of a conquistador's horse, was answered by the hungry cry of a sea gull spying its first catch of the day. But the woman barely recorded these early morning sounds, for her attention was directed toward the giant oak tree beyond the cypress wall.

A few minutes later, the swirling mist began its unhurried dispersal upward, revealing the lower limbs of the oak, clothed in Spanish moss. Then the trunk became visible, followed by the taller limbs, until the mist touched the crown of the tree and then was gone. Seeing the vast empty space at the top, the woman relaxed. She had been given another day's reprieve. Despite her lingering illness, Mary Musgrove Matthews Bosomworth, Queen of the Upper and Lower Creeks, sat erect, with the remnants of a strange, exotic beauty still visible upon her face. Hair the color of blackest swamp water, where no light fell, reached to her waist. For a moment her dark blue eyes, inherited from her English fur-trading father, held a regal serenity. But then in an instant they changed, taking on a passionate fierceness as she remembered the anguish and pain her father's people had caused.

This was her island, part of her Indian heritage that General Oglethorpe had promised to return to her on the fourth day of the Windy Moon. But like all men, he had forgotten his promise once he had achieved his purpose.

For twenty years Ossabaw, Sapelo, and the land around Pipemaker's Creek had been kept from her. And after the fighting and intrigue were over, only one island—St. Catherines— had been returned by the English. The years of denial now made the familiar smells and sounds all the sweeter—as much a part of her heritage as the land itself. Yet, as the sixty-five-year-old woman sat under the canopy of the silverlace vine and greeted the dawn, she knew that, too soon, she would be forced to leave everything behind.

She lifted her head in appreciation as the salt of the marsh mingled with the fresh aroma of acorn coffee. Mercifully, the sudden zephyr fluttering the palmetto fronds drowned out the kitchen whisperings between her third husband, Thomas, and her young bondservant, Sarah.

"Treats me like an annoyin' fly, she does; *her* with her uppity ways."

Thomas frowned as he watched the buxom young woman place the white porcelain pot of steaming coffee onto the serving tray.

"Don't complain, Sarah. Especially now."

Sarah's petulant voice softened. "No. The mistress can't last much longer, can she? I noticed how weak she was this mornin' when I helped her to her porch chair." Sarah straightened her linen lace-trimmed cap and turned to face the middle-aged man. "Ye haven't changed your mind from last night, have ye?"

The Reverend Bosomworth was not pleased at being reminded of his indiscretion. He deliberately pretended to misunderstand her. "No. As soon as I'm your legal owner, I plan to forgive your bond."

Sarah's coquettish smile turned into a pout. "I was talkin' about your other promise. To make me your wife."

"Everything in its order, Sarah. For appearance sake, I'll have to observe a proper period of mourning."

"And for appearance sake, Master Thomas, I hope ye won't mourn unduly long. I'm late for my time this month."

"Keep your voice down. I don't want anyone to overhear us. Now go and serve your mistress her morning coffee before it gets cold."

She did as she was told, leaving an alarmed Thomas behind. He reached for his own cup of coffee. Although his face was bland, the rattle of the cup against the saucer gave away his nervousness at Sarah's news. But then he took a deep breath, swallowed the hot coffee, and smiled. Even if Sarah were already expecting his child, it didn't matter. Mary would be dead long before Sarah began to show her impending motherhood.

Movements in the compound surrounding the plantation house indicated that the servants were already at work on the land. Hearing the commotion, Thomas straightened his shoulders and walked from the kitchen. He also began a praise to the morning. But it was not for the beauty of the land. His ambitions in leaving England were finally coming to fruition. Soon now he would be a gentleman of means—owner not only of St. Catherines Island, but of Mary's entire fortune.

As Sarah spanned the short distance between the summer kitchen and the long covered porch of the main house, she walked with a jaunty air. From the moment she'd been brought to this island paradise, she had pretended that she was the mistress issuing orders rather than the servant receiving them. Of course, she'd had to be careful, especially around the mistress, who always acted as if she could see straight through her with her sharp, piercing eyes.

With a shift of the silver tray to her other hip, Sarah paused, changed her expression to one of meekness, and then walked up the side steps to the long wooden porch.

When she had set the tray on the table in front of Mary and poured the coffee into the fragile porcelain cup, Sarah turned. "Will there be anything else, mistress?"

"Yes." From around her neck, Mary slowly removed a leather thong with a small key attached to it. "At the bottom of the linen press in my bedroom, there's a black wolf pelt. Bring it to me."

"What would ye be wantin' with that molty old thing?"

As soon as the words were out, Sarah realized she'd made a mistake. She wasn't supposed to know the contents of the locked linen press. She clapped her hand over her mouth, but it was too late. Once again, Mary's all-seeing eyes caused her to shiver.

"Just do as I ask."

"Yes, ma'am." Quickly the servant took the key and fled from the porch to do her mistress's bidding.

While Mary waited for Sarah to complete her errand, her thoughts returned to the oak tree. For the past three twilights, the vulture had come to roost in the top, and for the past three mornings, the bird had flown away. But it had been sent as a reminder. She could no longer put off the exhausting journey into the past, to make her final peace with the Great Spirit of her Indian ancestors and the God of the white man.

"Here's the fur, mistress. And your key."

With a nod of her head, Mary dismissed the servant. Wrapping the ancient black wolf pelt around her, she closed her eyes and began to stroke the furrows of fur, forcing from the hide latent memories that had been stored with it.

St. Catherines Island, the sea, and the marsh vanished. Caught up in a vortex of images, Mary was propelled backward to Coweta Town on the Chattahoochee River. And once again she was a small ten-year-old child—Princess Coosaponakeesa—waiting for the arrival of her fur-trader father, Ian....

# Chapter 2

"Come, Little Blue-eyed One. Your father's boat has been spotted. You must be at the landing to meet him."

At the sound of the old woman's voice, Princess Coosaponakeesa stopped her rocking back and forth in rhythm to the wind stirring through the trees.

"I have not finished saying good-bye to my mother," the young girl replied. "Go now, Sanawa. Leave me alone for a while longer."

The old woman sighed. "As you wish. I will wait at the end of the path for you."

Coosaponakeesa returned her attention to the burial mound before her and began to rock back and forth again. "Mother, did you hear Sanawa's words? My father is coming, just as you said he would.

"I know you told me not to be afraid to go with him, but I am. I would much rather stay here with Sanawa. But I gave you my promise." She brushed away the beginnings of a tear and continued. "You will always live in my heart, my mother. And I will look for you in the clouds, no matter where he takes me."

She reached into the small leather pouch at her side, took out four kernels of corn, and carefully placed them, one by one, in a pattern on the ground. In a singsong voice she intoned the litany taught her by her mother. "From the four corners of the earth, I will remember you...north, from whence all good things come; east, where the sun begins its daily journey; west, from whence all darkness of heart rests, and south, where memories are born and birds soar."

Coosaponakeesa stood and held up her hands toward the sky. "O Great Spirit, keep my princess mother on eagle's wings, with the softness of chanting winds for her gentle sleep."

She turned her back to the burial mound and, with certain steps, she walked to the edge of the grove where Sanawa waited.

By the time the two reached the riverbank of the Chattahoochee, Hollata, the young mico of the tribe, had already assembled his welcoming braves for the fur trader's arrival. Blood brother to them by marrying their princess, Ian had served as advisor, banker, and friend. But now the princess was dead and his association with them was coming to an end. There only remained the smoking of pipes in the council chamber, the exchange of gifts, and the final good-byes.

When the first boat, laden with gifts, came into sight, Coosaponakeesa hung back, content to watch from a distance. A ripple of excitement swept through the crowd as eager hands reached out to bring the boat to the landing. Then, a second one appeared, and then a third. But Coosaponakeesa still scanned the brilliant waters, swollen from the recent rains, to catch a first glimpse of the man she had not seen in so many moons.

Finally, the boat carrying Ian came into view. "Go, my child, and greet your father," Sanawa whispered, touching the girl on her shoulder, as if to prompt her. But Coosaponakeesa needed no prompting. She left Sanawa behind and walked proudly, to take her rightful place with the mico. And standing beside him, she waited as Ian clambered onto the landing.

His beard was grayer than she remembered, and the aging of many suns lay heavily upon his face. But his large frame was the same, and the same hearty voice boomed his greeting. "Peace, my brothers," he said, nodding first to Hollata and then to the others.

"Peace," the echo returned, repeated up and down the landing.

Coosaponakeesa stood patiently, waiting for Ian to notice her. All through her mother's illness, she had longed for his return and many nights had dreamed of being swept up into his comforting arms in a familiar hug. But at last, when his eyes sought hers, she spoke with the formality that all important occasions required. "Welcome, my father," she said.

He held out his arms for her. But instead of rushing toward him, she took a step backward, as if suddenly wary of him. Her startled manner was identical to the young fallow deer he had once saved and then released back to the wild. Thinking he would have to regain her confidence slowly, Ian lowered his arms and stood motionless, watching, lest she, too, would vanish.

Finally, he spoke. "You have grown taller, Coosa."

Recovering her composure, she said, "I am now ten years old by your calendar."

He smiled. "And past time for you to learn the white man's ways. Do you have your things packed?"

She nodded. "Sanawa has seen to that."

"Then be ready to leave within the hour."

His attention returned to the gift-laden boats. "Red Horse," he called to one of the Indians who had traveled with him. "Take the goods up to the council house so they can be distributed to the people."

Watching until the blankets and utensils had been removed from the boats, Ian left the landing with Hollata.

Coosaponakeesa waited until everyone had disappeared along the path to the council house. Standing alone by the water's edge, she became aware of a mockingbird singing in the nearby treetop, the waters softly lapping against the bank, and then in the distance she heard the excited voices of her people as they selected their gifts brought by her father. At that moment, Coosaponakeesa realized that she would not be hearing the sounds of Coweta Town again for a long time. She would be missing the festival of *puskita* as well, when the corn became ripe and new fires were kindled in celebration of the new year.

With a sense of imminent loss, she returned to the copse where Sanawa still sat.

"Sanawa, you should be with the others to pick out your new blanket," she admonished. "Soon all the pretty ones will be gone."

"I was waiting for you."

Coosaponakeesa looked at the old woman who had been her nurse from the moment she was born. In a voice filled with sadness, she said, "Oh, Sanawa, I'm going to miss you. I wish you could go upriver with us."

"That is not to be, Little One." Sanawa reached down and picked up two small sticks that lay near her. "You and I are like these two sticks," she said, crossing them and laying them back on the ground. "Our lives have touched for a time, because you needed me. But now our paths are pointed in different directions, ever farther apart. Go now, and get your things."

"Aren't you coming to help me?"

"No, Little Blue-Eyed One. Every new journey of the soul must be taken alone, no matter how many people are around you. This truth is my last gift to you. Carry it in your heart always.

"Now tell me good-bye, Coosaponakeesa, Princess of the Upper and Lower Creeks." Sanawa stood and inclined her head for final salutation.

The girl pressed her forehead against the old woman's. With the touch of the dry, withered skin, Coosaponakeesa felt a quickening of heart, as if the old woman had given her part of her own soul.

"Good-bye, Sanawa. May the Great Spirit keep you safe."

"And may the Earth Mother shield you from evil."

As Coosaponakeesa turned her back and made her way to the wooden dwelling where she and her princess mother had resided, she knew that Sanawa would not be at the landing to see her go.

Inside the room, Coosaponakeesa changed into her traveling clothes. Carefully, she rebraided her long black hair into two plaits, wrapping the leather thongs around each end. And with the prepared berry dye and wet clay, she daubed the design upon her face that proclaimed her royal lineage. Checking under her deerskin shirt for the amulet Medicine Woman had given her to ward off danger, she folded the wolf pelt from her floor bed, laced it to her other bundle and left the dwelling. By the time she approached the landing for the second time, Ian was waiting.

Only one of the three Indians was returning with them—Red Horse, the Muskogean, whose high forehead proclaimed his people's custom of binding the heads of their infant sons. He was already in the first boat filled with summer fur pelts. And even though his back was to her, Coosaponakeesa felt his power. It was his fierce stare at her earlier from the landing that had caused her to step back from her father, as if some evil presence were attempting to envelop her.

She would have to be wary of Red Horse, as her mother had warned. "He has much power, Little One. Show him that you are not afraid." Although her mother had never voiced it, she knew that Princess Rising Fawn had blamed Red Horse for her father's long separation from them. For he was the one who had persuaded Ian to build another trading post far from Coweta Town.

"You are ready now?"

"Yes, my father."

Ian hoisted her bundle into the second canoe. And immediately they began their trek upstream.

While the two boats sliced through the waters, Coosaponakeesa kept her silence. This was the time of day when poachers, intent on removing the wild game from Indian traps, might be roaming in the woods, or a war party of hostile braves returning home might be lying in wait for the unwary traveler.

With the hypnotic movement of oars breaking the waters, Coosaponakeesa became sleepy. The dappled sunlight, filtering in and out of the canebrakes, imprinted their opaque images upon her closed eyelids in fleeting tints of light and dark, while her skin responded to the warmth of the sun and then the sudden coolness brought by shade. Lulled into a near-dream state, she was able to summon up patterns of bright, exotic hues, forming a wheel of moving colors. But then the colors disappeared as she drifted into a deeper sleep.

Ian glanced back occasionally. He smiled as he saw the peaceful look on his daughter's face. It would be good to have her living with him, even though Red Horse had predicted that she would be nothing but trouble and that he would be wise to forget her.

Time passed, measured in stretches of regularly notched trees along the bank, in rocks and shoals avoided, and in the tiredness of Ian's muscles as he kept to a steady pace against the mild river current.

The raucous cry of a crow flying overhead finally caused Coosaponakeesa to stir. But it was the sudden vision of the Muskogean staring at her with catamount eyes that caused her to sit up, awake and alert.

Coosaponakeesa searched the river ahead for some sign of the other boat. But it was not in sight. Slowly she crawled toward Ian and held out her hand to touch his arm.

"What is it, Coosa? Have you finally awakened from your sleep?"

"Where is Red Horse?" she whispered.

"We passed him a half hour ago. He's now behind us."

"There's someone else on the river, too," she insisted. "Someone up to no good."

Ian frowned. Had he sired a timid child, afraid of her own shadow? That would not stand her in good stead where they were going. He looked into her eyes, so like his own. What he saw was not fear, but a primitive recognition of danger. And it was this that prompted him to quicken his pace, until he reached the shelter of a swampy peninsula jutting from the tangled green of a canebrake.

He brought the boat to rest, hidden from view of anyone traveling north, and there he sat in the curve of the red clay bank, with his loaded musket at his side. It was just as well that he had stopped for a while. This would give Red Horse time to catch up with them. For it would be much better to travel together now that it was beginning to grow dark.

Ian reached into his satchel and pulled out two elongated strips of tough, dried venison. He handed one to his daughter. She nodded in response but made no move to eat it, although her stomach rumbled with hunger. Her attention remained on the bend in the river.

The cry of the crow grew louder, yet no bird flew overhead. Five minutes elapsed, then ten.

Ian, waiting for the servant, began to frown. Red Horse should have appeared by now. Just as he was becoming concerned that something actually might be wrong, he saw two resting egrets flap their wings and move swiftly from their perch. That was a certain sign that there was human activity on the river. Red Horse's approach, more than likely. Yet, because of his daughter, Ian remained hidden, waiting until he was absolutely certain.

When the three canoes came into view, Ian was glad that he had waited. For it was not Red Horse, after all, but a scalping party of Shawnees, wielding their paddles in swift, rhythmic haste. It had been a long time since he had seen the Ohio Shawnees this far south.

An understanding Coosaponakeesa glanced at Ian, who now held his musket in his hands. Fearing that the strong scent of cured meat might attract the Shawnees' attention, she regretfully dropped her strip of dried venison into the water. Crouching low like an animal, she stilled her breathing until the birch-bark canoes had passed perilously near their hiding place.

# Chapter 3

Red Horse approached the first bend in the river with a curiously elated feeling. The Shawnees should have done their work by now, and it was time to catch up with the fur trader before he became overly suspicious at Red Horse's disappearance.

With his eyes on the treacherous surface of the river, Red Horse paddled swiftly. He rounded his canoe past the bend and then took the boat close to the river's edge to avoid the jagged rocks directly ahead.

He knew that Ian would be sad for a while, but then, with Red Horse's niece offered to him as a new wife, he would soon forget the child.

The Indian's sense of elation gradually diminished as he realized that he had heard no recent shot of musket, no sound traveling on the water to indicate that a fight had occurred. Of course, the arrows of the Shawnees would make no sound except for a slight whistle through the air as they headed for their prey. But Ian was not one to lose something without exacting revenge—unless he had been wounded in the surprise attack. But the Shawnees had promised Red Horse that Ian would not be hurt.

Perhaps Ian had moved faster than usual and the scalping party had not yet caught up with the boat. Yes, that might be the reason for the silence. He must be patient for yet a little while longer, until the deed had been accomplished.

Once past the larger rocks, Red Horse placed his paddle in the boat and began to drift haphazardly while listening for hostile sounds along the river. But as twilight struck the wilderness land the usual evening chorus of wild animals—panthers and wolves, bears and wildcats inhabiting the nearby swamps and thickets—blotted out the subtler sounds on the river.

"Look, my father. Is that not your other canoe?" Coosaponakeesa inquired.

Ian frowned. "It looks like it."

"But where is Red Horse? I don't see him."

"There's something wrong here. Get out of sight, Coosa," Ian commanded.

Swiftly, with his musket across his lap, Ian approached the other boat. As Red Horse's head suddenly reared from the pile of pelts, Ian raised his gun. But then, recognizing his servant, he immediately lowered it.

When Ian spoke, his voice was not one of a man overcome with grief. "Is there anything wrong, Red Horse?"

The servant searched for some sign of Coosaponakeesa. When he saw her, he realized his plan had gone awry. With the same stoical expression that signaled both joy and sorrow, he merely shrugged and said, "Furs shift. I stop to put them right."

"Then, let's hurry. The river is no safe place for Coosa to be this night. Shawnees are abroad, seeking mischief."

Once again, Coosaponakeesa felt an evil presence emanating from Red Horse. And once again, she put her hand on the amulet. Under her breath she murmured the power words taught her by Medicine Woman.

Red Horse shivered as he suddenly felt a sharp pain near his heart—like the jab of an arrow. He peered toward the child in time to see her removing her hand from her breast. So she had brought her medicine with her. For a fraction of a moment his undisguised hate overcame him. But then he grew calm again and took up his paddle. Her amulet might have spoiled his plans for her this time and saved her from the Shawnees, but she would soon be no match for Red Horse. It would be such an easy thing to steal the leather pouch when she was asleep. Then the princess would be powerless in an alien territory, far from the women of her clan.

A worried Coosaponakeesa was determined to stay awake. In the dark she watched, up and down the river, her eyes taking in the distant glow that told of campfires, while the wild, fierce symphony of the forest echoed the restlessness of her heart and spoke to her of danger and death. Never had she felt more alone than now. She wrapped the wolf pelt around her and ached for the comfort of Sanawa's soft voice lulling her toward dreamtime, toward safety. Yet, with each mile traveled, she already felt the thread of her familiar life unraveling.

Had she, herself, not watched and learned as the furry hide of the buffalo, the Bull of God, had been scraped and then woven into new cloth? Would she feel the same way as her Indian self was scraped from her and she was fashioned into an English daughter?

For many days they traveled. The river, portage, and Indian traces all indicated that they were getting farther and farther from Coweta Town. Finally, one evening as it began to grow dark upon the river, Ian turned to his daughter. "Are you awake, Coosa?"

"Yes, my father."

"Do you see the flicker of the lantern ahead?"

"Yes. Is that your trading post?"

"Not yet. My servant Muckross is waiting for us with the packhorse and ox cart. We will leave the river and travel overland."

"I am glad that the Great Spirit has allowed us to reach this far in safety."

"I, too, am grateful to the Great Spirit," Ian agreed.

The two boats approached the landing, and soon Coosaponakeesa was out of the boat, with her bundle at her feet.

"Let me take that for ye," a young man said. But he was not speaking to Coosaponakeesa. He walked past her as if she did not exist and stopped before her father.

"I'd rather you help Red Horse with the pelts, Muckross," Ian replied. "My daughter and I can manage the other goods."

"Yes, sire. As ye wish."

Within a few minutes the ox cart was loaded and the four were ready to leave the landing. "Here, Coosa," Ian said. "You're light as a feather, and I doubt Old Dolly can tell the difference between you and another pelt or two." Ian hoisted his daughter and dropped a surprised Coosaponakeesa into the cart atop the furs.

The near-constant vigil she had maintained on the journey had exacted its toll. Now, as the wheels of the cart rolled along the rutted trail, Coosaponakee's eyelids closed. She fell asleep and, as they traveled through the wilderness, she remained asleep, unaware when they eventually reached the steps of the trading post itself.

At that time of night, when the moon was beginning to fade toward the horizon, little activity surrounded the thriving compound that Ian had built two years previously. Crafted from native wood that had already mellowed into a soft gray, the outpost consisted of the store, an arsenal for guns, and the attached living quarters with its smoke chimney. In the pens beyond were his hogs, his cows and sheep. And closer to the house stood the melon and vegetable patches and peach trees watched over by his Indian servants and Muckross, his white indentured servant. But Red Horse was the one who helped him most, as a liaison with the Indians who brought their furs to Ian to trade for other goods.

As Ian stared down at the sleeping child he felt a tinge of regret for waiting too long to fetch her mother, once he had left Coweta Town. Most traders working for the Charleston fur-trading houses never considered a wilderness wife as anything but a business convenience. And once they had moved on to trade with a new tribe, the majority sought a new wife from that tribe. But Ian had truly loved Princess Rising Fawn and the child of that union. That was why he was determined to have Coosaponakeesa with him, to teach her his ways and make her a comfort to him in his old age.

Ian smiled at the proud, paint-smudged face, at the dark hair glistening with bear grease. At that moment, Ian could see little English heritage in his daughter. But all that would change once she was dressed in proper clothes and was taught to speak English in the same manner as the other young girls under Parson Beckett's tuition.

"I carry her inside for you," Red Horse offered. "Journey make you very tired."

"No, Red Horse. I'll do that myself. See to the storing of the furs in the back room of the store."

Ian hoisted Coosaponakeesa's belongings over his shoulder and gently lifted her from the cart. He unlatched the stile gate leading to the living quarters and then walked into his house.

Ian had no need to light a candle. In the waning moonlight, he could still make out the rough-hewn shapes of the furniture in the main room. But even in darkest pitch, he could still find his way across every inch of flooring. Ian walked past the chimneypiece, the rocking chair beside it, and stepped into the small room beyond.

It was this extra bedroom that he had furnished for his daughter, with the strong hemp-rope bed in the corner, the indigo-blue calico curtains at the single mica-paned window, and the two-tiered table holding the wash basin and chamber pot.

The room had an added comfort, too. For the warmth from the brick chimney on the other side helped to make it more comfortable on cold, rainy days. Of course, it was summertime now and no fires burned. But by wintertime, Coosaponakeesa would appreciate his well-thought-out plan.

She made a slight moaning sound as he placed her on the bed. Fearing that she might awaken during the night in a foreign place, with foreign smells, Ian took the familiar wolf pelt and placed it beside her, treating her as he would a puppy recently taken from its mother.

He debated about washing the paint from her face. But in the end, he decided to leave the chore until morning. "Welcome to your new home," he said softly. Ian leaned over, kissed the child, and then walked out, to seek the comfort of his own bed for the rest of the night.

Morning came far too soon for Ian. The odor of bear bacon wafted through the house and told him that Muckross was already preparing breakfast. For a moment he lay in bed and carefully summoned his muscles to obey him. Gingerly he sat up, balancing himself on the edge of the rope bed. Then he remembered Coosaponakeesa.

If she were still asleep, he would not waken her this early for breakfast. She could get something to eat later on. Once Ian had dashed cold water on his face, smoothed down his beard, and put on his shirt and breeches, he walked to the open door of Coosa's bedroom. At the sight of the empty bed, he grew worried. Had she gotten up so soon? Ian walked into the room and only then did he see his daughter. She was on the floor next to the bed, with her small thin body wrapped in the black wolf pelt. He smiled and tiptoed out of the room.

He sat down at the oak trestle table and began to drink the hot dark liquid that Muckross had poured into his mug. For Coosa's sake, he was glad he had a milch cow. Young girls needed fresh milk for their growing bones.

Ian was still enjoying his corn cakes dipped into molasses, along with the fried bear bacon, when Red Horse appeared at the door.

"Many braves come to trade," he announced, and then disappeared.

Quickly Ian washed down the last of his breakfast and hurried toward the store to start the business of the day.

Weights and measures, pots and pelts, hunting knives and venison hams now occupied his mind as he bargained for goods with the Indians, being careful not to shortchange them, as so many other fur traders were in the habit of doing.

With his mind so occupied, he completely forgot about Coosaponakeesa, asleep in the attached house.

The sun shone through the mica window, making colorful prisms in the air. As Coosaponakeesa opened her eyes, she was startled at the unfamiliar room. Then she remembered. This was her father's house. She was no longer in Coweta Town.

As she sat up she stared at the rope bed that had been so uncomfortable during the night, forcing her to find another sleeping place that did not sway like a tree bough in a storm. Standing up, she pressed both hands down on the bed. Immediately it moved under the pressure. She shook her head at its flimsy construction, so unlike her hard floor pallet.

Then she walked to the window and fingered the blue cloth hanging at the window. What a pretty petticoat it would make.

The two-tiered table beneath the window was a marvel, with its bowl and pitcher, already filled with water. Realizing she was extremely thirsty, she lifted the spout to her mouth, drank, and then returned the pitcher to its proper place.

On the lower tier of the table sat a large lidded pot decorated with flowers. She smiled as she reached out and touched it. Was it a cooking pot? It seemed almost too beautiful to be put into the ashes. As she lifted the lid to peer inside, the wooden frame holding the pot moved slightly. Delighted, she pulled it out on its hinge and pushed it back several times, until she lost interest.

Standing up, Coosaponakeesa again gazed out the window, until she noticed a group of bushes in the distance. She left the house to attend to her morning ablutions. A short time later, she returned to the empty house.

By now her stomach told her that it was past time to find something to eat. So she took her animal trap and small hunting knife and headed toward the wilderness to find her breakfast.

From the open door of the store room, Red Horse saw the young girl disappear from the compound. He hurriedly stacked the last of the recently traded furs onto their tall stilt racks. Closing the door, he, too, left the trading post.

# Chapter 4

Along the path to the river, small animal tracks were imprinted on the soft earth. The patterns were no different from those near Coosaponakeesa's own Indian village, where wild creatures regularly came down to water.

She stopped a few feet off the path and placed her animal trap into open position. From the nearby tangled mass of vines, she gathered a handful of fox grapes that had grown purple in the ripening sun. But she ate the grapes herself to stave off her own hunger, then gathered another handful to place into the trap, along with some succulent greens.

Instead of hiding and waiting quietly, Coosaponakeesa walked deeper into the woods in search of an old decayed hickory tree. Once she found one that had been shattered by lightning, she began to dig around its dead roots for a suckahoe truffle, or Indian potato, from which her people made bread.

Unaware that her actions were being closely monitored by Red Horse, she took her time, digging beneath the surface of dirt until she at last found the delicacy she'd sought. She took her knife, cut a large suckahoe from its anchorage, and wrapped it in the red triangle of cloth. She then covered up the remaining truffles with dirt, for use at another time.

A noise behind her caused her to look up. But seeing nothing but a small wampum snake slithering its way through the grass, she returned her attention to the business of breakfast.

Clearing a small space of vegetation on the forest floor, she began to gather small rocks with which to make a circle. And when that was done, Coosaponakeesa placed dry leaves and broken twigs inside the circle.

A young brown rabbit scampering through the woods stopped to sniff the cane trap. Overhead, the birds sang at water's edge, a deer drank, while a pike fish surfaced to catch a water bug. And then the snap of the animal trap spoke of success and tragedy in a primeval world of the hunter and the hunted.

"To thy spirit, little rabbit, I offer apology," Coosaponakeesa intoned as she removed the animal from the trap. And with deft action, she skinned the rabbit and made it ready for her roasting stick.

Later, when she had cooked and eaten the meat, Coosaponakeesa sat by the fire. She licked her fingers and then wiped them dry on the grass. "I feel better now," she said aloud to no one in particular, and then carefully covered the ashes with dirt.

Content to sit for a while in the woods that she had now claimed as her own—at least that small part near the dead hickory stump, with her own fire circle of rocks—Coosaponakeesa lay down and stared up at the sky. But her contentment was soon replaced with sadness.

If she only had someone to talk to—like Sanawa. Or to play games with. The children of her village were more than likely playing ball, or singing songs, or going for a swim at that very moment in the shallow river cove that resembled the one before her.

She gazed longingly toward the water. Sanawa's words echoed in her brain. "You must not go into the water alone, Little Blue-Eyed One."

"But Sanawa," she said aloud, as if the old woman were seated beside her. "There is no one here to swim in the river with me. And I do need a bath." She quickly made up her mind, for the water looked so inviting. "I'll go in for just a little while," she said. "But I promise to be careful, Sanawa. I'll stay close to the bank. You'll see."

With Sanawa far away in Coweta Town and in no position to scold her for disobeying, Coosaponakeesa removed her clothes and draped them on a nearby bush. Without thought, she removed the amulet from around her neck and also hung it on the bush next to her soft moccasins.

She approached the water gingerly, for with the recent rain she was unable to tell its depth. Holding on to the limb of a bush, she slid down the bank into the water.

At that point the water was still shallow and she smiled as the soft mud at the bottom squished between her toes. She walked along the river bottom for a few feet until the water came up to her shoulders. And with her eyes closed, she disappeared underwater, and only the telltale trace of her long black hair floating on the surface indicated that the ripples in the water had not been made by otter or fish.

Like all Indian children born near the water, Coosaponakeesa had learned to swim at an early age. She came to the surface, took a deep breath, and then went back under.

From his vantage point behind the pine tree, Red Horse watched the child. She was like a playful duckling, splashing and diving, and every bit as vulnerable as any other water creature to the larger animals attracted to the cove by the noise.

Red Horse left the safety of the tree and quietly crouched behind a stand of reedy cane. He watched and waited, and each time Coosaponakeesa's back was to the bank, he shortened the distance until he was within arm's reach of her belongings.

To take only the amulet would be a dead giveaway. So he grabbed up her shirt, her deerskin leggings, and her moccasins as well.

Overhead, a crow began to caw, but Coosaponakeesa merely recorded its flight as she gazed up at the sky. Content to float on her back for yet a little while longer, the young girl felt no sense of danger. But as a cloud passed over the sun she became aware of a sudden coldness. Shivering, she decided that she had been in the water long enough.

Rising naked from the shallows, Coosaponakeesa walked toward the bush where she had left her clothes. At first, when she did not see them, she decided that she must have floated downriver with the current. And so she began to walk in an easterly direction, all the time searching each protruding bush for some sign of her clothes. But they were gone.

As she returned toward the place where she'd climbed from the river she spotted the red triangle of cloth in which she'd wrapped the suckahoe. It lay on the ground next to her cane trap. Then she saw a broken twig on the bush above, indicating where her clothes had once hung. Coosaponakeesa's chagrin changed to an overwhelming anger when she realized that someone had deliberately stolen her clothes. But even worse, that person had also taken her amulet.

"Oh, Sanawa," she cried out. "Who could have done such a terrible thing?"

She sat down on the bank and began to rock back and forth in sorrow. Although it would take time, she could get another deerskin to tan and make into new clothes. But the medicine pouch was old, her legacy from the Wind clan. And in stealing that, someone had stolen a part of herself.

Standing up and gazing toward the gathering clouds, Coosaponakeesa made a vow that somehow she would find the thief and recover the amulet.

She twisted the water from her long, dark hair and, taking the red triangle of cloth, she tied it around her waist. With the animal trap in her hand, she retraced her steps through the woods to the trading post.

In Coweta Town, Coosaponakeesa's near nakedness would have gone unmarked, since she was still a child. But as she approached the side of the trading post porch, she heard a hoot of laughter. When she looked up, several of the white men and boys were pointing at her. Draped over the weathered railing was Red Horse, making no attempt to hide the sinister amusement on his features.

"What happened to clothes, river nymph?" Red Horse called out. "Did turtle who lives in underworld get them?"

"Maybe she lost more than her clothes," one of the white trappers suggested.

The mocking, humiliating words became a chorus of laughter trailing behind her as Coosaponakeesa dropped her animal trap and fled toward the living quarters that she shared with her father. At the stile gate she stumbled, but succeeded in righting herself and reaching the house before the triangle of cloth fell to the floor.

A few minutes later, Ian returned to his living quarters. "Coosa," he called. "Where are you?"

At first she did not answer. Even though she didn't understand some of the words hurled at her, she realized that she had somehow caused her father to lose face.

"Coosa," he called again. "Are you in your room?"

She drew the wolf pelt tighter around her thin body. "Yes, my father," she answered.

He stood in the doorway and, seeing her huddled into such a small, miserable ball, with her hair hanging in her face, he immediately felt sympathy for her.

"Where have you been?"

"I went for swim, my father."

"Alone? In the river?"

"Yes."

"That was a mistake, Coosa. Promise me that you will never go swimming by yourself again. It is not as safe around here as it is in Coweta Town."

Coosaponakeesa hesitated. She finally nodded.

"Now get dressed and come to the table."

When she made no move to get up, Ian came closer. "All right, Coosa, You can tell me. What's wrong?"

"I have no clothes to put on."

"What happened to them?"

"I lost them."

"Did you take them off before you went in swimming?"

She nodded.

"And you couldn't find them when you came out?"

Coosaponakeesa shook her head.

"Then someone must have stolen them when you weren't looking."

"I lost them," Coosaponakeesa stubbornly repeated.

At the unhappiness etched on her face, Ian did not press further. Instead, he said, "If that's the case, then I will get Mistress O'Reilly from the village to sew you some dresses. And you can even select the calico material. But in the meantime, I might have something on the store shelf for you to wear."

"Thank you, my father."

Later, Coosaponakeesa sat at the trestle table with Ian. A boy's homespun shirt and breeches tied at the waist with a rope clothed her. She sat silently and watched Ian demolish the food prepared by Muckross.

All at once Ian became aware that Coosaponakeesa had only drunk her milk. Her plate of food remained untouched.

"Eat up, Coosa. You must be starving."

"I have already eaten," she replied.

Ian smiled. "Surely a few berries found in the woods are not sufficient for you."

"I roasted a wild rabbit."

A surprised Ian said, "I thought only Creek boys went hunting."

"I know how to hunt as well as any boy."

"Yes. And that is a good thing to know, especially when there's nothing to eat. But food will always be provided for you here. There's no necessity for you to hunt again.

"There are so many other ways for you to spend your time, Coosa." He took a bite of venison ham and continued, "So many new things for you to learn before fall comes."

"I already know many things for my age, my father. I know how to find the suckahoe truffle. And how to make medicine from the bezoar stone. And how to catch shad without using a hook. I know four tongues of other tribes, and can sing all the songs of *puskita*, and keep the sacred fire burning. And I'm strong, too. I will be much help to you in the store."

Coosaponakeesa's proud recital of her accomplishments touched Ian. Gently he said, "Those are truly remarkable skills, Coosa. But I was thinking of things like improving your English. Parson Beckett is a hard teacher, and when you're placed under his tuition, I want you to be as fluent in your father's language as you are in your mother's. We'll work on your English in the evenings."

Quickly, he went on: "As for helping in the store, that really isn't necessary. I have plenty of servants for that. But when you're a little older, you can take over the supervision of the house and gardens."

"Thank you, my father." A soft glow began in her heart and spread throughout her being. Ian had seen to it that the thief had not taken everything from Coosaponakeesa that morning. She still had her father's love and respect. And one day soon she would also have her amulet back.

# Chapter 5

"I declare she looks just like a little princess in this new dress," Mrs. O'Reilly said, viewing her finished handiwork.

"But I am a princess," Coosaponakeesa replied. Yet looking in the mirror at her plain face and her ungreased hair caught up in a ribbon at the back, she didn't think she resembled one at all.

"Och, that's not the thing for the wee one to be answerin', Mr. Ian," the plump Mrs. O'Reilly suggested. "Some people might get the wrong impression—that she's an uppity lass."

"We'll work on that, Mrs. O'Reilly," Ian said. He turned to Coosaponakeesa. "When someone compliments you, Coosa, you must say, 'Thank you.' Nothing more."

"Thank you, Mrs. O'Reilly."

Mrs. O'Reilly smiled. "That's better, lass." She turned to gather up her sewing basket and scissors. "Well, now, it's time to be gettin' back to the settlement, it is. But I'll have the other dresses finished by the end of the week."

"I'll walk with you to your cart," Ian said, and left the keeping room with the seamstress.

As he helped her into the cart he said, "I can't thank you enough, Mrs. O'Reilly—making the dresses and then taking the time to bring Sally over a few days ago. Conversing in English with another child is quite beneficial to Coosa."

"All in the realm of my Christian duty," the woman answered. "And speaking of Christian duty, may I make a further suggestion, Mr. Ian?"

"Yes?"

"The lass can't keep that heathen name once she's enrolled in school. You must be thinkin' of a Christian name to give her."

"I'll set my mind to it tonight."

"And we'll see you at service this Sabbath?"

Ian hesitated. "Soon," he answered. "If not this Sabbath, then perhaps the next."

"Don't stay away too long, Mr. Ian. Devilish ways need to be attended to as soon as possible."

"I understand, Mrs. O'Reilly."

From the open door, Coosaponakeesa listened unashamedly to the conversation between her father and the seamstress. What did the woman mean, to change her name? If she did that, how would the Great Spirit know who was praying to him? And how could she be gathered to her ancestors when she was old if they did not know that she, Coosaponakeesa, was making the upward journey from the middle world?

"Coosa, I'm going back to the store," Ian called. "I'll see you at suppertime."

"Yes, Father."

Coosaponakeesa took off the dress and carefully folded it into the new linen press in her room. She climbed back into the shirt and breeches and quickly braided her hair again, for she had much to do before seeing her father again.

The deerskin was almost ready to be tanned with bark. It had been a chore, scraping the hair off with the shank bone and then soaking the hide in the pasty mixture of brains and water. Now it was time to scrape it again with the mussel shell until every bit of the moisture had been absorbed. All this she had done in secret, even drying out the sinews for thread. She had been particularly fortunate, too, in finding the large white bezoar stone inside the deer.

With the calciferous stone, the eagle's feather, and the dried herbs gathered in the woods, she had begun making another medicine pouch— not nearly so powerful as the one Medicine Woman had given her. That one could never be replaced. But at least the new one was better than having none at all.

A ripple of excitement spread across her body as Coosaponakeesa thought of the new deerskin dress she would make once the hide was ready. The pretty beads inherited from her princess mother could be used to decorate the dress and her new moccasins. The birds had also been kind to her, leaving a beautiful feather or two along the trail for her to find.

The old beads and the new feathers on the dress would serve as a bridge between her mother's village and her father's trading post. Yes, perhaps wearing it would help her to feel like one person, instead of two.

When Ian walked into the store, Muckross was waiting to make his daily report. "I kept my eye on her just like you asked me, but she's still a little savage, Master Ian," young Muckross complained. "And dressing her like Sally O'Reilly won't change her."

"Why do you say that?"

"It wasn't only killing the deer in the forest and carving the poor thing up like any hunter. But when she brought me the fresh venison ham to cook, I noticed she'd cut out a strange-shaped portion along the thigh. When I asked Red Horse why she did it, he said that all Indians throw that part away. They think it's polluted."

"And when you dress a wild turkey, Muckross, do you throw any of it away?

"Of course. The craw. It's not fit to eat."

"Polluted, maybe?"

"Well, it's got rocks and gravel—" Muckross stopped and grinned.

"So don't be too quick to judge Coosa, Muckross. Her life has turned upside down. And she can't be expected to learn everything new in a day or a week."

"I reckon you're right, Master Ian. It'll take quite awhile."

"Just continue to keep an eye on her, regardless of what she does. But if she looks as if she might get into trouble, then come to me immediately."

By late afternoon, when Ian left the store, he found a studious Coosaponakeesa leaning over the copybook and laboriously tracing the words and numbers he had set out for her to learn that day. And when supper was over, he sat on the porch steps with his daughter and went over new words. The drone of bees about the peach trees on that hot, summer evening combined with the music of Creek words translated into English.

"*Chelocco*," Ian said.

"Big deer."

"No. What the English call it," he prompted.

"Horse."

Ian smiled and nodded. "*Tohopki*," he continued.

Coosaponakeesa hesitated. "Fort?"

"Yes. That's very good, Coosa. Parson Beckett is going to find that you're a bright pupil."

The young girl moved closer to her father. She did not care about Parson Beckett. She only wanted to please her father.

Ian reached out his hand to his daughter, while ignoring the strong odor of raw deer hide coming from her homespun shirt and breeches.

As darkness came, with its wilderness noise, Ian and Coosaponakeesa left the porch and went inside. An open door was an invitation to any bear looking for food. So Ian placed the strong slat of wood into its iron pinnings, securing the door for the night.

Once the child was in her nightgown, Ian said, "I'll hear your prayers now, Coosa."

It had been a long, tiring day. By rote, Coosaponakeesa stretched out her arms toward the sky and began to speak in Creek. "O Great Spirit..."

Ian listened to the litany and didn't have the heart to make her speak in English. But he was gratified that she climbed onto the rope bed rather than spreading her wolf pelt on the floor.

A week passed, with Coosaponakeesa working diligently on her deerskin dress. When it was finished, she bathed herself in water from the basin and put on the dress. She quietly folded the clean homespun shirt and breeches along with the rope and relegated them to the linen press. A brief comment by the busy Ian that night at supper indicated that he had, at least, noticed her handiwork.

For the next few days, Coosa saw little of Ian. He remained busy at the trading post, with Red Horse at his side. The procession of Indian canoes upon the river, the heavy, lumbering carts going back and forth to the settlement, along with the packhorses being loaded down for the trip into Charlestown, combined to give the impression that her father was one of the most powerful men in the world. A sense of pride caused Coosaponakeesa to work even harder each day, learning to write her numbers and to read from the white man's Bible so that her father would be proud of her, too.

But her lessons did not occupy all of her time. She went often into the woods, digging up a suckahoe for Muckross to bake into bread or to gather herbs that were not grown in the garden.

She was aware that Muckross tracked her. How could she miss him, with his red hair and freckles as apparent against the brush as a red-throated bird. Even if she didn't spot him, she could tell that he was near, just by the snap of twigs. It was Red Horse that she didn't always see. Yet she sensed that he was there sometimes, too.

"Muckross," she called out one afternoon when he had been particularly heavy-footed."Why don't you help me, and then we go back to the house sooner?"

The young fellow lumbered out from the nearby bushes. "How did you know that I was anywhere around?"

"Your feet, Muckross. One day soon I sew you some moccasins like mine. Then you won't make big noise."

He continued to follow her until she reached a stagnant inlet of the river. Coosaponakeesa turned and asked, "Would you like me to catch fish for supper?"

"How can you do that? You don't even have a fishing line, Coosa."

"I don't need line or hook. I have something better."

He watched as she took a strange powder and sprinkled some of it upon the surface of the water. "The powder make them very drunk, like firewater."

In amazement, Muckross watched the movement in the water. A few minutes later, as several large fish floated lazily to the top, Coosaponakeesa took off her moccasins, held up her dress, and waded into the water. She threw one fish and then another onto the bank, where Muckross quickly gathered them up and wrapped them in his apron.

"Is that plenty, Muckross?"

"Aye."

It was then that Coosa and Muckross became friends. And although he still looked upon her as half-barbarian, he decided he was sadly lacking when it came to watching over her in secret.

The next afternoon, when they returned from gathering fox grapes, Ian was waiting in the keeping room. Quickly Muckross took the grapes and headed for the kitchen pantry.

"Your shoes came, Coosa. All the way from Charlestown."

Puzzled, she stared at the box her father held out to her. "But I have no need of other shoes, Father. See, I have new moccasins."

"These are for special occasions. Like going to meetings. Here, try them on."

She took the box, opened the lid, and stared inside. Strange-looking black shoes, with rigid, stiff bottoms, the kind that Sally O'Reilly wore, lay side by side, like two dried otters.

She walked to the settle, sat down, and removed her moccasins. But as she tried to push her foot into one of the shoes, her father said, "The other foot, Coosa. That one goes on the left foot."

Once they were both on, she tried to stand, but the pain in her feet caused her to sit down again. "They feel strange," she said.

"That's to be expected," Ian replied. "But walk across the floor in them a time or so, and you will soon become accustomed to them."

Wincing, she put one foot in front of another. She felt clumsy, and she made as much noise as Muckross.

"They'll feel better once you put on your stockings," Ian said, and smiled. "Now that you have your shoes to go with your new dresses, I'll take you to the settlement meeting house this Sabbath. You'll meet Parson Beckett then, and we can talk about your baptism."

"Will I have a new name for that, Father?"

"Yes."

"Who will choose my name? Parson Beckett?"

"No. We can do it together if you like, Coosa. Tonight."

He continued, "I still have work to do. A supply of powder horns and muskets has to be unloaded and stored in the arsenal. But why don't you take the Bible and look through it for names while you practice walking in your new shoes?"

"I like Sally," she said. "I want to be called Sally."

Ian stopped at the door. "I don't think that's such a good idea. Two Sallys in the same classroom would only cause confusion.

"But what about Eunice, or Lois, or even Rebekah? Do you like any of those?"

"No, my father."

"Then, we'll discuss it later."

Ian disappeared. Coosaponakeesa limped to the small table by the rocking chair, where the Bible lay open, and there she sat, turning one page and then another.

Her new name would have to be chosen with great care and satisfaction. For one day she would be queen. And when her uncle, Old Brims, died, her son would become emperor of all the Creeks. That was her destiny, as her princess mother and Sanawa had taught her.

# Chapter 6

"Mary, child of the covenant, I baptize thee in the name of the Father..."

Coosaponakeesa knelt before the stern-looking parson in his black frock coat. She tried not to show her confusion as the water was placed upon her head. Despite Ian's reassurances, she could not still the voices of her ancestors within her. As long as she could remember, the stories of the Spaniard, Tustanugga Hatke, or De Soto, and the black-clad priests had been recalled around the sacred campfire—stories that told of cruelty and crucifixion. Had Tomochichi's own father not been crucified upside down by the Spaniards when he refused to renounce the Great Spirit: "He who sitteth Above and is in all Places."

She was supposed to be a heathen, brought into Christianity, with her name inscribed on a page of the church records. Yet, in studying with Ian each evening, Coosaponakeesa could see little difference in the two Gods, little difference in the religious tenets, except that the white man, smoking the calumet of peace, would usually go back on his word. Her people could never do that, for once the sacred smoke reached *Sotolycate*, the promise was sealed.

But perhaps there was more to this Christianity than the immortality of the soul, or punishment or reward after death. She was willing to learn, if it pleased her father.

Coosaponakeesa closed her eyes as Parson Beckett prayed. When the *amen* had been echoed throughout the congregation, the ceremony was over. As she stood beside the parson, Ian was the first to greet her.

"Welcome into the Lord's fellowship, Mary."

"Thank you, my father."

Sally O'Reilly edged her way forward with her mother. She was extremely fair of skin, with golden curls. "Oh, Mary. I'm so happy for you," she said. "This is a wonderful day, isn't it? And you look so pretty in your new dress and shoes."

"But my feet hurt, Sally," Mary whispered. Sally giggled and whispered something into Mary's ear.

Now standing slightly apart from them, Parson Beckett also conversed in whispered tones to one of his other female parishioners. "I have no hope that the child will remain in the arms of the church for long. I've seen it happen before. They all fall back into their heathenish ways, sooner or later."

"But you are truly a man of God, Parson," the woman answered, with an understanding smile, "to take even one of the little barbarians under your tutelage. I understand she is to attend your school, too."

"Yes. And that may be even more of a disaster. But we shall see, Mistress Whitaker. We shall see."

Ian frowned at the woman and then glanced quickly at Mary. But she gave no indication that she'd overheard.

"This is a special day for ye both, Mr. Ian. The Lord be thanked."

"It is, indeed, Mrs. O'Reilly," Ian replied.

Many in the congregation followed Coreen O'Reilly's example, shaking hands with Ian and making appropriate remarks to Mary, *née* Coosaponakeesa.

Soon the crowd began to disperse, some walking, others climbing into their carts and conveyances for the ride back to their homes built on the outward rim of the settlement called Ponpon. From the corral, Muckross and one of the packhorse drivers, Colin, brought the two Indian piebald ponies and hitched them to Ian's carriage standing in the shade of a large poplar tree.

As soon as Mary climbed into the carriage she eased off her shoes and wiggled her toes. As she sighed in relief Muckross laughed, reached under the carriage box, and brought out her moccasins. "Are these what ye be needin', Mary?"

Just as a grateful Mary reached out to take them she saw Mistress Whitaker and her son Billy walking on the side of the rutted road. "Later, Muckross," she whispered. "Hide them. Quick."

Mary squeezed her feet back into the black leather shoes and placed her hands carefully in her lap. "Father, tell me the story of Ruth and Naomi in that foreign land," she requested as the carriage overtook the woman. Ian tipped his hat and nodded civilly before he began the story.

His eyes were merry as he recited, "Once, a long time ago, there was a famine in Israel...." As soon as they had gone a short distance, Ian stopped the story. "All right, Muckross. You can hand Mary her moccasins now. We're safely out of range of Mistress Whitaker."

He gazed into Mary's innocent blue eyes and laughed. Once she had put on her moccasins, Ian made no attempt to finish the story. Instead, he began to talk to Colin about the trading trip into Charlestown. And Mary was content to listen.

The rest of the summer vanished quickly, with an ambivalent Mary torn between two cultures. By sunlight, she resembled the Indian girl, Coosaponakeesa, in her deerskin dress and her hair in plaits. But by lantern light each evening, she became Mary, the dutiful daughter, dressed in calico, with her hair tied back by a ribbon. The English veneer was still thin, fragile.

But Ian could not expect a complete metamorphosis, especially during the four-month mourning period for her mother. Soon, though, the time would be up for both child and husband. Then, perhaps, all Indian ties with Coweta Town would be easier to forget.

Ian was not the only one keeping track of the mourning time for Princess Rising Fawn. Red Horse was doing the same, patiently waiting until he could present Bending Cane, his niece, as new wife to Ian. She was a pretty little thing—with her graceful hands and her walk that resembled a reedy cane bending against the wind.

He had thought that he would be rid of Coosaponakeesa long before now. But Muckross had been her constant shadow in the wilderness. So, devising another way, Red Horse had quietly sent out word that he would swap an ax and a pint of contraband rum for either a horn snake or a coral snake.

That very morning the exchange had taken place between him and his kinsman, Long Bone. Now there remained only one thing to do—to put the snake in the girl's room when the cabin was empty. Red Horse smiled at the thought of the snake. No amulet or medicine made by the child was strong enough to work against the reptile's venomous strike.

"Do you need me this next hour, Ian Yonahlongi Hatke?" Red Horse inquired, using Ian's Indian name. "I help Long Bone bring in pelts from the landing."

"No. Go with him. It's a shame, though, that he didn't get here a few hours ago. We could have sent his furs on to the Charlestown warehouse with Colin."

Red Horse left the store and disappeared in the company of Long Bone. But rather than going all the way to the landing with him, Red Horse circled back, unobserved, to the north edge of the woods, where he had secluded the divided basket containing his quarry.

Quickly, he retrieved the basket hanging from the tree limb and hurried toward the attached cabin. Stealthily looking around him, Red Horse crept onto the porch. He already knew which boards sagged and groaned, so he avoided those. He opened the cabin door and stepped across the threshold. The keeping room was deserted, as he had known it would be. Earlier he had seen both Coosaponakeesa and Muckross going off toward the lower shoal of the river, some distance from the landing. And at that time of morning, the servants were always busy, seeing to the hogs and poultry in the folds and coops and weeding the garden where musk melons and vegetables struggled for survival amid the rampant native weeds.

Red Horse walked into the small bedroom behind the chimneypiece and, kneeling, he placed the basket on the floor next to the chamber pot. From under his shirt, he brought the leather pouch he had stolen that day at the river. It held no magic for Coosaponakeesa now. Inwardly laughing, he finally placed it amid her clothes in the linen press, for her to find—devoid of bezoar stone, herbs, and feathers, which he'd kept for himself.

No remorse touched his heart as he walked back to the chamber pot and removed its glazed enamel lid. With singular intent, he loosened the thong of the two-sided basket.

As used as Red Horse was in handling snakes, he was extremely careful with this one. Quickly turning over the basket onto the empty chamber pot, he jammed on the pot lid with his right hand, trapping the snake in the second receptacle, even as he removed the basket with his left.

The sudden rattle of the horned snake tail against the inside of the pot and the ensuing odor of the released poison indicated the ferocity of the trapped snake. Long Bone had done well. Far better than the Shawnees. Although Red Horse would have gotten much satisfaction knowing that Princess Rising Fawn's proud daughter was slain by some Shawnee, he nevertheless realized that, however dangerous, this method he was now using to get rid of the girl was even better. A sudden childish laughter brought Red Horse from his vindictive reverie. Coosaponakeesa and Muckross were returning far too early. Red Horse grabbed up the empty basket and headed out of the bedroom. But then the sound of footsteps on the porch told him that he was trapped, with no way out.

He darted into Ian's bedroom just as the two came through the front door.

"Mary, I can't do it," Muckross complained.

"And why not?"

"Your father would have my hide."

"But I thought you were ordered to follow me wherever I went."

"Only up to a certain point. If ye were headed for dire disaster, then I was to go to Master Ian and tell him. And I will, Mary. If ye try to do such a dangerous thing."

"Are you afraid for me, Muckross? Or for yourself?"

"Both."

Mary sighed. "In the village of Tustacatty, there is a man like you. He was afraid to go to war with the other warriors. So now he lives among the women. The mico took away his bow and arrow, and he lives in shame, tending the cooking fire every day."

Muckross laughed. "Ye can't shame me, Mary. For I already tend to your father's cooking fire. And ye forget. I have only three more years as a bonded man. Then I will be free to go."

"And where will you go?"

"Back to Charlestown, where civilized people lie abed and don't have nightmares of being massacred in the night. Begging your pardon, Mary. I'll own me a tavern one day, where fine gentlemen and even ladies come to dine."

Misinterpreting the wary look in Mary's eyes, Muckross said, "What's the matter? Don't ye believe me?"

Mary held up her hand for silence. The young man watched as a primitive transformation came over the girl. She lifted her head and sniffed like a wild animal catching the scent of an enemy.

She motioned for Muckross to take down the loaded musket from the wall. And she turned toward the larger bedroom. "Father, is that you?" she called out.

When there was no answer, she removed the hunting knife from its leather sheath at her waist and took a step toward the bedroom, with Muckross at her side.

At the unmistakable sound of something at the window, the two rushed into the bedroom. It was not unusual for some wild animal to force its way into a cabin, especially when there was food around. But as Mary and Muckross quickly surveyed the room they saw nothing.

Muckross walked to the open window and looked out. "I guess we scared it away. Whatever it was."

Mary closed the shutters. "My father must have forgot to bolt the window this morning."

"See, this is what I meant, Mary. A body is not safe in the wilderness—either from man or beast."

While Muckross put the gun back in its rack, a subdued Mary walked into her own bedroom. The mica window was still intact. Nothing had been disturbed. Yet there was a presence in the room, as if something or someone who had no business being there had left a lingering odor.

With Muckross attending his cooking pots, Mary went into the kitchen garden to gather some bay leaves for the soup. But before returning, she walked along the back of the house—stooping to examine the prints upon the soft earth.

Less than a yard from her father's window, a large moccasined footprint was apparent in the dirt. But it proved nothing. Too many people came and went in the compound for the print to be significant.

Once she had given Muckross the bay leaves, Mary went into her room and closed the door. The same odor that she had smelled earlier now permeated the room. For a brief moment, Sanawa's face seemed to be reflected in the windowpane. "Look around you, Little Blue-eyed One." Startled, she blinked her eyes. When she looked again toward the window, the face was gone. She decided she had only imagined the likeness and the voice because she was homesick.

Her desire to return to Coweta Town for the celebration of the corn festival was the reason for her argument with Muckross. Ian was far too busy to take her, but if Muckross were willing to travel with her, then she could visit with her people and still be back in time for the first school day.

"Mary," Ian's voice called to her.

She opened her door and walked into the keeping room. "Yes, my father?"

"Muckross here tells me that you had a scare."

She shrugged. "It was nothing. Some animal fled through your window."

"Are you certain that it's gone? Did you see it?"

"No, Father."

Ian was aware that he had made enemies, regardless of how fair he had tried to be in his trading.

"Muckross, you haven't seen Chitunga hanging around here, have you?"

"No, Master Ian. Not since that day that you refused his"—he hesitated—"his, er, goods to take to Charlestown."

The trader was relieved at the bondsman's sensitivity. It was just as well for Mary not to hear that Chitunga had tried to sell him two young Indians. If they had been captured in battle, then they could legally be sold as slaves in Charlestown for shipment to the plantations in the Indies. But Chitunga had kidnapped them, instead, and lied about the circumstances. By refusing to deal with Chitunga, Ian had made an enemy capable of retribution at any time.

"I think I'll take a look around the cabin," Ian said. From the hearth, Ian took a long, two-pronged stick and began a careful search of every nook and cranny of the cabin.

With a curious Mary following him, he walked into his own bedroom first. Using the long stick, he carefully removed the bedclothes, layer by layer. Finding nothing out of the ordinary, he walked to the sea chest and opened it. Using the same procedure, with his pistol in one hand and the stick in the other, he proceeded to empty the chest of its contents.

The tobacco box in the keeping room, the flour bin in the pantry, all were carefully examined by Ian. Then he walked into Mary's room.

Again using the long stick, he attacked the linen press, removing all of his daughter's clothes and even running the stick along the wall behind the press. Satisfied that it was more than likely an animal and not Chitunga who had invaded his living quarters, Ian put his pistol back into its holster.

All at once Mary spied the leather amulet that lay half-hidden between the folds of one of her dresses. "Look, Father. My old leather pouch. I wonder how it got back into my room."

Just as she stooped to pick it up, Ian's sharp voice warned her. "Don't touch it, Coosa."

The sudden words, spoken in Creek, surprised her. Her hand poised in mid air. She remained quite still as Ian lifted the pouch, catching its leather string with the pronged stick.

As the medicine pouch swayed from the long stick, a sudden movement of the soft leather casing indicated that some small living thing was confined inside.

Now speaking in English, Ian said, "Lift your window, Mary."

She walked to the window and, moving the tiered table a little out of the way, she pushed up the window and propped it open long enough for Ian to thrust the stick outside.

"All right. Put the window down."

The sash closed, anchoring the stick like a small fishing pole, with the leather pouch dangling at the end of the pronged stick.

"What do you think is inside?" Mary asked.

"Something deadly, God's truth. That's why I'll kill it outside rather than risk having the thing escape inside the house."

"I'll go with you."

"No, Mary. Watch from the window to make sure it doesn't get away."

Disappointed, she stood close to the window and waited until her father appeared outside with a garden hoe. She watched as he placed the pouch on the ground and gingerly loosened the thong. Standing on tiptoe, she saw a small red and black snake poke its head out and then quickly slither toward freedom. But Ian, with one stroke of the hoe, cut the deadly coral snake in half and crushed its head with his brogan.

Mary remained by the window and stared as Ian gathered the two halves upon his hoe and hung them side by side on the small fence. Although the snake was now harmless, Mary knew that the spirit would not depart until sundown.

With the window lifted only several inches, merely high enough to remove the pronged stick, Mary pulled it inside and then shoved the tiered table back in place. But as she did so, the chamber pot lid rattled and then slid off to the floor with a clatter.

Ian returned the hoe to the small shed and retraced his steps to the front porch. He was convinced that the culprit had been Chitunga, intent on getting back at Ian where it would hurt most—through his daughter, who had grown closer to his heart every day. But soon, school would start. And that would be much safer for Mary, working under Parson Beckett's care rather than spending hours in the wilderness, with only Muckross to watch over her.

Seeing Ian, Muckross began dipping two bowls of soup from the kettle. "Your meal be more than ready, Master Ian."

"Have you called Mary?"

"No, sire. I think she be in her room still."

"Then I'll get her."

Her back was to him as he walked to the threshold of the bedroom. "Mary..." He made a guttural sound in his throat as the image of his daughter standing motionless, with the pronged stick outstretched, seared itself into his brain. Coiled around the stick was a snake the breadth of Mary's arm.

"Don't move, Mary," he warned. Realizing that she was only inches away from death, Ian quickly drew his loaded pistol, aimed, and fired.

The blast of the shot knocked the stick from Mary's hands. And still she remained motionless, until Muckross came running at the sound of the discharge.

"What's the matter?"

"Don't look, Muckross," Mary answered. "You have weak stomach."

That evening as the sun went down and the two deadly snakes hanging together upon the fence finally ceased their writhing, Mary stood at the window for one last glimpse. To her people, the snake had always been a symbol of new life emerging from the old.

With sadness, she traced the face of Sanawa upon the window. How she longed to see her old nurse again.

Later that evening, as Ian came to check on his daughter before going to bed himself, he found Mary, wrapped in the black wolf pelt, once again asleep on the floor.

# Chapter 7

A frustrated Red Horse, returning from a trip to his village, paddled swiftly toward the trading post landing. Seated in the canoe was Bending Cane, his niece, with her worldly goods wrapped in a trading blanket.

The Indian had exchanged an expensive ax and a pint of rum for two dead snakes hanging on the fence. But matters could be worse. Ian Yonahlongi Hatke did not suspect him, and for that he was grateful.

But it was no longer feasible to try to get rid of Coosaponakeesa. She had some secret power that protected her. He would have to rely on Bending Cane to lure the trader's affection away from his daughter instead.

Red Horse tied the canoe to the wooden pole of the landing. "Come, Bending Cane," he said. "I will take you to the trader's house."

"Is the Englishman handsome, Uncle?" she inquired. "And is he kind?"

In a gruff voice Red Horse said, "It does not matter whether he please you or no. You are here to please him. If you fail, I give you to Chitunga."

Bending Cane shuddered. Chitunga had been banished from her village for his crime against the Fox clan. They had searched for him to bring him to justice, but he had eluded the warriors for the required number of days in the wilderness. They had been forced to return home without him. Now, if the outlaw could disguise himself and sneak back to the village for the corn festival and the lighting of the new fire without being found out, he would be free to remain in the village without punishment.

"I will please Ian Yonahlongi Hatke, Uncle. Or I will kill myself. Chitunga will never have me."

Red Horse grunted. Bending Cane was too full of fireside stories. She would never be brave enough to turn the knife on herself, as some of the earlier women of her tribe had done, slaughtering their children first, rather than be put in chains and neck collars of their conquerors. No, Bending Cane was meek and gentle—not like the proud Coosaponakeesa who constantly challenged him with those dry-scratched eyes.

Red Horse turned and looked at Bending Cane. Her hair, dressed in bear grease and cinnamon, glistened in the sun. And her large, dark eyes were much prettier than the sky eyes of the *Hatke*, who came from across the waters.

But it was her beauty that had begun to get Bending Cane into trouble. She should be thankful that he had whisked her away from the village this time before she was found out. Else her ears might have been cut off for punishment.

Red Horse knew that Ian, although getting old, was just as susceptible to Indian beauty as all the other English, Spanish, and Frenchmen. Had the trader not set great store in Princess Rising Fawn, who had remained faithful to him until she died? Of course, Creek women were not like those of other tribes. They were expected to be chaste and faithful.

But white men were different. They chased after all women with the resolve of a buck gone a-whoring. Yet Ian had remained faithful to Princess Rising Fawn too, in his own way. He bore little resemblance to the trader down the river who had three wives—an Indian one, a black slave one, and a *hatke*, left in a house in Charlestown with their chalk-colored children.

Now, with his wife mourning over, it was time for Ian to bed a new wife and sire other children. And when that happened, Red Horse, as Bending Cane's kinsman, would have more power in his village.

Red Horse had chosen his timing well. Today was first-school-day for Coosaponakeesa. And Muckross had been chosen to deliver her to the settlement school. Red Horse would take Bending Cane to the deserted cabin and then go to the store to tell Ian Yonahlongi Hatke of his good fortune.

Down the long rutted road toward the Ponpon settlement, the pony cart traveled, with Mary holding on to the sides. The morning air held a hint of fall, while the leaves of the dogwood trees visible from the road had already begun to turn red, to match the berried bracts.

"This is an exciting time for ye, Mary," Muckross said. "Your first day at school. I'm only glad, I am, though, that ye be under Parson Beckett's brimstone eye today, and not me."

"Don't make me feel worse, Muckross," Mary said. "I have much to be nervous about."

"Just keep your mind on your lessons and stay away from little Billy Whitaker. He likes to get other people into trouble."

"Do you think he will say anything about that day when my clothes were stolen?"

"And ye came running past the trading post porch with only that red cloth around ye?" he finished with a laugh.

"Don't tease me, Muckross. That was a day of shame for me."

"Aye. But don't put it past him to taunt you. Billy's a crafty one, like his pater. Pay no attention to any of them, Mary. Behave like the true princess ye are, and ye will get by."

"Yes. That is good advice, Muckross."

For the next several minutes, Mary was silent, but her mind was busy. Did she dare use the sacred powders that she had brought with her?

The pony cart kept to the path through the wilderness stretch of land, where little light filtered through the thicket, where litters of howling wolf pups cavorted before their rocky dens, with little fear of being discovered. Then, the darkness gave way to light in the same manner as the wilderness to civilization. And on its edge where the two met, the wild animal sounds diminished as the steady, sharp ping of the blacksmith's anvil announced the encroaching town.

On one side of the blacksmith's shed, a creek fed into a small pond, where ducks and geese waddled through the reeds toward their morning swim. And up ahead, beyond the wooden railing, Mary saw the meeting house with its belfry, protected by the houses built around it. Although she couldn't see it yet, Mary knew that the log schoolhouse lay directly beyond the meeting house, in its own small grove of trees.

"Muckross, stop here. I will walk the rest of the way."

"But I promised your father I would deliver ye safe."

"And so you have. To the village. Now turn around and go home. I want no one to think that you have brought a baby to school."

"Are ye sure ye'll be all right, Mary?"

"Yes. Stop here and let me out."

Reluctantly he did so. And when she had climbed down, Muckross handed her lunch basket to her. "I fixed an extra special lunch for ye, Mary."

"Not snake meat, I hope."

"Oh, nothing of the kind..." He realized then that she was making a joke.

"Thank you, Muckross."

Still he hesitated, although Mary was beginning to show her impatience at his dallying. "I'll come back for ye when school is out at three o'clock."

"Wait for me at the blacksmith's," she ordered. "Don't come for me at the schoolhouse."

Mary watched while Muckross turned the pony cart around. Slowly, deliberately, she began to walk the rest of the way toward the village. As the sound of the wheels in the ruts grew dimmer, she gazed over her shoulder just in time to see the pony cart disappearing.

Mary quickly changed direction, heading instead toward the duck pond on the other side of the blacksmith's shop.

She didn't know when she had felt so plain, with the stark white apron over the somber gray calico dress, and her hair, stripped of bear grease, pulled back so tightly by the ribbon. And her feet hurt, too, for she had been made to leave her moccasins at home. She now wore the uncomfortable black shoes that had already rubbed blisters on her heels.

Unhappily, she sat down by the pond and gazed into its still waters. Her plain, colorless reflection gazed back at her. How could she act like a princess today if she did not look like one?

She could change that, though, with the sacred pigments hidden in her apron pocket. Polished and ground, the powders had been made from the dry rot of heart pine mixed with iron oxide, yellow clay taken from the bluff of the river, and dried blue delphinium flowers, mixed with bear grease.

Using the small shell from the pouch, Mary scooped up some of the pond water. And then, waiting for the water to become calm and placid again so that she might see her reflection as she painted herself, she mixed the powders, taken from the separate compartments. When the mixtures were ready a few minutes later, she began.

With circles and lines and the jagged streak of lightning beneath one eye, her face took on the patterns of Creek royalty. She was sister to the Moon, reflected in the yellow clay crescent on her forehead; kinswoman to Brother Sun, proven by the red circles upon her cheeks, and daughter of the Wind, confirmed by the white, two-fingered curve across her chin.

Gazing into the water, Mary was satisfied. This was a special day, and by painting her face in the traditional way, she was showing that the Great Spirit had awarded her much power in her walk upon the earth.

In the distance, a warning bell began to sound. The school. Parson Beckett. The painting ceremony had caused her to lose all track of time. Quickly Mary grabbed up her shoes and her lunch and, barefoot, she sprinted toward the log schoolhouse. She arrived five minutes later, at the ringing of the second bell.

Parson Beckett, flanked by the boys and girls of the village, stood in line and watched her approach. When she saw them, Mary stopped, as though facing a camp of enemy warriors.

The silence seemed interminable as they all stared at her. A timorous giggle from one of the girls broke the silence. And soon the air was filled with humiliating sounds. The giggle grew into laughter and then guffaws. Open mouths gaped at her and twitching fingers pointed at her. Billy Whitaker hit his thigh in glee. And even her friend, Sally O'Reilly, was laughing. She felt completely betrayed.

"Hamish Pettipoole," Parson Beckett finally said to the largest boy. "Take the children inside and keep them quiet until I deal with this...this little barbarian."

The children followed the boy into the schoolhouse while Parson Beckett returned his attention to Mary, with the wrath of God upon his brow.

"Mary, I baptized you in good faith. But I see that the heathen is still within you. What shall we do about that?"

"I...I don't know, Parson Beckett."

"Then shall I tell you?" he asked, showing his teeth as if to smile.

His black frock coat flapped in the sudden breeze as he took a step closer. "First, you will go to the horse trough, Mary, and wash the paint off your face. When you have finished, I shall expect you in the classroom, clean of face and suitably shod."

His glance left the shoes in her hand, and he continued. "You have been put in my care for a purpose, Mary. To save your soul from perdition. And I intend to do that."

"Yes, Parson Beckett," she replied, although she wasn't sure who Perdition might be.

Dejectedly, Mary headed for the horse trough in the middle of the village. And as she had been instructed, she splashed the water on her face to remove the decoration she had so carefully painted on. A few minutes later, she stood in the doorway and waited for Parson Beckett to notice her.

"Come in, child," he said finally, motioning her toward a roughly hewn log at the front of the class.

"There will be no laughter," Parson Beckett scolded the other pupils. Then he returned his attention to sorting out the students according to their learning.

At the trading post, Red Horse approached Ian, who was busy measuring out a pound of sugar for Tall Chief. "Master," he said, "I bring Musqua gift. You take looksee at cabin."

"Red Horse, I'm busy with Tall Chief. I'll go and see it later."

"No, Ian Yonahlongi Hatke. Go now. I finish trade with Tall Chief."

A curious Ian, sensing the urgency in Red Horse's voice, handed over the measuring cup, nodded to Tall Chief, and then left the store.

Bending Cane, scrubbing the long trestle table, heard Ian's footsteps. She looked up from her work as he walked inside the cabin.

"Hallo," he said, coming close to the table. "Who are you?"

"I am Bending Cane," she answered. "I be much help to you. You see."

"Did Red Horse bring you?"

"Yes. He said you need woman. You want me to stay?"

Ian hesitated. She was so appealing, standing there and looking at him with that saucy expression, her head bent to one side.

She smiled at him and recited, "I cook and clean. I preserve meat and make nut bread and dry berries for winter."

Muckross could do with extra help, especially now that he was taking Mary back and forth to school.

"All right, Bending Cane. You may stay."

The girl nodded. "You tell Red Horse?"

"Yes. I tell Red Horse," he repeated. He added, "When my servant Muckross returns, ask him to come to the store."

As Ian left the cabin, Bending Cane finished scrubbing the table. Then she removed her belongings to Ian's bedroom. There, she spread her blanket on his bed.

# Chapter 8

Mary sat, ostracized from the other pupils. The marks of the cane upon her palms made it difficult for her to hold the chalk steady as she slowly traced the letters of the alphabet on her slate.

The school had been divided into groups, not according to the age of the pupil, but according to the answers given to the questions Parson Beckett had asked.

Sally was in the Homer group, with Billy Whitaker and Hamish Pettipoole in the Aristotle group. Polly and Maggie, the only other girls, were in the Socrates group. The rest were boys whose names she did not care to learn.

Mary stopped her writing and watched while Polly made eyes at Hamish Pettipoole, seated on the nearby bench. It was not so much that she cared about any of them. Only, she was curious to understand the customs between English boys and girls.

"Mary, keep your mind on your work," Parson Beckett admonished.

She took up the chalk and once again began to trace the letters. And when she had finished, the teacher came and gazed over her shoulder.

"All right. You may take your seat with the Homer group."

She left the corner of the schoolroom, next to the teacher's table, and walked slowly toward the Homer group. At first, there seemed to be no room for her on either log seat. But then Sally smiled shyly at her and moved over, giving Mary barely enough space to sit on the end.

"Now we will have our history lesson for the entire school. Listen carefully. If you know the answer, raise your hand."

Parson Beckett posed one question after another. All over the room, boys and girls stood when called upon and recited the answers. Even Sally knew the answer to one of the questions. But Mary, with the shame of the morning still fresh upon her, was unable to answer a single question.

Finally, Parson Beckett said, "Name the first Spaniard who explored this area of the colony, east of the Mississippi River."

Mary smiled and raised her hand.

A surprised Parson Beckett nodded to her and said, "All right, Mary. You may stand and give the answer."

All eyes turned to Mary as she stood. And with a sense of pride, she said, "Tustanugga Hatke."

At the laughter in the schoolroom, Parson Beckett struck his cane across the table. "Silence," he commanded. "All of you."

The room became quiet again, almost as quiet as his voice when he said, "Can someone give the correct answer?"

Maggie raised her hand.

"Yes?"

"John Ferdinand Soto."

"Thank you, Maggie."

Tapping the cane gently across his open hand, the teacher looked again at Mary. "Come here, Mary."

She could tell that she was in worse trouble than before. But this time her eyes were defiant as she faced him.

"Do you know why you will have to be punished again?"

"No, Parson."

"You tried to show off in front of the class when you did not know the answer to the question."

"I spoke the truth," Mary defended. "Tustanugga Hatke and Hernando de Soto are the same man. That I know. But how was I to know that you English changed his name?"

"I will not have insolence in my schoolroom," Beckett bellowed, the vein in his neck standing out against his collar. "Go and sit on the stool for the rest of the afternoon, Mary. I will deal with you after school."

Long before school was to end, Muckross hitched the piebald pony to the small cart and began his journey to the settlement. The day had been filled with unusual happenings, not the least of which was the sight of Bending Cane at work in the cabin.

"Red Horse's niece has come to be with us," Ian had told him. "She will be a lot of help to you, and company for Mary, too."

"Yes, sire."

From that, Muckross wasn't certain what her position was to be. Yet the sight of Bending Cane's belongings in Ian's room, with the trading blanket spread across his bed, left no doubt later on. Poor Mary. How was she to take this, with her mother being supplanted in her father's affection by a woman from another tribe?

While he sat under a beech tree near the blacksmith's shop and waited for Mary, he debated whether he should tell her on the way back home of Bending Cane's arrival or just wait and let her father explain.

The minutes, like gathered pelts piled one on top of the other, spread into the late afternoon, and still Mary did not come. Each time he heard a child's voice, Muckross thought it might be Mary. But then the voices vanished. The sun traveled through the sky to a position barely to the treetops. And by that time the pony had turned as restless as he was.

Just when he had decided to go to the schoolhouse, Muckross heard a great uproar in the settlement. When he jumped down from the cart and moved toward the road to get a better view, he saw Mary walking slowly, with the other children laughing and taunting her as she passed.

"Heathen, heathen, are ye leavin'?" a voice called out.

"Teacher's pet, teacher's pet, has he finished caning you yet?"

As she walked on, Billy Whitaker danced around her and made a war whoop with his hand across his face. "Who has a painted face and skinny-dips in the river?"

Together, in chorus, the crowd of children answered, "Indian Mary. That's who."

A distressed Muckross, ready to go to her aid, changed his mind as a woman's voice admonished, "Children, stop that noise right now. And Polly, you come inside immediately."

He watched as the children ran off. A relieved Muckross slowly walked back to the pony cart. Mary would be all right, now. And it would be far better not to let on that he had seen what had happened. Mary was proud. Sometimes too proud for her own good.

He began to whistle an Irish tune and, with his back to the road, Muckross became occupied with the pony's bridle. He didn't look up again until she approached the cart.

Seeing her, he climbed into the cart and, holding out one hand, said, "Here, Mary. I'll give ye a lift-up."

But at his grip, Mary withdrew her hand as if she had touched fire, "No, Muckross. I climb in, myself."

"All right, Mary. Then give me the basket anyway."

She allowed him to take the empty lunch basket. He noticed she was favoring her left hand. But then she climbed into the cart and sat down beside him, with her hands folded in her lap.

Clucking his teeth to the pony, Muckross turned the cart toward home. For a few moments neither spoke. Finally he said, "How was your first school day, Mary?"

Without answering, she changed the subject and began to talk about the mallards on the river. Muckross was not surprised. He had been around Indians long enough now to know that they did not lie. If it was something they didn't want to answer, then they began to talk of something else, as Mary was now doing.

The darkness of the woods seemed intimidating to Muckross. He listened uneasily to every small sound. The pony shied as a deer bounded across the road directly in front of them. Then a whir of wings filled the air when a covey of bobwhites, chased by a hawk, descended to the safety of the thicket.

At that time of the day, with the sun low in the sky, Mary's reaction to the forest surrounding her was different from Muckross's. She began to feel at peace again amid things she knew about. And she tried to close her mind against Parson Beckett and think only of the pleasant evening to be spent with her father, Ian.

When the pony cart reached the trading post, Muckross could see that Bending Cane had been busy in his absence. Already, beyond the enclosed fence bordering the house, the beginnings of a sweat oven was taking shape.

To anyone who knew of such things, the style was unmistakable—the hollowed-out hole in the ground, lined with small rocks, and over it a mound of clay, formed like a butterfly's cocoon, with an opening at one end.

"Who is building the oven?" a curious Mary asked when Muckross stopped the pony before the fence.

"Probably Bending Cane."

Mary's eyes clouded. "Who is she?"

"Ye'll have to ask your father that, Mary. For I cannot truly say."

Mary jumped down from the cart and opened the gate. And Muckross, silently cursing the treachery of life, hurried to the barn shed to unhitch the piebald pony.

When Mary entered, the keeping room was empty of people. But the signs of a visitor were there. With a heavy heart, Mary passed through the room and continued to the small one on the other side. There, she removed her gray calico dress and black leather shoes for the more comfortable deerskin dress and moccasins.

Sitting on the bed, she gazed down at her raw, swollen hands, where Parson Beckett had struck her repeatedly with his cane. This punishment was new to her. No one in her clan had ever beaten a child in this way, for each was considered a gift sent by the Great Spirit. Of course, her people could be severe with the lawbreakers who did not follow the ways taught by their ancestors.

They could be banished for their crimes. Or have their ears cut off. Or if caught for the second time, have their noses cut off. As Mary picked up the small looking glass and touched her face, her mind was on Bit Nose. Could Parson Beckett punish her in the same way? She would ask her father that night, after supper.

But first, she would attend to her hands. And after that, find out about this Bending Cane that Muckross had mentioned.

From her linen press, she brought forth the torn strips of linen. And from her medicine pouch, Mary withdrew the healing herbs that she had gathered earlier in the woods. Mixing the herbs with bear grease, she rubbed the salve onto the palms of her hands and then wrapped them in the coarse strips of cloth.

As she sat on the rope bed and waited for the herbs to work their magic, Mary heard a stirring in the keeping room.

It couldn't be Muckross, for his shoes always made a dull noise as he walked across the wooden floor. No, this was someone in moccasins, with a light step.

Mary stood up and walked to the door. Ever since the episode of the snakes, they had all been careful of intruders. "Hello. Is anyone there?" she called.

When there was no answer, Mary walked out of her room and looked. No one was there.

Remembering that it was from her father's room that the culprit had escaped before, she walked from the keeping room to check the other bedroom. She frowned at the brightly-colored trading blanket draped across her father's bed. And at the sight of someone's belongings in the corner of the room, she grew even more puzzled.

The moccasined footsteps sounded again, and Mary whirled out of the room to face the intruder. Standing before her was another Indian girl, older than she, with her long plaits glistening as Mary's had done before she had been made to remove the bear grease.

"Who are you?" Mary demanded.

"I am Bending Cane."

"What are you doing inside my father's house?"

"Red Horse bring me. I be Yonahlongi Hatke's wife."

Mary didn't know which made her more furious—the fact that Red Horse had brought her, or that the girl claimed to be her father's wife.

"My mother, Princess Rising Fawn, is Ian Yonahlongi Hatke's wife," Mary shouted. "You lie."

Bending Cane also grew angry. "The princess is dead. Red Horse tell me so."

"But my father is still in mourning for her."

"No, Coosaponakeesa," she said, even though Mary had not told Bending Cane her name. "Mourning time is over. Now I be English fur trader's wife. And we have many plump babies together. You see."

In her heart, Mary realized that Bending Cane must be telling the truth. The blanket, the sweat oven—all pointed to Bending Cane's welcome by her father.

Feeling doubly betrayed, Mary fled from the cabin and ran toward the river.

# Chapter 9

Mary sat by the river's edge and waited for her anger and hurt to subside. As a much smaller child, she had gone often to an isolated place by the waters when she was feeling sad.

But it had never lasted long. Sanawa or her princess mother would always know when to come for her and coax her home. Now, no one cared. She could remain by the river as long as she wanted.

Mary gazed out on the quiet waters, with the slight breeze stirring up small, singing ripples. The nearby canebrake also stirred, with a whispering in the air that summer was over. And the new season's message was confirmed by the mallard winging toward the water for rest before flying farther south.

As Mary watched the deceptively tranquil scene before her, she knew that the peaceful surface told only part of the story. A gray, roughened object, like an old log, floated slowly in the water toward the duck. At first, she wanted to call out a warning. But she had no right to interfere. She merely watched the drama unfold—the log floating closer, the duck oblivious of danger. And then, with a powerful snap of the jaws, the alligator found its meal.

Mary's attention turned from the water to her hands. The herbs had been on long enough to work their magic. And so she unwound the white strips of cloth and gazed down at both hands. Opening and closing them, Mary realized that they were better, with the swelling much subsided.

She walked to the water's edge to rinse the strips of cloth. And as she hung them on a nearby bush, she remembered another day when she had done the same, with her clothes. But she would be more careful this time. No one would pilfer the cloths waiting to dry.

It was not long afterward that she heard the telltale sign of movement in the woods. Mary had long ago learned to recognize Muckross's walk, with his clumsy shoes. But the two-legged one approaching had moccasined feet. With a wariness born of the instinct to survive, Mary stood up and hurried toward the canebrake to hide.

From her vantage point she watched until the person became visible. It was not Red Horse, as she had first thought, but her own father. What had possessed him to come to the water? Surely not to look for her.

She watched as he walked to the bush and examined the strips of cloth, now nearly dry.

In the water, the alligator made a swift splash with his tail, and an alarmed Ian stepped back.

"Mary," he called out. "Are you close by? Answer me, Mary."

"Here I am, Father," she answered immediately, coming from her hiding place.

"Thank heavens, child. I was afraid you had gone in swimming again."

"No, Father. I remembered what you said."

Ian knelt on one knee and stared in the direction where the river widened. But he looked as if he were searching for something far beyond the river, far beyond the horizon. Mary stood beside him. She waited for him to speak.

"These are hard times, Mary."

She remained silent.

"A man gets very lonely for family out here."

"But you have me, Father," she said in a suddenly accusing manner. "I thought you were happy with me."

"I am, child. And I had hoped that you would be happy too, living with me."

The words sounded ominous. He was sending her back to Coweta Town because of Bending Cane.

"But I'm not sure that I have done the right thing, taking you away from your clan and the people you love—to put you into such an alien society, with different rules and a different language."

"I understand, Father. You do not want me, since you have Bending Cane. I will pack my things and leave."

"Oh, Mary. The new servant has nothing to do with this. I'm talking about the other children being so cruel to you today. Muckross told me what happened."

He had called Bending Cane servant—not wife. She looked into her father's eyes. "Bending Cane is not your new wife?"

"No. There was a big misunderstanding. But it has been set right. Now, to get back to the trouble at school. I will go to Parson Beckett tomorrow and—"

"No, Father. I will manage."

He smiled and reached out for one of her hands. He turned it palm upward and gently traced the welts that had not completely disappeared. "If that is how you wish it. But know this, Mary. If things get too difficult for you, I will intervene."

She did not understand the English word. But she knew from his voice that her father wished to help her.

Ian stood and shook his tall, lumbering body. "Now get your linen cloths off the bush and let us go home. Muckross and Bending Cane have prepared a delicious supper for us."

As they took the path back to the post, Ian's mind was on Parson Beckett. He, also, had evidently been harsh with Mary, judging from her caned hands. But the man would have sense enough not to go too far; else Ian would withdraw his considerable support from the school. The parson might be a servant of the church, but he was well aware that he could not live on the pittance awarded to him each year by the Missionary Society for the Propagation of the Gospel.

Mary's mind, like her father's, was on Parson Beckett and the school. The children did not matter. They could no longer hurt. But she was determined that one day she would be the best student in the school. And on the way to her goal, she would ignore the slights and the pettiness. Had she not seen how brave men ran the gauntlet without flinching? She would be equally brave. For in her soul she was Princess Coosaponakeesa. And that was enough.

That winter, the months rolled by. Fur trading reached a feverish pitch, with luxurious winter furs brought to the trading post. In the afternoons, Mary took to sitting in a corner of the store, doing her lessons as well as listening to the trading going on. It was partly, too, to get away from Muckross and Bending Cane, who were constantly at each other's throats concerning the house, the dependencies, and the pantry. Mary suspected that Bending Cane's bad temper had something to do with the times the servant made eyes at her father and he didn't seem to notice.

Toward spring, Colin, the master of the packhorse caravan into Charlestown, became her friend, bringing back small mementoes to her from the city to the trading post.

"What is it like, Colin," she would ask, "this great city with hundreds of people?"

"Oh, it's not much different from here, Mary," he would tease. "The people have heads and hands, and they walk the same as—"

"No, Colin. Stop teasing me. What are the houses like?"

"Well, now, they're different, I must admit. They look like great redbrick castles, with real glass windows and slate roofs brought from England. Or else they're built of the finest wood, with porches facing the rivers. And some even face the ocean, with huge waves rolling in with the tide."

"And the ships. How big are they?"

"They're like giant birds, with sails for wings," he replied. "They can hold a herd of horses, a hundred slaves, and vast stores of molasses and flour and other staples that you see around you. It's quite a sight to watch the men unloading them."

"One day I will go to the wharf and see for myself."

"Maybe when the country settles down a bit, your father will take you."

"Yes. I will ask him."

But Ian had no desire to take Mary on the hazardous trip through the wilderness. There was an unrest in the primitive land, with small tribes constantly at war, not only among themselves, but with the invading settlers, who cleared more and more land, forcing the Indians ever westward to search for sustenance. White hunters, carrying lighted pine knots in metal pans, stalked their prey at night and killed the animals by the thousands, carving the small part they wanted from each animal and then leaving the rest of the carcass for the wolves.

The animals were not the only victims. As the lawless vagabonds traipsed through the wilderness from place to place, they also kidnapped, raped, and murdered the young Indian women. This information Colin kept to himself as he told Mary of the caravan trips to Charlestown.

But one afternoon, as Mary slipped quietly into the store and took her place behind a molasses barrel to study her lesson for the next day, she overheard an unsettling conversation between her father and Colin, who had just returned from one of his trips.

"Ian, something will have to be done soon about the Indians," Colin said. "They're getting awful restless, and I can't say as I blame them much."

"Why? What did you see this time, Colin?"

"I spotted some Indian braves with war paint on their faces. Rumors are flying that Old Brims is stirring up the Yuchis and the Yamasees and calling them together for a war council."

Ian nodded. "I was afraid of that. We can't keep breaking the treaties and expect the Indians to do nothing about it."

"It's not only the treaties, Ian. So many of the fur traders I see are a sorry pack of thieves, beggin' your pardon, Ian. Why, I hear that Martin Petros has his Indians so deep in debt to him that they can bring in their pelts till doomsday and still be owing him."

Mary remained still. Her first inclination, to make herself known to her father, vanished when she heard the name of her uncle, Old Brims, Emperor of all the Creeks. The news of his displeasure with the white fur traders and settlers was disturbing. For she remembered her princess mother's stories of her brother's prowess in war. And of his sense of honor among his people. Retribution, swift and terrifying, walked at his side. There would be no mercy for his enemies once he was stirred to action.

As soon as her father and Colin disappeared into the storeroom, Mary slipped from her hiding place. But as she made ready to leave she saw Red Horse walking from the direction of the landing. If she left now, she would bump into him. And she didn't want that.

Quickly deciding on her course of action, she opened and shut the door and retraced her steps into the store. "Father," she called. "Are you in the store?"

She watched as he appeared from the storeroom. "Hello, Mary. I'll only be a minute. Colin is here."

When Red Horse walked into the store, Mary was laughing and talking with the two men. But seeing Red Horse, she said," I'll go back to the house now, Father."

"All right. I'll see you in an hour."

The sound of Muckross arguing with Bending Cane greeted her as Mary reached the cabin.

"The master does not like deer tongues, Bending Cane. I'm preparing him a nice slice of hog's ham."

Bending Cane made a sneering sound. "Hog meat is unclean. Animal that eats other animals is unclean."

"But your people eat bear meat," he argued.

"That different. Bear sacred. Only one."

Seeing Mary, Muckross drew her into the conversation. "What do ye think, Mary?"

She gazed from Muckross to Bending Cane and back. That year at school she had learned the definition of the word her father had used earlier—*intervene.* Now she understood what it actually meant. She had no wish to antagonize either Muckross or Bending Cane, and so she said," Why don't you prepare both? I like deer tongue. And perhaps my father will change his mind. But we know that he will enjoy the ham."

"I fix deer tongue," Bending Cane said, staring at Muckross.

"Fine with me. I'm fixing the ham."

Another year passed. And although the situation between the two servants did not get any better, Mary's situation at school improved tremendously.

On the day Parson Beckett moved her up from the Homer class to the Aristotle class, Polly was waiting for her after school. "Mary, would you like to stay tomorrow and help at Mama's quilting party? Sally and Maggie are coming, and I thought you might enjoy it, too."

"I'll ask my father tonight."

That was the beginning of her acceptance. By the time she was thirteen, it became a common occurrence for Hamish Pettipoole to find some excuse to walk with her to the blacksmith's shop, where Muckross was accustomed to wait for her.

But by the next fall, when she was promoted to the Socrates class, Hamish had left school to go to work. Her Indian dreams of setting out a bowl of hominy for him to eat, signifying that she was willing to marry him, vanished with him. But of course, that was not the way it was done in the English world, anyway.

Her disappointment at his leaving school was compounded by Muckross's imminent departure. The red haired, freckle-faced youth had worked out his indenture to her father. He was now free to go to Charlestown.

"Good-bye, Mary. I'll never forget ye," he said.

"Good-bye, Muckross. One of these days I'll come to Charlestown. And I'll look for your splendid tavern."

"And I'll fix ye a meal fit for a queen."

Mary laughed. "I want to see the town while I'm still a princess," she whispered. Then her merry eyes grew sad. "Here, I've packed something sweet for you to eat along the way. And you must wear this under your shirt for protection." She took a small leather pouch and handed it to him along with the dried peaches and fox grapes.

"I thought ye'd given up your heathen ways, Mary," he teased.

"There's a rabbit's foot inside."

"Aye. Well, that's all right, then."

Mary stood on the trading-post porch with her father as Muckross joined Colin's horse train. She waved until he was out of sight. With a sober face she left the porch and went to the cabin to supervise Bending Cane, who was already celebrating having the kitchen to herself.

# Chapter 10

"Ian, it's a strange thing about Indians," Parson Beckett began. "They certainly have an ear for the English language. They're much more adept at proper pronunciation than the foreigners who come to these shores."

Ian nodded. "But only if they learn it from the proper source. One of my Indian traders speaks like a German immigrant—and it's all because Kraus Moeller lived in his village at one time." Ian smiled. "I'm certainly glad that Mary was tutored by you and not Herr Moeller."

"Yes. Hearing Mary speak now, you might take her for the most elegant young lady in an English drawing room." He leaned closer to Ian. "I would not tell Mary so, for she is still struggling with the sin of pride. But I have never seen anyone improve so much in five years. Of course, I couldn't help but give her the award as the most outstanding student."

"I know she views it as an honor, Parson. We're both grateful to you."

"Oh, it wasn't my doing," the parson said quickly. "Heaven knows I looked for someone else. But if I had given the award to another, then I would have been guilty of a grosser sin.

"No, Ian. Do not be grateful to me. For I'm not sure that what we did was right—to take a half savage and put her into our world."

Mary, dressed in the fine blue silk dress, with a white fichu at the neck and her dark hair swept upward, waited outside the schoolhouse for her father to finish his conversation with the parson.

She was now fifteen years old. Although still tiny and slender, she possessed a regal look. Her once-sallow complexion had taken on a flawless, creamy glow, with the blue of the dress setting off the dramatic blue of her eyes. And her great mane of hair, long without benefit of bear grease, held a fine sheen in the late afternoon sun.

"Congratulations, Mary," Coreen O'Reilly said, passing by with her daughter, Sally. "What will ye be doing, now that school is out?"

"Oh, I will remain with my father and help him with the trading business. He's not too well, nowadays."

"Yes. I thought he was looking a bit peaked."

"And you, Sally?" Mary inquired. "Have you and Billy set the date for the banns?"

Sally blushed. "Sometime in the fall, I think."

Mrs. O'Reilly spoke up. "Mrs. Whitaker had a letter from him just yesterday. He's building a house on the Edisto River. He has two Negro slaves to help him with the house and to clear the fields. Yes, my Sally is awful lucky, even if she didn't go as far in school as ye did, Mary."

"But I'm not as smart as Mary is, Mama."

"Don't put yourself down, Sally. Ye have a beau, and Mary doesn't."

Mary and Sally exchanged glances. They both knew that Billy Whitaker was no catch, despite Mrs. O'Reilly's bragging.

"Good afternoon, Mrs. O'Reilly," Ian said, approaching the three.

"Mr. Ian," she replied, nodding her head. "A fine dress Mary is wearin'. Did ye have it sent from England?"

"Yes. But since she seemed to be outgrowing all of her clothes, I bought some bolts of muslin and calico, too. I hope you won't be too busy getting ready for Sally's wedding that you won't have time for my Mary's sewing."

Mrs. O'Reilly seemed slightly mollified. "Well, now, I can always make room for Mary. Wasn't I the one to sew her very first dresses when she came here? It would be a poor soul who would turn her back on her now."

"Good. I'll talk with you later about the time. Right now we have to get back to the trading post. I have an important visitor coming from Charlestown."

"Oh? And who might that be, Mr. Ian?" Coreen asked.

"Captain Musgrove. He's visiting these parts on behalf of British and Carolina fur-trading interests."

Mary and her father walked to the small carriage. It was a more elegant one than the cart pulled by the piebald pony. As she climbed up, Mary said, "I miss Muckross. I wish he could have been here today."

"Maybe Colin will have a message from him."

Mary watched as Ian took the reins in his hands. Her father had lost most of the dexterity of his fingers, even though Mary had sought to keep them supple by regular hot oil rubbings. But the trouble was not only in his hands. His illness was rapidly spreading to the rest of his body, despite anything she could do.

That was why Mary was glad that her schooling was completed. She had long taken over the domestic supervision of the house, the gardens, and the animals in the folds. Now she could devote more hours in helping Ian with the store and watching Red Horse more carefully, for his loyalty to Ian seemed to be waning. She and the Muscogean had always been enemies, but ever since the episode of the two snakes, he had treated her with a certain wariness, as if she possessed some secret power that it would be healthier not to challenge. Lately, that wariness, too, seemed to be waning.

Other changes had also occurred at the trading post. Once Muckross had left, a pair of indentured twins, Ruby and Sandy, had been added to the household. The cabin had been expanded, with the dogtrot addition built to shelter the visitors who happened along. With its own fireplace and bedroom off the smaller living area, it was completely separated from the cabin, yet attached to it by the covered porch, or dogtrot.

As the carriage wound its way back to the post, Mary's mind turned to their coming visitors. "I hope Ruby has finished airing the bedclothes properly and brought in the sweet shrub branches, as I told her."

Ian smiled. "I think you're more excited about Captain Musgrove's visit than any other. Or could it be young John, coming with him, that has you in such a dither?"

Mary's blue eyes sparkled at her father's teasing. "I have never seen anyone even close to my age who lives in a fine house in Charlestown."

Ian cleared his throat as he often did when he was ready to say something not to Mary's liking. "Living in a fine English house, Mary, does not make a man better than another. And despite Captain Musgrove's standing as an assemblyman, he has been censured by that same assembly for some of his questionable dealings with the Indians."

"I understand, Father. But we must be hospitable to them both, is that not so?"

"That is so," he admitted.

Mary clutched the school parchment to her breast. She was happy. At that moment she felt as if she were standing upon a great threshold. This was a new beginning—a time of joy and of hope. The uneasiness that had nagged at her with each tale of increasing hostility between the Indians and the settlers was dismissed from her mind as she turned her thoughts to the coming visitors.

In five years' time, the wilderness between the town and the trading post had dwindled, as the town, like Ian's cabin, had expanded. New settlers had felled the trees and planted their crops of corn, enclosed their folds of sheep against night predators, and made orchards of apples and peaches. With the advance of civilization, even the settlers' hogs felt safe, rooting around by day for nuts in the nearby woods and coming home toward sundown with the call of "soo-ee," each recognizing the distinctive inflection of his owner's voice.

But as the carriage rolled down the well-worn path, Ian felt the silence, different from a few hours before, when he and Mary had traveled the opposite way into town. No sound of grunting pigs, no calls of birds overhead greeted them.

"There's something different about the woods," Ian said. "Do you feel it, Mary?"

She came out of her reverie and listened. Her transformation was startling. Despite the elegant silk dress, despite all the other outward trappings that proclaimed her a lady, she changed swiftly into a more primitive being, taking in the scent of the wind, drawing out the secrets of the trees and thickets.

Then, once again, she became the English daughter. "It is too quiet, Father. Something or someone has scared the animals and birds. Let us hurry home."

Ian nodded. With a sense of urgency now, he clucked his tongue and slapped the reins to increase the horse's gait. Without speaking, Mary and her father sped through the woods, with only the rhythmic crunching of the carriage wheels in the ruts of the road marking the passing minutes.

Up ahead, the trading post seemed peaceful, with the smoke of the cooking fire visible through the trees. Ian's sigh was one of relief. For the past several months, he had been uneasy about leaving, even with Red Horse there to take care of the store.

Ian brought the carriage to a stop before the gate. He motioned for the boy, Sandy, to take the vehicle on to the barn shed. "Walk Tallassee a bit, Sandy, to cool him off. And then when you've put him in the barn, come to the store."

"Yes, Master Ian."

As Mary walked with her father onto the porch she said, "Do you think Captain Musgrove will get here in time for supper?"

"It's hard to tell, Mary. But why don't you set a place for them at the table, anyway?"

Mary nodded and went to her room to take off her expensive clothes and put on an everyday calico, with apron. In the other bedroom, she heard her father doing the same—removing his good clothes for his work clothes. By the time she came into the keeping room, her father had left the cabin.

As Mary surveyed the room she saw that Bending Cane had not finished her chores. And the cooking fire had been left unattended. With a firm set to her chin, Mary called out. But Bending Cane did not answer.

Exasperated with the Indian woman, Mary went in search of her. Not finding her in any of the usual places, Mary finally walked to the servants' quarters at the back of the garden. Built like an Indian long house on the outside, the wooden building was divided inside, with a separate door for each small apartment,

She knocked on one of the doors. "Bending Cane, are you in there?"

She waited and then knocked again. Finally, Mary pushed the door open. Bending Cane was not inside. Neither were her belongings. The red trading blanket had been removed from her bed. Puzzled, Mary retraced her steps back to the cabin.

From the open window, Mary could hear Ruby's voice as she sang. Gratified that the indentured servant, at least, was where she was supposed to be, Mary walked across the dogtrot to the guest quarters.

On the hearth by the fireplace stood a large earthenware jug. From it, fresh branches filled the air with a wonderful, woodsy perfume. The two rocking chairs, the small table, and the lantern were well polished. And the woven rag rug on the floor gave a homey coziness to the half-logged room.

Pleased with the way the room looked, Mary proceeded to the bedroom, where Ruby had her back to the door. "Ruby?"

The girl turned around. She would always be undersized, Mary thought. For when Ian fetched them, both she and her twin brother looked like two abandoned pups put outside the den to die. No one had offered to pay their transportation, for they had almost died aboard ship, and neither looked capable of working a week, much less twelve years.

Feeling sorry for them, Ian had purchased their bond at half price, which was more than the captain of the ship expected. And now, with their health back, the two were good and willing workers, if a bit slow.

"Ruby, have you seen Bending Cane?"

"She left, Miss Mary. Not long after you and Mr. Ian set out."

"Where did she go?"

"I don't know. I saw her talkin' to an Indian on the tradin' porch. He was awful to see—half-naked and all daubed in red, with blue marks across his nose and a black streak down his arms. I went inside and bolted the door, I was so scared. And pretty soon, I saw her walkin' across the garden with her things. That was the last I saw of her."

Mary was clearly out of sorts with the news. "Well, come with me, Ruby. That is, if you've finished in here."

"Yes, mum."

"You and I will have to hurry and set the table and finish cooking the supper. I'm not sure what time Captain Musgrove will arrive. But we have to be ready. Men are always hungry after a long trip."

Ruby followed Mary across the dogtrot and into the cabin. There, the two began their preparation, roasting the wild turkey on the spit. And amid the coals on the hearth, Mary placed the heavy black iron skillet that contained the cornbread.

Later, peach tarts, melons, and fresh vegetables from the garden graced the trestle table. But the wood of the table was not visible. For Mary had covered it with the white linen cloth reserved for special occasions. At each place, she positioned the flatware and the blue china. Flowering pea vines and forest trillium filled the small vase in the middle of the table, and on each side sat tall, tallow candles ready to be lit.

Mary returned to her room, where she took a bath. Once again, she swapped her calico for the blue silk dress. When she had finished combing her hair, she walked back into the keeping room just in time to hear the sound of a wagon approaching the trading post.

# Chapter 11

"I think I'll go to bed, Mary," Ian said. "Looks like Captain Musgrove won't get here today after all."

A disappointed Mary sat in the rocking chair by the hearth. Two clean plates remained on the trestle table, with the cold meat platter and vegetable dishes covered by napkins. The wagon that had arrived earlier belonged to one of the settlers and not the Musgroves.

"I'll stay up a little longer, Father," Mary said. "But if he doesn't come within the next half hour, then I'll go to bed, too."

By the light of the tallow candles, Mary continued to read. But each time she heard a noise, her attention immediately left the book. Finally, she marked her place, closed the book, and took a candle into her bedroom.

Mary took off her dress carefully and put it away. When she had gotten on her night clothes, she then sat down at the small dressing table and removed the pins from her hair. With her thoughts lingering on the events of the day, she picked up her hairbrush. It was when she had almost finished her hundred strokes that she heard the knock at the door.

Had the Musgroves finally arrived, after all? Mary dropped the hairbrush and gazed toward the linen press where she had put up her beautiful dress. But at the sound of a second knock, she realized there was no time to get dressed. She would have to let them in immediately.

With a shawl thrown over her shoulders to hide the white stroud gown, she took her candle and rushed toward the door. But before opening it, a cautious Mary called out, "Who is it, please?"

"Musgrove," the reply came.

Mary unbolted the door and opened it. Standing on the porch were two tall figures silhouetted against the pale aura of the moon.

"Come in," Mary said, standing aside for them to enter. With the candle held high, she introduced herself, as she had been taught. "I am Mary, and I bid you welcome on behalf of my father. I'm afraid he has already gone to bed."

The older Musgrove nodded. "We had hoped to get here before nightfall, but we met with some difficulties." At the frown of the younger man, he abruptly broke off. "This is my son, John Musgrove."

He nodded toward Mary and said, "A pleasure to meet you, ma'am."

He was a beautiful young man, broad-shouldered, with a strong face. His infectious smile caused Mary a momentary speechlessness. But then she regained her composure. "Your quarters are ready. I'll show you to them. And then, if you are hungry, I can offer you a cold supper and something to drink."

"Very kind of you," the younger Musgrove responded.

Within a few minutes, Captain Musgrove and his son had put their belongs in the rooms off the dogtrot. And by the time they returned to the main house, Mary was already bringing the food from the pantry and placing the platters upon the trestle table.

The two candelabra were ablaze with candles, lighting the trestle table and giving Mary a better view of the two men, who had both washed the dried mud from their faces and combed their hair. After one glance toward the captain, an older version of his son, Mary continued her interest in the younger man.

Although about the same height as Hamish Pettipoole, he was far more handsome, with his damp, sandy-colored hair curling about his neck. Despite the loose-fitting buckskins, she could tell that his body was strong and sturdy, the muscles of his arms and thighs as well developed as her father's before the wasting disease had come upon him.

As she set a tray of warm bread beside him, John Musgrove's eyes—a startling blue—not like the sky, but the color of the majestic herons on the marsh—met hers for a brief moment before she glanced away.

Mary felt unsure of herself in the younger Musgrove's presence and she didn't like the feeling. She was used to serving as hostess with her father's visitors, but never in her nightgown. Even though it was as thick or thicker than most of her dresses, and the tied shawl completely covered her shoulders, she still regretted that she had been caught in this manner. Why had she not kept on her beautiful blue dress, with her hair pinned up, rather than having it sprawl over her shoulders?

But then Mary took herself to task for such thoughts. The men were tired and hungry after their long trip. They probably had not even noticed what she was wearing at all. And so her mind returned to food and drink, and to making her father's guests comfortable.

As she filled the captain's cup, he said, "I understand from your father's letter that Parson Beckett has been tutoring you."

"Yes. For the past five years," she replied. There was a pride in her eyes that made them sparkle.

"Quite a long time. For a girl."

"For your society, mayhaps," she answered, aware of the differences between his English traditions and her own Indian culture, where the women had more power than the men.

John laughed appreciatively, even as his father scowled. "How much longer will you be in school?"

"Today was my last day."

"What will you do now?" John asked.

"Continue to run the house. See to the gardens and the flocks. And then, to help—"

She stopped. No, it would not do to mention Ian's failing health, especially in front of the man surveying the fur-trading empire of the business house in Charlestown. "To help the servants with the preserving of meats and fruits."

Mary continued to see to their needs. When their hunger was finally assuaged, the two rose from the table.

"We won't keep you up any longer," Captain Musgrove said. "But thank you for that most tasty repast."

John added his thanks to that of the captain.

Mary nodded and replied, "My father will be pleased to see you both at breakfast."

From the candelabra on the table, Mary relit the single tallow candle in the holder and, handing it to John, she said, "Sleep well."

With his father already headed to the door, John smiled at the young girl. "Good night, Mary."

"Good night, Mr. Musgrove. Captain."

Mary then bolted the door and listened until the footsteps across the dogtrot porch vanished. Hurriedly, she returned to the table, put up the bit of remaining food, stacked the dishes for Ruby to wash the next morning, and then went to her bedroom.

As soon as the captain and his son, John, were inside their own quarters, with no chance of being overheard, John asked, "What did you think of Mary?"

"She's a capable lass," he answered. "Evidently the apple of Ian's eye, else he wouldn't have spent all that money on her education."

"Comely, too, don't you think?"

The captain laughed. "Bound for you to notice that." The captain held the candle closer and examined his son's face. "You're not interested in the girl, are you, John?"

"It's too early to say," he replied. "Remember I only met her an hour ago."

That night the captain and John lay in bed, each thinking his own thoughts, but of the same girl.

The captain, remembering their narrow escape that day from the scalping party, saw Mary in terms of what she could do for them. After all, she was not only Ian's daughter, but a Creek princess, and Old Brims' niece. With increasing danger for anyone in the fur-trading business, the one who took the Creek emperor's niece to wife would be assured of safety and a thriving livelihood. But let matters work themselves out without his interference. He was tired and wanted a good night's sleep.

John was not nearly so business-minded as his father. His thoughts of Mary that night took on a more personal direction. Her manners were every bit as elegant as Eleanor Mimms's. In fact she spoke in a more refined manner than many of his Charlestown acquaintances. He was amused at her proud manner, at the way she'd answered his father as if she were every bit as good as he. He liked her exotic look, too. He'd had an urge to reach out and touch that long mane of black hair, but of course he had restrained himself.

Thinking of it now, it wasn't the only urge that he had been forced to restrain. Despite her civilized façade, there was something of the forest about her, making him recall the stories swapped by the men who had taken Indian women to wife. He'd known of trappers who completely disappeared, so governed by love for these women that they had turned their backs on white society.

That night, John's dreams were filled with Mary. And when he began to awaken, he slowly stretched and reached out to feel the long hair he had stroked during the night. But when he opened his eyes, he realized he was clutching the pillow instead.

"Time to get up, Johnny. Breakfast is ready."

His father was already dressed. So John hurriedly washed his face and put on his buckskins that he had worn the previous day. Of softest leather, his shirt and breeches were protective as well as serviceable. No thorns had penetrated the leather, even through their forced flight past the thickets.

By the time John arrived in the keeping room, Ian and his father were already at the table and drinking hot mugs of tea.

"Ian, this is my son, my namesake."

Ian nodded. "Have a seat, John. I trust you slept well?"

"Yes, sir. Very well."

Ian continued. "Mary is seeing to the servants. The breakfast should be on the table shortly."

Ruby and Sandy, the two indentured servants, entered with trays of food. Mary was beside them, directing them. She smiled at the men seated at the table.

"Sit down, Mary," Ian said, motioning for his daughter to take her place at the other end of the table. He glanced from the captain to John. "I believe you both met my daughter, Mary, last night."

"Yes. Good morning to you, Mary," John said as his father nodded in her direction.

"Good morning to you both."

"Eat up," Ian urged as soon as the food was served. "We observe the Indian tradition in our household of giving thanks *after* the meal."

"A sensible thing to do," John said.

"Keeps the food from getting cold," Captain Musgrove agreed, and immediately dug in.

"Sometimes we're more thankful than at other times," Mary offered.

"Especially if there's been a calamity in the kitchen, eh?"

"Oh, there's little chance of that, Captain, with my Mary watching over things."

The conversation turned to business, and Mary sat quietly and listened as she ate. At intervals, she motioned for either Ruby or Sandy to replenish the mugs, the bread, and the bear bacon. When the men had finished and pushed themselves back slightly from the table, Ian bowed his head and gave thanks.

The rest of the morning was disappointing for Mary. She was busy enough seeing to the daily chores, especially without Bending Cane to help her. But she missed going off to school. And by afternoon she missed taking her customary seat in the store to listen in or even bargain with the Indians and settlers.

With a hearty breakfast and an early supper, a midday meal was not necessary, so Mary knew she would not see the visitors or her father again until suppertime. But with the cabin cleaned, the pantry inspected, and preparations made for the evening meal, Mary grew restless.

"Ruby, I'm going for a walk," she said to the servant. "I'll be back within the hour."

"What do you want me to do about the peach pies?"

"Watch them until they're done, and then put them out to cool. But make sure that the raccoon can't get at them."

"Yes, Miss Mary."

Dressed in one of her more flattering muslins, Mary left the porch of the cabin and began to walk in the direction of the river landing.

From the open door of the arsenal, John saw her walk by. His father and Ian were still engrossed in their conversation. Although John would have been interested in the conversation, he was more interested in talking with Mary. So he left the two men and began walking in the same direction as the young girl.

Deep in thought, Mary sat on the dock and languidly dipped her hand into the water. No one watching her would have suspected that she had a single care. But actually, she was troubled. Something was wrong. She knew that Bending Cane's disappearance the day before was tied to the uneasiness she felt in the air. And now Red Horse's canoe was gone from the landing. She peered downriver, hoping to catch a glimpse of the Indian she had seen slip away at midmorning. If he returned, that would be a good sign that all was still well.

"Mary?"

She turned around at the sound of John's voice. "Yes?"

"Do you mind if I sit with you for a while?"

"No." She moved over and made room for him on the dock.

As they sat together in silence and listened to the river running and watched the hawk glide lazily overhead, Mary knew that a new danger had entered her life. With his easy conversation, his handsome face, John Musgrove was much more harmful to her soul than anything Red Horse had ever dreamed up. For Mary could feel John's power over her, and even worse, she had no desire to counteract it.

# Chapter 12

From east to west, north to south, the emissaries of the Creek emperor rode—to the chief towns of the Yuchi, the Yamasee, the Catawba, the Saraw, Waccamaw, Appalachee, and Santee. Each carried the bloodied staff of war in his hand, and on his tongue the words of the emperor.

"My brothers, our lands have been taken from us by the English. We have been cheated of our furs by their traders. Our women have been ravished and our children sold into slavery. For too long we have watched and done nothing as the white man grows like a plague among us, slaughtering our game and breaking our treaties.

"Now let the calumet of peace be broken and let the tears of our people rise up as warriors from the ground. Let the traders and settlers be slaughtered even as the deer. And let the Earth Mother be nourished with the blood of their women and children.

"Join me, my brothers, in a holy war, to drive the white man from our land.

"As a surety that you are with me, tie your blood pledge upon my staff."

From one Indian village to another, the emissaries rode. Their long staffs became heavy with the strips of bloodied flags representing each tribe and each town that had pledged its warriors to the emperor of the Creeks in his holy war against the English.

This was the reason for Red Horse's disappearance from Ian's store and for Bending Cane's flight the day before. The Creek Nation and its allies had been called to war, and no one at any settlement or any wilderness trading post was safe.

At the Ponpon settlement, Coreen O'Reilly finally finished packing. She had stayed up all night, after Billy's letter arrived, saying that he wanted Sally to come to Charlestown immediately so they could be married there.

It had certainly given her little enough time to plan and to get someone to drive her wagon in Colin's packhorse train. But before she and Sally left, Coreen knew she'd have to send a message to Mary and then find out what time the caravan would be leaving.

Coaching the young driver she had hired, Coreen said, "I expect Mary already knows from Colin that Mr. Whitaker has sent for my Sally and that we're both leavin' tomorrow. But I want ye to tell her that because of leavin' so soon, I won't be able to make her any new dresses. Now, you have that, Elrod?"

"Yes, mum."

"And ye'll check with Colin again about the time he's leavin'?"

"Yes, Mrs. O'Reilly."

"Well, get on the way, I prithee. We don't have all day."

Early the next morning, just before daybreak, Mrs. O'Reilly, Sally, and Elrod took their places in the caravan headed for Charlestown. They would travel only as far as the way station where Billy would be waiting to take them on to his house. Coreen was not a good traveler, but for Sally's sake she would not complain, no matter how uncomfortable the trip.

"What's that, Elrod? Up ahead. See? In the woods?"

Coreen was startled at every movement, every sign of wildlife. She even jumped when the packhorses snorted suddenly, blowing like bellows through their nostrils.

"Looks like a bear cub, Mrs. O'Reilly. Probably stealin' some wild honey, judgin' from that angry buzz of bees."

Coreen immediately brought out a large piece of muslin. "Here, Sally. Put this over your head. Wouldn't want your face swollen out of shape when Billy sees you."

"Oh, Mama, it's too hot for that," Sally complained.

"Maybe so. But do it, lass, for me. Ye remember little Charlotte Mundy and what happened to her when she fell into that wasps' nest."

"Yes, Mama. I remember. She died." Sally took the muslin and draped it over her sunbonnet as her mother continued talking.

"I had that dainty little white dress almost sewed for her when it happened. I had no idea that it was goin' to be her funeral dress. She looked so pretty in it. Could hardly see the wasp stings. I had to stay up all night, finishin' it in time, just like I did two nights ago with your weddin' dress."

"I hope my wedding dress will have happier memories than Charlotte's dress," Sally said, her sad countenance hidden by the muslin.

"Of course it will, Sally. No use to dwell on morbid things during this happy time."

The hum of disturbed bees grew louder as they came together in a swarm along the Indian trace. A sudden neigh, a bolt of one of the horses, and soon bedlam began.

Colin swore as the sound mounted. He had hoped to get through this particular part of the forest with a minimum of noise. Instead, their whereabouts might as well be broadcast to the entire wilderness.

Fifteen minutes later, the horses were all back in line. But the damage had been done. The lone Yamasee scout, dressed in his war paint, had spotted them.

Through the forest the Indian warriors crept, with all traces of civilization and kindness purged from their minds and bodies three days previously by the sweet sage and steaming rocks of the sweat lodge.

Like the greased shafts of arrows and polished musket stocks they carried, their painted bodies glistened in the filtered light of the sun. As the young warrior chief took cover behind a tall oak tree, he rubbed his hatchet with dirt to remove the dried blood of the settler's family who had been ambushed by the creek, and at the same time he watched for the approach of the horse caravan.

Down the worn trail, Colin led his group, signaling for each person to remain quiet. Only the occasional sound of a hoof hitting against a rock, a nervous neigh, or the steady squeak of the wheels of Coreen's wagon marred the wilderness trek.

And then a sudden bird call was answered in like manner farther down the trail.

"Mama, did you hear that? I'm so scared," Sally whispered.

Coreen put her trembling hand on her daughter's shoulder to indicate her sympathy, but she spoke no words of comfort. She was too busy examining every slight movement on each side of the wagon.

As they continued through the forest, the unnatural silence brought terror to the heart. No animals crossed their path. It was almost as if the wild ones had sensed danger and fled to their rotted logs and underground burrows.

Then, at the most dangerous bend in the trail, where the caravan was least able to defend itself, the band of Indian warriors gave an eerie howl and rushed forward.

The horses, with the stings of the bees too new, too recent in memory, were spooked by this fresh onslaught from another source. They again bolted as the warriors attacked.

"Elrod," Colin shouted. "Get the women back to the settlement."

But the mare pulling the small wagon cart had other ideas. She took off across the woods, with Elrod, Coreen, and Sally barely managing to hold on.

"Don't look back, Sally," Coreen cried.

Her warning came too late. Sally had already turned her head. She gave a stifled cry as she saw one of the drivers knocked from his horse and an Indian raise his hatchet to strike.

"Poor man," she mourned, and began to cling to her mother.

As the mare continued her frenzied escape, saplings broke under the weight of the wagon, while the lower limbs of oaks slapped at the women's faces. The wagon did not stop until it suddenly became wedged between two large loblolly pines. The abrupt action tossed Elrod, Coreen, and Sally headlong into the brush.

At Ian's trading post, Captain Musgrove was in no hurry to leave. The company was pleasant, the hospitality cordial, and the comforts of food and bed far better than he'd expected. Then, too, Ian was quite a source of information on the way an Indian trader could make money for himself and the business house he worked for. So many of the traders were such a sorry lot that they gave the rest of them a bad name. But not Ian.

"I believe my son is smitten with your daughter, Ian," he said, watching their two children from his seat on the trading porch.

Ian gazed down the vista where Mary and John were returning from the dock. "She has that effect on most men, I've noticed. At least this past year." His expression was noncommittal, as if he were merely stating a fact, nothing more.

"What are your plans for her?"

"That's up to Mary. She has her Creek inheritance coming to her, of course. It doesn't seem to be important to her at the moment, though. And I'm glad. A man in his old age needs his kin around him as long as possible." Ian rubbed his arm which had grown increasingly numb since morning.

Mary smiled and waved to her father as she approached the porch. "I'll be in the house, Father, if you need me," she said.

He nodded and watched the two young people separate. As Mary continued past the porch John walked up the steps to take his seat near the two men.

On a broken-down horse, borrowed from the blacksmith, Parson Beckett raced down the road towardthe trading post. His clerical frock coat flapped around him as both he and the horse wheezed from exertion.

"O Lord, hear your servant's voice crying in the wilderness," he intoned, between gasps. "Save us, your God-fearing people, from the heinous savages of this new Canaan."

Each breath of the wind, each cry of a bird, had the same effect on the parson as the most maniacal howl of a marauding Indian. Every moment he expected his life to end. By the time he reached the trading post, none was more surprised than he that he was still alive.

"Ian, Ian," he called, seeing the man on the trading porch. "There's an Indian uprising. Hamish

Pettipoole just crawled into the settlement, with a hatchet in his skull."

The parson climbed down from his horse and stumbled up the steps. Ian reached out to steady him before he fell.

"Sandy, go get the parson some rum from the cask," Ian said to the young indentured servant. "And you, Parson, sit down and catch your breath."

Within a few minutes Parson Beckett had quaffed the rum as if it were water. Once his nerves became steadier, he told a fragmented story of Charlestown already under siege and the murder of Thomas Naire, an Indian agent, by the Yamasees at Pocataligo.

"He was burned at the stake. A horrible death. And the settlers around were killed, too. Governor Craven has called out the militia to protect Charlestown from the savages."

"Then I'll have to leave immediately," Captain Musgrove said to Ian.

"I'll go and pack our belongings, Father," John said.

"And I'll see to the horses," Captain Musgrove responded.

"Go with him to the barn, Sandy," Ian urged.

The two Musgroves and the servant disappeared while Ian remained with the parson.

As John hurried to the cabin, he felt a tremendous disappointment. From the moment he had seen Ian's daughter that first night in the dim candlelight, his heart had known that he could be happy with her. But he had been content to court her gradually, realizing that she was young and he could not tell her of his feelings too soon, for fear of alienating her. Now those words would have to remain unspoken. Because of this war, he might never see her again.

"Mary," John called out at the door of the cabin.

"Yes, John?" She wiped the flour from her hands and walked to meet him. Her smile vanished when she saw his sober expression.

"Did you hear? Charlestown is under Indian siege. My father and I will be leaving immediately."

"John..."

He saw the distress in her blue eyes. At that moment he wanted to take her into his arms, to taste the sweetness of her lips. Instead, he forced a smile and said, "May the Lord watch over you, Mary."

"And you, John."

He turned his back and hurried along the dogtrot porch to gather his belongings.

With her heart close to breaking, Mary thought of her princess mother. Was this how she had felt when Ian Yonahlongi Hatke had left her?

But they were husband and wife. She was nothing to John Musgrove, who had so stolen her heart. "How could you do this to me, Uncle?" she cried, angry with Old Brims, reaching out from his home in the hills to ruin her life so far away.

Later, with a feeling of dread and fear for the safety of John's life, she stood at the closed gate and watched him go. He lifted his hand in farewell—the tall, beautiful man with the engaging smile and genial nature.

"Will he be leavin' for good?" Ruby asked, coming to stand beside her mistress.

"Yes," Mary said. "I'll never see him again."

She brushed away a tear. In a voice more stern than usual, she said, "Go and clean the guest quarters, Ruby. And then bolt the doors."

Toward the river, heavy gray clouds passed over the sun. The tall hardwood trees swayed in response to the hostile wind, and in the distance a roll of thunder became the fanfare for the gathering storm.

# Chapter 13

"What are we to do, Ian?" Parson Beckett asked. "When they get here, the savages will show no mercy for anyone. Our poor little settlement will vanish from the face of the earth."

Ian gave only a strangled sound in response, but the parson did not notice. The effects of the second mug of rum had loosened the parson's tongue, urging him to lament his ever leaving England, his ever giving up Charlestown for a backwoods settlement.

But finally, when Ian made no effort to commiserate with his sufferings, Parson Beckett turned his head and looked at the fur trader. What he saw made him even more fearful, for Ian had slumped against the railing, and his eyes had taken on a glassy appearance.

"What's the matter, man? Are you ill?"

Ian lifted his hand and then dropped it into his lap, as if the effort were too great.

The parson fled toward the cabin and called out, "Mary, come at once. Something has happened to your father."

She sat in the rocking chair by the hearth and stared down at the flower she had pressed between the pages of the book. John had given her the flower—fragile and beautiful—the only thing she had to remember him by.

Into her reverie, Parson Beckett's voice intruded. "Mary, where are you? Come quickly."

At the urgency in his voice, Mary dropped the book and began to run. She nearly collided with the parson on the porch.

"What is it, Parson? What's happened?"

"It's your father. He's slumped over on the trading porch, Mary. Looks like he might be dying."

"No."

With the parson behind her, Mary ran as fast as she could to reach her father. Had the war party come upriver and gotten to her father without her knowing? She knew that the Creeks were vicious with their enemies, cutting off their heads or scalping them and leaving them to die a painful death.

By the time she reached the trading porch and saw him, Mary felt a momentary relief. There was no sign of blood.

She knelt beside him. "Father?" she called out.

Ian merely stared at her, without speaking.

"It's all right, Father," she crooned to him softly. "You will be all right soon."

Mary began to rub his hands gently and in a low voice said to the parson, "Please go and find Sandy.

Tell him to bring me the strongest deerskin. We will have to carry my father to his bed."

Within a short space of time Ian was lying upon his rope bed. His eyes communicated with Mary, even though he could say nothing. But she understood. "Rest now, Father," she urged. "Go to sleep for a little while. I'll take care of things until you are better."

She waited for him to close his eyes, and once he was asleep and breathing evenly, she tiptoed out of the room. Signaling Ruby to take her place, she went onto the porch where the parson was still praying.

Seeing her, he got off his knees. "What are we to do, Mary? About the Indians? They may already be at the settlement now, killing my poor parishioners."

She looked toward the sun, low in the sky. "No. They will not come today. Tomorrow, perhaps."

"Then I suppose I should return to the settlement. We will fast and pray..."

Mary had no patience with an inept man. "No, Parson. We will work and pray.

"While Sandy gathers the guns and powder from the arsenal, you ride back to the settlement and post a lookout in the meeting house belfry immediately."

He nodded and said, "Yes. I suppose that's the thing to do."

As Mary walked to the tree where Sandy had tethered his horse, she continued, "Then get a brigade to draw every available pail of water to put out any fire that starts, and have the women get together as much food as they can. When that is done, gather all the people inside the meeting house and bolt the door.

"Sandy will be along presently with the guns and powder from the arsenal."

As the parson nodded again and climbed back on the old broken-down horse, Mary called out, "Don't raise a general alarm. Instead, send someone quietly from house to house."

There was a calmness about Mary as she walked into the cabin. She had no time to spend in sentimental reminiscences. Her father had taken ill. The settlement and trading post were in danger of being destroyed if she did not act quickly.

Once again she checked on her father. His breathing was still even. So she motioned for Ruby to follow her into the keeping room.

"Stop sniveling, Ruby," she ordered the young girl.

"But we're all goin' to be killed. You heard the parson, clear as I did."

"Not if you do what I tell you. Now hurry up and get the spare hams and other things I told you. When Sandy leaves with the guns in a few minutes, I'm sending you with him."

Ruby wiped her eyes with her apron and ran into the pantry for the requested supplies while Mary walked into her bedroom and began to search among her old clothes in the bottom of the linen press.

Later, with the candles and bread, fresh fruit, and cured hams laid out on the strong white tablecloth, Mary tied a great knot, and the two dragged the provisions out onto the porch to await the wagon filled with guns.

When Sandy stopped the wagon outside the gate to the cabin, he jumped down to help the two young women lift the provisions into the wagon. Ruby then climbed up beside Sandy, but Mary remained on the ground.

"You want me to come back for you and Mr. Ian?" Sandy asked.

"No, Sandy. We'll stay here at the trading post."

Ruby began to cry again, but Mary ignored her. She spoke again to the indentured servant.

"Sandy, hang this flag from the belfry so it can be seen from a distance."

"What is it, Miss Mary?"

"Never mind. The Indians will recognize it."

She handed him her own royal flag that she had brought with her from Coweta Town. Painted on it were the same signs with which the small schoolgirl had decorated her face more than five years previously.

Sandy took the flag. He looked at it and then back to her. She knew he had no idea what she was doing—claiming the settlement as her own, placing it under her protection. But would it work? Did she have sufficient power even to save herself, much less save an entire English village?

"The Lord keep thee and watch over thee, Miss Mary," Ruby called out as the wagon left the yard.

Mary waved and went back inside to check on the condition of her father, Ian.


"Mama, Mama," Sally O'Reilly cried. Wake up." She tightened the piece of muslin about Coreen's bleeding head as her mother lay moaning on the ground.

A wheel had come off the wagon, and now they were stranded in the forest. In the distance, the sound of guns and the barbaric howls continued, indicating the fierce battle raging between Colin's packers and the hostile Indians.

"Elrod, do you see anything?" Sally whispered to the boy stationed behind one of the wagon wheels with his musket poised on his arm.

"Not yet, Miss Sally. But if they come, I'll be sure to get some of them before—"

"Oh Elrod, don't even speak it. We're goin' to be scalped, I just know it."

"If your mama would only wake up, we could try to make it back to Ponpon."

"But she can't, Elrod. She hit her head hard. And I can't leave her by herself."

They waited and listened. The fighting seemed farther away now, judging from the gunfire that came in sporadic bursts. Noticing this, Elrod pondered what to do. They couldn't stay where they were forever. He had hidden the wagon as best he could with tree branches, but he had no hope that they would not be discovered eventually.

"Miss Sally," he whispered. "I think we should try to leave now."

"Not without Mama, Elrod. I told you I wasn't leaving her."

"It will be dark soon. We'll put her on the horse. And the two of us will walk beside her. That's the only way."

He handed Sally the gun while he untethered the horse. The boy had difficulty lifting the woman from the wagon onto the horse. But when he had done it, he realized that he had another problem. Coreen O'Reilly was in no condition to sit. So finally he draped her over the horse, distributing her weight evenly as he had seen Colin do with his packhorses. The three set out on the trail back to Ponpon.

Regretfully Sally looked back at the wooden box barely visible from the wagon. "My clothes," she lamented. "I wish I could save my wedding dress, at least."

"It's better to save your skin, Miss Sally. The walkin' will be hard enough without being weighted down by somethin' you can do without."

The unnatural silence of the woods gave an eeriness to their flight. An occasional hooting of an owl, answered by another farther down the trail, caused Elrod to stop and listen.

"That's not an owl, is it, Elrod?" Sally whispered.

"It might be," he said. But his reassurance was not convincing. They both knew that it was more than likely an Indian signaling to another ahead that they were coming.

The unnatural silence extended to the trading post, where Mary sat by candlelight before the table in her bedroom. No trace of the English girl was visible in the mirror. Her muslin dress had been exchanged for the soft deerskin dress, fringed with beads. On her feet were moccasins of like design.

Gone were the pins from her dark hair and the ribbon that had matched her dress. Now, the long, luxuriant mane was plastered with bear grease and tied into two plaits that hung down past her young bosom. And on her face she wore the sacred pigments of red, blue, yellow, and white, her heritage visible for all to see.

She was now Coosaponakeesa, princess of the Creeks and niece to the emperor who had stirred her people to war against the fur traders and settlers.

She had been busy far into the night. Now nothing was left to do—except to wait for morning and for what the new day would bring.

Coosaponakeesa took her candle and walked into her father's bedroom. She leaned over and examined the spots that she had painted earlier on her father's face—resembling the dreaded pox of the white man that had wiped out entire tribes. Satisfied with her work—that is, if no one came too close—she blew out the candle.

On the floor beside her father's bed, she wrapped her black wolf pelt around her and went to sleep for the rest of the night.

In the darkness, ancestral dreams visited her. It was a long journey, past the life that she had lived with her father, past all remembrance of her childhood in Coweta Town, to the time when she and the wolf had been sisters in the spirit world.

Past the vestiges of the wilderness, Sally O'Reilly, Coreen, and Elrod came, until the crude palisade of logs bordering the settlement loomed in the distance. An exhausted Sally whispered, "Mama, we're home."

Coreen, now awake but still dazed, responded, "The Lord be praised."

In a few minutes, judging from the lightening of the horizon, the sun would be coming up soon. The three had been traveling all night, stopping only long enough to rest the horse.

Now Elrod pushed the gate open, and the three entered the settlement. The horse, sensing that food and water were near, whinnied in anticipation.

Up in the belfry of the meeting house, Parson Beckett was finishing his portion of the night watch. In the stillness of the past hour, he had dozed. But at the sound of the horse, he came alive.

The Indians had finally come, as he had known they would, to slaughter them all. He saw their stealthy movements along the lane toward one of the houses. With a trembling arm, he brought the gun into position and, closing his eyes, he shot in their direction.

Coreen O'Reilly, propped up by Elrod and her daughter Sally, had taken only a few faltering steps when the horse dropped dead at her feet.

As a second shot rang from the belfry the woman cried out, "Don't shoot. It's me—Coreen O'Reilly."

The sound of the gun reached the trading post, where Coosaponakeesa still slept. Instantly, she was awake. She fled to the window to peer out, but it was not yet daylight. It was too soon for the Indians to be attacking the settlement.

She bolted the window and, a few minutes later, she carefully made her way through the passage to the arsenal and into the deserted store. As she placed her hand upon the floor, she felt a vibration, barely discernible to the palms of her hands. But from that, she knew that the war canoes were approaching from downriver.

As the sun crested the hill Red Horse, with his warriors, quickened their pace, dipping their oars in and out of the water in double time. And Coosaponakeesa, standing on the trading-post porch of her father, Ian Yonahlongi Hatke, waited to challenge her mother's people.

# Chapter 14

The fifteen-year-old Coosaponakeesa looked toward the landing with the same expression as old Brims himself. Though small in stature, she possessed an ageless quality that spoke of command and power in the matriarchal society of which she was a part.

The white man had never understood the power of women. The house, the fields, the children, all belonged to the woman. She could tell an errant husband to leave her hearth, could negate the decisions made in the council chamber. It was the woman who allowed the hunter or the warrior his own way, unless it conflicted with the good of the clan and the tribe. And the daughters of the Wind were the most powerful.

As she watched the warriors slide their canoes past the reeds and dart in silence from tree to tree, Coosaponakeesa touched the amulet about her neck and recited the almost forgotten words of Medicine Woman.

Suddenly, the Indians, brandishing their hatchets, made a great rush toward the trading post. But the sight of this Indian girl standing on the porch, with her hands outstretched in welcome, caused them momentary confusion.

Taking advantage of their surprise, Coosaponakeesa smiled and in the Creek language said, "Welcome, my brothers, to my village."

One of the warriors moved in front. Beneath the war paint, Coosaponakeesa recognized Red Horse. "Kill her," he shouted. "She is the enemy."

"No, my brothers. I am of your people— Coosaponakeesa, Princess of the Upper and Lower Creeks."

"She is Ian Yonahlongi Hatke's daughter," Red Horse said with a sneer. "Have we not sworn to kill all English traders and their families?"

Speaking in his own tongue, Red Horse was a powerful adversary. He was no longer the trading-post Indian speaking the white man's language in broken sentences, but a silver-tongued Muscogee orator.

She could see that Red Horse's words were beginning to take effect. A frenzied restlessness now rippled through the war party and several of the braves moved forward, aligning themselves with Red Horse.

"It is true, my brothers, that Ian Yonahlongi Hatke is my father—just as it is true that my mother was Princess Rising Fawn, sister to the Emperor Brims."

At her announcement a murmur arose among the Indians. Pressing the advantage it gave her, she said, "Whoever harms one hair of my head will have to answer to my uncle for the crime. Who among you would wish to stir the wrath of Old Brims?"

"Let us kill the trader instead," a voice offered.

"We will kill them both," Red Horse said. Yet he himself made no move toward her.

"Will you listen to the words of this...this *parch corn* Indian?" Coosaponakeesa asked, using the most disparaging term she could think of. "His war paint and his feathers today cannot disguise his heart."

Her words hit their mark. For Red Horse had worked for Ian for a long time, choosing to leave his village. If he were not exactly like some of the others, who had moved closer to the white settlers and relied on them to protect them from their enemies, the accusation, nevertheless, was severe enough to humiliate Red Horse before the other warriors.

"I will kill the trader myself," he announced, now brandishing the hatchet above his head.

"Ian Yonahlongi Hatke is ill, with the white man's plague."

"You lie, Coosaponakeesa."

"He is ill, Red Horse. If you do not believe me, I will show you. Who among you is brave enough to come with me?"

Red Horse motioned for two of the braves standing beside him to follow. Coosaponakeesa led them past the trading post toward the house. She had no fear that the Indians would take the few things from the store that remained in view. For the fireside story of the trading blankets and trinkets that

Tustanugga Hatke had brought with him over one hundred and fifty years before was embedded in their memory—an unfair exchange of their pelts for a blanket and the white man's pox.

From the open porch of the cabin, Coosaponakeesa motioned for the three Indians to enter. Red Horse was first, with a hesitant pair behind him.

Inside the bedroom, Ian lay motionless on the rope bed. In the semi-shadows, he was a terrible sight, with the illness prominent upon his face. But the fact that he did not stir as they entered reinforced Coosaponakeesa's words.

The two braves, staring over Red Horse's shoulder, took one look and fled. "Coosaponakeesa speaks the truth," the two Indians said, returning to the others.

Red Horse also wanted to run, but he walked with dignity back to the post. He had lost enough face already, dealing with Coosaponakeesa. But it would be foolhardy to take the scalp of a man with pox.

With his chest out, he motioned for the braves to return to their canoes. "Come, we will go upriver," he announced. "Many other scalps wait to be taken."

Red Horse did not look back. Watching him disappear toward the landing, Coosaponakeesa remained on the steps until the sound of the war drum was swallowed up by the wilderness.

Her legs began to tremble. The confrontation with Red Horse had left her weak. But she had done what she had set out to do. How long this truce would last, she had no way of knowing.

Another war party, coming from the opposite direction along the horse path, gathered around the broken-down wagon abandoned by Coreen and Sally. In curiosity, one Indian poked at the wooden box until the top opened, revealing Sally's trousseau.

For the next few minutes the braves forgot their vendetta against the settlers and fought among themselves, tearing at the dresses and grabbing the decorated bonnets, ribbons, and camisoles.

It was a strange, motley war party that approached the settlement. At the head of the procession through the woods came Eagle Feather, wearing his symbol of bravery in his hair and part of Sally's wedding dress draped across his bare chest. Behind him walked his younger brother, who had tied ribbons through the slits in his earlobes. Other portions of the trousseau were visible throughout the band of Indians.

When the sun had risen at the settlement, the men and young boys had stationed themselves at the loopholes of the meeting house, and Sandy had taken over the lookout post in the belfry from Parson Beckett. At the sight of one of the Indians darting behind a tree, Sandy called out, "They're here. The Indians are here."

Down below, a baby cried. Parson Beckett got down on his knees to pray. Hamish Pettipoole, still weak from the head wound, rose from his pallet, reached for a musket and took his place at one of the loopholes.

Sally, who had tended both her mother and Hamish, followed Hamish with a supply of gunpowder. Throughout the meeting house, women stood beside the men and boys to supply them with additional powder, while at least one or two of the women took up muskets themselves. The small children, urged to be as quiet as possible, were watched over by Ruby, the indentured servant.

The flag that Mary had given Sandy now flew in the breeze overhead. But it was forgotten by the people who crouched inside the meeting house and waited for Sandy to give them the signal when the Indians began their attack.

"Are they coming?" one of the men finally called out.

"I see three or four of them standin' near the clearing," Sandy called back. "Looks like they're havin' a conference of some kind."

As one of the Indians pointed toward the belfry, Sandy ducked. He was afraid they had spotted him.

"What are they doing now?' another voice called out.

Sandy carefully peeked through the belfry opening to take another look. "I think they're going toward the cornfield."

"Maybe they won't attack us," Hamish said to Sally, trying to sound reassuring. "Maybe they'll steal some food and animals and then leave."

A few minutes later the bleat of a sheep and the low of a cow seemed to corroborate his hope. A few war whoops were mixed with the sounds of animals, and then silence returned to the settlement.

After a half hour, Quinton, the blacksmith, motioned for the parson to take his place at the loophole. He then climbed the small, narrow steps to the belfry to survey the settlement himself. Coming back down the stairs, he said, "I believe they're gone for the day."

"Did they do any damage to the barns or the houses?" a man asked.

"Not as far as I can see. But I expect some of us will be missing things. Sandy said they'd already stolen some women's dresses. One had on a bonnet with blue ribbons..."

"My trousseau," Sally moaned. "I'll bet that was my bonnet they took."

"Better your bonnet than your blonde curls, Sally," Hamish said.

But his comment did not make her feel any better.

"I wonder why they changed their mind about attacking us?" Coreen asked.

"Probably thought we were too heavily armed, what with all the guns poking out of the loopholes," Elrod offered.

"No, it was the flag," Ruby said. "It was Miss Mary's flag that saved us."

"What flag?" Sally asked.

"The one she gave Sandy to hang from the belfry. It has all those strange Indian signs on it—a crescent moon and a bolt of lightning."

Hamish Pettipoole propped himself against the wall of the meeting house. His head was aching but his mind was still clear. "Sally," he said to the girl beside him. "Do you remember that first day when Mary came to school? She had those same designs painted on her face."

"I remember. And I remember how much fun we made of her, I'm ashamed to say."

"Do you believe that she's an actual Creek princess?"

"I'm not sure. She told me so one time. Said she was going to be a queen someday. But I thought she was making it up."

Parson Beckett's voice intruded. "My friends, let us get on our knees to give thanks for being spared this day."

Once again the parson was in charge of his flock. But as he offered his prayer of thanksgiving to the Almighty, Sally and Hamish Pettipoole also gave thanks to Him for their former schoolmate, Mary.

Within several days the settlement returned to near normal. Sandy and Ruby went back to the trading post, but the flag remained flying over the belfry of the meeting house. Although Parson Beckett was not too pleased, he would not risk disaster by taking it down too soon.

All over the Carolinas, the Yamasee War continued. Traders and settlers were caught in a bloodbath; Charlestown remained under siege. English colonization of that part of the New World appeared in jeopardy, despite militia reinforcements sent from Virginia.

During that time Mary cared for her father, Ian. A few of the friendlier Indians came to the trading post to swap their furs for English goods. But once the supplies in the store were gone, there was no way to get more. Colin and the packhorses had disappeared. And it was too dangerous for the periaguas, the large, flat-bottomed boats, to take the river route.

Ian lived on for the remainder of the year—never speaking. His only communication with his daughter was through his eyes. In them she saw her own love reflected.

Toward the end of the year, Ian died. She buried him by the river, with Parson Beckett praying the funeral service. But later, on that same afternoon, she went once again to the small mound, and there she recited the litany taught her so many years before by her mother.

Taking the four kernels of corn, she placed them in a pattern on the ground. "From the four corners of the earth, I will remember you, Ian Yonahlongi Hatke...north, from whence all good things come; east, where the sun begins its daily journey; west, from whence all darkness of heart rests, and south, where memories are born and birds soar."

She then stood and held up her hands toward the sky. "O Great Spirit, keep my father on eagle's wings, with the softness of chanting winds for his gentle sleep."

With those words, she not only buried her father, but the hopes and dreams of the English girl, Mary.

A few days later, word came. The war was over and a new trader was coming to take over the post, the house, and the indentured servants. There was now nothing left for her.

With the black wolf pelt, her sacred pigments, and a few other personal remembrances, Coosaponakeesa fled back to Coweta Town, to her mother's people.

# Chapter 15

In the year 1716, with the Yamasee War finally over between the Indians and the English settlers of the Carolinas, delegates of the peace commission rode from Charlestown to the chief Indian towns so that the chieftains could make their marks upon the new treaty and seal it with the sacred tobacco of the peace pipe.

For Coosaponakeesa, living in the capital town, the period of mourning for her father was over. Now she could no longer put off choosing a husband. Outside the village, two rival micos, both pressing for the hand of the princess, waited impatiently while the female members of their clans called on her with their gifts.

"I do not know these micos," Coosaponakeesa confided to her elderly cousins seated around her. "How can I choose between them if I don't know what they look like?"

"Sarak is very brave and strong," the sister of Sarak replied. "He wears many eagle feathers in his war bonnet and many scalps on his staff."

"I would not wish to marry a coward," Coosaponakeesa said, "but we are now at peace. No, there will have to be something else for me to be interested."

One of the sisters of the other mico, Chillikeepi, said, "Oh, Princess, our brother is as brave as Sarak. But he can dance and play the flute, too."

For the first time, Coosaponakeesa appeared mildly interested.

"And how did he learn these things?"

"From the French dancing master who came to our village."

"Accept the one who has sent you the most beautiful gift," her cousin seated at her right urged.

She looked at the array of gifts spread before her. She had seen so many like them at her father's trading post. So she was not impressed.

Coosaponakeesa stood. "I cannot make up my mind today. Come back tomorrow."

The disappointed sisters of the two micos carefully folded the blankets holding their gifts and left Coosaponakeesa's quarters.

"You cannot wait forever, Coosaponakeesa," her cousin, Marsh Flower, admonished. "Soon you will have spurned all the micos of our tribe. There will be no one left for you to choose, except some old, snaggle-toothed one in the sunset of his life."

Back in the two camps of the micos and their kin, the disappointed female relatives retreated. When Chillikeepi had been told all that Coosaponakeesa had said, he decided to act quickly. He sent a challenge to the camp of Sarak. If the other mico agreed, they would enter Coweta Town themselves on the next day to fight for her. Then she would be forced to choose the winner as husband.

Sarak, in his camp, listened to Chillikeepi's messenger. Confident that he was the stronger, Sarak agreed.

That night Sarak went through a purification ritual, as he usually did before going into battle. His servants set up a tent of buffalo skins and, building a fire inside, they brought large rocks and waited for them to absorb the heat.

A naked Sarak sat inside the tent, with the water from the creek causing a great hissing sound as it was poured upon the hot rocks. The tent filled with steam and the odor of sage. Hotter and hotter the tent became, with Sarak sweating out the poisons from his body. When he could finally stand it no longer, he raced from the tent and jumped into the creek to cool off.

At the other pitched camp, Chillikeepi polished his lance with bear grease and tested his elkhorn bow. When that was done, he brought out his flute, played a lilting tune, and then went to bed.

The next morning word had spread throughout Coweta Town of the impending fight between Sarak and Chillikeepi. "See what you have caused now, Coosaponakeesa," Marsh Flower admonished her young cousin.

"But Marsh Flower, I did not ask them to fight over me."

"Nevertheless, you will be obligated to marry the winner. I pray to the Great Spirit that the one you wish for husband will not die."

The younger John Musgrove, traveling with his father in the peace delegation to Coweta Town, heard a great commotion as they approached the village. He was familiar with most of the Indian festivals, and he had deliberately set the time of their arrival for a quiet time. Evidently, he had chosen wrong.

There was an air of festivity, of merriment, and great shouting. When he and the others had tied up their canoes and walked a few paces toward the village, John saw what had captured the people's attention.

One horseman, with shield and lance, was attempting to unseat another. The fast Indian ponies, coming from opposite directions, kicked up a cloud of dust as they raced toward each other. The two bare-chested braves were magnificent, with their bodies groomed for battle. Rubbed down with bear grease, they wore nothing but a loincloth, leggings, and moccasins.

John watched as a lance hit the decorated buffalo shield held by one of the braves. At first he thought the brave would be unseated by its great force. But the mico held on and regained his balance as he raced to the end of the course and turned.

Seated in a place of honor was a young Indian girl, alongside the wizened Brims, Emperor of the Creeks. John smiled when he realized that she must be the prize—like the jousts of old, when knights fought for a lady fair.

Not wishing to intrude in the middle of this important festivity, John and the others with him remained where they were. When the challenge was over, they would make themselves known, although he knew that the emperor was already aware of their coming.

John's eyes strayed back to the Indian girl. There was something familiar about her, the way she held her head in such a regal manner. Where had he seen her? He focused his entire attention on her face.

His heart knew first. It began to beat rapidly. His breath came in short gasps. It was Mary. The one he had searched for. The one he had given up all hope of finding. She had disappeared, with the new trader who had taken Ian's place unable to provide a single clue.

In spite of himself, he began to walk toward her.

From the corner of her eye, Coosaponakeesa saw the moving figure. Her attention left the two in combat and latched onto the visitor dressed in buckskin.

It was John. John Musgrove. The love of her life.

Coosaponakeesa stood. She began to walk rapidly in his direction.

"Mary," he shouted, oblivious to everything else around him.

"John. John Musgrove."

He held out his arms, and she ran to him.

Now the eyes of the village left the two ponies and the men on them. Only a few saw the two braves unseat each other at the same time. A much more interesting event was taking place off the field.

For John, the peace mission and the treaty were momentarily forgotten. Holding Mary close, he said, "I thought I would never see you again."

"I stayed at the trading post as long as I could."

"But when I went back, you were gone. Harrison, the new trader, didn't know what happened to you. And neither did anyone at the settlement."

His relief at seeing her was suddenly marred with fear. He looked down into her eyes and said, "I haven't come too late, have I, Mary? Tell me that you are still free to become my wife."

She looked in the direction of the two warriors on their ponies and back to John. "The micos are fighting for me now, John. Although I have not agreed, it is the custom to marry the winner."

"Then let's stop the contest immediately. Tell them that you're already promised to me."

As she hesitated, he cried, "You do love me, don't you, Mary?"

"Yes. With all my heart."

"Then what is to stop us?"

"Not what, but *who*."

John looked at the small, wizened man seated on a large wooden chair in the distance. Beside the chair stood a large ceremonial staff of vulture feathers.

"The emperor?"

"Yes."

"Introduce me to him before he declares a winner. We'll explain our—"

"You will have to wait for him to recognize you, John. But I will do what I can."

John motioned for his father to join him, and soon all three approached the seat of honor.

Mary cleared her throat. "Uncle, may I present..."

Old Brims held up his hand. He did not wish to be disturbed while the joust was still in progress.

In disappointment, Mary motioned for the two Englishmen to take their seats beside her. When it seemed that John was going to protest, Mary shook her head. "We will have to wait." She gestured toward the two micos, who were poised for another pass to unseat each other.

"Settle down, Johnny," his father advised in a low tone. "Don't do anything to jeopardize the peace treaty signing."

As John reluctantly took his seat and waited, the old emperor pretended to be absorbed in the action on the field. But in truth he had given himself time to think.

He was not only the emperor of the Creeks, but its elder statesman, constantly juggling allegiance from the French to the Spanish and then to the English, back and forth, for his people's survival. Despite aligning one son with the Spanish and another with the French, he still felt an uneasiness concerning these English. Were they not the ones who had burned his towns and killed his warriors with their superior weapons? If he signed the peace treaty they had brought, what guarantee did he have that they would not break it?

Unobtrusively, he glanced toward the impatient young man seated beside his niece. And then he saw the expression on her face as she gazed at him. What he saw confirmed his suspicions. This man was the reason why Coosaponakeesa had shown little interest in any of the micos.

Like the alliances made by most enemy nations in times of truce, a marriage between Coosaponakeesa and the Englishman would suit his purpose. For he needed the ensuing years of peace between the two nations to give his people time to become strong in number again. But he would have to be careful of Sarak, if he were winner of the joust. The young mico would have to be suitably compensated for the loss of his prize.

Down on the field, Sarak scowled at the strangers who had taken the attention away from him. Determined to bring the joust to a spectacular ending with his victory over Chillikeepi, he dug his heels into the ribs of his pony, gave a shout, and rushed headlong toward his adversary. In brute strength, he was the superior man. Sarak had only to remain astride as he knocked Chillikeepi from his pony.

When the distance between the two was a mere hundred yards, Sarak suddenly threw his protective buffalo shield to the ground. The crowd gave a great gasp, for he was now vulnerable to Chillikeepi's lance. Balancing his own lance, he urged his pony faster and faster. And when Chillikeepi was almost upon him, Sarak hurled his weapon with all the strength his arm possessed and then quickly twisted his body to the protective side of the pony.

The other lance, missing its victim, whistled through the air as its owner, Chillikeepi, fell to the ground.

By the time Sarak righted himself and looked back, he realized that he had won. He took his time, letting the pony cool down while the stunned Chillikeepi's relatives removed the defeated mico from the arena of battle. And then Sarak left his pony and began to walk toward the emperor to claim Coosaponakeesa.

"Uncle, I must speak with you immediately." The distress was evident in Mary's voice as she motioned toward John and his father to come and stand beside her. "May I present John Musgrove and his father, Captain Musgrove."

As Brims took his time in acknowledging the two, Mary said, "I do not wish to marry Sarak, Uncle. This is the man I love."

"Does he love you, Niece?"

John could no longer keep silent. "I do indeed," he said, using the Creek language. "I want to marry her."

"Sarak would have to be compensated for his loss."

"Marsh Flower's daughter is of an age to take a husband," Mary argued. "She has already said how much she admires Sarak."

"Is this true, Marsh Flower?" he inquired of the woman on the platform.

"Yes, Cousin."

"Then speak to her to see if she is willing to take Coosaponakeesa's place." He turned back to his niece. "There are other considerations, besides a wife."

"I will compensate him," John offered, "with horses and gifts."

"John, are you sure...?"

"Yes, Father."

The captain said no more.

By that time Sarak had reached the platform where the dignitaries stood. With no indication that he had decided one way or the other, Brims reached out his hand toward Sarak, bringing him to stand beside him. The crowd, seeing that their emperor was getting ready to make a speech, settled down, and not even the cry of a baby marred the afternoon.

"My people," he began, "you have seen the bravery of Mico Sarak today on the field."

Sarak's chest expanded in pride, as all eyes were upon him. He was savoring every moment until he realized that the emperor was not saying the words he expected. Was Coosaponakeesa not going to select him as husband after he had won over Chillikeepi? He continued listening, with his anger mounting. No, it was the Englishman she had chosen, as a token of friendship between the Creeks and the English.

His victory turned to ashes, despite the emperor's promise of gifts. He was ready to refuse them and leave when a young girl, Angel Blossom, suddenly appeared. She was beautiful and looked toward him with great admiration.

After a brief consultation with Brims, she spoke to the mico. "Sarak, I am of an age to marry," she began. "And you are looking for a wife. I would bring to you honor, for my mother, Marsh Flower, is of the Wind clan and cousin to the emperor. Our children would be blessed with a royal heritage." Then with downcast eyes she waited for Sarak to indicate his willingness to accept her proposal.

Before he had a chance to make up his mind, Brims added, "I would release you, Sarak, from staying here a year to work for the family. If you accept Angel Blossom's offer, then you are free to take her and return immediately to your own town. But know this. If word ever comes that you have not been kind to her, she and her children will be free to return to Coweta Town."

This sudden break with tradition had been a difficult one to decide. But Brims wanted no disappointed suitor around to make trouble for Coosaponakeesa and her Englishman.

Sarak, looking at Angel Blossom, liked what he saw. She was almost as lovely as Coosaponakeesa, but did not appear to be nearly so haughty. That was in her favor, as well as the absolution from the year of work. Too, his pride was still intact. Coosaponakeesa had not actually spurned him. It was the emperor who had decided her fate, and no one would dispute the emperor's wisdom in times of war and peace. Mollified, Sarak nodded to Angel Blossom, and she left her place by her mother to come and stand beside her new husband.

With the matter of Sarak disposed of to everyone's satisfaction, Old Brims had cleared the way for Mary and John to marry. Now his attention could be turned to the matter of the peace treaty with the English.

# Chapter 16

For three days, as the peace delegation met with Brims and his council, Mary saw little of John Musgrove. But that was as it should be, for she was surrounded by the women helping her to get ready for her wedding.

Her wooden living quarters were cleaned, with fresh boughs gathered for fragrance and new stones brought from the river for the cooking fire. Gifts of deer skins and beaver were sewn together for the marriage bed, and the women took turns helping Coosaponakeesa prepare her own wedding dress of soft doeskin decorated with fresh water pearls taken from the mussels in the river, and edged with small, colorful beads.

She had few English clothes left. Part of her heart regretted that she would not be wearing a beautiful white dress like the one Sally's mother had made for her wedding to Billy Whitaker. But she was the Princess Coosaponakeesa and, as such, she would be dressed in the Creek manner, with her face proclaiming her royalty. This she would do, to show honor to the emperor and her mother's people.

By late afternoon of the third day, when everything had been done and she was alone, Mary heard John calling to her outside the dwelling. "Mary, may I come in?"

"No, John. I'll come out instead."

He smiled as he looked at her. "Are you allowed to go for a walk with your future husband?"

"Yes."

She fell into step with him as they began to walk toward the river.

"The treaty has finally been agreed upon and signed. All is well."

"I'm glad," she replied. "I was waiting to hear. Now there is nothing to stand in our way."

"Except that the missionary is leaving for Charlestown early in the morning."

"Then the wedding ceremony must take place before the sun goes down today. Is that agreeable with you?"

"Of course it is. The sooner the better. My mind has scarcely been on the peace treaty these past three days."

"Then go and tell your missionary, and I will speak to my uncle. The celebration feast tonight can be our wedding supper, too."

"But where will I meet you? And what time?"

"In the square, before the council house. Within the hour."

He held onto her hand for a moment longer, and then they departed.

On her way back from speaking with Brims, Mary stopped before Marsh Flower's house. "Marsh Flower, gather my kinswomen together," she called. "I am getting married in an hour."

By the time the women had helped her to braid flowers in her hair and paint the royal pigments upon her face, Mary was aware of the afternoon air, heavy with the scent of roasted meat and delicacies for the celebration feast. This was to be a wonderful night, filled with peace and love.

As Marsh Flower and the other women accompanied her to the square, Mary said, "I am sorry that Angel Blossom is not here to share my happiness."

"She has already shared in your happiness, Coosaponakeesa," Marsh Flower replied. "Because of you, she has a fine husband. I hope this Englishman will make as good a husband as Sarak."

All of Coweta Town had gathered to see their princess married in this strange English ceremony. Much talk in a language they did not understand and a scratching of paper, like the treaty signing, caused them a slight uneasiness. But in seeing Coosaponakeesa dressed in the doeskin dress with the pigments upon her face, they were reassured. The older ones even remembered another time, when Princess Rising Fawn had also become wife to an Englishman.

The one who was least aware of the significance of the marriage was the missionary who had volunteered to travel with the peace delegation. As he stood before them in his black surplice and intoned the words that made Mary and John man and wife, he thought he was merely performing a Christian ceremony between a simple Indian girl and a fur trader, both having been baptized in the church. What he did not know was that Mary was making a rite of passage from princess to the queen of her people.

When the words had been spoken and the vows made, Mary looked at John, standing so tall beside her. He was wearing the white linen shirt she had sewn for him, with the buckskin trousers. Her smile was intimate, mischievous, and loving.

Amid congratulations from the captain, the missionary, the others from the peace delegation, and the host of Creeks, Mary and John left the square and walked to their place of honor for the feast. As he sat down on the blanket beside her, John leaned over and whispered, "I can hardly wait to scrub the paint off your beautiful face."

"That will not be your only duty tonight, husband."

John moaned and said, "How long do we have to stay? My appetite is not for venison."

"After the emperor makes his speech and your father answers him, we will be free to go."

"Then I will ask my father not to be long-winded."

"Unfortunately, I cannot do the same with my uncle."

It was much later in the evening, as the stars shone overhead in the black sky, that Mary and John finally slipped away from the festivities. Their absence was noted with knowing smiles.

Tenderness and love were no strangers that night in the wilderness. With her face cleansed of all traces of paint and her dark, lustrous hair unbraided, Mary drew John to her on the soft marriage bed of deerskin and beaver. Chaste, as all Creek maidens were taught to be, she nevertheless knew what was expected of her. There was no shame in her naked body. She welcomed the exploration of John's hands and the birth of feelings that had always lurked beneath the surface, waiting to be shared with the right man.

"You're beautiful, Mary," John whispered. "I love the feel of your skin next to mine—like the finest silk."

She returned his lingering kiss and said, "I have slept in dream time, waiting for this night with you. Love me, John."

He needed no further urging. As an owl hooted in the distance, and the night music of the wilderness answered, John and Mary consummated their love, their spiritual vows changing to flesh and passion that ignited and became part of the sacred fire that would never go out.

With his father returning to Charlestown to take the signed treaty of peace to the assembly and Brims returning to his peace town, John remained in Coweta Town with his wife.

Once again life took on a familiar, satisfying pattern for Mary. John built his trading post on the river, and she moved into the quarters so similar to the ones she had shared with her father, Ian. But she did not remain in the house long. With servants to do the chores, she soon began working by John's side at the post, as much a trader as he. He did nothing to discourage it, for her influence with the Creeks brought many riches to the trading post. If there was a problem, it was usually Mary who could solve it, since she understood the Indian culture so well and was part of the English heritage, too.

One afternoon, when John had finished his trade with an Indian from downriver, he turned around to say something to his wife. But she had left the store. When she did not return after a few minutes, he began to grow worried. He left the store and walked into the house, where he found her sitting in the chair near the hearth.

Seeing him, she smiled. In her hand she held the treasured book that Ian had given her.

"What are you doing, Mary?"

"Dreaming," she responded. "Do you remember the day you gave me this red flower? When we were sitting together at the river landing?"

She held the book open for him to see. "I pressed it between the pages, and it's been here all this time."

John nodded, but he was still puzzled. "What is this sudden attack of melancholia all about? What is really the matter, Mary?"

"I felt the need to rest."

"Are you ill?" He moved toward her to feel her forehead. "I hope you're not coming down with the swampy fever."

She reached up and took his hand from her brow and placed it on her stomach. "Your child grows within my body," she said. "That is why I must take time to sit and dream."

"Mary."

She watched his face as she told him. His smile, his eyes, reflected what she wanted to see—that he shared her joy.

The winter passed rapidly. By springtime, new life clothed the forest. The deer and her fawn, the wolf with her playful pups, all were a part of the creation of the world. Their cries echoed throughout the wilderness and spread to the trading post, where another cry—a human child's—joined in this primeval order of things.

"You have a fine son," Marsh Flower said to Mary. "It is as Medicine Woman predicted." She leaned forward and whispered in Mary's ear so that no one else could hear. "Guard our little emperor well."

The child, with his noble brow, grew. Sturdy and plump, he was the best of two worlds. He had inherited the dark, straight hair of the Creeks, with his father's startling blue eyes. Mary and John called him David, but the Creeks in the village knew him as Running Elk, for the child, once he learned to walk, ran more often than he walked. Bilingual, he touched the hearts of the Indians who came to trade.

Swiftly, a fever spread from village to village. The burial mound in Coweta Town grew larger, with the kernels of corn sprouting into lush green stalks with the rain.

Overnight, the child became ill. No amulet tied about his neck, no Christian prayers had the slightest effect. David, the little emperor, died in Mary's arms as the sun crested the hill.

"My heart is breaking," Mary cried. But John could not comfort her. His own heart was breaking, too.

Several days later, after the burial of the child, John had made up his mind. He looked at his wife, who now carried the seed of another child. He could not risk losing them, also.

"Mary, would you like to go to Charlestown to live?"

"Do you mean—leave Coweta Town and this trading post?"

"Yes. The fever only seems to be getting worse. David is gone, but we must now think of you and the unborn child. It will be safer in Charlestown."

Earlier in her life, Mary would have been overjoyed to hear those words, that she would finally be getting to live in that thriving city. Now, it no longer mattered.

"I will go, if that is what you wish to do," she answered.

Once again, Mary packed the few items that meant so much to her, but left her other possessions behind. With the wolf pelt and medicine basket containing her amulet, her dried herbs, a rock from the sacred fire, and a lock of David's hair, she bid farewell to her cousins and the village and went to the landing place to wait for John.

The periagua came into sight. Sensing that it might be years before she returned to Coweta Town, Mary whispered, "From the north, I will remember you..." The words choked in her throat. In sorrow, she climbed into the boat, without looking back

# Chapter 17

Charlestown, in the year of 1723, was a town of strong-minded, independent men and women. Having survived the Yamasee War, fires, hurricanes, pestilences, and pirates, all without the help of the lords proprietors, the people had thrown out the inefficient proprietors' agents and petitioned the King of England to make them a royal colony. But in the intervening two years, the people had virtually governed themselves.

Added to this independence, the Charlestownians had a different view of life from some of the other colonies. Coming by way of the Antilles and Barbados, they had brought with them their laughter, love of gambling and racing, and sense of honor that sometimes resulted in dueling under the oaks. Their zest for life and its gaieties was clearly different from their dour-faced Puritan cousins who had settled in the colder climes of the north. Only the threat of the Spanish and French fleets could dampen their spirits.

This was the town to which Mary and John Musgrove moved in 1723.

Brick houses, made from the ballasts of the ships from England, dotted the harbor. Warehouses of native wood held furs to be loaded on ships to the mother country and exchanged for needed goods for the colony. For entertainment, professional actors regularly came from Europe with the latest plays. And public houses, or taverns, sprang up everywhere, with rum and ale in quantity.

At the Golden Swan, the newest public house near the harbor, Muckross, the former indentured servant, surveyed the public and private rooms to make sure they were in readiness. The large slabs of beef were roasting in the kitchen at the back and the casks of ale were filled to overflowing.

"Ye may open the door now," he said to Emmett, his own indentured servant.

People came and went all day, eating and drinking, with some staying far into the night. Muckross did not mind the hard work or the late hours. He had wanted all his life to have his own tavern.

About a month after he had opened the tavern, Mary and John came to the Golden Swan. At first, Muckross did not recognize Mary. She was dressed fashionably for the day, in a dark blue muslin, with a matching bonnet and shawl draped over her shoulders. She could easily have been one of the ladies escaping from the miasma of a rice plantation, tended by slaves to reside in her healthier town house for the summer season.

"Welcome to the Golden Swan," Muckross said as the couple entered.

"Muckross? Is that you, Muckross?"

His hair was as fiery red as ever, even though his freckles were not quite so obvious. He had put on weight, too. But Mary, staring at the boy who had grown into a man, waited for him to confirm his identity.

"Aye, I'm Muckross, the proprietor."

He took a closer look at the young woman beneath the bonnet. And the recognition caused him to smile with joy.

"Mary? Miss Mary?"

"Musgrove. I'm Mary Musgrove now. And this is my husband, John."

"Come. I'll take ye to a private room upstairs that catches a fair breeze from the sea. And I'll serve ye myself, so happy I am to see ye."

John's eyes twinkled as he listened to two friends catching up on the gossip between courses.

"I always wondered what happened to Sally O'Reilly," Mary said. "Whether she married Billy Whitaker."

"That I can tell ye, with authority. The two did not wed. Billy has been a steady customer every night, and I think it's his loss of Sally that has given him a grog nose."

"Did she die?"

"No, Mary. She married Hamish Pettipoole."

"Oh, I'm so glad." She looked at John shyly. "I could not imagine being wed to a man that I did not love."

Muckross stared down at John's empty mug. "Here I am, going on about the settlement people, when your cup is empty. I'll fix that soon enough."

From that night, Mary and John were regular customers at the Golden Swan, until political events suddenly changed their lives.

The Creek peace treaty that had been signed with the English soon disintegrated. New demands that Brims' Confederacy make a complete break with its former allies, the Yamasees, who had gone over to the Spanish, was met with resistance. And to make matters even worse, Brims discovered that his own enemies, the Cherokees, were secretly armed by the British. He had never forgiven the earlier treachery of the Cherokees in massacring his emissaries, and so the warfare between the two Indian nations began again.

Retributions from the Creeks brought similar retributions from the Cherokees. And when the Charlestown authorities showed their displeasure with the war by putting an embargo on trade with the Creeks and refusing their entry into the city, Mary and John Musgrove decided to move to the family's plantation property outside the city.

The next few years were unsettling ones in their marriage, for while John, a captain in the Carolina militia, was leading an expedition against the Yamasees in Spanish territory, Mary was busy receiving and advising her Creek relatives and corresponding with the Beloved Woman of the Cherokees. As Beloved Woman of the Creeks, Mary was determined to do what she could to end the animosity between the two Indian nations and put the Upper Creeks back into the good graces of the English.

But her duties as queen of her people did not let her slight her duties as wife and mother. Her love for John remained strong. By the time a truce had finally been established and the fur trade embargo lifted, Mary had borne John four sons—David, the child who had died in Coweta Town, and three others—John, Jamie, and Edward, called little Edward Walking Stick because of an affliction to one of his legs shortly after birth.

With the Cherokee and Creek War finally behind them, Mary and John became customers again at the Golden Swan. And it was Muckross who served them on a special evening in 1732 when they arrived with the royal governor Johnson, Colonel Bull, and the agent for Indian affairs.

After they had been shown to a private room upstairs and Muckross had personally taken their order, Governor Johnson got down to business.

"The Spanish situation is growing graver by the hour, John," he began.

John Musgrove nodded. "Our fur traders in the south have certainly found that out. Several have already been ambushed. It doesn't speak well for the resumption of the industry."

"Nor for the life of our colony," Johnson added. "If we don't do something about it soon, the Spanish and their allies will completely wipe us out."

"What we've always needed is a buffer zone between Charlestown and St. Augustine," Colonel Bull said, entering into the conversation.

"Well, I have good news on that score," Johnson said, smiling. "A little over a year ago, I proposed the idea to the King's Parliament. Yesterday, I finally received a reply. Parliament has given us permission to set up a trading post near Spanish territory so that our enemies' actions can be monitored more closely."

"Where?" Mary asked, immediately interested in the idea of establishing another trading post with her husband. These past few years, she had missed that portion of her life.

"Near the mouth of the Savannah River, at Yamacraw Bluff."

"But there's not a single Indian tribe, friendly or unfriendly, within fifty miles of the bluff," the agent argued. "Not much of a buffer zone, I'd say, unless we can come up with some friendly Indians in our camp."

"That's the obstacle to be surmounted, and the reason we're here. Any suggestions?" Johnson looked as each one at the table and waited for someone to speak up.

The silence mounted. Mary finally said, "Mico Tomochichi, my uncle's lifelong ally, is looking for a place to settle down in his old age. His band is small, about a hundred. But he might be persuaded to settle in that coastal area."

"Do you think he would be friendly to an English trading post?"

Mary smiled at John. Neither Colonel Bull nor the other two men understood.

"I think my wife could see to that," John relied, with a trace of irony.

"Then would you two take on the trading post, Johnny?"

Muckross, overhearing part of the conversation as he replenished the food and drink, was saddened as he saw Mary nodding her assent to her husband. Their answer meant that the two would be leaving Charlestown behind.

Within a few weeks, after Mary had sent her nine-year-old son John to Brims for his tutelage, as was the custom for the future heir of the Creeks, Mary and John made ready to leave for Yamacraw Bluff.

"I wish Jamie could go with us, too," Mary said as she took one last look at their fair-haired younger son, standing on the wharf with his grandparents, John and Margaret.

"It's still not too late to take him with us, Mary."

Mary shook her head. "No, Johnny. His education is more important. It's just that I will sorely miss him."

"But we still have *ticibane* here to keep us company."

"Yes." She smiled at her youngest, little Edward Walking Stick. He returned her smile and reached out to take his mother's hand.

In London, about the same time, another conversation was being held about the Spanish danger to the Carolina colonies. This fear, discussed over a period of time, was now helping to bring a certain landed gentry's dream to fruition.

James Edward Oglethorpe had always been something of a firebrand, with his zeal for causes more than likely inherited from his strong-willed Jacobite mother, the Lady Eleanor. But in his thirty-six years, he had gradually learned to channel his zeal into a more acceptable behavior. As the elected representative from Haslemere to the House of Commons, he had discovered many inequities in life. At last he had a chance to resolve one of England's worst injustices while, at the same time, dealing with the Spanish danger.

As he waited for the other trustees to arrive for the important meeting he turned the pages of a book, *The Villa of the Ancients,* privately published by his old friend, Robert Castell. Once again, he admired the drawing of the villas, the gardens, and the layout of the town squares. One day, perhaps, he might be able to pay a special tribute to this friend.

Although his white powdered wig hid a healthy mane of golden red hair, the sadness in James' gray eyes could not be disguised. He would always be haunted by the architectural book. Its enormous cost had turned Robert's fortunes to disaster. With the sales smaller than expected, Robert could not pay the printer, and so he had been thrown into debtors' prison in Fleet Street.

Only by chance had James discovered him in his investigation of the prison system by the House of Commons Committee.

"I have no more money to pay the warden's bribe," Robert had confided. "He says he's going to throw me in the pest quarters now. That's a sure death sentence for me, Jamie. I'll never survive."

Despite James' intervention, the warden could not be budged. So his talented friend had died of smallpox.

Too late for his friend Castell, James had, nevertheless, spearheaded the new law that dealt with the way debtors were treated. Thus began his concern for the treatment of the poor and the oppressed. His dream to establish a new colony where the worthy poor could make a fresh start had been born that day in Fleet Street.

At a sound of voices, James closed the book and waited to greet the other members of the trustees.

"The situation looks good, James," Percival, the president of the trustees, said. "I have it on the highest authority that our plans will be approved and the money forthcoming."

"Walpole should be pleased. We are actually killing three birds with one stone," another offered. "Doing something for the worthy poor, providing for the propagation of the Gospel, and protecting the Carolinas from the Spanish."

"I will begin the publicity preparations immediately. It's not too soon to start attracting the kind of citizens we want for a new colony," a delighted Oglethorpe said.

The campaign was extremely successful, with many families eager to be interviewed. By the time the ship, *Anne,* was ready to sail, one hundred and fourteen people had been selected. Ironically, not a single debtor was in the group.

Carpenter, wigmaker, tailor, merchant, baker, wheelwright, apothecary, vinedresser, the men all had occupations that could be used in the New World.

Only a surgeon and a minister of the Gospel waited to be added to the list—and a leader to oversee the founding of the colony.

At the last minute the surgeon and minister were enrolled. But who, among the trustees, would lead the expedition?

"I'll go myself," James Edward Oglethorpe said, setting sail on November 17, 1732.

In the latter part of January 1733, Mary Musgrove watched a small sloop winding its way through the inland waterway that connected the Carolinas to the Savannah River and Yamacraw Bluff. With several of her Indian servants, she waited at the top of the bluff, while three white men began to climb upward from the riverbank.

She waved as she recognized one of them—Colonel William Bull, the engineer from Charlestown. "Quick," she said to one of the servants. "Go back to the house and prepare some refreshments for our visitors."

For Colonel Bull, Mary was scarcely recognizable as the smart, well-dressed woman he had last seen at the Golden Swan. Her hair was in two long plaits that hung to her waist. Instead of muslin, she wore a dress of soft deerskin to counteract the wintry wind. On her feet she wore her comfortable moccasins.

"Colonel Bull, welcome to Yamacraw Bluff," she said.

"I have brought a visitor, Mary. May I present Colonel James Oglethorpe of London. Mistress Musgrove, wife of John Musgrove, the fur trader."

"How do you do, Colonel," she said, acknowledging Oglethorpe's nod.

Tall and handsome, the stranger towered over her. She smiled at the quizzical expression on his face as she spoke to Skee, her other Indian helper, concerning the rangers who had come with the two, and then immediately changed into English to address her visitors.

"I am sorry that my husband is not here to greet you, as well. He left several days ago on a hunting expedition to replenish the larder. But come to the fire and warm yourselves. Refreshments will be ready soon."

Within a few minutes the rangers had disappeared into the trading-post side with Skee, while the captain of the rangers joined them inside the house. As food and drink were served to Bull, Oglethorpe, and the captain, Oglethorpe was gratified that Mary had provided for their entire scouting party.

Observing the social amenities, Colonel Bull did not discuss business until the meal was finished. After a complimentary word or two, he handed over a letter addressed to Mary and Johnny from the governor. He gave her time to read it and then he said, "As you can see, the governor has requested that you and your husband render all possible aid to Colonel Oglethorpe."

Puzzled, Mary looked from one man to the other and waited for further explanation.

Bull continued. "Colonel Oglethorpe has brought a ship of a hundred English settlers to this New World. He hopes to build a settlement for them somewhere on the south bank of the Savannah River, but he does not wish any harm to come to his people."

"So what is the governor specifically asking of us?" Mary inquired.

"First off, he wants you to help the colonel get permission to land from the Indian mico here."

"You realize, of course, that the treaty recognizes this as Indian land."

Before Bull could respond, Oglethorpe said, "We have no wish to push the Yamacraws off their land. We come in peace and want to be friends with them."

Mary remained silent, thinking of the possible repercussions; for Tomochichi and his band had little love for the English. Finally, she spoke. "I will do what I can. But it is late now. Remain here for the night, and I will send a servant in the morning to tell Tomochichi that you wish to speak with him."

Mary looked up and smiled as she saw her small son, Edward Walking Stick, peeking from behind the door. He disappeared again when he saw that he had been discovered by his mother.

That night the two visitors slept in the guest quarters off the dogtrot porch, while the rangers camped near the boat. When morning came, Oglethorpe rose early to follow Mary to Yamacraw village, where she became the interpreter between the handsome Englishman and the elderly, six-foot Mico Tomochichi.

# Chapter 18

Tomochichi, the fierce war chief of one of the Creek towns, had refused to sign the treaty of 1716 with the English and make a final break with the Yamasees. For although he was considered a Creek because of his mother, his father had been a Yamasee. And so, by refusing both orders, he had been banished.

But unlike Red Horse and some of the others from the Creek Confederacy who also hated the English and had gone south below the Altamaha River to trade with the Spanish, Tomochichi, remembering the Spanish cruelty to his father, had chosen instead to gather some of his loyal followers and wander along an unsettled area of the Creek territory, between the English and the Spanish colonies.

Mary's invitation in 1732 to Tomochichi to settle near her trading post was received with great relief. It was fitting for him, at his advanced age, to return to the burial mound of his Yamasee ancestors, and to give his polyglot tribe, all of Muscogean stock, a name—Yamacraws—taken from the bluff itself.

Now, one year later, Tomochichi, whose mind had become almost as simple as a child's, was treated with respect as the mico of their tribe, but the real power of the Yamacraws rested with their medicine man, Tallapoosa, the Tall (to distinguish him from a mico of the same name), and their Creek empress, Coosaponakeesa.

Mary's message, that she was bringing an Englishman from far across the waters to powwow with Tomochichi and his council, had caused a great stir in the Yamacraw village.

"We should kill him at once," Tallapoosa, the medicine man, said.

His suggestion brought a murmur of approval among some of the braves.

"No," Tomochichi replied. "Coosaponakeesa is bringing him. Let us listen to the white man's words."

A similar murmur of approval to his suggestion was voiced. The council was clearly divided.

The next morning, as the sun filtered through the giant cedars and pines and the smell of sassafras lay gently on the mild wind, two lone figures wound their way from the trading post toward the village. Mary knew that the sight of the rangers would cause immediate enmity, and so she had persuaded Oglethorpe to come alone.

She was aware that their every step was being monitored. She was not surprised that the council had gathered, with Tomochichi seated in his place of honor, by the time they arrived.

Mary had already instructed Oglethorpe on the protocol and the presentation of his gift to Tomochichi. She herself had provided the gift from her own personal storehouse. The trinket gifts that Oglethorpe had brought with him were no more appropriate for a mico than the ones that had been offered to her earlier in Coweta Town.

The council house was built of the same rough material as the trading post, the bark of the half logs still visible from the outside. The smoke from the sacred fire in the middle rose upward and vanished through the hole in the roof. Around the fire, a semicircular tier of seats made from the clay of the riverbanks was occupied by the members of the council, the seats facing a high wooden throne, upon which Tomochichi sat. His great-niece's son, Toonahowie, his heir apparent, according to the matriarchal custom of the Creeks, sat on his right. But the seat to his left, usually reserved for the medicine man, Tallapoosa, was vacant—not a good sign.

Mary and Oglethorpe approached the throne. Oglethorpe bowed low, as if Tomochichi were King George II himself.

"My lord, Tomochichi—" Mary spoke in the Creek language—"I have brought an Englishman from across the waters to speak with you. His name is James Edward Oglethorpe, a great chief of his own village in the land across the waters."

A small hissing sound came from one side of the council. At the hostile reception, James reached for the sword at his side, an automatic gesture from the days he'd fought under the Prince of Savoy. But the sheath was empty. Mary had insisted that he leave it outside. He was now at the mercy of the hostile Indians.

In a flash, Mary turned in the direction of the sound and, in a stern voice, spoke a few words that caused instant silence. Reassured by her that he was not going to lose his head, James again took up the mission that had brought him to the village.

"I come in peace, O great Tomochichi," he said, waiting for Mary to translate.

The mico was a giant of a man, even taller, James noticed, than he himself, though Tomochichi remained seated. Around his shoulders the Indian wore a buffalo cape. Although his chest was bare, he wore a collar of otter skins around his neck. His head was shaved except for a warlock hanging over his right ear.

In shock, James realized that the Indian had the same gray-colored eyes as he had. But he could not tell if the color were true or merely the gray-colored film that obscured the vision in many old men.

"Present him the gift," Mary urged.

As James unfolded the scarlet velvet cape lined in gold silk and trimmed in white ermine a pleased sound rippled through the council chamber.

Tomochichi stood, removed his buffalo cape and, with the help of Toonahowie, placed the lush red velvet around his shoulders and sat down again.

"Now tell him what you want."

Mary again prompted Oglethorpe, who began to speak of his wish to land a small group of his people to settle upon the land. He had no way of knowing if Mary translated everything he said. He only knew that she seemed eloquent in his petition, speaking not only to Tomochichi but also to the council.

Back and forth, questions came. When he saw Tomochichi nod and the council voice a more pleasing sound than the hiss he had been greeted with, he looked at Mary for confirmation.

"He has given his approval, sanctioned by the council, for you to land your people."

The treaty to be signed was in his coat, but he had left his quill and ink outside. "What about the treaty?" James asked. "Will Tomochichi sign the treaty between us now?

"No. That will come later, with much ceremony. Smoke the sacred tobacco with him now. That will be sufficient."

She spoke to Tomochichi, who then motioned for Oglethorpe to come and take the seat to his left.

"I will wait outside for you," Mary said and, nodding to the assembly, she left the council house.

Her eyes were wary as she looked for Tallapoosa, the medicine man. She finally spotted him near the far wall of the council house, where he had been eavesdropping. Stationed at other strategic spots were the braves of the village, with their weapons handy, in case the powwow had not gone well.

Once Oglethorpe emerged from the council house and his sword was returned to him, Mary said in a low voice, "We will walk slowly through the village. Do not hurry, regardless of what you hear or see."

In the distance a sharp rattle filled the air. A black wolf pup, tied to a post, gave a small growl as he passed. James had not seen a single woman or child in the entire village.

He took his cue from Mary, who smiled and walked slowly, ignoring the braves stationed along the way. The closer they came to the trading post, the more James began to realize what this tiny woman at his side had done. She had not only saved him from an unpleasant end, but had given him what he wanted—the chance to begin a new colony without fighting for the land.

As the trading post came into sight he turned to the woman. "Mary," he said, "I have a great need for an interpreter and a diplomat between these Indians and my colony. If you would agree to take the position, I will pay you a hundred pounds sterling a year and build you one of the first houses in our new town."

Mary was silent for quite a while. Her silence puzzled him. He was being extremely generous, offering her as much as the highest official would make.

Finally, she answered. "I will think about it and let you know my decision before you leave tomorrow."

That afternoon, as James and Colonel Bull, eager to survey the land where they would build the new colony, took a long walk over the land along the bluff, a thoughtful Mary remained at the trading post.

Did this Oglethorpe not realize the heavy burden he was asking her to take upon her shoulders? Would it be worth it, the added heartache of placating two cultures who were so prone to misunderstandings because of the subtleties in each language?

Her heart was still aching at the loss of her second son, John, who had died that past summer along with Brims, when an Englishman had unknowingly brought yellow fever to the Chattahoochee. Losing two children had made the others even more precious to her.

How thankful she was that Jamie was such a sturdy fellow. She missed him, but she knew that he was happy, going to school in Charlestown. It was frail little Edward who worried her. Soon he would be of an age to begin his education, too, far from her.

Yet had she not translated Oglethorpe's hopes and dreams to Tomochichi, to establish a school for all the children and to live in peace with their brothers, the Yamacraws? If the colony were successful and Oglethorpe accomplished all he set out to do, then Edward, her heart, would not have to leave her for a few more years.

By the time Colonel Bull and Oglethorpe returned, Mary said, "I have made up my mind. If you wish me to do so, I will be your interpreter and liaison with the Indians. But remember this, Colonel. The way will not be easy for either one of us. The Creeks are a fierce people. If you do not keep your promise to them, they will turn on you and your colony, and there will be nothing I can do to stop them."

"I understand," he said, satisfied to have gained Mary's help. The trustees were sure to object to the amount he had offered, but if Mary Musgrove were able to assure the welfare of the colony, then she would be well worth the price.

"A word of advice, Colonel," she offered.

"Yes?"

"You saw Tomochichi's throne?"

"Yes. A very handsome piece of cypress."

"Then I suggest that you have a larger, more impressive throne made for you in time for the signing of the treaty. I have painted you as a great chief in a vast kingdom over the sea. Your throne will be a symbol of that power."

His gray eyes twinkled at the thought. His sisters at the Jacobite court of James, the Pretender, would enjoy the joke. He must write them soon and tell them that he, too, might be considered a "great pretender."

The next morning, Mary stood on the bluff and watched the boat with the rangers, Colonel Bull, and James Edward Oglethorpe disappear. A sudden wind flapped her skirts about her ankles.

She looked out toward the sea, to the horizon that now promised the long-delayed cold of winter. As the freezing rain squall moved toward land Mary hurried to batten down the windows of the trading post.

# Chapter 19

"Mother, I see the boats coming upriver," Edward Walking Stick announced as he rushed into the trading-post store.

For the past two weeks the child had gone back and forth to the bluff to peer downriver for the boats that would bring the new settlers.

"There are six of them," he continued. "A sloop and five periaguas."

"Would you like to go with Singing Rock to tell Mico Tomochichi?" she asked. "He will want to be here to greet them after they disembark."

"Yes. And I will tell Senauki and Toonahowie, too."

John would be disappointed that he had missed Oglethorpe for the second time and that the settlers had arrived before he returned from Charlestown. But it couldn't be helped. Winter was an extremely busy season at the trading post, with the most luxurious furs brought in. It had been necessary for him to get the loaded periaguas to the Charlestown warehouse in time for the next shipment to England. But the rangers were on hand to help Oglethorpe.

As the colony's boats drew closer to the opposite shore Mary left the trading post and came to stand upon the bluff. Dressed in her osnaburg shift and a stroud petticoat of red—the color of women's power—she watched the people begin to walk up past the sandy beach and struggle to climb the crude earthen steps of the steep embankment to reach the even ground above.

Soon Mary was joined by a few Yamacraws, who had also seen the boats approach. She knew that many of the people in the Indian village had been uneasy about this new invasion by the English. But they trusted their queen, Coosaponakeesa, in her decision to allow them to land. Although she had left it to Tomochichi as mico to make the formal treaty, the village knew that she would be constantly watchful. One word from her, and they would rise to drive these colonists out; for she had not given away the land of her heritage—merely allowed the colonists to use part of it.

The storm the past week had left its blustery, chill wind as a legacy, causing great havoc with the construction of a crane to unload the vessels and the setting up of the four large tents.

When one of the tents took wing and threatened to blow away before it was properly staked, Skee, the Yamacraw brave at Mary's side, said, "Not so smart, these people. Plenty heap cold to live in tents."

"They will build wooden houses later," Mary explained.

The Indian nodded, satisfied.

Mary watched as one man seemed to be supervising everything. Even from a distance, she could tell that it was Colonel Oglethorpe, presiding over the unloading of the cattle and other animals. She noted the seven horses that were brought from the sloop and tethered beyond the tents. She smiled as a massive wooden throne chair was also unloaded.

Mary, realizing the formalities to come later, finally left the bluff to return to the trading post. Tomochichi and Senauki and most of the village would be gathering at her house before marching to greet Oglethorpe and his colonists.

Shortly before dusk, a small English child, playing before one of the tents, looked up when he heard the jingling of bells in the distance.

"Mama, Mama," the child screamed, and ran inside the tent.

"What is it, Willie?" she asked.

"The Indians are coming. Are they going to scalp us, Mama?"

The frightened colonist, holding an infant on her hip, rushed to the opening of the tent. Her eyes sought out Colonel Oglethorpe first, to see if he were going to raise an alarm. Instead, he smiled and began to walk toward the procession.

"No, child," she responded, trying to disguise her relief. "Father Oglethorpe said the Indians would be coming to welcome us. And see? Some of them are even bringing gifts of food."

With Mary Musgrove coming to stand at his side, Oglethorpe bowed first to Tomochichi, with whom he already felt a kinship. Through Mary, as interpreter, he met Senauki and Toonahowie, who would one day become mico of the tribe. But the most important one that day was Tallapoosa, the medicine man.

"Whatever Tallapoosa does, do not flinch or draw back," Mary warned.

So with a calm politeness, James stood and listened as Tallapoosa began his speech.

With words punctuated by grunts, shouts, and grimaces, Tallapoosa recited the history of the Creeks—their origins, their power and prowess in war. Included in his speech was a vivid portrayal of the manner in which they dealt with their enemies. As he spoke, the ferocity on his face was designed to bring terror to even the most hardened soldier of the crown.

At times, Tallapoosa paused, waiting for Mary to translate his terrible words to the Englishman.

If she did not see fit to translate every threat, Mary nevertheless knew that Oglethorpe understood the seriousness of the occasion, and the power that Tallapoosa enjoyed in the village.

Baffled at the bravery of this man standing before him, Tallapoosa changed his stance. Coming even closer, the medicine man took the feathered fan with the attached bells, and began to stroke Oglethorpe with it, to ascertain his power.

"Do not step back," Mary warned again.

James gritted his teeth and stood his ground, allowing the feathered fan to touch him, near his heart, his head, and along the course of his humors.

Earlier, James would have drawn his sword if any man had taken such liberties. But the duel with one of his political enemies ten years before had resulted in his incarceration. It had been through his mother, the Lady Eleanor, that he had been set free. From that time on he had allowed his head to rule his temper—just as his head now told him that he must not be pushed into rash action by this medicine man before him.

Tallapoosa suddenly withdrew the fan and Mary, still cautious, translated his words. "Tallapoosa says that you are a man with a brave heart. And that you have brought much power to this land."

For the first time Oglethorpe also smiled. But before he could respond, Mary continued, "He wishes to meet your medicine man that you have brought with you."

"My medicine man?" For a moment James looked baffled. "Oh, he evidently means our surgeon, Dr. Cox."

Dr. Cox, watching the proceedings from the side ranks with his wife, Frances, and their two children, heard his name. At Oglethorpe's signal, he left the crowd to come and stand beside him. Dr. Cox, realizing that Tallapoosa could be an enormous help in finding local medicinal plants he needed, asked for his words to that effect to be translated. But hearing them, Tallapoosa stepped back and his face became guarded.

Only Mary understood Tallapoosa's jealousy and the threat this second medicine man might be to him. But no one else seemed to notice the Indian's reaction, for now Tomochichi stepped forward with his gift to Oglethorpe. With speeches back and forth, and the Indian women setting up the food that they had prepared, a spirit of camaraderie overtook the group. The colonists, so many malnourished even before the long sea voyage, relaxed and began to eat the plenty that the land had bestowed.

Remaining aloof, Tallapoosa did not join in the festivities. Mary, seated beside James Oglethorpe, saw that the medicine man was monitoring Dr. Cox's every move, even to noting which tent he and his family had been assigned.

With much ceremony, Tomochichi finally rose from his place of honor. It was time to go back to the village. Within a few minutes, the colonists were left to themselves.

"Thank you, Mary," James said at last. "Once again you have been a tremendous help to me."

Mary nodded. "If you have no further need of my assistance, then I will go back to the trading post."

The blustery wind began to howl, with the tent openings flapping in the distance. Mary could see the smoke coming from the chimney of the trading post, where Justice, her black servant, had built a fire for the night.

She hesitated. "I would welcome you as our guest, Colonel, if you would care to stay at the trading post rather than remaining here for the night."

James shook his head. "I must set an example for my people. It would not look good if I chose the comforts of a fireside tonight."

"I understand," Mary replied, knowing even before she had spoken that he would not accept her invitation. "But what about Dr. Cox? I noticed that he has a cough, and the chill wind will do him no good. Mayhaps he and his family would wish to accept my offer?"

"A good idea," James replied. "We cannot have our surgeon getting ill. He's much too important to our little colony."

Mary's son Edward had already gone ahead with Toonahowie. And so it was Dr. Cox's little boy who trotted by her side as Mary led the way for the surgeon and his grateful wife, Frances.

From the corner of her eye, Mary saw Tallapooosa moving cautiously in the pine grove, not far from the newly erected tents. Seeing him lurking there, she was now certain that she was not being overly concerned by putting Dr. Cox under her personal protection.

"Mother, Mother," Edward greeted her as she approached the trading post. "Father and Jacob have returned from their trip."

His words brought joy to Mary. She had missed her husband, as well as the genial bondservant, Jacob Matthews. With little more than a year left to serve, Jacob now seemed more a part of the family than hired help. When they had left Charlestown for Yamacraw Bluff, John had been extremely lucky to buy out Jacob's remaining time from the man who had chosen to return to England.

"That is certainly good news, Edward," Mary replied. She then turned to Dr. Cox. "My husband had hoped to get back in time to welcome all of you. There will be much to talk about around the fire tonight."

"I hope we will not be intruding," Dr. Cox began.

"Not at all. We're used to having visitors stay with us. After all, there is hardly any other suitable place between here and Spanish St. Augustine."

"Which I have no desire to see," Dr. Cox interjected with a laugh.

When John appeared on the porch, Mary rushed to greet him. She was shy before her guests, but John had no such hesitation in showing how much he had missed her. He lifted Mary as if she were a tiny doll and gave her a resounding kiss.

"So, our guests have arrived," John said, finally putting her down and looking toward the Cox family.

"Yes. And this is their surgeon, Dr. Cox, and his family." With pride written across her face, Mary said, "This is my husband, John Musgrove."

The two men shook hands. "And my wife, Frances, and our two children."

"How do you do?"

Dr. Cox's cough caused Mary to cut the formalities short. "Come, let's all go inside to the fire."

That evening, as a late supper was served, Frances Cox did not recognize the woman who had served as interpreter to Colonel Oglethorpe that day. A transformation had occurred. At one end of the table sat another Englishwoman, dressed in English clothes—simple, but still in the English style. The woman's dark hair was no longer in two plaits that reached to her waist. Instead, it was swept back from her face and pinned at the nape, in much the same way that her own hair was fixed.

Yet Mary Musgrove's appearance was not the only surprise. Their bondservant, Jacob, also sat at table with them. In England, that would never have been allowed. The rigid social rules to which she was accustomed seemed to have vanished in this wilderness. How else could she explain supping with a half-breed and a bondservant and considering herself extremely fortunate?

"I understand from my father that Carolina is sending some sawyers to help cut the trees for the new houses."

Dr. Cox looked at his host. "A godsend. We have only one good carpenter among us, Noble Jones. All the other men have had little experience with building. And only one or two with farming."

"They'll all learn soon enough," Jacob assured him. "In this wilderness, you have to learn things quick, or you won't survive."

Seeing the alarm in her guests' faces, Mary said, "Tomochichi has promised that the entire Yamacraw village will help Colonel Oglethorpe. By spring, the crops should be planted and many of the houses built."

"Father Oglethorpe has promised that we will have one of the first houses," Frances said, as if to reassure herself.

"And that is as it should be," Mary replied. "Your husband is an important man to the colony."

John Musgrove smiled at his wife. Although she was speaking to the Englishwoman, she did not take her eyes from her husband's face. A surge of desire swept over John. He knew that Mary was just as eager as he to say good night to their guests.

Finally turning to Frances, Mary asked, "Would you care for anything else?"

"No, thank you. The evening has been a delight. But if you don't mind, I think my husband and I will retire."

"Yes. It's been an unusually long day for you, I know."

As everyone stood, Jacob said, "I'll clear the table while Justice sees to the animals."

With regret, the servant watched Mary and John bid good night to the Coxes and then walk arm in arm to the adjacent bedroom.

Inside the darkened bedroom, Mary lay in John's arms. "I've missed you, Husband," she uttered against his warm mouth.

"How much?" he teased, suddenly turning and lifting her on top of him, causing the bed to creak.

At the noise, a dish clattered in the serving room. Mary, stifling a giggle, whispered in John's ear, "We're disturbing Jacob."

"Then he should get on to bed like the others instead of listening to us from the pantry."

"That's not fair, Johnny," she admonished. "I'm grateful that he volunteered to do Singing Rock's chore tonight."

"And wishin' he could take over mine," John answered.

His kiss prevented Mary from replying.

# Chapter 20

Several months later, as James Oglethorpe walked past the few buildings and houses already erected in the first tything, or district, his impatience mingled with his sense of pride. The bakery, the stranger's house where visitors to the colony could find a bed, and a widows' house were already up, with the public building nearly finished, too.

But the race to build houses and clear the land to plant crops had proceeded at a much slower pace than James had imagined. If they did not get extra help soon, the majority of the people might have to spend another winter in the tents. As for food, they could not continue relying on the larder and beef cattle belonging to the Musgroves. The colonists would have to start supplying their own food or risk starving. That is, if they were not massacred by either the Indians or the Spanish, or didn't all die of disease within the next few weeks.

When Dr. Cox had died so unexpectedly, James was saddened. But his sorrow had suddenly changed to alarm when other colonists soon followed, several a day, until now more than a third of his people were dead of the bloody flux.

The survival of the colony and the colonists were his main concerns—not the peccadilloes of one Irish ne'er-do-well on which the trustees had wasted their energy and ink.

As he continued to walk in the direction of the experimental garden, where both his interpreter and his vinedresser were waiting, James thought of the latest letter of instruction from the trustees that had arrived the previous day. After one quick perusal, he relegated the letter to the box containing all the others, but the message still rankled.

"It has come to our attention that this Irishman smuggled a whore, disguised as his servant, onto a ship for his own pleasure during the long voyage to Georgia. We cannot allow these types of dangerous persons to pollute our colony. You are to send them both back to England on the next ship...."

Since the trustees didn't want the man in Savannah, then James would send him with his two indentured servants to Hutchinson Island, instead. At least that way, there would be two more men to bear arms in the defense of the colony.

"Good morning, Father Oglethorpe," a young boy along the square called out.

"Good morning, Willie," he answered, recognizing the Cox boy. "I trust your mother and sister are well."

The boy hesitated. "The baby was feverish this morning."

"I'm sorry to hear that. Maybe Mistress Cox should get a nostrum from the apothecary."

"Yes, sir. I'll tell her."

James's gray eyes quickly glanced over the boy from head to toe. He was gratified that he seemed to be such a sturdy lad. If anything happened to Willie, Mistress Cox would have to move into widows' quarters and give up all rights to both the new house and the land already under cultivation.

James's frown lessened at the sight of Mary Musgrove, waiting for him at the edge of the palisades. He waved and moved forward at a faster pace.

How different Mary's position was in the Indian culture from that of the women in his own—just one more thing that the trustees would never understand about this new land. But it would not be to his advantage to suggest just how much he had come to rely on Mary.

"Colonel," she said, nodding to him as he approached.

"Good morning," he said.

The two fell into step together, the tiny woman and the tall, austere man. They were comfortable with each other, as if they had walked the earth side by side for many moons.

"I hope you don't mind seeing the garden with me while we talk. The Piedmontese wants to show me the condition of the vines and mulberry trees."

"I am free this morning. John and Jacob are tending the trading post. And Singing Rock is watching over Edward. The child seems better today."

"That is good news. I pray his recovery will soon be complete."

James was sincere in his wish, for he knew of the tragic loss of her two eldest sons. Death had never been a respecter of persons, either in the Old or the New World. But at least in this wilderness, cruelty was mixed with hope, a minute commodity in the back streets of London Town.

While they walked, James's mind returned to the reason for his conference with Mary.

"You have thought of the wording of the treaty?"

"Yes. And the ceremony accompanying it."

"What about the invitations to the chiefs?"

"They have already been sent by Tomochichi's runners."

"And Tallapoosa? Do you think he will cause trouble?"

"More than likely. He's drunk with power now that Dr. Cox is dead. He is saying among the people that his medicine is greater than yours. You must get another doctor in the colony at once."

"I wish to heaven that it were that simple—to snap my fingers and have one appear."

The Trustees' Garden, laid out in squares and crosswalks, soon enveloped James's interest. At the northern boundary stood a grove of trees, left in a primal state, with hickory, oak, sassafras, and tulip poplars. The rest of the ten acres had been cleared to make way for the rows of orange trees and mulberry trees, the hope of the colony to supplant the silk imports from China. Each colonist had only to request his ten mulberry trees from the garden, but so far it looked as if few had taken advantage. James sighed. It was his fond hope to take back on his next trip to England the first woven silk as a gift to the queen. But like so many of his dreams, this one was far from being realized.

Seeing the Italian gardener ahead, James quickened his pace. "Good morn, Signor Batalli."

*"Buon giorno*, Colonel."

Amalfi Batalli, the small, dark-haired man, quickly stood up from his kneeling position. In his hand he held a curved knife that he had used to snip an errant tendril from the espaliered grapevine.

"The vines seem to be growing well," James said, indicating the nearby plant.

"For such young plants," he acknowledged. "But the wild ones are much stronger."

Mary smiled at his words. "Yes. Our muscadines do not need such constant care."

"Ah, but the golden vino from these, one day," Amalfi said, touching his lips with his fingers.

James laughed. "But it will be several years before our vines give us fruit. Is that not so, Signor?"

The Piedmontese nodded to Oglethorpe.

"So I suppose we will have to be content with the wild muscadines in the meantime."

"But not for wine," Mary cautioned. "Between the children and the bears, there are never enough to ferment."

Together, the three walked among the rows, lingering from time to time to examine the trees and other plants. And then, as Oglethorpe and Amalfi stopped to discuss the garden, Mary walked ahead, toward the orange trees planted on a small ridge. These, she knew, probably would not survive the coming winter, for they were planted in an unsheltered place, where the cold winds would sweep in from the sea. But she had not been asked here to give her opinion of the plantings.

The treaty was her primary concern—to help James Oglethorpe write the words that would be acceptable to the majority of the headmen. It was a delicate matter; for from the time that her uncle, Brims, the Creek strength had lain in keeping the French and Spanish guessing as to their intent toward the English.

Mary, seated on the half log that served as a bench, looked up when she heard Oglethorpe's approach. As she started to stand, James quickly said, "Don't get up. Why don't we both stay here? It's much more pleasant than my tent." He too sat down on the half log.

From her apron pocket, Mary pulled out several sheets of parchment. "For the past few days I have been working on the wording of the treaty...."

From time to time Amalfi glanced up from his work. Without seeming to be overly interested, he watched the two, their heads together, looking down at the parchment, their voices weaving together, with an occasional phrase caught by the wind. Hers was the musical one, with the other holding a rather strident, earnest quality. Amalfi knew they were both oblivious of him as he began to rake the small clippings in a pile for the other workers to remove later.

As he put his knife away and left the Trustees' Garden, the Piedmontese shook his head. A garden was for lovers, not for the discussion of business matters. If he had been in the colonel's place, he would have wasted no time in stealing a kiss, with thoughts of bedding that delectable creature as soon as possible, husband or no husband.

A few minutes later, as James gazed down at the drafted treaty, he said, "It's a pity that Old Brims is dead, and that I never had a chance to deal with him face-to-face. He was a legend through Europe—that wily old statesman that the Spanish called *Le Gran Cazique*."

Mary made no comment at the mention of her uncle's name. She waited for the colonel to indicate that they were finished so that she could return to the trading post. Instead, he seemed reluctant to let her go. "Tell me about this new mico of Coweta."

"You mean Youhowlakee?"

"Yes."

"Actually, he's the guardian of the late emperor's twin son, Essabo."

"Oh, yes. The young heir apparent."

Mary did not contradict him. Her Creek fear that a malevolent spirit might overhear and harm her child kept her from explaining that Jamie, still at school in Charlestown, was the chosen one. Even though Essabo would be a mico some day, it was Jamie who was destined to become the emperor now that his two older brothers were dead.

Not wishing to say anything against Youhowlakee, whose power was tenuous, at best, Mary said, "Youhowlakee serves as regent for now.

Not everyone in Coweta Town follows him, but his mark on the treaty will be sufficient, with the other chiefs, even if he is replaced later."

"You mean when Essabo takes over?"

"Essabo. Or one of his cousins," she added under her breath.

"Then we must make sure that Essabo comes, too," James insisted. "To give the treaty more validity, even if he is still under age."

Mary smiled. "And to give Toonahowie the joy of seeing him again."

A raucous noise suddenly invaded the primeval Eden—that of a woman's shrill, high-pitched voice coming from the waterfront.

James laughed. "I believe Markham's wench, Alice, must be protesting their forceful removal from Savannah."

At Mary's puzzled expression, James explained, "I gave orders this morning for a periagua to take Markham and his household to Hutchinson Island. It was either that or sending them back to England, at the trustees' request."

Mary stood up and gazed in the direction of the small island across the harbor. "You might be sorry that you did not banish them from the colony altogether."

The mere hint of criticism wounded James's feelings. His decisions had not been questioned by anyone since he'd set sail from England. What did this woman know of governing a new colony? With a sense of hostility he glared at her, but there was a challenge in her eyes that caused him to forget his resentment. In good grace he smiled, for at that moment she reminded him of his mother, the Lady Eleanor, scolding him for some misdeed.

"For better or worse, it's done. Come, let's go to the bluff to see the noisy little baggage off."

With the treaty secured, James began to walk beside Mary toward the bluff. After a few minutes the melee on the beach was forgotten as James stood alone and watched Mary trace her way down the path to the trading post.

# Chapter 21

The clamor in the square attracted immediate attention. Sensing that something alarming had occurred in the colony, the baker left his bread unattended in the giant oven; the tything man cut short his rounds, and the children stopped their games to run toward the square.

"Something's happened at the bluff." The message was passed one to the other as the people crowded together.

"Have the Spaniards come upriver?" an anxious voice inquired.

"Maybe it's a pirate ship," a childish voice suggested.

One of the militiamen, coming off watch, hoisted his musket to his shoulder and motioned for the children to be quiet as he strained to hear the three-way conversation taking place between an unsmiling Indian messenger, Mary Musgrove, and Colonel Oglethorpe.

From her position on the stoop of one of the houses nearby, Coreen O'Reilly sat, with her needle following the intricate smocking pattern on the baby dress. She had not wanted to leave Charlestown, but Hamish had been hired to oversee the sawyers cutting the timber for the new houses. Wherever Sally and Hamish went, Coreen also went.

At the noise, Coreen left her needlework and began to walk in the direction of the square.

"What's wrong?" she asked as she reached the small group of women standing at the edge of the crowd.

"I think there's been a murder," Frances Cox answered.

"I'm not surprised. It's like I said the moment we stepped on this heathen land," another woman whispered. "Our lives aren't worth tuppence. If the Indians don't get you, the Spanish will."

"I survived the whole Yamasee War in Carolina," Coreen confided. "That was a terrible time. I even had my horse shot out from under me. My daughter Sally can vouch for that."

"But we're at peace with the Indians, aren't we? So it must be the Spanish."

"It might be the French."

Unable to hear what was going on, they watched as Mary and James disappeared from the square to walk in the general direction of the Indian village. But as Willie wove his way through the crowd from the place where he had been listening, his mother, Frances, stopped him.

"Willie, did you hear what happened? Who was killed?"

"An Indian brave. I heard Mary tell Father Oglethorpe that Tomochichi thinks that one of us did it, and he's demanding revenge."

A woman moaned and clutched her child closer to her breast. "Then we'll all be scalped for sure."

The militiaman fingered his musket and said, "We'll protect you. Don't worry."

Coreen snorted. "A rusty musket or two isn't going to save us."

"What will happen to the poor unfortunate who did the crime?" the baker asked.

"Well, they'll have to have an inquiry first..." the militiaman began.

"And then the Indians will burn him at the stake," Willie finished for him.

"Willie," his mother admonished. "You don't have to scare us unduly."

The baker lifted his head and sniffed the air. "Faith, I think it's my bread that's burnin'," he announced.

As he began to rush back to the bakery a second militiaman stopped him. "Get your musket and powder and take up your position at the palisades at once. Colonel Oglethorpe's orders."

The crowd quickly dispersed, the women gathering their children and taking refuge in the few completed houses, while the men and older boys gathered their muskets to defend the small colony against possible attack.

Along the wooded path to the Yamacraw village, Mary hurried, her fleet-footed steps keeping pace with the long stride of the man beside her. The messenger had disappeared almost at once, leaving the two alone.

As Mary and James approached the village the beating of Indian drums had already begun.

Recognizing the war rhythm and hearing the warriors chanting, Mary said, "Tallapoosa is getting them into a frenzy. It will be difficult to stop them."

"It looks as if it's almost too late, Mary."

James caught a glimpse of the village scene—the sight of the young dead Indian, his litter placed upon a high ceremonial mound near the sacred fire. He had not been dressed for burial, merely had his arms folded across his bare chest. Bending over him was Tallapoosa, touching him with his feathers, while the bells gave an eerie, menacing sound interspersed with the grunts and shouts of the medicine man and the rhythmic, compounding beat of drums and moccasined feet.

For a brief moment, Tallapoosa glared at Mary and the intruder. Then, turning his back on them both, he renewed the pace of the ceremony, louder, faster.

The dim outline of the cypress throne greeted Mary as she went inside the council chamber. She knew that Tomochichi was seated there. She sensed his presence even before her eyes adjusted to the darkness.

Motioning for Oglethorpe to remain behind, Mary slowly walked toward the throne. When she reached it, she stood before it and waited, seemingly oblivious to the noise outside.

A shaft of light pierced the darkness from the small opening in the roof and touched the gold talisman around Mary's neck. She did not move, but was content to stand, until the old man deigned to acknowledge her presence.

Finally, Tomochichi spoke. "And why does the Beloved Woman of Coweta and Kashita honor us with her presence?"

Mary's manner was different from the first time when James had accompanied her. As she greeted Tomochichi, there was a charming sweetness, even a hint of deference to her voice.

"To request your permission to address the council."

"The time for words is gone. Tallapoosa was right. We should never have allowed the English to land, for they have brought grief to our people. Your words cannot breathe life again into the dead."

"That is true. The young brave I saw cannot be brought back to life on this earth. But perhaps my words can save others."

"Like the English?"

"No. Only you and the council can save the English in this colony. But in doing so, you will be saving the remnant of your people. For if the colonists are massacred, more will come and take their places, like the shells from the sea at every tide."

Standing where he was, James understood few words. He had listened intently to the exchange, trying to grasp the meaning in the inflection of the two voices. But then the measured silence between Tomochichi and Mary became just as eloquent as the words spoken between them. James had seen this same type of silent ritual on the battlefield, an inherent respect to an ancient warrior before the younger drew his sword.

Finally, Tomochichi said, "Tooawhi's death demands revenge. Tallapoosa said so."

"Then let us find the perpetrator and punish him alone."

"The English stand together. They would not give up one of their own."

The medicine man had evidently coached Tomochichi well.

"Ask James Edward Oglethorpe to his face, Tomochichi." Mary motioned for James to come and stand beside her. As the mico phrased the question, Oglethorpe waited for Mary to translate.

"Tomochichi wants to know if you will give up the murderer to be tried by his people. Decide carefully, Colonel, for the fate of the colony rests on your answer."

James hesitated. If he agreed, a slow, painful death awaited the culprit. But if he did not agree, then the colony would be wiped out.

"If there are witnesses who would swear to the truth, that one of my men killed the Indian without provocation, then I will punish him myself."

Mary smiled. She nodded to the mico and said, "Call together your council, Tomochichi. Allow me to speak so that we might settle this in peace."

Again there was silence. Then Tomochichi clapped his hands and one of his headmen, hidden in the shadows behind the throne, came out of hiding to walk with the mico.

Once Tomochichi had gone from the council chamber, James voiced his uneasiness. "What will happen now, Mary?"

"First, I will speak to plead your case. And if the council agrees, then the trial will be held."

"Will I be allowed to question the witnesses?"

"Yes. And to examine the body, to determine the manner of Tooawhi's death."

Outside, the drums seemed to beat interminably. But when they ceased, James was more uneasy than ever. Yet, when the council began to appear, he gave no indication of his inner turmoil. Standing at attention, with his spine straight and his face showing no emotion, no curiosity, he didn't flinch when Tallapoosa walked by, suddenly shaking the rattle in his face to show the medicine man's contempt for the entire colony.

Tomochichi, wearing his buffalo robe around him, took his throned seat, and only then did the mico motion for James to come closer, to sit on the circular rung directly below the throne, thus putting the Englishman at a physical disadvantage.

There were no hisses this time as Mary spoke. But the faces were hostile as their attention was directed to the woman speaking on James's behalf. If only he could understand what Mary was telling them, then he would have felt a little better.

For a half hour she continued, with no clue to James. For all he knew, the Indians might be planning to scalp him and send his head back on a post for all the village to see.

Once she had stopped, the air was as silent as when she'd begun. She appeared to be waiting for something to happen. One hand went up. Slowly, another joined the first hand. And another, until a majority of hands was up in the air.

With the show of hands, Tomochichi signaled the two braves standing at the opening. Within a few moments the body of the Indian, accompanied by his family, was brought forward on its litter and placed before Tomochichi.

Back and forth now, the words went. "Tomochichi wishes you to examine the body and tell him what you find."

"Will I be allowed to touch the body?"

"Yes. The purification has not yet begun."

Before the body of the young man, Oglethorpe kneeled. He had seen many a man killed in war, by gunpowder. But there did not seem to be a musket hole in his body. He lay in an unnatural position, despite an attempt to lay him out otherwise.

"This brave has not been shot," James announced. Mary translated his words.

"His neck appears to be broken," James added.

That, too, was translated. His finding was corroborated by a grunt.

"Did he fall from a great height?" James questioned. "For he appears to have other bones broken, as well."

Mary translated and then prompted James. "Ask for Tallapoosa's witness," she urged.

He did, but no one came forward.

"Then, let me talk with the ones who found him."

Two young boys came forward. But when questioned, they professed that they had not actually seen the murder. They had discovered his body at the base of a cliff, after it had happened.

It took another hour to piece together what must have occurred. As the evidence mounted, with the father testifying that the young man had been despondent, refusing to eat since the girl he loved had spurned him, James began to sense a change in Tomochichi. His wrath appeared to be waning. But the hostility of the council had not abated.

With sharp words exchanged back and forth, the drama unfolded. Finally, in disgust, Tallapoosa gave a signal to one of his followers, who began a rhythmic stamping of feet. In a threatening gesture, Tallapoosa moved closer to James, as if to make him a prisoner. But the medicine man had not understood the link between Mary and the old mico.

Tomochichi suddenly placed himself between Oglethorpe and Tallapoosa. "He who would harm my friend must kill me first."

In the end, justice won. Unable to prove that any colonist had been seen on the bluff at the time of the Indian's death, the council reluctantly decided that it had been suicide, and that no one was to blame.

And so, on that day, the old mico challenged Tallapoosa's power and took a firm stand as a friend to Oglethorpe and the English colony. He motioned for Oglethorpe to join him. "Come, my friend. Let us smoke the pipe in peace."

"And may we settle any other dispute in the future, as this was done," a relieved James answered through Mary. "In honesty and among brothers."

That night, as the great wailing for the dead filled the night sky, James sat in his tent and listened. So close. His little colony had come so close to being wiped out completely.

Not far away, on the porch of the trading post, Mary sat with her husband, John. Little Edward Walking Stick lay heavily in her arms.

"Here, let me take the boy," John said, reaching out for the sleeping child. "I'll put the little fellow to bed."

When he returned, Mary was gazing up at the North Star, and she seemed to be just as far away from him as the star. "You were gone so long today, Mary. Oh, don't get me wrong," he hastened to reassure her. "I'm not complaining. Skee and Justice were more than enough help. I just wondered if anything unusual happened."

"No more so than any other day, Johnny. There was a slight misunderstanding between Tomochichi and the colonel. But they smoked the sacred tobacco and everything is right again."

She reached out and took his hand. Together, they sat and listened until the sad wailing in the distance ceased.

# Chapter 22

In May, when the rivers were running mud red from the abundance of spring rains and a canopy of lush new green clothed the forest trails, the chiefs of the eight Lower Creek Indian towns came to Savannah to sign the English treaty with James.

Mary and John Musgrove had made careful plans for the week's celebrations, for numerous feasts, the exchange of gifts, and the singing, dancing, and games that the Creeks so loved.

As was the custom in all Creek treaties, Mary had seen to it that a large area of the land she claimed outside Savannah along Pipemaker's Creek had been set aside for the exclusive use of her people as a resting and camping place as they traveled back and forth between their Creek towns and the settlements. This area the settlers were not to encroach upon.

But to show honor to her proud young cousin Essabo, the regent Youhowlakee, and her elderly cousin Wilimico, at the official signing of the treaty,

Mary had arranged for them to spend the nights in her Savannah town house rather than camp on the outskirts of the town with the others.

"Take good care of them, Skee," she said to her servant the day before they were to arrive. "And make sure that they don't get into any trouble."

"I take good care," he said.

"And no rum," she warned as she left the small clapboard house to go back to the trading post.

Megan Tutwiler stood at her open door and watched Mary disappear down the street. "I don't understand why Father Oglethorpe ever gave that woman a house here in town with the rest of us."

Her husband, scraping the mud from his shoes before coming inside, made a noncommittal grunt. He had been careful not to cross Megan, ever since she had given him a black eye on the ship.

"Did you hear what I said, Mr. Tutwiler?"

"Yes, dear. You're right, of course."

"Coreen told me today that Mary's even invited some of the savages to stay in her house. If that's true, I won't get a wink of sleep the entire time they're here."

"Rather dangerous, I would say. They might even try to scalp someone." Henry Tutwiler sighed. If he had been born lucky, the Indians would scalp Megan. But he'd never had a lucky thing to happen to him.

"That's why you're going to start sleeping on a pallet by the door, with your musket loaded."

"Yes, dear."

The next night, when the candles in the houses had been snuffed out one by one and the sliver of moon had given up its struggle against the dark, overhead mists, Henry took up his guard position as instructed. In the distance he could see the faint glow of the bonfires and hear the beat of drums that had begun at suppertime and still showed no signs of stopping.

Megan's heavy breathing from the rustic bed at the back of the small house combined with the bloodcurdling yells from the Indian encampment to keep him awake. But then, despite them both, he finally dozed.

"Mr. Tutwiler!"

The small man quickly came awake.

"Yes, Megan?"

"I hear something down the street. Look out and see what's happening."

Henry pushed back his pallet and edged open the door only wide enough to get a bird's-eye view of the open lane.

"There're some Indians coming, Megan. But it's all right. I think I recognize Skee."

"Well, keep watching them. And make sure they don't step foot on our little plot."

To that, Henry made no comment. Even if the Indians decided to come inside his house and take everything he owned, he would never be able to do anything about it. He couldn't shoot at anybody, despite the brief arms training he had gone through with all the other men in the colony. He was a wigmaker, not a soldier.

A good wigmaker, too, even if Megan never gave him the proper credit. But the rows of wigs on the dummy heads lined along the shelves at one side of the room attested to his artistry.

A nervous Henry watched as the Indians disappeared inside Mary's house. For some time he stood and listened to the noise. But gradually the night became quiet and he went to sleep.

The next morning, a hung-over Wilimico awoke as the sun pierced through the open window of Mary's town house. The Indian had celebrated far too much with Skee the previous evening and he was in no condition but to cover his head and remain in bed as Essabo and Youhowlakee set out for the encampment. In the quiet, he rolled over and went back to sleep.

Later that morning the pleasant aroma of blackberry pie drifted from Megan's house, curled past the open window, and caused Wilimico to stir. He sniffed the air several times and realized that he was hungry. There on the window ledge of the next house, three pies sat cooling.

Quickly, he arose, put on his loincloth and moccasins, and crept out the door.

Moments later, Megan's enraged voice pierced the air. "Mr. Tutwiler!"

"What is it, Megan?"

"That bloody Indian is eating my pies. Stop him!"

Henry turned around from the table where he was working on the new wig for the Reverend Herbert. His eyes met those of Wilimico, who was standing at the window and enjoying Megan's offering on the ledge.

At that moment Henry feared Megan's rage much more than the sight of the old Indian. He knew he would have to do something to satisfy his wife. So he picked up his musket and walked out the door to confront Wilimico.

In a quivering voice, Henry said, "I know you don't understand a word of what I'm saying, but please leave Megan's pies alone."

The Indian stared at him. In desperation, Henry held up one finger. "One pie. You take." He pointed to the other two pies and shook his head. "You leave alone."

As if he understood, Wilimico nodded, took the remainder of the pie he had been eating, and began to back off. "Tustanugga. Friend."

Baffled at the benign behavior of the Indian, Henry watched until he disappeared from sight. Behind him, he heard Megan. "I don't know how you did it, Mr. Tutwiler. But I'm proud of you."

A sense of accomplishment, a new feeling permeated Henry's mind. But to hide the shaking of his limbs from his wife, he walked inside and sat down in his chair to take up his work again. "You have to be firm with these Indians," he said. "I guess the sight of the musket must have scared him away."

But the wily old Wilimico had scarcely noticed the gun in Henry's hands. He had seen something much more impressive—the row of his enemies' heads, barely visible in the shadows. The man was a great white warrior—a tustanugga—one who deserved respect among the Creek warriors.

Wilimico finished the pie as he walked in the direction of the trading post. He would find out the name of the Englishman from Mary so that he could request his presence at the treaty signing. It would be an honor to smoke the peace pipe with such a warrior as that.

Toward the end of the week, Henry sat in a place of honor beside Wilimico and watched the historical signing of the treaty by the headmen of the Lower Creeks. He still had no idea why the Indian had taken such a liking to him.

Mary was puzzled too, but said nothing. Her job had been completed. During the days of festivity, she had constantly entertained and seen to it that nothing occurred to mar the important signing that would bring peace to her land and her two peoples. She had stood at the colonel's side as interpreter, making sure that the ceremony was without flaw and that the gifts were distributed, according to rank. On the next morning, after the final feast, she bade farewell to her Indian kinsmen as they began to depart for their forest homes.

"This was a momentous week, Mary," James said. The austere man rewarded her with a rare smile.

"Yes, Colonel. A momentous week."

Together they stood at the intersecting path and looked on as Wilimico embraced his friend Henry. "Now, that's a strange friendship, wouldn't you say?" James asked.

"Wilimico has evidently seen something in Henry Tutwiler that your colonists have not."

"Whatever that quality is, it has certainly improved Henry's worth, even in his wife's eyes."

"Just as your treatment of Tomochichi has improved his worth in the eyes of his people."

"Despite Tallapoosa..."

"Yes. He will try to find some way to undermine the treaty. You must still be wary of him."

James moved back quickly as Mary's kinsmen surrounded her. He headed for his tent under the great oak tree and there he stood, watching the displays of affection for the small, dynamic woman. He thought of his sisters and what they would say about her. They would probably like her, too. But not as a sister-in-law.

James caught his breath in surprise. Where had such a thought come? Mary Musgrove was married. And happily, too. He must not allow her importance to him in matters of the colony to spill over into his personal life.

"My dear little cousin," Mary said to Essabo. "You have brought honor to our people. Go now in peace, and may the winds carry you safely home."

The proud young man was wearing the mantle that Oglethorpe had presented to him, a replica of the ones the Micos Tomochichi and Umpyche had also received. "I take with me the memory of our visit with you," he replied in a formal voice, for Youhowlakee was within hearing distance. But he leaned forward and, in a softer voice, he said, "And I count the days until Running Bear joins us in Coweta Town."

"Yes. He will be leaving the house of his grandfather soon."

"Essabo," Toonahowie called out. "Wait for me. I have a present for you to take to Malatchee."

The neighing of a pony, the polyphony of voices raised in a series of spine-tingling whoops, combined with the swirl of dust as Mary's relatives finally departed, leaving a relieved Savannah behind.

# Chapter 23

With Tomochichi's firm friendship and the signing of the peace treaty, James Oglethorpe saw the danger to Savannah lessening from the north and west.

Another of his worries had also been dealt with by the sudden arrival of a new doctor—Samuel Nuñez—to take the place of Dr. Cox.

Late one afternoon, as James made his way to the trading post, he knew that he had been right to ignore the trustees' instructions and to allow the exiled Portuguese Jews with Dr. Nuñez to land in the new colony. It was much more important to attend to the people's health than to give in to the prejudices of his fellow trustees. To prove it, the sick were already improving, with fewer deaths. The advice of Mary, to get another doctor, had been sound in another way. For Dr. Nuñez's arrival had not only been a boon to the sick. His presence had also served to deflect some of Tallapoosa's power.

But now another problem had reared its head to threaten his colony, a danger from the south along the Altamaha River.

The Spanish had grown increasingly bold with their forays, striking at the English footholds and arming the Indians hostile to the English to join in the attacks. For quite a while now he had mulled over in his mind what to do about this serious situation.

As James reached the trading-post porch he hoped with all his heart that Mary and John Musgrove would agree to the only viable solution he could see at the moment—to open a second trading post; this time on the Altamaha, where they could also serve as lookouts against the Spanish.

"But are these not your own people, Mary?" James asked, sensing her hesitancy at his suggestion.

"They're Creeks, all right," John answered for her. "But that doesn't mean they're friendly. It was always a loose alliance, with one tribe free to choose their friends and enemies."

"And the ones below the Altamaha have chosen the Spanish as their friends," Mary added.

"I realize that what I'm asking you to do will be dangerous, but there's great reward, too, in the trading rights."

Already the Musgroves controlled one-sixth of the entire fur trade going through the warehouses of Charlestown. But for Mary, the additional money would not be the main consideration.

"And you will have military protection," James added to his argument. "I understand that the captain of the rangers, Jacob Matthews, was once an indentured servant of yours."

"He's a good man," John acknowledged. "At least when he worked for us, we were always able to depend on him, weren't we, Mary?"

She did not confirm or deny his observation. Instead, she said, "How do you feel about it, Johnny? Is this something you would wish to do?"

The idea of new vistas, new avenues of trade, had always appealed to John. It was the same excitement that gripped nearly all traders—that combination of danger and reward, of living on the edge of civilization.

Without trying to sound too eager, John said, "We could always try it, Mary. And if it doesn't work out, we still have the post here."

James suppressed a smile. It would not do to show his relief. "Then does this mean that you will do it?"

Mary nodded to her husband who, in turn, affirmed James's request. She poured another cup of tea for the colonel, who was content to linger for a few minutes longer before walking back into town.

Within a few weeks, Mary and John founded Mount Venture, the wilderness outpost on the Altamaha. With help from their servants and Indian friends, they quickly cleared the land, felling the trees to turn them into half logs that became the walls of the trading post. Nothing was thrown away. Even the extra bark was fastened to the roof with the thatched palmetto fronds to help keep out the rain.

The Musgroves were now in more hostile territory, where one could never be certain of friend or foe—only in their willingness to trade, whether in animal skins or human scalps.

But from the beginning, the post seemed especially blessed, for the Spanish had never been dealers in furs like the English. Mount Venture became the market where the Indians could exchange their pelts for needed goods—hatchets, yard goods, flour, molasses, and rum.

With the presence of the rangers, the danger of the wilderness did not seem so great. But on the morning that Mary and John left for Mount Venture on their trip back to Savannah, Red Horse, serving as a spy for the Spanish, hid in a blind and watched them pass.

His eyes narrowed when he recognized the woman. So it was true. After all these years, Coosaponakeesa, the enemy who had bested him at Ponpon, had finally been brought to him. Today he was alone, and she was too well protected by the rangers, wielding their muskets. But she would return. He had waited this long. He could afford to wait a little longer.

In Savannah, James sat outside his tent in the shade of a large oak. He had also been thinking of the Indian woman, but not in the same terms as Red Horse. Now, as he was getting ready to leave on his first trip back to England with the Indian delegation and John Musgrove as interpreter, he realized how important Mary had always been for the colony.

As much as he would like to have Mary see England, he knew that it was imperative to leave her behind. No one else in the Creek hierarchy had her power and influence, certainly not Tomochichi. But if James was able to single out the old mico and allow him honor by taking him on a voyage, then perhaps Tomochichi's influence would widen.

James felt reasonably sure that Savannah's five hundred residents would defend the town in his absence. And even though taking up arms was against their religion, the sturdy Salzburgers, newly settled in at Ebenezer, would serve as an added deterrent to a raid, just by their presence. But as far as the rest of the surrounding settlements, he had more reservations. As a military man, he realized the inadequacy of the small string of defenses, from Fort Argyle on the Ogeechee to the nearly abandoned Fort St.George on the bluff looking out on the inland waterway to the south.

Until Mackay could recruit some of the ferociously fighting Scottish Highlanders for the settlement in the Altamaha delta, he would have to rely totally on Mary and the rangers to help counteract the constant Spanish danger from that direction.

All in all, though, James felt that his long, exhausting months spent in the New World had been successful. His major disappointment rested with the mulberry trees and the slow progress on the filature—the silk factory—to spin the silk. The industry had not taken off the way James had envisioned. But as he looked toward the avenue of trees in the Trustees' Garden, he had to be content that he had enough silk cloth made in the colony to present to the queen.

As soon as the man he had recently appointed as the magistrate approached the tent, James stood up. "You've finished gathering all the reports?"

"Yes, Colonel. They've been taken to Mr. Gordon."

"And the silk for the queen?"

"It's here in the packet, carefully wrapped for the sea voyage."

"Then I suppose it's time to get to the landing."

Inside the trading post on the bluff where Mary and John had been busy for the past week, Mary was helping her husband, John, with his last-minute packing.

"I'll miss you more than you'll ever know, Mary," John said, with the sound of regret in his voice.

Mary smiled at him. "I doubt that. You'll have your hands full keeping Toonahowie and the others out of trouble." Suddenly her eyes showed her concern. "Look after them, Johnny. Especially Senauki and Tomochichi. They're never been so far from their people. And they're certain to feel alienated, surrounded by strangers whose speech they can't understand."

John nodded. "I'll write you about everything."

"And I'll let you know what goes on at the trading posts."

At the mention of the posts, John's expression changed to anger. "It seems that my father could have sent someone better than that pompous lout Watson to help oversee this trading post while I'm gone."

Mary knew that her husband spoke the truth. But agreeing with him would not make his departure any easier. "Watson may surprise us both. But I'll be traveling back and forth from Mount Venture. So I'll keep an eye on him from time to time."

"That's another thing, Mary. Sometimes you act as if you're invincible. Promise me you won't travel alone while I'm gone. It would be far too dangerous."

"Don't worry abolut me, Johnny. Jacob has promised to keep a close watch."

John's eyes took on a teasing glint. "But not too close, Mary. He's still in love with you. I wouldn't want him to steal you away from me."

Mary laughed. "Have I ever given you cause for concern, Johnny?"

He shook his head and grinned. "I guess you can't help it that half the male population is in love with you. Even the indomitable Oglethorpe."

"That, my husband, is quite an exaggeration, and you know it."

"Well, let's just say that I'm glad he's coming along on this trip, and not staying behind."

"He's probably on the bluff waiting for you. Justice," she called to her black servant. "It's time to take the master's belongings to the dock."

In the end, it was Skee who followed them to the landing, for Watson had already sent Justice on some unknown chore for which he had not bothered to apprise either Mary or John.

In the harbor, the masts of the periaguas pointed toward the billowy April sky, seeded with the rain that would come later in the day. Even from a distance, the sounds of the workers making ready to get underway carried up to the bluff and mixed with the chanting sounds made by Tallapoosa as he led the Indian delegation to the appointed place of departure.

Nine Indians in all had been selected to make the trip to England with James; first along the intracoastal waterway to Charlestown to await the ship, H.M.S. *Aldborough*, and then across the sea to London. Besides Tomochichi, Senauki, and Toonahowie, the party also included the war chief, Hillispulli, and Senauki's brother, Umpyche, another mico.

A half hour later, Mary stood on the bluff, while below, the boats cast off, to the salute of guns guarding that portion of the harbor. Over a year had passed since she had first greeted the Englishman, James Oglethorpe. Now he was leaving and taking her beloved husband with him. In sadness, she lifted her hand in farewell as both men waved to her.

Suddenly she picked up her child and held him in her arms. "Wave to your father, *ticibane*. It will be a long time before you see him again."

She stood until the boats disappeared from view. Lost in her thoughts, she at first did not hear the voice speaking to her.

"Mary?" the voice called again, a little louder.

"Yes?"

"Come back to the house and have a cup of tea with Mama and me," Sally Pettipoole invited. "And bring Edward. He can have some molasses cookies with Annabelle and Patrick."

"I like cookies," little Edward responded, struggling to get down from his mother's arms.

Grateful for the promised diversion from her sadness, Mary lowered the child to the ground. "It seems that Edward has already accepted your invitation," she said, watching her son run toward Sally.

Nostalgia surrounded her as she sat at the small table in the cozy house so like her own and sipped the boiling hot tea with Sally and Coreen. The days at Ponpon seemed so distant, yet her fondness for Sally had never wavered.

"It's good to be sitting here, isn't it?" Sally asked. "As if we were still schoolgirls studying under Parson Beckett."

Mary deliberately entered into the charade. "You were the prettiest girl in the school, with your blonde curls and the pretty dresses made by your mother. How I envied you."

Sally's mouth twisted in embarrassment. "But look at me now, Mary. I've grown plump and my hair has faded. Yet you look almost the same. The years haven't touched you the way they have settled on me."

Coreen, coming to her daughter's defense as she usually did, said, "Hammish likes you the way you are, Sally. Don't belittle yourself."

"She's right, Sally," Mary agreed. She looked at Annabelle, sitting primly between the two little boys, Patrick and her own son Edward. "And your Annabelle looks exactly like you."

Suddenly, Mary laughed. "Look. She has Edward just as bewitched over her as Billy Whitaker and Hammish were over you."

"I think it's the molasses cookie," Sally whispered. "I noticed she slipped one of hers to him."

Coreen took another sip of tea and then cleared her throat, a sure sign that she was going to speak her mind, regardless of the consequences.

"Mary, you know I don't like repeating gossip, but—"

"Mama..." Sally protested.

"It's for her own good, Sally. I think she should know about the rumors that vile man is spreading."

"What are you talking about, Mrs. O'Reilly?"

"If you and my Sally were not such good friends, I probably wouldn't say anything. But I think you should be warned. Megan Tutwiler told me just yesterday that Mr. Watson is telling everybody in Savannah that you're a witch. And that you have us all under your spell, including Father Oglethorpe."

Mary dismissed the gossip with a shake of the head. "Poor man. Everyone must realize how ridiculous his accusation is."

"I'm not so sure. Mary," Coreen said. "If he keeps on sayin' such terrible things about you, he might cause a great deal of harm. Bein' called a witch is a serious thing."

"I'll be leaving tomorrow to go back to Mount Venture. He'll probably stop talking about me then." Mary looked up as Hamish entered the house.

Seeing her at the table with his wife and mother-in-law, Hamish grinned. "Mary, what a nice surprise."

Coreen quickly stood up. "Would you like a cup of tea, Hamish?"

"Did you bring any rum with you, Mary?" he teased.

"You know I didn't, Hamish."

He made a face. "Then a cup of tea it is."

Little Annabelle sidled up to her father and pulled a molasses cookie from her osnaburg apron pocket. "I saved a cookie for you, Papa."

"That's my girl," he said, taking the half-crumbled cookie and giving her a hug.

When the child had gone back to the steps where Edward and Patrick sat, Hamish leaned over and said, "What's this I'm hearing all over town about you, Mary?"

"Just an amusing rumor, spread by Watson, I understand."

"Don't take it too lightly, Mary. If I were you, I'd go to the magistrate immediately and complain. He could do great harm to you."

"I doubt that, Hamish." Mary finished her tea and suddenly stood. "Come, Edward. We must be going now."

Coreen and Sally walked to the door with her. "Godspeed to you, Mary," Sally said, touching her cheek with her own in a gesture of friendship.

Mary responded with Creek words that Sally could not understand. Then she said, "I have called upon the Great Spirit to watch over you and your house while we are apart."

"Thank you, Mary," Sally replied.

As Mary crossed over to her own small clapboard house she held steadfastly to little Edward's hand. Although she had been careful to disguise it, a sense of uneasiness had invaded her at Coreen's revelation about Watson. That's why she had used her mother's language to invoke a blessing on them all. But now she consciously pushed the rumors aside. She had no reason to fear anything that Watson did or said. She was merely lonely for Johnny. Yes, that was what it was. Nothing more.

"Well, Edward. A good night's sleep and then we'll be on our way."

"Where?"

"Back to Mount Venture."

"But I wanted to sail with Papa and Toonahowie on the boat."

"I know. So did I. But we have to take care of the fur trading. And keep a watch on the Spanish."

"Will Jacob and the rangers be there when we get back?"

"Better than that, Edward. They'll be meeting us halfway."

"I like Jacob."

"So do I."

"And Papa?"

"Yes. Papa likes him, too."

In his other hand, Edward held the remaining molasses cookie. As it broke and a few crumbs fell to the ground near the wooden steps, a black crow suddenly swooped downward, coming dangerously close to Edward's face. With a protective gesture, Mary shielded the child with her arms and rushed him toward the door and safety.

# Chapter 24

John Musgrove sat at the library desk belonging to the Earl of Egmont and began penning a letter to his wife. For days he had been caught up in the festivities that had swept over London like a brilliantly orchestrated *puskita*, the Creek celebration of a new year. He hardly knew where to begin, he had so much to tell Mary.

He dipped the sharpened goose quill into the brass inkstand and finally put his thoughts to paper—telling her about the voyage and the royal liveried oarsmen who had met them and brought them down the Thames to London, with crowds gathered on the banks to view these "magnificent savages" from the New World.

"You wouldn't believe the reception, Mary," he wrote. "For weeks now, Tomochichi and the others have been entertained by half of London, it seems. The old mico has taken it all in stride. He behaved with great dignity at the formal reception in Old Palace Yard, and he has quite won over Egmont and the other trustees.

"Today is the most important day of all; for we have an audience with the king and queen at Kensington Palace. King George is sending his royal coaches-and-six for us, and Toonahowie has memorized the Lord's Prayer to recite in English to the queen.

"One sadness has occurred. Umpyche died of smallpox and was given a Christian burial in the cathedral. Other than that, we have all been well. Although the colonel will be staying in England longer, he has invited us for a visit to his country house before we sail for home.

"I hope you and the boys have been well. I miss you, my wife. And I pray that the winds will be kind and send me swiftly back to you...

Your husband, John"

At the sound of Tomochichi's voice calling to him, he hurriedly sealed the letter with wax and then turned his attention to the mico.

In Savannah, Mary's thoughts of her husband had been pushed aside as she attended to the latest crisis over Watson.

Ever since John and Tomochichi had left with James Oglethorpe, she had done more than her share in trying to keep the peace in the colony. The trips back and forth through the hostile wilderness from one trading post to another had been a strain on her; yet she had no choice. For seizing on Tomochichi and Senauki's absence, Tallapoosa had wasted no time in

225

causing dissension in the Yamacraw village. And Watson's behavior had further compounded the troubles. Only through her periodic visits was Mary able to ward off a direct confrontation between the English and the Yamacraws.

There was trouble, too, among the colonists themselves. The civil authority left in charge of the colony by Oglethorpe was now near collapse, with divided factions, power struggles, and decisions made from vindictivenesss rather than fairness. In disgust, the baker as well as many of the other settlers had left Savannah for the more civilised Charlestown.

Mary was surprised that the officials had put aside their squabbling long enough to take Watson to court and order him to cease his libelous accusations against her. She had demanded compensation, too, for Skee's relatives, since Watson had bragged about causing his death by deliberately keeping him so drunk that he finally died in a stupor. But it was too much to hope that the authorities would retrieve the money that Watson had skimmed from the trading post in her absence and spent.

From the moment the man had come, he had clearly been a thorn both in her side and in the colony's. Most had tried to look the other way at his smaller infractions, but that morning, Watson had gone berserk—painting himself, running naked through the streets, and shooting at the friendly Indians who had come to the post to trade.

Incensed at his behavior, Mary had marched in and taken his gun away from him. "I won't be responsible for you any longer," she'd said in disgust.

"Get out, Watson, before the Indians come back and kill you."

Mary had immediately left the post to alert the magistrate and to find Isteche and the others who had been treated so rudely, to appease them. Finally mollified by Mary's willingness to trade their skins for the goods they required, the small group now returned with her.

Inside the trading post, Watson, with a deerskin draped over his naked body, was still taking his time, stripping the shelves of the items he wanted for himself. Beside him was Justice, whom he had commandeered to help him. But at the sound of Mary and the Indians returning so soon, Watson panicked. He quickly locked the door, grabbed Justice as hostage, and barricaded himself in the arsenal, where the muskets and powder horns were stored.

When Mary walked onto the porch and reached out to open the weathered wooden door, it didn't budge. It was barred from inside. She listened to the voice of her servant Justice pleading with the man she despised.

Concern for her servant prompted her to motion the Indians out of sight. She remained on the porch and called out, "Justice, are you in there?"

She waited, and a frightened voice finally replied, "Yes, mistress."

"Then unlock the door. I need you to help me unload a periagua down at the dock."

After a few moments of frantic whispering, Justice called out, "Mr. Watson say he won't let me go with you."

"Watson, can you hear me?"

"Yes, I hear you. What do you want, witch?"

Mary ignored his epithet. "Let Justice go. He has no quarrel with you."

Still hidden behind the trees, the Indians led by Isteche waited for the man to obey their Beloved Woman.

But a shot suddenly rang out instead, and Mary ducked as a piece of timber post split near her head. Another shot close at hand caused her to leave the porch.

Hamish, Peter Gordon, Noble Jones, and Henry Tutwiler, alerted to the drama unfolding, raced into the clearing in time to hear Isteche. "Not treat Beloved Woman with respect. We take fellow now."

"Wait," Mary cautioned Isteche and the others. "Let me try to get Justice out first."

"No, Mary. That's suicide, for sure," another voice called out.

She recognized Hamish Pettipoole's voice, but she paid no attention to him. With soft fleet steps, she ran past the porch and toward the living quarters. Tiptoeing into the large open room with its fireplace and comfortable chairs, Mary avoided the squeaky plank in the floor and headed for the other door to the arsenal that opened directly into the cabin. But when she gently tried to open it, she discovered that this door was locked as well.

Had Johnny told Watson about the extra key hidden under one of the hearth bricks? She knew that she had not, and no one else had ever been told, except Jacob. As she crossed the room again, she prayed that the key was still there, undiscovered.

Trying to make as little noise as possible, Mary pried up the brick. But before she had a chance to retrieve the key, the uneasy truce outside ended, with shots exchanged and the sudden rush of feet upon the trading post porch.

"No," Mary cried. "Wait." But it was too late. The Indians had evidently decided not to allow their queen to walk into danger by herself. With a ramming log, they battered down the trading post door.

By the time she had found the key and was able to open the door to the arsenal, Mary saw only Isteche and the other Indians standing amid the stacks of muskets. There was no sign of Watson—only the dust-laden sunlight pouring through the open back door.

"Watson not go far," Isteche assured the disappointed Mary. "White men chase him. Catch him soon."

"Good. He's a lunatic. They'll have to commit him now for sure. And we'll be rid of him once and for all."

She looked from Isteche to the others. She was grateful that the Indians had not bothered to chase after Watson. She knew that they had only done what they set out to do—to protect their Mary from harm.

When she walked over to lock the back door and return to the store to begin trading, Mary heard a slight moan coming from the other end of the arsenal. It was then that she remembered her black servant, Justice.

She discovered him lying on the floor behind a stack of muskets. "Oh, Justice," she said, kneeling beside him. "Are you hurt?"

"I'm dyin', mistress."

He coughed and, in the dimness of light, Mary saw the telltale stain of blood on his rough, homespun shirt. The stain began to widen, prompting Mary to tear a remnant of cloth from her petticoat and press it tightly like a sponge against his chest. But it was of little help. The wound was too severe, even for healing herbs to do any good.

"Why didn't you run? I never wanted this to happen."

Justice's voice was weak. "I was scared, mistress. Mr. Watson say they were comin' to get me, to sell me to the Apalachees."

"They were only coming to get him. Not you."

At the end, a sad Mary sat, cradling her servant's head so that he could breathe a little better. She began to sing a soft, plaintive chant to alert the Great Spirit that Justice was beginning his journey home.

*** 

"Tomochichi, you can't go out into the street dressed like that," John said, aware of the mico's near nakedness. "Put on the new clothes the trustees gave you."

"White man's clothes are not comfortable," Tomochichi argued.

John looked out the window at the splendid white horses and the king's three royal coaches waiting to take the Indian delegation to the palace.

A magnificently dressed Oglethorpe walked into the room, his war medals pinned to his military uniform proclaiming his bravery in battle as clearly as the eagle feathers attested to Tomochichi's. "Is there a problem, John?" he inquired.

"Tomochichi does not wish to wear the white man's clothes."

"My friend, you must wear at least the coat and top hat to show honor to the king."

James spoke directly to Tomochichi, with his friendly gray eyes never wavering from the old mico's face. Beside him, John translated his words.

Finally, an understanding Tomochichi nodded to James Oglethorpe and proceeded to allow the servant to help him with his mantle, but he kept on his moccasins, his breechclout, his royal collar of otter skins, and the decorations upon his face.

Through the streets of London, over the rough cobblestones, the wheels of the royal carriages rolled. Curious onlookers stared, hoping to catch a brief glimpse of the passengers. Finally, the carriages stopped before gilded wrought-iron gates.

Down the long labyrinth of palace corridors, the Indian delegation walked. Scarlet-liveried servants, the gleam of gold ceilings and marble floors magnified in the light of ornate candelabra heightened the awareness that they had come to see a rich and powerful king. This audience was the reason they had undertaken the long sea voyage—to ratify the formal treaty and to present to the English king, as a symbol of their good faith, the white eagle feathers that had been gathered and sent from the Creek Indian towns along the Chattahoochee, the Ocmulgee, the Oconee, and the Savannah.

Doors opened before them and closed behind them until they reached the inner doors to the great hall and the throne. The royal court, lining the approach to the seated king and queen, watched the proud procession. Discreet whispers followed them, dukes and duchesses, lords and ladies speaking in great surprise at their majestic demeanor. The few who were looking forward to making fun of these children of the forest suddenly lost their desire to do so.

As the court held its breath the tall, regal Tomochichi bowed to the king. And in strange accents spoken with the equal elegance of any other foreign diplomatic emissary to the royal court, the mico began his speech.

"This day I see the majesty of your face, the greatness of your house, and the number of your people.

"I am come for the good of the whole nation called the Creeks to renew the peace which long ago was had with the English. I am come in my old days, though I cannot live to see any advantage to myself. I am come for the good of all the children of all the nation of the Upper and Lower Creeks...."

He waited for John Musgrove to translate his words before proceeding to the most important part of the audience with the king. And when John had finished, Tomochichi held out the eagle feathers and intoned, "These are the feathers of the eagle, which is the swiftest of birds. These feathers are a sign of peace in our land and have been carried from town to town there, and we have brought them over to leave with you, O great King, as a sign of everlasting peace."

When the king had received the gift, the mico continued, "O great King, whatever words you shall say to me, I shall tell them faithfully to all the kings of the Creek nation."

John was disappointed at the king's brief, uninspired reply. For Tomochichi's sake, John added a few polite phrases that in no way changed the basic meaning of the king's words.

Then Tomochichi turned to the queen, his speech acknowledging her importance in the same way that the Creeks acknowledged their Beloved Women.

"I am glad to have the opportunity of seeing the mother of this great people. As our people are joined with Your Majesty's we do humbly hope to find you the common mother and protectress of us and all our children."

Later, as John re-created in another letter to his wife, Mary, this command visit to the palace and relayed the words that Tomochichi had spoken, his sudden impatience to return home was mixed with pride in Mary's people. But they were scheduled to remain two more months in England.

"The Archbishop of Canterbury will send his barge to take us to Putney to dine with Lady Dutry, and from there we will proceed to Lambeth Palace. But for Tomochichi's sake, I hope the archbishop will not wish to talk about the Creek religion. Tomochichi is very superstitious now. He feels that by talking about it at all, he offended the spirits and thereby caused Umpeche's death...."

This letter was sent, like the others, on a ship bound for Charlestown. But as to whether Mary would ever get to read it, that was left in the hands of destiny. On the day the ship left port in England, hostile forces along the Altamaha were at work, planning her imminent destruction.

# Chapter 25

A darkness of heart trod beside Mary, casting its shadows on the trail—more visible than things seen: the bird, the deer, the beaver. Its voice became that of the owl hooting from the tall tree; the bull alligator bellowing from the swampy marsh. Princess, queen, mother, wife. The darkness struck at her, like the slap of a willow branch, reminding her of the fragility of all names gathered around her. But that of "mother" seemed the most fragile.

She looked back at little Edward Walking Stick, trying so hard to match Singing Rock's stride and failing. It was still not too late to turn back, to leave the child this time, as Sally had suggested, with her own Patrick and Annabelle.

But no. She was being foolish. Losing Justice had affected her more than she wanted to admit. As Mary walked she began to pray a silent prayer, weaving strong threads around her son, like an arachnid protecting her young. But the prayer, the touch of the amulet around her neck gave her no comfort in the early twilight. Stronger forces were at work in the wilderness ahead.

Mary stopped and waited for Singing Rock to catch up with her. She had decided. Edward would not come this time to the trading post along the Altamaha. Her decision, weighed carefully, had nothing to do with a fear of death for either her or her son. Death was the other side of life, as constant as day/night, sun/moon, English/Creek.

But when death came, it had to be on her own terms, not on some enemy's—waiting to entrap her. The dishonor was not in dying, but in defeat. So there was nothing cowardly in returning her son to Savannah and refuge.

"You will take Edward back to Sally's," Mary commanded. Singing Rock's questioning eyes met hers. "And you can help Sam Everleigh in the store. He will need your guidance until I come back."

Singing Rock protested. "It is dangerous for you to travel so far alone. And what about the supplies? How will you carry them?"

"Charlie Bowlegs and I will manage. Go now. Swiftly. Before the darkness catches you.

"Edward?"

The child came to his mother. "Why are we stopping? Is it time to make camp for the night?"

"No, my heart. I have decided to send you back to stay with Patrick and Annabelle."

"But I want to go with you."

"It's such a tiresome journey, Edward. And see? You're already being eaten up by the swarming gnats.

Go back with Singing Rock, and I promise you can come with me next time."

"You won't be lonely without me?"

"Of course I will. But I can manage for two weeks." She gave the child a reassuring smile. "Just as you'll be able to manage eating a few more molasses cookies."

A few minutes later, Mary watched Singing Rock and her son disappear beyond leafy trees that obscured the narrow trace. Then she gave the signal to Charlie Bowlegs to continue south.

It was about the same time of evening—early twilight—several days later, when Mary and Charlie Bowlegs finally arrived at the prearranged rendezvous point.

The two approached the place carefully. Seeing signs that Jacob and the five other rangers were still camped at the deserted ruins of the old fort, Mary made herself known and walked in.

Part fort, part Spanish mission, the ruins were a living reminder of past cruelties. If Mary had anything to do with it, the ruins would remain a mere relic to a former time, and the Spanish would have no opportunity to rebuild.

Jacob immediately came toward her. "I was worried about you, Mary. You're a day late."

"I'm lucky to get here at all."

"Why? Did you have trouble along the way? Or was the trouble in Savannah?"

"Both. But it's all right now."

He had known the woman long enough to realize that, whatever the trouble, she had no desire to talk about it once she had dealt with it. He went about his chores, sending one ranger to gather more wood for the cooking fire and posting two of the rangers for evening sentinel duty. He saw Charlie Bowlegs secure the packs high in the trees and begin to make camp for the night in the shelter of the fallen sassafras tree.

But he had not seen Edward. The child usually rushed to greet him after a short absence.

Later, as he knelt by the small fire and poured hot coffee into his tin cup, Jacob said, "Where is little Edward?"

"I left him in Savannah." Mary continued stirring the stew, a chore usually done by her servant.

"And Singing Rock?"

"I left her in Savannah, too."

Few other words were spoken that night. In silence they ate the cooked food, heaped dirt upon the ashes, and then prepared for the long night in the protection of the low tabby wall. Fresh leafy boughs under Indian blankets became their separate beds, the two within arm's reach, yet as far away as the stars that shone over them.

Jacob slept lightly, the night sounds causing him to rise quietly on his elbows and then, recognizing the noises, to lie down against his loaded musket, his constant companion from the day he had joined the rangers.

Old resentments shared company with his musket—the quirk of fate that had brought him young and penniless to this new land; the years he had wasted in working off his debt while other men became property owners; and then the same maddening way in which Mary seemed to look past him, even though he was now no longer her bondservant.

He was a handsome man, tall and strong, a sturdy sort of fellow who would be a strength to the colony, if the stingy snobs and nabobs would give him half a chance. But perhaps, without realizing it, that was exactly what Oglethorpe had done in making him captain of the rangers stationed on the Altamaha. Jacob knew that the man held Mary Musgrove in the same high regard that he did. So in keeping her safe from harm, Jacob might be helping himself as well.

Yes, he would guard Mary with his life. That was what he'd sworn to do, anyway. But in the process, if it helped to advance his own cause, then all the better.

Too restless to go back to sleep, Jacob arose and went to check on the guards. Passing Charlie Bowlegs, he murmured to him in Muscogean, a habit that had protected him more than once in this land so close to the Spanish, where a few English words, spoken in innocence, might reach the ears of a spy hidden in the marsh grass.

By early light, the trading post named Mount Venture seemed particularly vulnerable to Red Horse. Any day, for the past two weeks, he could have torched the place and seen its supplies and skins go up in flames. But that would have given him little satisfaction, with Coosaponakeesa not present to witness the destruction. Or better yet, to die in the flames.

But she was on her way. Ohoopkee's son had spotted her, surrounded by the rangers. Soon though, even the rangers would be no protection for her. They would be destroyed by Capitàn Rivera and his soldiers, coming from St. Augustine. That would leave Red Horse free to deal with his longtime enemy in any way he pleased.

Close to midafternoon, Mary, Charlie Bowlegs, and the rangers paddled lethargically toward the landing on the Altamaha. The incessant sun, the gnats and mosquitoes, the potato lice covering the wilderness plants had all taken their toll on the rangers.

Between the rhythmic pull of the oars, Jacob rubbed at the large red welts encircling his waist, where the lice had burrowed into his skin. He looked over at the implacable Charlie, his skin glistening in the sun from the rancid-smelling bear grease. Not once had the Indian scratched or indicated in any way that he was uncomfortable.

With sweat running down his brow, Jacob longed for a cool swim to ease his sunburn and to drown the lice still clinging to him. And he longed for a tankard of rum, contraband in Savannah, but available at the trading post to both the rangers and the Indians who came to trade.

He looked over at Charlie, one of the few who could drink him under the table. "You getting thirsty, Charlie?" he asked with a wink.

"I be thirsty when time come," he replied, with no visible emotion etching his weathered face.

"I'll give an extra tankard to every man, if we make the post by sundown," Mary wagered. At her words, the rhythm of the oars picked up considerably.

An hour later, with no prior warning, a jagged streak of lightning flashed across the cloudless blue sky and was answered by a loud crack of thunder in the distance. Mary frowned at this sudden change in the weather, and she watched uneasily while the rapid gathering of angry clouds turned the steadfast blue into a menacing gray.

She had no need to look at Jacob's face to discern his reaction to the impending storm. He had been among her people long enough to be affected by their beliefs. She watched the rippling of his arm muscles and felt the forward thrust of the canoe in a spurt of energy, catapulting it past the dangerous rocks that drummed with the sound of giant raindrops falling from the sky.

Soon a sheet of rain slashed at them, with the wind rising in shrieking tones, while the Bull of God, loosened from its cage, roared in deep displeasure at the wanton slaughter of its offspring upon the earth.

How long the Great Spirit would allow the bull to remain unleashed, Charlie Bowlegs had no way of knowing. But he, too, kept up the intense pace, for there was no safe place in the wilderness to hide from its wrath. Their only recourse lay in reaching the landing as soon as possible.

Unlike Mary's retinue, the soldiers approaching the trading post from the south with Capitán Rivera, stopped to find shelter. Their polished armor, designed to protect them, had already served as a lightning rod, causing one of the men to be knocked senseless to the ground. So Rivera gave orders for his men to remove the protection that had now become a danger.

While Arroyo Rivera huddled under the dripping palmetto fronds hastily erected into an overhead shelter for his men, he took comfort in the knowledge that the weather seldom played favorites. The same storm was keeping the rangers from their destination, too. His only disadvantage that he could see, aside from the one injury, had to do with his superstitious Indian allies, who might not join the fight in the darkness of the night.

Soon the storm lessened enough for Arroyo Rivera to give the signal to move out. But with the lightning still a danger, the men left their armor behind, to be retrieved from its hiding place upon their return.

A short distance from the trading post, an angry Red Horse listened to the laughter, the merriment coming from inside the post. While he and his braves had waited patiently for Capitán Rivera and the soldiers coming from the south, Coosaponakeesa and the rangers had gotten through. Because of the unexpected storm, they had slipped quietly past his scouts and were now celebrating their safe journey through the wilderness.

Once again, Coosaponakeesa had bested him. Red Horse started to give a signal for his braves to disperse for the night, but then the sound of men afoot in the forest made him change his mind. Peering through the steady sheet of rain, he was able to make out a small band of Spanish soldiers cautiously approaching the crossroad. Leading them was Arroyo Rivera.

Red Horse gave no formal greeting of friendship to his ally. Instead he complained, "They have gotten through. You can hear them inside the trading post."

Rivera listened for a few minutes and smiled. "All is not lost. Give them time to drink a little more. Then we will surround them and strike when they least expect it."

When Red Horse did not comment, Rivera eyed him in the dark. "You are still with us, Red Horse?"

The Indian struggled with his beliefs. But hate superseded any other factor. "Yes, Capitán."

"*Bueno.*"

With the downing of the second tankard of rum, Charlie Bowlegs got up and began to dance and chant. His movements caused the floor to creak and the oil light to sputter. The rangers, seated at a long wooden table, encouraged him to continue by slapping their hands and stamping their feet to keep time. Jacob, with his musket leaning against the railing, watched Mary instead as she refilled his tankard from the oak cask. Diminutive in height, she was barely visible over the long slab of wood that served as a bar.

As Mary turned around she noticed one of the rangers stagger from the table and peer out the partially shuttered window.

"What is it, McRae?"

"I thought I saw someone outside. Guess it was a limb moving."

"More than likely," Jacob responded. With a suddenness he put down his tankard and grabbed Mary's arm. "Let's join Charlie," he said, pulling her toward him.

Mary laughed. "You're drunk, Jacob."

"Not too drunk to dance with the Queen of Savannah."

At the rangers's urging, Jacob bowed. "May I have this dance, m'lady?"

It had been so long since Mary had enjoyed any frivolity at all. Her husband, Johnny, was the one who had always provided the levity, the fun in her life. At that moment she missed him more than ever.

"Only if it's a gavotte," she replied.

"Faith, if the wee one hasn't entertained the French dancin' master," one of the other rangers teased. "If ye don't know the steps, Captain, I'll be more than willin' to oblige."

"That's not necessary, Laddie," Jacob said, reeling Mary to his side for the start of the set dance.

With Charlie Bowlegs dancing to his own music and Mary and Jacob urged on by the humming tenor voice of Laddie, Arroyo Rivera signaled his men one by one to cross the cleared land between the forest and the trading-post compound.

Red Horse and the few braves who were not afraid to fight in the dark had already taken their places at the back of the store. There they waited for Rivera to initiate the action, engaging the rangers. Then they would move in, taking Coosaponakeesa as their prize.

With a sudden rush of feet on the porch and the bright glow of fire as muskets exploded, Jacob and

Mary fell to the floor. Tankards, swept from the table, spilled their brew as the rangers grabbed their muskets.

"Quick, douse the light," Jacob called out. But Mary was already crawling toward the timber post where it hung.

Mary, Charlie, Jacob, and the five other rangers were completely outnumbered. But they were all fighting with a grim determination. The Spanish were cruel enough. But the greater cruelty for any survivors lay in being turned over to their Indian allies. Death, too horrible to comprehend, kept the rangers fighting. For them, it was far better to die in battle.

Just when the sheer force of the unarmored Spanish threatened to turn the tide of battle, muskets fired from across the clearing mingled with the sounds coming from the trading post.

Laddie, peering through the slit in the shuttered window, saw, in the brief musket glare, a second flank of Spanish soldiers, dressed in armor.

"Jesus, we're finished," he said.

But as he watched, a strange thing happened. The two Spanish groups seemed to be fighting among themselves, with dire consequences for the ones surrounding the post. The armored ones, with their muskets aflame, rushed across the clearing. Caught in the crossfire, Rivera's men began to fall.

A sickening realization came over Rivera. The battle was over. He had failed in his mission and lost his armor, too. Helping one of his bleeding men, he quickly retreated.

At the trading-post door a voice shouted, "Jacob, we're here."

"Christ's blood, what took you so long?"

"Well, now. We came across all this armor hidden under some palmetto fronds," he began. "And since we were so outnumbered..."

Mary lit the oil light again. "Charlie, come and help me," she said. "These men deserve a little reward for their trouble."

The Indian who had appeared so drunk earlier took his place beside the rum cask. And Jacob, watching the two go about their business of filling the tankards, smiled. "You were a brave one, Mary. Dancin' with such frivolity, and knowin' you had a Spanish audience."

"But you cut it too close, Jacob. Next time see to it that your men get here a little sooner." The words, sounding harsh, were softened by the appreciative look Mary gave the captain of the twenty rangers.

Farther down the Altamaha, toward the mouth of the delta, as the sun came up, a bitter Red Horse watched as the few remaining Spanish soldiers limped to their boat.

A still-proud Rivera stood at the prow and waved in farewell to Red Horse. "Until the next battle," he called.

Red Horse grunted and then turned to Ohoopkee. "Next time we not bother with Spanish. Next time we burn her out."

# Chapter 26

In December, with the return of Tomochichi and John Musgrove from England, a great celebration took place at the Yamacraw village, and at Cowpen, the home of the Musgroves. Summoned by Tomochichi, the braves of his village and their families soon gathered to hear all the stories of the trip and to examine the lavish gifts sent by the English king and queen. These, Tomochichi had promised to share with his village and with his other Indian allies.

None had more cause to celebrate the triumphant return than Mary. She had missed her husband considerably. But beyond that, the Spanish, during John's absence, had stepped up their efforts to destroy her; for they had rightly discerned that she was the one with the power to keep the peace between the English and the Creeks. Destroy Mary Musgrove, Queen of the Creeks, and the peace treaty would soon disintegrate.

But that night, with her husband and her people gathered around her, Mary put danger out of her mind. In contentment, she sat before the great bonfire, smelled the enticing aroma of tender young beef and wild turkeys roasting in the open air, and listened to Tomochichi. For several hours he talked, impressing upon his braves the importance of the mission he had made to England. Once he had repeated for them the words of good-bye to his friend Oglethorpe—"I am glad to be going home, but to part with you is like the day of death"—Mary knew that Tomochichi's oration was finally over and that the dancing and songs of celebration and thanksgiving could begin.

The drums began to beat; the mood lightened, and the braves who had sat in repose for so long, dispersed, some to join in the dancing, some to admire the gifts in which they all shared.

"It is good that Toonahowie is nearly well," Mary said to Senauki, seated beside her.

On the other side of the bonfire, in a sheltered blind from the wintry wind, the young Toonahowie sat, wrapped in a warm buffalo robe while he watched the others his age taking part in the stylized dance around the bonfire.

Taking her eyes from her great-nephew, Senauki turned to Mary. "Yes. On board ship, we despaired that he would ever see the land of his ancestors again. We feared that he might die like my brother, Umpyche. But the Great Spirit was kind."

For the celebration, Senauki wore the same long scarlet satin dress in which she had her portrait painted, the clothing a gift from the trustees. Like Mary, who was also dressed formally for the occasion, she had her hair done in the English manner, with a winter rose tucked behind one ear.

A male voice suddenly boomed behind Mary. "Are you both ready to eat? Edward tells me the feast is done."

Mary nodded to her husband and laughed. "The child should know. He's kept his nose close to the hissing grease for the past hour."

"Then I'll send Singing Rock for your food," John replied.

A few minutes later, the two women, attended to by Mary's servant, still sat apart from the men and enjoyed their time of talking alone.

"Your husband is a fortunate man," Senauki remarked, after a moment or so of eating. "I was told that the trustees gave him a hundred pounds sterling for serving as interpreter, and also five hundred acres of land."

"Very generous of them," Mary responded, remembering that she had yet to be paid for her own services.

"But what I cannot understand, Mary, is how can the English give away your land to anybody? Even to your husband."

"The colonel knows the situation concerning the lease of the land. That is sufficient for now."

The two ate in silence for a while longer. Then Mary said, "Did Colonel Oglethorpe mention when he would be returning to the colony?"

John, coming to sit down beside his wife, answered, "I expect he will have that in his letter to you."

"What letter, Johnny?"

"Why, the one he sent by me. I guess, with all the excitement, I forgot to give it to you. Remind me tonight. And I'll dig into my sea trunk for it."

She tried not to appear impatient at the news of the waiting letter. But once the festivities began to wind down, she searched for her son and went home.

It was not long before her slightly drunk huband followed. It was clear that he had other things on his mind besides searching for a letter.

"Come to bed, Mary," he insisted. "The letter can wait until morn."

Intent on showing her how much he had missed her, John made love several times, whispering to his wife his innermost thoughts in a slurred but loving voice. "There wasn't a wench in all of England could compare with you," he said. "I looked at the young ones in the palace..." Satiated, he yawned and went promptly to sleep without finishing the sentence.

But Mary had trouble going to sleep. The letter was on her mind. Knowing that she would not disturb her husband, she arose, put a shawl over her gown, and lit a candle.

In the chair by the hearth that still glowed with embers, Mary sat and held the unopened letter. It had not been hard to find amid the mementoes in Johnny's sea trunk. Her finger, tracing the design embedded in the red sealing wax, sensed the strength of James Oglethorpe's presence. For a time she clutched the letter to her breast and then finally broke open the seal. Holding the letter close to the candle, she recognized the familiar bold strokes of the quill.

"My dear Mary," the letter began. "It will be some time before I see you or the colony again. There are so many details to take care of here in England before I return to Savannah...."

Mary's breath eased. So he was planning on coming back. She read on, both delighted and disappointed, understanding how much he needed her to take care of matters in the colony, yet feeling apart from his life at Westbrook. As she finished the letter she sensed that he was surrounded by enemies in his own country, men who would be content to destroy him and his dream, just as the Spanish would be content to destroy her.

Mary touched the amulet around her neck. Loosening the string, she took a pinch of sacred tobacco, and with words so ancient that no one remembered their origin, she threw the tobacco onto the embers. It gave a small, singeing hiss as the aromatic smoke filtered upward beyond the chimney, wafting its way to the Great Spirit above. Feeling better, Mary folded the letter, laid it on the hearth table and, blowing out the candle, she went back to bed. Soon she was in dream time, where her ancestors showed her more clearly her path, to help her divine her destiny and to give her the strength needed for the dark days ahead.

Within six months, when the warm spring days had given way to summer heat and the miasmas that rose up from the low places to plague the marshy land had spread insidiously, John Musgrove became ill.

At first, Mary was not alarmed. But when her usual remedies seemed to have no power or effectiveness, and each day saw the worsening of John's condition, she decided to leave the wilderness

of Mount Venture and take her husband back to
Savannah, to seek help from Dr. Nuñez. She had not
forgotten his care of the sick earlier. With the help of
Jacob and the rangers, she prepared John for the
hazardous trip ahead.

"Is my father going to die, like Jamie and my
other brothers?"

The pain pierced her heart as Mary looked at
Edward, her last remaining child. "I do not know,
*ticibane,*" she answered, afraid to use his real name
for fear some evil spirit might be listening, to mark
him as well. "If the Great Spirit wills it, he will live."

For three months now, she had been in deep
mourning for her older son, Jamie. Sent to Coweta to
begin his training as the royal heir to the Creek
Nation, he had not even had a chance to complete his
initiation. Both he and Essabo had been killed in the
forest. The rain had obliterated the signs of their
enemies. Not even the arrows in their hearts had
given any clues as to who had done the dastardly
deed. Now the burial mound that held her princess
mother, her firstborn David, and little John, held her
Jamie as well. Her cousin Malatchee, with ties to the
French at Mobile, was now King of the Cowetas.

They moved out, with Johnny placed on a strong
buffalo hide supported by poles and carried by the
Indian bearers—Charlie Bowlegs, Sam Talking
Bear— and two of the rangers, Laddie and McRae.

From time to time they stopped to rest. Mary,
wiping her husband's fevered brow, would force
spring water onto his parched lips and see that a little
found its way down his throat. When the time came to
move on, she wrapped him once more in her black

wolf pelt to cause him to sweat, and then gave the signal to continue.

By the third day, when they had stopped for a while, Jacob whispered to Mary. "He's getting worse. Do you still want to go on?"

She did not hesitate. "Yes. The only hope for Johnny is in Savannah. My herbs have lost their power, as if someone has put a curse on them. We must go on."

In certain ways, the water journey became easier with each new day, even though they were constantly struggling against the current. Mary tried to still her mind, to make it as calm as the mirrored waters that reflected only the blue of the sky. At times she was successful. But then Johnny would call out in his fever, not knowing where he was, not realizing that she was beside him. And then all serenity would be lost, to be replaced by visions of harmful, mystical creatures too horrible to behold.

"Johnny, we'll soon be home to the Cowpen," she said, leaning close to him. "You'll get well there. You always loved the place. And once you're well, you'll be walking over your new plantation with the overseer...."

She waited to see if he would show any response. She smiled when he opened his eyes.

"Mary?"

"Yes, Johnny?"

She leaned closer to hear his weak whisper.

"My head is hurting."

"I know. You have the fever. Here, let me pour some cool water on your brow...."

He put up his hand, as if to stop her. "We must talk... When I'm gone..."

"You're not going anywhere, Johnny. Except home, where Dr. Nuñez or Surgeon Pensyre can take care of you and get you well."

He acted as if he did not hear her. "Let Jacob help you. He's one of us. The colonel will only cause you pain."

Seeing the toll that the talk was taking on him, Mary said, "Hush, now. And rest. We can discuss Jacob later."

Farther ahead, in another boat, Jacob looked back toward Mary. Little Edward sat beside him, with the ranger's musket across his knees.

Mary smiled and waved to them both. Jacob nodded, assured that she did not need to stop. He increased the rhythm of the oars, for they were near journey's end. Stopping at Tybee Island, where they entered the mouth of the Savannah River, the Rio Dulce, Mary learned that Pensyre had died a few days earlier from the same fever that was sweeping the coast. There was nothing to do but to continue to Savannah. More bad news greeted her at Yamacraw Bluff. Dr. Nuñez had left the colony in her absence.

"We're home, Johnny," she said. His only response was a peaceful look that softened his face. It was almost as if the fur trader had held on to life merely long enough so that he could die, not in the alien wilderness, among his enemies, but surrounded by friends—Tomochichi, Senauki, Toonahowie, and the Indians who regularly came to trade at the post built by him and his beloved Mary, the Princess

Coosaponakeesa. For like Oglethorpe, his heart was Indian.

For two more days he lingered. Then, on the third day, at sunrise, when the eagles took flight over the majestic forests of the New World, the drums began to beat in slow, mournful rhythm. Later, Tallapoosa, who swept aside his animosity toward the Queen of the Creeks only long enough to participate in the burial ritual, accompanied the sober, impersonal service of the Anglican priest with a more volatile chant of his own. Punctuated by bells and rattles, the song of Old and New World combined, rose upon the wind and swept out to sea.

Beside Mary, to share in her sorrow, were her kinsman Tomochichi, with his village, Jacob and his two rangers, Laddie and McRae, with Sally and Hamish, Coreen O'Reilly, the Tutwilers, and the entire colony of Savannah. The only one missing from the service was James Edward Oglethorpe.

# Chapter 27

On a cold February day in 1736, with the stiff wintry breeze taunting the golden palms along Yamacraw Bluff, Mary Musgrove, a widow for the past eight months, finished counting and examining the deerskins of Coosahatchee, who had come to trade.

While she waited for the Indian to look over the wares on the shelves, she glanced toward the corner of the post where her son, Edward, recovering from a cough, was unusually quiet. Seeing that he was still engrossed in drawing on the buffalo parchment with the black gum ink, she returned her attention to the trade.

"You have twenty-one fine skins, Coosahatchee. The hatchet costs three, the calico petticoat fourteen. So you have four left. What would you like in trade for the last four skins?"

"What can I get?" he asked.

"Do you need any flints?"

He nodded.

"You can have twelve flints for one of the skins."

"Need bullets, too."

"Thirty bullets for another skin. Now you have two left."

She waited for him to make up his mind.

"Ax."

"No, that takes five skins. Unless you want to give something back."

The Indian shook his head.

"Do you want a knife? Or a pair of scissors?"

"Want shirt."

"No, that costs five skins, too. But if you'd like, I can let you have either the shirt or the ax if you promise to bring me two extra skins next time."

"Shirt," the Indian said, satisfied at the trade.

As Mary began to take down the goods from the shelves Sally Pettipoole entered the store. "Mary," she said in an excited voice, "a boat carrying Father Oglethorpe has just been sighted on this side of Peeper Island. I know you've been waiting for him to come ashore. He should be here soon."

"Charlie," she called out to one of her helpers. "Take over for me. And watch Edward, too," she said.

Mary grabbed her red shawl from the hook and hurried out the door with her friend.

Down to the bluff they both went. Already a crowd had begun to gather to welcome the founder back to the British colony.

"They say he's bringing another missionary of the Gospel with him—a John Wesley—to take the place of the Reverend Herbert."

"And none too soon," a woman's voice countered. "Such godlessnesss—men going hunting on the Lord's Day. And getting drunk and swearing on all the other days..."

"And old hags gossiping all seven days about what doesn't concern them," a male voice piped up.

"Hush now," Coreen O'Reilly said to the group. "What a fine homecoming for Father Oglethorpe, hearing nothin' but complaints."

"Coreen's right. At least let him land before he's deluged with all our complaints."

"He's bringing other colonists, too, I hear. For a new town farther south."

"Good. Savannah's getting much too crowded."

All around her Mary heard the sound of voices, but she paid little attention; for her thoughts had turned inward.

For eight months she had kept busy, working night and day, pushing her body beyond its physical limits so that her mind would be too tired to think and remember in the nights, when she missed her husband the most.

But knowing that James had depended upon her all this time had given her the courage she needed to maintain the peace and run two trading posts so far apart.

It had been less than a month since the Scottish Highlanders, recruited by James, had reached Savannah. While their wives and children remained in town, she, as interpreter, and some of the Yamacraw braves had led the able-bodied men and their indentured servants down the inland waterways to the Altamaha delta.

There, near the mouth of the river, the Highlanders, under Oglethorpe's orders, had felled trees, built houses and a chapel for their families, and given a Scottish name, New Inverness, to their new little town. But the land upon which they built was ancient, honeycombed with ruins of Spanish missions interspersed with burial mounds and vast heaps of oyster shells that spoke of past Indian feasts.

Images of the old and new seesawed back and forth, like the antiphonal chanting that Mary's ancestors had learned from the Jesuit and Franciscan priests and had handed down to each succeeding generation.

Remembering the colorful plaid tartans of the new colonists against the ancient coastal ruins of missions, Mary was startled to see a tall man, who was also dressed in Scottish plaid, standing in the prow of the boat coming into the Savannah harbor. From the set of his head, proud and stern, Mary knew that it was James, even before she could see his features.

She watched him climb the forty steps of the bluff, where the crowd merged to give him a hand, vying to be the first to welcome him back to the colony. James nodded to one and then another, but his gray eyes, searching the crowd, did not show any pleasure until he had spied Mary, half-hidden in the mob.

"Mary, it's good to see you again," he said.

"I'm glad you're finally home, James."

He reached out and touched her hand in sympathy. "I'm sorry...about John. He was a fine fellow."

His attention was immediately challenged by the bailiff. After a few words he came back to where

Mary was standing. "We'll finish talking tonight," he said hurriedly. "In town. At your house."

"For supper."

"It will be quite late."

"The time does not matter."

Directly behind him came another man, winded from climbing the steps. "How do you do," he said, holding out his hand to the waiting magistrate. "My name is William Stephens. I'm on my way to Charlestown to do some surveying. Can you direct me to the strangers' house?"

"I'll take you there myself," the magistrate replied.

William narrowed his eyes as he watched the intimate exchange taking place between the general and the half-breed woman. Ignoring Mary, he smiled and nodded to the row of colonists as he rushed to keep up with the magistrate.

Mary did not attempt to follow the crowd. James was back in Savannah, as he had vowed in his correspondence that he would be. She had waited this long to talk with him again. And although it would be difficult, she could wait a little longer.

That evening, beyond all reasonable hours when one would normally expect to eat an evening meal, James walked from the square, where he had taken a room at Widow Hawkins' house. His boots made a squishing sound in the mud that lined the lane leading to Mary's house.

From what he had heard in the past few hours, he had merely left one group of troubles behind in England for an equally onerous set in the colony.

But he was a military man, sworn to protect the English interests against both the French in the west and the Spanish in the south. Let the letter writers, like Francis Moore, whom the trustess had appointed as recorder and storekeeper of the new settlement, take care of reporting back to the trustees. He had forts to build, new towns to settle, and battles to win. But for him to do it all, in increasingly hostile times, James knew that he needed the support of Mary more than ever.

Megan Tutwiler peered out in the dark when she heard the sound of footsteps on the neighboring stoop and then the light tap on the door, "Mr. Tutwiler, come here," she whispered.

Her husband, getting ready for bed, hastily finished putting on his nightshirt. "What is it, Megan?"

"Looks like Mary is entertaining Father Oglethorpe. At least he just walked inside." She clucked her teeth. "It's not seemly for a widow woman to let a man in her house this late at night."

"It's none of our concern, Megan," Henry said in a stern voice, "what time the two choose to get together. They won't be doing anything more than discussing the colony's business. So come away from the window, and let's get to bed."

Megan sighed and did as she was told. Henry inwardly thanked his friend Wilimico for the change in his life. He still did not understand what he had done to win the man's respect. But being given a place of honor to witness the treaty signing had done something to him. Feeling worthy at last, Henry had taken charge of his own family.

At Mary's house the food and wine were quickly put on the table. Soon the two—James and Mary—sat down and began to eat.

"I thought the meeting would never end," James complained. "I had to hear about every spat, every misunderstanding, as well as all the punishments meted out...."

"Yes, your officials were extremely busy while you were gone," Mary said, with a twinkle in her eye.

"You were busy, too, weren't you, Mary?"

"With far more to show for it, I hope."

James nodded. "Your work with the Choctaws was truly splendid—getting them to come to Savannah to trade."

"I'm not so sure Carolina is too happy about that. The assembly has tried for years to persuade them to come to Charlestown."

The slight awkwardness between the two vanished as Mary kept the conversation from taking on a too personal note. James, feeling at ease once more with the woman who understood so many of his problems, turned his discussion to the new settlers who had come back with him.

"I'm not sure how these new colonists will fare, remaining, as they will, on Peeper Island for the next several weeks." He sighed and added, "But there's no help for it, even if they do get restless."

Mary acted as if she had no interest in the new settlers. Instead she asked, "What are you going to do about the Salzburgers?"

He glared at her with set lips, as if she had no business bringing up the Reverend Boltzius's petition to move their settlement. "Nothing. They'll stay at

Ebenezer, where they are. The land is good, and there's no need for them to give it up for something that may not be nearly so healthy."

"They're determined to move."

"Then we'll see who has the most resolve—their leader or me." James's attention returned to his plate.

"Tomochichi has asked the Carolina Assembly for permission to move his village farther north," she said. "Sometimes land loses its strength to grow food."

On purpose, she did not tell him the real reason Tomochichi had given to her for wanting to move farther away from Savannah. "These civilized white people pollute the land and the water with their open privies. We go where sky is fresh with smell of sassafras and pine, and fish swim in clear waters."

James took several sips of wine and spoke again. "I need to travel down to Frederica, to design the fort and the town and see to the building of temporary huts. And, of course, I need you to come with me, Mary, to parlay with the Indians."

He stared at the woman sitting across the table from him. How different she looked from that afternoon. It was amazing her ability to change, almost like the little chameleons at his country place at Godalming. Yet it had less to do with what she was wearing—whether the deerskin dress or the fine blue silk tonight—than with her manner. When she was among the Creeks, she was one of them, taking on their ways, their speech. When she was with the English, the metamorphosis was equally swift. Yet James knew that the English veneer could also vanish in an instant. It was this dual quality that held such a fascination for him.

"You heard me, Mary? That we need to go to St. Simons?"

She hesitated. "When would you leave?"

"As soon as possible. Could you be ready by tomorrow?"

"An escort takes time to arrange. The Spanish and their allies are a constant threat nowadays..."

"I thought mayhaps Tomochichi could supply some of his braves to go with us."

She nodded. "And who will build the huts?"

"I brought some able-bodied settlers this time on the *Symmond.* Some of them will go ahead with us. And Hamish Pettipoole has agreed to go, to help them." He did not add that Hamish had consented only if Mary were along to assure safe passage.

In the end, with her son Edward left with Sally again, Mary started the journey down the waterway with James. Following behind them were Hamish and the ablest of the new settlers, with the Yamacraw warriors in other boats. While the braves were on guard for possible signs of a French or Spanish ambush, Hamish kept his eye on the periagua that held the saws and axes for the construction ahead.

The trip was not without danger to them all. But the presence of Mary was like a talisman when they encountered other Indians. Soon after they reached their destination, the men began to build the temporary huts with palmetto fronds woven together for the roofs, while James's attention turned to the design of the fortress and its ramparts. Once he had explained the course of the intended moat, he was content to allow the men to finish the project without him.

Within a few days he and Mary and a small contingent of Yamacraw braves left, to return to Savannah.

"On the way, I need to stop off at New Inverness and see how Mackay and the Highlanders have progressed with their new fort," he said to Mary.

"Is that why you're wearing the plaid today?" she inquired. "In honor of your visit with them?"

James laughed. "That, and the coldness of the wind." He did not mention his family's lifelong loyalty to the Stuarts as the rightful heirs to the throne of England. He had distanced himself from his Catholic sisters living at the court-in-exile at St.-Germain-en-Laye. But with their constant letter writing and carrying secret messages back and forth to the Jacobites in England, he was lucky that his loyalty to King George II had not been questioned.

By the time they reached the Scottish settlement, James was delighted with what he saw. The men, dressed in Highlander habit, with their broadswords and muskets in top fighting condition, made him proud of his new settlers. Yes, they were the type he needed—fierce, strong—to sire and defend his colonies. He must make a note to request soldiers with wives and families.

That night, James refused the bed offered him in one of the tents. It seemed particularly important to gain the men's acceptance of him as their military leader. And so, by the guard fire, James wrapped his plaid about him and slept out in the open, sheltered only by one of the giant oaks. It did not endear him to

Hugh Mackay and the other officers who felt it necessary to keep him company. But the rank and file of men who would later follow him into battle applauded his Spartan-like decision.

By the next day a group of rangers, including Jacob Matthews, arrived on horseback. They had blazed a trail all the way from Savannah to New Inverness, opening up an overland route between the two colonies.

"Mary," a surprised Jacob called out, seeing the woman in the square.

An equally surprised Mary said, "Jacob, what are you doing here?"

"I might ask you the same thing," he replied. "Charlie Bowlegs told me that you and the colonel had gone to St. Simons."

"And so we did," a stiffly formal James responded, coming to stand beside his interpreter, as if to protect her from the attention of the ranger.

"We stopped over on our way back to Savannah," Mary informed Jacob, ignoring James's proprietary air.

"From what Charlie said, Mary, I think you should go first to Mount Venture. Things aren't too good at the post right now."

"I doubt that I would have time…"

Jacob said, "If it's all the same with you, Colonel, I can take her there myself, in the morning."

"Mary…?"

"You don't need me anymore," she said. "But evidently Mount Venture does. I'll speak to Wasatchee. He will guide you back to Savannah."

Seeing the frown, Mary smiled and added, "After all, Colonel, I do have a business to run."

By the next morning, as the early sunlight began to filter through the hoary beards of moss clinging to the oak next to the campfire, the neigh of a horse awoke James. Propping himself up, he saw the ranger Jacob help Mary onto a palamino pony. Not understanding his feelings in seeing her leave, he watched until the two disappeared into the wilderness.

# Chapter 28

Within a few weeks Mary was back in Savannah. It was good, she thought, to become reacquainted with her child and to be at her plantation, where she could now supervise her servants in the spring planting of crops.

The cattle were fat on the bountiful yield of corn, and the vast folds of sheep, pens of hogs, and coops of turkeys and chickens promised that there would be enough meat and eggs to share with the colony. Yet for all her generosity, the trustees had been slow to reimburse her.

"Thomas," she inquired of the storekeeper in Savanah. "You sent the trustees the bill for last season's purchases?"

"Aye, Mary. But you know how slow they always are. You'll get your money. Just be patient a little longer."

He hesitated. "By the by, could you let us have a few extra shoats and sides of beef? We've got that shipload of new colonists to feed. Thought they would be in Frederica by now, but there's not a ship's captain that will sail that close to Spanish waters."

"All right, Thomas. But let me go home and talk with my servants first. It might take a day or two to get it done."

"No need to send word back to me. My niece Sophia can call on you tomorrow to get the particulars. I know how much she enjoys visiting with you."

By the afternoon of the next day, when Singing Rock answered the insistent knock at her door, Mary expected her servant to usher Sophia into the keeping room. Instead, an Englishman appeared. He was small—almost as small as she was—with long curly hair hanging to his shoulders. From the three-cornered hat in his hand to the long black frock coat and knee breeches, she had little trouble in surmising who he might be.

"Mrs. Musgrove?"

"Yes?"

"My compliments, ma'am. My name is the Reverend John Wesley, lately of Lincoln College, Oxford. I have been recommended to you by Colonel Oglethorpe."

"Come in and sit down, Mr. Wesley."

Within a few minutes, with a glass of muscadine juice to assuage his thirst, he began to tell her of his lifelong dream—not to become a minister for the Savannah parish, but to serve as a missionary among the southern Indians.

"And that's why I am seeking your help, Mrs. Musgrove. To teach Benjamin Ingham and me the Muscogee language."

"It's a difficult language," she countered. "Colonel Oglethorpe has been here for more than three years, Mr. Wesley. And during that time, even he has not been able to master that language, much less any of the other dialects."

Mary and the minister continued talking as another tap at the door sent Singing Rock scurrying to answer it.

"But I daresay it will be easier for me, Mrs. Musgrove. Languages are my speciality—Greek, Latin, French..." Wesley stood at the sight of the beautiful young woman who walked into the room.

"Oh, Mary, I'm so sorry. I didn't realize you had company. I'll come back another time."

"Come in, Sophia," Mary encouraged. "Mr. Wesley, may I present Thomas Causton's niece, Miss Sophia Hopkey. Sophia, this is the new minister, the Reverend John Wesley."

She smiled inwardly as the two beautiful people took silent measure of each other.

As he helped the young woman to her seat Wesley said, "I do hope you are going to be one of my parishioners, Miss Hopkey."

"Oh, yes. And did I hear that you are fluent in the French language? I have been looking for a tutor, sir, these past six months."

"Then I will be happy to oblige. It's so refreshing to see young women pursue the strengthening of their minds as well as the Spirit."

The two did not remain for long; for Mary was called to the trading post to meet a large Indian delegation come to trade.

"Mr. Wesley, if you and Mr. Ingham are determined, then I will try to arrange time to teach you." She stood up. "And Sophia, I think you came here for a message to take back to your uncle."

Sophia blushed, for her reason in coming had completely skipped her mind.

"Tell Mr. Causton that he can send his carts tomorrow morning after ten for the dressed meat."

As Mary hurried to the post, she heard the young minster's voice behind her. "Oh, Miss Hopkey. If you're going back into Savannah, then I will be happy to walk with you...."

Again, Mary smiled. It was spring, that season of the year when the earth blossoms and yearns for fulfillment. The signs were all around her—the swelling of leaf buds, the bellies of she wolves distended with their unborn pups, and the primeval stirrings within her own soul, reminding her that she had been without a husband these past nine months.

She remembered Johnny's words. "Look to Jacob. The colonel will only cause you pain."

Although she did not agree with Johnny on the latter, heaven knows, during these difficult times, she could do with someone sympathetic to help with the trading posts, the land, and overseeing the servants. Jacob came nearest to understanding her. He had made it clear that he would be more than willing to take Johnny's place in her life.

With the escalation of hostilities between the Spanish and the English, and the Indians actively courted by St. Augustine with a shower of expensive gifts and the promise of money for each British scalp brought to them, Jacob was forgotten.

James needed her to help stem the change of allegiance to England's enemy.

For the next several months, with Mary constantly at his side, he held parlays and peace talks with the various tribes of the Upper and Lower Creeks, distributed gifts, and played for time against the day when the opposing forces would have to meet in hand-to-hand combat.

Then, toward the end of the year, when Mary had seen to the Creeks' continued loyalty, James left again for England to raise a regiment of soldiers to bring back to the colony.

In 1737, William Stephens, who thought little of Oglethorpe's friends in the colony, arrived in Savannah from Charlestown to serve as the personal representative of the trustees and to try to make some sense out of Causton's muddled financial accounts. Tomochichi, ninety-five years old, moved his people to the new Yamacraw village.

In that same year, another change occurred as well. Mary, tired of being a widow, began to welcome Jacob's attentions.

Late one evening, when Edward Walking Stick was already asleep, Mary and Jacob sat on the steps of her house not far from the bluff and listened to the night sounds around them.

"Mary," Jacob said suddenly. "I've been thinkin'. You've been a widow long enough. It's time for you to be marryin' again."

"Oh?" she answered, with an amused note to her voice. "And I suppose you've come up with a list of possible husbands for me to consider?"

"It's not a long list, for truth," he admitted. "Only three. There's the colonel, of course. But there's no tellin' how long he'll be stayin' before goin' home to England. Besides, I don't think he's the marryin' kind." Dismissing Oglethorpe, Jacob said, "Then there's the Reverend John Wesley...."

Mary laughed. "So you think that now his love affair with Sophia has gone sour and she's married someone else, the Reverend Wesley will want to fall in *my* arms?"

"Not exactly. Especially since he's supposed to stand civil trial for his libelous attack on little Sophia. But I'll tell you one thing. I fully expect him to flee the colony before it comes to that."

"Poor, unhappy man," Mary sympathized. "He hasn't been too successful in anything. Despite his hard work in trying to learn the language, none of the Creeks can understand a word he says."

"And I hear old Tomochichi doesn't like him, either. Is that true?"

"I'm afraid it is."

The sounds of a cougar in the distance and the nervous lowing of one of the beef steers caused Mary and Jacob to halt their lighthearted conversation. Finally, when no further sounds were forthcoming, Mary's attention returned to the conversation.

"So, who is the third possibility?"

"Me."

"Oh, Jacob, are you proposing to me?"

"You might say that."

"But don't you know, it's the *woman* who proposes in my mother's culture?"

"How does she do that?"

"Sometimes by accepting a man's gift and then setting out a plate of hominy for him."

"Blast it, Mary. You're half English. And I'm English." He got up from the steps and walked over to the bed of flowers that was Mary's joy. Pulling up one of the blue cornflowers by its root, he came back and thrust it in Mary's hand. "Here's your bloody gift," he said.

"Thank you, Jacob." She broke off the stem and carefully placed the flower into the bosom of her dress. And with laughter in her voice, she said, "Now, Jacob. Would you like a bowl of hominy?"

For a moment he said nothing. And then, with a great roar of laughter, he picked up the tiny woman and held her in his arms as he began to dance on the porch.

"Stop it, Jacob. Put me down," she said. "You'll wake Singing Rock and little Edward."

"Then they can join in, too. It's not every night that an Englishman gets proposed to."

But he stopped his dancing. Still holding her in his muscular arms, he leaned down and kissed her slowly on the mouth.

A short time later, Mary's newfound happiness as Jacob's wife was marred by tragedy. In one of the last entries in his diary, before fleeing the colony, the Reverend John Wesley wrote: "On November 23, I buried the last of Mary's sons."

Perhaps it was for this reason that the bereft Mary set such great store in her younger husband, Jacob. Her sons were all gone, with little hope of having more.

Whatever Jacob wanted, she gave him, generous with all her possessions. She was now the wealthiest woman in Georgia, yet so far, she had not been paid her one hundred pounds a year for her work as interpreter, diplomat, and liaison, or for the goods sold to the colony. The fourth day of the Windy Moon had come and gone, but still her islands, Ossabaw, Sapelo, St. Catherines, had not been returned to her, as promised. However, she said little about this, for she knew that James Oglethorpe had his mind on other things.

But in December, Tomochichi held a great feast in her honor, to present the land of his old village back to Mary. He, at least, had not forgotten that it was the Queen of the Creeks who had invited him and his people to come and settle on her land. So it was proper and right that as he moved farther north, the original land be returned to her in a formal ceremony.

On that late afternoon of the celebration, the winter breezes were gentle. In the center of the abandoned village, where the sacred fire had once burned, Mary and Jacob sat together on a blanket spread on the ground. Across from them sat Senauki, now grown old, with her husband.

William Stephens, coming from his acreage outside Savannah to his home in town, took a shortcut from the bluff. He was surprised to hear the excited shouts of children playing at the old village. As he drew closer he smelled the aroma of meat roasting in the open air.

"Good evening, Mr. Stephens," Jacob said as he came into view.

"Good evening," he replied, nodding to the couple on the blanket. "I'm surprised to see you here."

Tomochichi spoke to Mary, who in turn said, "The mico invites you to share a glass of wine with us."

"Why, thank you. I don't mind if I do."

Room was made for him, and the elderly man sat down on one of the blankets. "To your health," he toasted, nodding to Tomochichi.

Mary's translation brought a smile and a nod from the mico. "I am much pleasured," Tomochichi responded, repeating the only English phrase he had ever learned.

But Stephens saw the brief flicker of recognition as he spoke. The old buzzard pretended he couldn't understand English, but if he were a wagering man, Stephens would wager his entire salary from the trustees that the old mico could understand everything that was said around him.

"You are having a celebration of some kind?" Stephens inquired.

Jacob became the spokesperson, as Mary remained silent. "Yes. Tomochichi is officially returning Mary's land to her, since he has moved on."

Again, Mary translated for Tomochichi.

William Stephens knew that the trustees would not approve of the mico's gesture. For the action to be recognized, Tomochichi would have to deed the land back to the trustees first, who in turn would deed it to

Mary and her husband. But now was not the time to tell Mary what she needed to do. Let the old Indian have his ceremony.

When his glass was empty, William said, "I fear that I will not be able to stay longer. I must be getting back." He attempted to rise, but like many men his age, he had difficulty. Seeing this, Jacob stood to give him a hand up. With his dignity gathered around him, Stephens left the old town.

On the way home he mulled over how far he had fallen. Fleeing from creditors and desperately needing a job, William had taken what was offered to him in this rough new world. The gentleman's life on the Isle of Wight was far behind him. And his degrees meant little here in this colony, where even most of the judges could neither read nor write.

"I don't believe he likes you, Mary," Jacob said with a laugh.

Mary smiled, unconcerned. "But you like me, don't you, Jacob?" she teased.

"You're the darlin' of my heart. Come, let's show Senauki and Tomochichi how we danced while the Spanish soldiers surrounded the trading post."

He pulled her to her feet as he called out, "Toonahowie, get your flute. We need some music."

For a few moments Mary forgot her sorrow, for she was among friends. But then she begged to sit down, and a sympathetic Jacob complied.

After the feast, Tomochichi began the formal presentation, speaking from the heart the long oration that he had rehearsed for the past week.

Later, as Jacob and Mary walked back to the plantation house, he said, "Well, there's nothing wrong with the old mico's endurance. I thought he was going to talk all night."

"Jacob, have more respect for my ancient kinsman," she admonished with a smile.

That night, as the two lay side by side, Jacob nuzzled her ear. "You remember the night almost five years ago when Johnny and I came back to the bluff and you were entertaining the Coxes?"

"Yes. Tallapoosa was jealous of the surgeon. I had to protect him."

"And I was jealous of Johnny," he confided. "I dreamed of being in his place, in bed with you."

"You have a place of your own in my heart, Jacob. Don't ever be jealous of what Johnny and I had together."

Assured of her love for him, Jacob tightened his arm around Mary and went to sleep, their bodies curved together as one.

# Chapter 29

While James Oglethorpe chose to ignore the shortcomings of his Georgia colony, there were those in both Carolina and Georgia who were more than willing to inundate the trustees with accounts of supposed injustices and favoritism, and the poor health conditions that plagued the people.

From Charlestown, the recently released Watson, who had aligned himself with William Stephen's son against his father and the Georgia colony, generated more than his share of complaints. Added to these letters that crossed Egmont's desk were the monthly petitions for the restrictions against the importation of rum and Negro slaves to be rescinded, together with requests for large land grants.

Rather than become self-supporting after the first year, Georgia had now cost the most of any of the colonies, thus putting a tremendous drain on the public coffers.

Egmont knew that these matters would also have to be added to the long list about which to question his friend Oglethorpe.

Yet the greatest danger for Georgia came from an old enemy, Sir Robert Walpole, who did not like James.

"The man should be stopped. And the southernmost settlements dismantled. Oglethorpe is provoking a war with Spain by building these new colonies dangerously close to Spanish Florida."

"War with Spain is inevitable. You know that, Robert," Egmont said, defending Oglethorpe. "James is merely trying to build a strong defense system to protect our other colonies—Carolina, and even Virginia."

"You are repeating James's words, Egmont."

"And you are parroting Queen Caroline's pacifist leanings."

The two laughed, neither changing his opinion.

Yet, in the end, James was successful in doing what he had set out to do in England. He was appointed general of all troops in Georgia and Carolina, and colonel of his own regiment of British regulars.

By the time he returned to Georgia, he could not ignore the delicate state of affairs.

"It seems that everyone is angry," a hurt James said to his friend Tomochichi through Mary, as interpreter. "Carolina is angry because the fur trade is now licensed in Savannah. And Georgia is angry because Carolina has slaves to work their plantations."

"Many of the Indians are angry at the English fur traders for bringing smallpox and killing their people," Tomochichi recited in Muscogee.

Mary was unusually quiet, doing nothing but serving as interpreter between two old friends, until James spoke directly to her. "You and Tomochichi are keeping something from me. I can feel it. Tell me what it is, Mary."

With a few words to the old mico, who had aged considerably in the time that James had been away, Mary began to relate the potential disaster that James would have to deal with immediately. That is, if it were not already too late.

"Chigilly and Malatchee have sent word that they can no longer guarantee the loyalty of their warriors to the English."

For James, that was indeed bad news. "How many?"

Mary hesitated.

"Six hundred? Seven hundred?" James prompted.

"Seven thousand."

The bile rose in James's throat. Suddenly he felt sick. "That's nearly the entire confederacy."

"Not only the Creeks," Mary said. "But the Choctaws, the Chehaws, the Chickasaws, and the Cherokees."

"How did this happen?"

"The Spanish."

"Then our little colony is lost. We have been defeated already."

"Perhaps not," Mary replied.

"What do you mean?"

"There's still a chance, if you go to Coweta Town to hold a peace talk with all the chiefs."

James's voice sounded bitter. "Over four hundred miles through swamps and forests with a Spaniard and a hostile Indian behind every tree is not something my inexperienced troops would look forward to."

A quick exchange of words between Mary and Tomochichi took place while James waited.

"Tomochichi says that you should not take troops with you. Go alone, with only a small escort, so that the warriors will know that you come as a friend, not an enemy."

"You would be willing to go, Mary?"

"Yes. Tomochichi apologizes that he is too old to come along also. But he will provide a few braves as guides and send a runner ahead to let them know you are coming."

James quickly made up his mind. "Then, we will leave tomorrow. Tell my old friend to send his runner."

Mary smiled. "Thloco left yesterday."

The three parted, for Mary and James, especially, had much to do before morning.

"You're going all the way to Coweta Town? Are you out of your mind, Mary?" Jacob faced his wife with an angry look.

"No. It's necessary, Jacob."

"When the high and mighty Oglethorpe calls, you always go running. I thought that was over with, Mary. Especially since they haven't paid you a shilling they promised. And you've done all the legal things they told you to do to get your old land back, but I don't see the trustees sayin', 'Thank you, ma'am, and here's the deed.'".

"Mayhaps you can check into it while I'm gone."

"And what if you don't get back?"

"Then the plantation is yours, as well as the trading post. So please, Jacob, try to stay sober and take care of the properties."

At that moment, Jacob and Mary's marriage seemed to be wilting as surely as the porch flowers under the hot July sun.

By the next morning, with the black wolf pelt, a hunting knife in its sheath, and Johnny's musket at her side, together with an English canteen slung over one shoulder, Mary left her house for the new Yamacraw village, where she joined James, his three indentured servants, Charlie Bowlegs, and two other Indian braves chosen by Tomochichi: Massony and Yakee.

Already the heat was rising from the earth's floor and a swarm of stinging gnats left their dark place in a rotten tree limb and began to travel in ever-widening circles, until the small group and their horses were surrounded.

Five rivers lay before them, but all flowing from north to south—the Ogeechee, Oconee, Ocmulgee, Flint, and finally the Chattahoochee. For centuries, the rivers had been a blessing to her people, who used them as highways through the wilderness. But on this trip, they would be obstacles—for the group was headed due west.

"I see that you travel light," James said, finally coming to ride beside Mary.

"Yes." She glanced back at his two lagging men, walking beside two packhorses that were weighted down by vast supplies, cooking utensils, and even a tent. "And I see that you travel with all your worldly goods."

James smiled. "I told my man Hanson he was packing too much. But he insisted a general needed his tent and a change of sheets."

"You will need only the gifts for the chiefs and a little dried venison. Your servants will realize that when the packhorses start going lame."

Two evenings later, as the group stopped to make camp for the night, Mary and Charlie Bowlegs looked at each other. They had been traveling in relatively friendly territory, but had made very little progress. The most difficult part of the trip was ahead. But if they continued, even at the same pace, they would never reach Coweta Town within the next three weeks.

Around the campfire that night, while James's tent was set up by his servants, Mary, Charlie, and Massony prepared their sleeping places by the fire in the usual manner, piling freshly cut limbs and leaves for a bed. Yakee had been given the task of guarding the hobbled ponies and horses.

In the darkness, the feral, luminous eyes of the forest creatures watched, but the guard fire kept them at a distance. Toward morning, the sounds of the forest animals suddenly vanished as prey of the human kind burst upon the tented camp. Muskets were fired at each of the bedded leaf mounds, while a half-naked Indian warrior with a hatchet pounced upon the tent where James still slept.

In a few seconds Charlie Bowlegs and Massony, having used the typical Creek trick of sleeping elsewhere, rose from their hiding places and shot two of the culprits. But the third—the one with the hatchet—had them at a disadvantage. For if they shot toward him, then they might hit the general, instead.

But then, from another direction came a shot, bringing the enemy down, along with the tent.

All eyes turned in the direction of the nearby thicket from where the shot had come. Seeing Oglethorpe with his smoking musket in hand, a relieved Mary said, "We thought you were in the tent."

"You forget. My heart is Indian, too. I decided to sleep nearer the ponies."

Charlie Bowlegs laughed. "General's red hair worth much money in St. Augustine."

"But it's worth more for me to keep it," James joked, trying to forget the latest price—a hundred English pounds—offered by the Spanish for his scalp.

"We'd better break camp and get on our way."

"But General," Hanson protested. "I haven't fixed your morning coffee. And it will take an hour to clean your tent."

"Leave it. From now on we travel light. We have to make better time today."

He looked at Mary, and she nodded her approval.

But from that day onward, the trip was a constant struggle, through marshes, where the packhorses sank to their knees; at the banks of swollen rivers where the guides searched in vain for a shallow place to cross. And each day, braving the added dangers of snakes, alligators, and stinging insects, and not knowing what was ahead or behind, James was aware of his greatest enemy: time. Would he be too late to persuade the tribes to remain friendly to the English? Had the war already started, with his colonies being attacked at that very moment?

When they had been traveling for more than a week, Mary assured James, "Today will be a little easier, for we are traveling along an old buffalo trail toward a salt lick."

He looked around at the rampant overgrowth, every inch of the ground between the trees taken up with weeds and vines and grasses.

"Your eyes must be better than mine, Mary. If we are following a trail, I certainly can't see it."

"It doesn't matter. Charlie Bowlegs can see it."

A curious James said, "How can he tell that it's a buffalo trail? Why not deer or bear?"

"All animals have their special trails—each different. Muskrats, birds—"

"Birds?" he questioned. Then he said, "Oh, yes. A path of flight."

"Charlie calls them trails in the sky."

They grew silent, for it was not good to speak too much in hostile territory.

Several hours later, Massony, who had gone ahead to scout, returned to the main party. At a sign from him, they quickly wheeled their horses and ponies together, hiding in a thicket. In the silence of the forest, they listened.

Other horsemen were in the forest, and from the sounds, they were Spanish. James might not be trained in the ways of forest creatures, but when it came to soldiers—especially the enemy—he was more knowledgeable. But it didn't take much military prowess on his part to ascertain that the horsemen going through the woods greatly outnumbered his own little band.

Later, deeming it safe, they moved out.

Hanson, the trustees' servant assigned to Oglethorpe, had come down with fever and was of little help. "Leave me here by the river, General. I can't go on."

"No, Hanson. You wouldn't last a day out here alone."

His suggestion was repeated several more times until they came across a man tied to a tree. Seeing how he had been tortured and burned, Hanson no longer requested to be left behind.

Along the Indian trace that connected Coweta Town with the old trading post at Savannah Town, now called Augusta, a small group of rangers, stationed at Augusta outpost, together with their Indian guides, finally met up with Oglethorpe's party. But the rangers were in no better condition than those who traveled with James. They were all weak with hunger, suffering from fever and the bloody fluxes brought on by drinking the river water.

On that day Hanson was finally left behind in a shallow grave covered by rocks, to shield it from the wild animals.

As they began the last fifty miles to their destination, James's spirits were at their lowest ebb. But then Mary said, "Look, James, in the trees."

Hanging from the limbs were bags of flour and tuckahoe cakes, sustenance for them from her kinsmen. And from that, James knew that he was not too late.

With a little food in their bellies, they pushed on. By the time they reached another ten miles on the trail, a veritable feast was spread for them—venison, turkey meat, melons, and muscadines.

Mary greeted the Muscogee escort waiting for them there on the eastern side of the Chattahoochee River and introduced General James Edward Oglethorpe, the Englishman, who had left the coast and braved between four and five hundred miles of the roughest inland terrain to meet with them in their own capital.

They all sat down together and ate, with Mary translating Oglethorpe's words. Once they had rested, they began their final passage, under safe escort, to Coweta Town.

# Chapter 30

For ten days the formal ceremonies took place, with Mary being careful to translate the important words that must be accurate and understood by both sides.

While the negotiations were going on, James sat on a bearskin-covered log and, with the chiefs, drank their strong black tea made from cassina leaves. He disguised his distaste for the beverage in much the same way that he disguised his illness from them, with a face that showed no emotion. The symptoms of malaria had come upon him gradually, after the long trek through the wilderness. But from earlier bouts with the disease, he knew that the worst was yet to come, with the headache and feeling of malaise giving way to fever and chills.

Carefully Chigilly, Malatchee, and the chiefs of the other tribes went over the points that concerned them, and James finally breathed a sigh of inward relief when the numerous conditions were resolved and the Creek Confederacy reaffirmed its allegiance to King George II, despite the Spanish attempt to lure them to the opposing side.

James had promised that the English would observe the land boundaries of the earlier treaty, and since the white man had brought sickness to the villages, making the people unable to tend their crops, James also promised fifteen thousand bushels of corn to see their people through the winter. The money for this would have to come from his own private coffers; for Egmont had made it clear that the trustees would not be responsible for any more unauthorized expenses.

With Mary's job completed, she left James smoking the calumet of peace with the chiefs. Walking down the path to the burial mound, she, too, felt at peace. And for the rest of the afternoon, she remained there with her memories.

The next day, as the small retinue pulled up stakes and started the long trek homeward, this time by way of the fort at Augusta, James said to Mary, "Young Malatchee has a regal bearing. From his manner, he would be completely at home in any of the drawing rooms of Europe."

"Do not be deceived by his polished surface that shines like a mirror in the sun," she cautioned. "At heart he is fickle, bending the way the wind blows."

"Are you warning me, Mary?"

"Yes. But for now, keep him satisfied with presents. They are the way to his heart."

With the successful signing of the treaty of Coweta behind him, there was not the same great sense of urgency to propel them homeward. So a more lesiurely pace was set.

By the middle of the journey, James could no longer disguise his illness. His horse stumbled and, too weak to hold on, James fell into the canebrake. At once Mary and one of the rangers dismounted and rushed to him.

"Are you hurt, General?" the ranger inquired.

"Yes, he is," Mary said; for she saw that a cane had broken in two as he fell and pierced his side. Already, the blood was oozing through his shirt.

"I'm all right," he insisted and, refusing their help, he climbed back upon his horse.

But by the time they reached Augusta, James was quite ill, and the wound in his side was infected. With the man out of his head, and his body convulsing with malarial chills, the trip had come to a stop. They would be forced to stay in Augusta until he had improved enough to travel again.

"I need to get back to Savannah, Mary," he complained in one of his more lucid moments.

Mary turned a deaf ear. Instead she gathered herbs for the local apothecary to use on the infected wound, and she herself fed him the bitter waters made from the bark she carried in her leather pouch.

As Mary smoothed the pillow at James's head, he said, "I feel as if I'm home again in the nursery, being taken care of by my mother."

"You're weak as a baby, that's for sure," she agreed. Her smile became impish. "But I'm not sure that I like being looked on as your mother. After all, James, you're older than I am."

He reached out as if to take her hand. And then he remembered. No man touched a married Creek woman. "You know what I mean, Mary. You've saved my life and I'm truly grateful to you."

His serious response caused her to drop the levity in her own voice. "Then stay in bed until you're well, James." She reached over and dipped a cloth in the gourd filled with cool springwater and began to bathe his fevered brow.

The effort of talking had taken its toll. With the soothing ministration, James closed his eyes and went back to sleep.

After several weeks the fever subsided, and the wound began to heal. But James was still weak when the message from William Stephens arrived. "Open it, Mary. And read it to me."

For a moment she was silent. Then she read aloud the message that the representative of the trustees in Savannah had sent to the general of the troops in Carolina and Georgia.

"Spain has declared war against England."

"Then our trip to Coweta Town was just in time, wasn't it? We now have our Indian militia to fight *with* us rather than against us."

"What are you doing?"

"Why, getting out of bed. I must return to Savannah as soon as possible."

This time, with the horses left behind, they journeyed down the river. The periaguas holding the rangers, Charlie Bowlegs, the general, and Mary kept in close proximity to each other.

Unknown to the group, Tomochichi lay dying, with his village gathered around him. Senauki, sitting by his bed, fanned him with the feather fan belonging to the medicine man, Tallapoosa. The little bells made a pleasant, tinkling sound in the quiet autumn afternoon.

"I am sorry to be leaving when my good friend needs my help against the Spanish," he said to Senauki.

She leaned closer to hear his whisper.

"I wish to be buried in the white man's town," he said. "Tell Oglethorpe. He will understand." For nearby was the burial mound of his father and his Yamasee ancestors.

Before Mary and James reached home, the old mico died. As they walked up the steps of the bluff the two were greeted with the sad news.

Oglethorpe honored his old friend's request. Tomochichi was buried in the middle of Percival Square, with full military honors. The skirl of the bagpipe provided the funeral music as James himself led the procession and helped to support the bier.

The town of Savannah and her Indian allies were drawn together that day to celebrate the life and death of Tomochichi, the ninety-seven-year-old mico of the Yamacraws. In respect, an armed escort accompanied the procession and fired volleys over the grave as the cannons along the bluff answered.

No words were spoken. Toonahowie, the heir of the Yamacraws, led Senauki to the open grave, and there they gave up Tomochichi's eagle headdress, his beads and arrows, and his blanket, to accompany him into the next world.

When the silent ceremony was over, Mary led the grieving Senauki back to her house to rest and to receive the condolences offered by the colonists.

But Mary had little chance to rest. With Spain planning an imminent invasion from the island of Cuba, she was sent by James to alert the chiefs of the Indian tribes and call for the warriors that had been promised, while he himself went to Charlestown to arrange for the Carolina regiment.

Jacob Matthews now became indispensable. As a ranger, he went on forays with Oglethorpe, organized Indian hunting parties to secure game for the colonists, helped to oversee the two trading posts, with Mount Venture gaining in prominence because James urgently needed spies near the border to keep an eye on the Spanish. As Mary's husband, he entertained the Indians who came to Savannah.

Jacob was a product of the rough frontier—young, impetuous, and inclined to drink too much. When he did, he was often embroiled in brawls, but the town officials were afraid to censure him because of his wife's importance to the colony.

As the coastal road came under patrol, enemy ships were often spotted along the horizon. The threat of invasion, the illness of the people, the spies captured in their midst, and the attempted murder of James by one of his mutinous soldiers all combined to keep the colonists in a state of alarm.

It was during this time that Thomas Bosomworth arrived in Savannah as clerk for the extremely busy William Stephens. Approximately the same age as Jacob, he was tall, imposing looking, and intelligent. But he was a younger son who would inherit nothing from his family in those days when the eldest received the inheritance. He turned to the New World to seek his fortune.

He had not been in Savannah long when he decided that he needed a post more suited to his many talents and with a higher-sounding title than clerk. His persistent letters back to England paid off. He was appointed Secretary of Indian Affairs, and in that role he came in contact with Mary.

But the meeting was a disappointment. She was not impressed with either him or his title.

"I can't understand it, Mr. Christie," he said to the new bailiff. "You would have thought that the woman would have known how important I am to her livelihood."

Christie laughed. "Mr. Bosomworth, the trustees have saddled you with an empty title. If the truth be known, Mary could have you removed at any moment, she's that powerful."

His words gnawed at Thomas all day. What was the good, then, in having a title that even a woman, and a half-breed at that, could take away?

Mary was not aware of Thomas's thoughts. She was far too busy.

By early summer James had finally received his military support. A group of rangers, the Highland Regiment from New Inverness, or Darien as it soon would be called, and the Indian militia, with Toonahowie as head of one legion, all came together at the mouth of St. John's River near Amelia Island. The invasion of St.Augustine by General Oglethorpe had begun.

At Fort Moosa, James won his first victory. And leaving a colonel, part of the Scottish Highlander regiment, and forty Indians behind to patrol the wooded area, James took the main body southward to St. Augustine.

"Change camp every night, Colonel," James, once again ill with the fever, had admonished the officer. "You don't want to be caught by surprise if the Spanish come back to attack."

But his orders were not carried out. Near the gates of Moosa they camped every night. In the middle of June, an overwhelming Spanish force attacked at dawn, killing most of the Highlanders.

In his report to King Philip, Governor Montiano in St. Augustine duly noted the defeat: "The Battle of Moosa destroyed the settlement of Scotchmen and people in whom Oglethorpe had the utmost confidence."

In the battle for St. Augustine, Oglethorpe met with defeat as well. Six half galleys, with their nine-pound brass cannons, had already arrived from Cuba to thwart any taking of that Florida city by the English.

For Mary, James's disappointment had personal repercussions. Her large plantation had been left unattended and her cattle driven off, as her overseer was conscripted into the force and then killed in battle. And while she was caring for her ailing husband, Jacob, who had caught the fever that had plagued the land, another disaster was unfolding at Mount Venture.

Red Horse had waited in vain for Mary to return to the trading post on the Altamaha for their last confrontation. For years, the woman had been his anathema. But the Spanish were on the move, and the defeat of the English was certain. This time, he would win. But Red Horse was old, almost too old to fight. After this last battle, he would become an *istechaque*, an old man sitting around the village with other old men, recalling past days of glory until he, too, was buried in the mound of his ancestors. Only his hate for the woman had kept him going this long.

"Red Horse," one of the warriors called to him. "The Spanish captain has given us orders to move out at once."

"Where are we going?"

"North. That's all I know," Hoosela replied.

Red Horse had to make a decision quickly. "Go on. I will catch up with you later. I have something to do before I leave this place."

Hoosela looked at the old warrior and nodded. It would be just as well if he remained behind.

The sound of many horsemen taking flight from the wilderness caused the ground to vibrate under Red Horse's feet. His old war pony lifted his ears at the sound, but a whistle from Red Horse kept the pony from following the others.

Later, from the cover of the trees, Red Horse stared at the trading post. All was silent. The cabin looked deserted, but he took no chances. He circled around the compound, looking for some sign of the caretaker. The man was either hiding or had fled with word of the Spanish invasion.

Taking his time, Red Horse walked onto the front porch and tried the door. It was not even barred. So he pushed it open with his hatchet and then jumped back at the sudden creak of the iron hinge. He waited, but hearing no further noise, he crept inside.

The store was filled—with brightly colored cloth on the shelves and barrels of flour on the floor. A mug of liquid sat on the counter, as if a customer had been interrupted before finishing it. Red Horse walked over, stuck his hand in the mug, and then tasted the liquid that dripped from his finger.

Rum. Fiery, golden rum. He picked up the mug and downed its contents before moving on. Using his hatchet, Red Horse took great pleasure in destroying the store and its goods. Then he walked into Mary's living quarters, piling her personal items into a heap in the middle of the floor and dousing them with the oil from the lamp. Within a few minutes, he had started the fire that smoldered and smoked, the flames in no more hurry than he was.

He went back into the store and found the cask of rum. Pouring himself another mug and still another, he finally felt its effects in his belly. And with the feeling came fresh courage. He was Red Horse, warrior and enemy to Coosaponakeesa, and at last the winner of a personal blood feud that had started many moons before.

In ecstasy, he swung his hatchet, chopping at the wood everywhere—the poles, the supports to the rafters, the counters, the flooring. And then he stopped. In the grayness of his surroundings, he saw at the back of the store a basket of unspeakable beauty. His eyes began playing tricks on him, as if the basket were changing shapes and colors. Coosaponakeesa's medicine basket. It seemed to be alive—with the throbbing of life itself. To him, the basket *became* Coosaponakeesa, and he was seized with the feeling that he must destroy it too, that in doing so, he would actually be killing his adversary. With his hatchet poised, he took several steps toward the basket. But as he reached out to destroy it, Red Horse lost his balance and stumbled against one of the poles supporting the roof.

Pine bark and palmetto thatch drifted downward, before the roof fell on top of him, pinning Red Horse under its timbers. For how long he lay there, he had no way of knowing. But at last, as he began trying to extricate himself, he smelled the fire and heard the crackling of flames. He began to struggle in earnest, but the harder he tried, the worse the situation became. It was as if he were bound by some invisible rope.

A few minutes later, as smoke filled the trading post and flames shot from the roof, a riderless war pony left the Altamaha wilderness and raced toward the sound of battle.

By May of 1742, Jacob died, and Mary was a widow for the second time. But her period of mourning was cut short. Little more than a month later, James sent for her to come to Frederica. Again he needed his interpreter and diplomat.

"I was sorry to learn of Jacob's death," James said as he and Mary sat in the shade of the orange grove that surrounded the two-story residence on St. Simons Island.

"There have been many sad losses this year," she replied.

"And more to come, I'm afraid," James added.

Spanish ships were headed toward Cumberland Sound. It was necessary to apprise the Indian troops of their role in the impending fight.

"The French are becoming more warlike, too," she mentioned. "Licka sent word to me of their recent battle against the French."

"Lucky for us that he is in our camp. A pincer movement from both enemies at the same time would annihilate us. Tell Licka, though, that he must be careful not to start a full-scale war on that frontier."

Later, as word came of the nearness of the Spanish fleet, James left to meet it. Mary was gratified to learn that the attack by the Indian militia and some of James's troops drove the Spanish, with heavy casualties, from the sound.

But the Spanish had shown their hand. They were determined to wipe out the coastal colonies. Knowing that the enemy ships would return soon, James brought the new regiment of Scottish Highlanders that had recently settled in Darien and called for more Indian militia.

"You will have to distribute presents to the new Indian recruits," Mary said.

James nodded. Once again, he would have to pay for the gifts from his own pocket. But too much was at stake not to heed Mary's advice.

# Chapter 31

On St. Simons Island, the July day began with a red sun spewing its hot rays over the alligator-infested marsh. Guarding her nest of eggs, a female alligator watched and waited for the gray heron to plunge its long beak into the algae-rich shadows. Then she lurched, her body moving swiftly toward her morning snack. With a powerful snap of the jaws, she crushed the heron and swallowed, still hungry, as she lumbered once again to her hiding place to watch and wait for other prey coming within easy striking distance.

Other eyes also kept an early-morning watch— those of the young lookout on the British ship commanded by Captain Thompson. Pressed into service by Oglethorpe to help guard the harbor, the ship's captain heard the ominous words, "Sail, ho! Enemy ships on the horizon."

Captain Thompson took his spyglass and looked in that direction. The boy was right. Riding upon the wind and high tide, Spanish ships, more numerous than he could count, appeared in the distance in battle formation, with their flags hoisted and cannons primed for battle.

"Prepare to defend harbor," he barked. "Man your stations!"

Signals sent to the land batteries brought the cannons swiveling into alignment, their mouths waiting for a closer approach of the enemy before the firing. And on the smaller guard schooner, the ninety Highland troops under the command of Captain Dunbar also prepared for battle against the fleet. They were already veterans from the Cumberland Sound engagement.

For more than four hours the battle was fought, with the Spanish attempts to board both ship and schooner held off. During that time casualties for the Spanish were already heavy from the battery and ships' guns.

Finally, with the harbor unbreached, the Spanish ships, thirty-six in number, pulled away and set sail in the direction of Frederica, where it would be easier to land the soldiers and then return south.

Realizing their intent, Oglethorpe issued his orders: "Get the ship and schooner out to sea for Charlestown harbor immediately."

The merchant ships had no hope of being saved. Taking the fighting men off them, James had those ships destroyed, with all stores and provisions. Then the entire group of men set out on a forced march to Frederica, to arrive before the Spanish ships.

Two days later, a scout returned to Oglethorpe. "Spanish soldiers are marching in the woods toward Frederica."

"How many did you see?" James inquired.

"Didn't wait to count them. A lot more than us, though," he said. "They were spread out all over the woods."

"Then we'll get to them before they can form battle lines," James said.

Taking his Indians, his rangers, and the company of Highlanders, James rode out to meet them. In the deep woods where the startled deer fled and the woodchucks disappeared into their hollowed-out homes, the air came alive with the eerie sounds of Highland yells intermingled with Indian war whoops, as tomahawks and claymores, musket balls and arrows found their mark.

In disarray, the Spanish fled, with James and his men in pursuit. They followed for some distance before the general finally called a halt. There would be other days, other battles. The men needed to save their waning strength for the second wave of enemy troops.

It was not long in coming.

Over the wide swath of savannah, that area where no marsh grass grew, two hundred foot soldiers and one hundred grenadiers, the specially trained elite of the Spanish army, together with their Indian allies and escaped slaves from the Carolina plantations, marched. Also accompanying them was the steady sound of their drums, whose rhythms echoed from the walls of the Alcázar and the Alhambra, and from the jungled temples of the Aztec kings.

Listening to the roll were James's men, hidden in the wooded area beyond.

All around them the Spanish captain, Don Antonio Barba, could see nothing but the vast stretch of savannah. It went on for miles, it seemed. Because the men were tired, wet, and hungry, he deemed it a good place for them to stop and cook their meal of the day.

"Ho, Don Antonio," another captain called. "Do you think our Indian friends will find any scalps today?"

The captain smiled. "If they can dig the English out of their burrows. I hear this Oglethorpe can disappear like a fox."

"A red fox, at that," the other man said, laughing.

The grenadiers and the other men stacked their guns together, content to relax in camaraderie while the food was being prepared.

As the blue haze of the cooking fires gradually joined the mist rising from the marsh, a sudden volley of arms sounded from the woods beyond. The man standing beside Don Antonio fell. The surprised captain realized that they were under siege from an unseen enemy.

"To your muskets, men," he shouted. Then he felt the fiery pain in his hip. He had been hit.

The rigid formations and battle patterns of the grenadiers, who were used to meeting their enemy face-to-face, were no good in this land, where James and his soldiers had learned well how to fight Indian-style. Shooting from the protection of the woods, they more than balanced their small, pitiful numbers against the larger Spanish force. Routed, the Spanish fled, taking refuge in the fort, their leaders either killed or wounded. Disillusioned and defeated, they were soon driven from the island.

The fight that day at Bloody Marsh had far-reaching consequences. But not realizing its significance until much later, James made another foray, with full troop support, to try and take St. Augustine once more.

Fort Diego, on the St. John's River, fell. But when he reached the city, the capital of Spain in the New World, Oglethorpe could not get the Spanish at the Castillo de San Marcos to come out and fight. So he and his men went home to Frederica, where he and Mary rejoiced in the temporary cessation of hostilities.

By November they were in conference again; for there were always problems among the various tribes to be dealt with.

"I hear that our Secretary of Indian Affairs has left for England," James said.

"Yes, he came to tell me good-bye. It seems that Mr. Bosomworth will be taking holy orders and becoming a man of the cloth."

"Did he say whether he will be returning to Savannah later on?"

"He did not mention any future plans. I know the administration of the orphanage at Bethesda has upset him. He believes the poor children are abused every day in the name of religion, but his complaint to the trustees was not met in the spirit he wished."

James shook his head. But then he smiled. "I understand the bishop was questioned on why he keeps sending such poor specimens to the colony for the propagation of the Gospel."

"Did he have an answer?"

"Yes. That it was better for a field to be plowed by asses than for the ground to be given over to thistles."

"The followers of the Great Spirit would not agree with him."

"And neither do I. I see too much damage done by the asses of the world."

James became introspective. So few people understood the problems, the calamities he'd faced. Why could they not be more like Mary, without his having to explain, ad nauseum? Yet, he knew that he should have written to the trustees more often, to let them know what was going on and to defend himself against unjust accusations.

He should have written William Stephens more often, too. But when had he had the time? Yet, for the man to correspond with his German servant behind his back had hit him as being a particularly underhanded way of keeping up with his whereabouts.

The year passed, with more forays to defend the colony against the Spanish. And in 1743, as Mary returned to Frederica, she learned that the brave Toonahowie, still wearing the gold watch that the Duke of Cumberland had given him on his visit to England, had been killed in battle. His death put an end to an era, severing a link with the past.

Outside Orange Hall, the small two-storied tabby house which James had built, he and Mary sat in silence and watched the full moon hovering over the water, its pale reflection scattered in the waves that softly surged to shore.

Feeling old at the age of forty-seven, with seasonal bouts of chills and fever, James turned to look at Mary. In the moonlight she appeared no older than on the day he'd first met her. Yet he knew her age, younger than he, as she had reminded him earlier, but not by that many years. Only five or six.

They had been through a lot together. She was the best friend he'd ever had—besides the old mico, Tomochichi. But it was Mary who had encouraged that friendship for the good of the colony. He couldn't understand why Stephens should have such objections to his few remaining friends, when they were the ones who had saved the colony.

Now it was his enemies in London that he would have to be concerned with. After all his blood, sweat, and sacrifice, he had been ordered home to face a court-martial stemming from the first ill-fated march against St. Augustine, when nearly the entire Highland Regiment left at Moosa had been wiped out.

Finally, James spoke. "Mary, I'll be leaving soon for England."

Mary did not respond. Instead, she waited for him to continue, for during the past few hours, she had sensed a struggle within James, a yearning to bring to life those feelings and emotions that he had never allowed to blossom for fear of the strange, forbidden fruit they would create.

Mary knew him well. For at that moment James was trying to come to grips with all that he felt. But he had no words to describe the pain that tore at him at the mere thought of an enforced separation from her. She was a part of him—his heart, his love for this new land, all the hopes and dreams and ambitions that he had ever known.

My God, was this what love was about? That emotion he had ridiculed without ever having felt its power?

Yes, that's what it must be. With the realization that he loved this woman as he had never loved another, he wanted to shout it for all the world to hear. But when he found his voice again, his words were barely audible over the whitecapped waves that lapped against the shore.

"I love you, Mary."

"I know, James."

"But how? I didn't know, myself, until a few moments ago."

"Your English eyes did not see the old buffalo trace, either. But it was there, nevertheless."

"Then, is there something else I haven't seen as well? Do I dare hope that you might love me a little bit, too?"

"I've loved you for a long time, James," she replied. "I think it began the day you stood before Tallapoosa and gritted your teeth, when you really wanted to run him through with your sword."

James smiled. "I remember. I hated his liberties with those bell-jangling fans."

The old memories intruded, postponing for a short time what was to come. Then James removed the heirloom diamond ring from the little finger of his left hand.

"Hold out your hand, Mary," he urged.

Looking into his serious gray eyes, she did as she was told.

"I want you to wear this ring, Mary. Always. As a symbol of our love. Never take it off; for tonight we are irrevocably joined together."

She felt the warmth of the ring as he slid it onto her finger. Tears came to her eyes. "I have nothing to give you in return, James. Such a valuable gift demands one of equal value."

"Take care of my little colony until I return. That will be a far better present for me."

He held out his arms for her, and she gladly came into his embrace. With his lips, he kissed away her tears. "I don't know what the future holds for us, Mary. Whether we will have years together or just this one night. I only know that you are mine and I am yours, heart and soul."

He did not have to say any more. Together they rose from the crude bench and walked upstairs to James's bedroom.

There was no bed of soft deerskin and beaver for them to share. Only a military cot was witness, as Mary became James's wilderness wife in the Indian way. The day he returned from England, cleared of all charges, would be time enough for a Christian ceremony. Until then, their love would remain a secret.

Much later, James whispered, "Orange Hall is yours, my darling, to use anytime you wish."

"No, James. The day you return is the day I'll come back to Frederica."

"Then I pray to God that it will be soon."

That night the sand dunes along the shore sang with the wind in an ancient ritual, recalling the earlier days of Spanish missions and Indians paddling silently by. Lying in James's arms, Mary heard the island's antiphonal song and was content.

# Chapter 32

Eight months later, the Reverend Thomas Bosomworth returned to Georgia. Wearing the surplice of the Anglican Church, he had been duly ordained by the Bishop of London and then promptly appointed by the trustees to take care of the religious welfare of Georgia, with power to perform all ecclesiastical tasks.

According to the appointment, he was now the possessor of three hundred acres of land, with two indentured servants to aid him, a trust house in Savannah to be used as a parsonage, and fifty pounds a year as compensation for his work in promulgating the Gospel to the colony.

But in order to carry out his duties, he needed a wife. He had prayed about it on the return voyage and discussed it with the ship's captain in the evenings.

"Aye. A man of the cloth needs a helpmeet," the captain had agreed. "And a healthy one, at that, who won't be comin' down with the fever. Sturdy stock. That's what you need, Reverend."

"Mayhaps you can tell me, Captain, if there are any young ladies aboard this ship, who might be of a kind, Christian nature?"

"Well, there are some young ladies to be sure, but as to their dispositions, that would be for you to discover."

"Yes, of course." Thomas waited for the captain to reveal the names.

"Mistress Oxford is traveling with her daughter, Nellie. But I fear that if you get one, you get both. I don't know how you would feel about having her mother live with you."

Thomas hesitated. "Do you have others to recommend?"

The captain smiled. "There's this pretty little poppet named Purgia Smithfield. She's an orphan with little money. Her uncle is paying her fare across. But if a dowry doesn't mean that much to you, I could introduce you to her."

It would not sound good if he said that a dowry was of importance, even though it was. And so Thomas forced himself to smile. "By all means, I shall look forward to the introduction."

The moment he saw her, he knew that Purgia would be quite suitable. And after talking with her, he found that she was reasonably intelligent, although not on his level. A pity that she had no money.

"Shall we take a turn on deck, Miss Smithfield?" he asked.

She looked at her rather stout, red-faced uncle for permission.

"Well, I suppose it would be all right," he said. "After all, if you can't trust a reverend with your niece, who can you trust?"

Thomas gritted his teeth at the coarse laugh. "Quite," he said, nodding to the man.

"What are your interests, Miss Smithfield?"

"I like music, sir," Purgia said in a quavering voice.

"Do you play an instrument?"

"The harpsichord. And I sing a little, too."

"The hymns of the church?"

"Yes, sir."

A sudden, cold wind whipped the cape about her and tore at her blonde hair. Seeing it, Thomas said, "You must not remain out in this wind any longer. I will take you back to your uncle."

They walked hurriedly to shelter, but Thomas had decided. Purgia was sweet and docile. She would do for his purpose. That is, if he found no other with a dowry by the time he reached shore. "Until tomorrow," he said, turning her over to her uncle.

But the next day he did not see the young woman. When he finally encountered the uncle, Thomas said, "I do hope Miss Smithfield is well. I had hoped that, mayhaps, we could take another turn on deck this afternoon."

"She's feeling poorly today, Reverend. My little Angus has just gotten over measles. And I wonder if Purgia might not be comin' down with the same thing."

"Then give her my regards. And tell her that I will pray for her recovery."

Thomas's prayers did not help Purgia. She became worse, and within the week it was Thomas who performed his ecclesiastical duties for his first burial at sea. Angus, Sr. and his wife commented several times on the beauty of the service. But for Thomas, the words were empty. God had decided that Purgia was not a suitable helpmeet for him.

But whom had he chosen for him as a wife? Not Nellie, Thomas hoped, for one look at the robust girl had sent him scurrying to his cabin.

That evening, in the candlelight, Thomas took up his Bible. He would be led by the Lord to the name of his future bride, if he prayed hard enough. After kneeling in supplication for an hour, he rose and, with his eyes closed, he opened the Good Book and pointed.

Then he read where his finger led him. "And the angel appeared unto Mary...."

Mary? He frowned. The only Mary he knew was Mary Matthews. She certainly was not his idea of a loving, docile wife. She was headstrong, independent, and older than he. Surely the Lord didn't have her in mind for him. And yet...

She was the wealthiest woman in Georgia. So there was the dowry. And although a tiny woman, she was of sturdy stock, as were so many of the offspring of English fathers and Indian mothers. She was used to entertaining well. And there was no denying that he had been attracted to her in an embarrassing way, causing him fleshly discomfort. Just thinking about her now made him feel sinful. But did St. Paul not say that it was better to marry than to burn in hell?

All that night Thomas remained in his cabin and thought of Mary. And by morning he had convinced himself that God had chosen her as his wife.

Now he only had to convince Mary.

"You are out of your mind, Thomas Bosomworth." She glared at the man who had just set foot on her property and announced that she had been chosen as his wife. "If I ever decide to get married again, it certainly will not be to you."

She twisted James's ring in agitation at the effrontery of the man standing before her. "If you're so set on getting a wife, why don't you call on the Pettipooles? Annabelle is the one looking for a husband. I'm not."

Thomas merely smiled. "You'll come around," he assured her. "You only need a little time to get used to the—"

"There's not enough time left on this earth to get used to such a proposition. Go home, Thomas, and pray some more. You have misunderstood the Lord."

"No, Mary. Your heart may be hard this day. But God will soften it toward me. I can afford to wait."

"Then wait somewhere else, Thomas. I have work to do."

He hesitated. "I won't trouble you again, Mary, by speaking of this. But when your heart is ready, you can reach me at the parsonage that formerly belonged to the late Reverend Christopher Orton."

With his dignity intact, he left Mary's house.

In London, James Oglethorpe found that his old enemy, Walpole, had been forced to step down, while his friend, Egmont, had grown tired of dealing with the trustees and so had voluntarily resigned from that body.

Still, James was kept busy, in both Parliament and the Trust, answering to the many petty accusations hurled against him from both Georgia and Carolina, as well as from England.

Yet the most serious accusation was dismissed—that of military negligence. From the court-martial he emerged victorious. But it was a humiliating experience, one that James would always remember with little desire to forgive those responsible for the charge leveled against him.

When the trial was over, he sat in the office of his solicitor, where he had come to discuss the state of his affairs, too long neglected.

"What do you plan to do now, General?" the solicitor inquired.

"I'd like to go back to Georgia—"

"I'm afraid that's out of the question," the man said before James had finished. "You can't afford it. Your personal finances are in shambles—ninety thousand pounds of your own money spent in the colony. And I have it on good authority that Parliament will not reimburse you one pence."

James nodded. It was true. His request had been turned down.

"And your estate in Godalming has been mortgaged. Your sister, Mistress Anne, tells me the roof leaks, and there's not enough money left to repair it.

"And think of this. Even the little stipend coming from your seat in Parliament would be lost if you left.

Haslemere would elect someone else to represent them. So in the end, you would lose both money and prestige."

James did not like the direction in which the conversation was going. Yet he had come for advice. If it were unpleasant to hear, he would nevertheless have to hear it.

"Then what do you suggest?" he inquired, trying to keep the irritation from his voice.

"You'll have to do what other men of your station do when they find themselves in pecuniary difficulties—marry an heiress."

James stood, irate at the suggestion. "If that is the only solution, then—"

"God's truth, sit down, James," the solicitor urged. "I've known you too long for you to get your dander up with me."

He sat down again as the solicitor continued.

"It's not as if an arranged marriage is anything out of the ordinary. It's done all the time to save estates from falling under the ax."

"But one would hope that there might be a little love between the—"

"Aha! So we have come to the real reason for your objection. Is it that you have, heaven forbid, fallen in love with one of your penniless little colonists?"

"Not exactly."

"Your protest sounds rather weak to me. But let me remind you again, James. You have an obligation beyond your own desires—to stay here and save your father's estate and to put a roof over your sister's head. If you turn your back on your family obligations, then

I predict nothing but Fleet Street for the entire Oglethorpe family."

Although his heart protested, James knew in his mind that his old friend was right. After all he'd done, he was no longer wanted in the colony. And Mary, drained of so many of her possessions, would eventually be pushed out, too, her earlier contributions forgotten by the new regime headed by William Stephens.

But when that time came, Mary had others she could depend upon. His own family had only James.

By the time he left the solicitor's office, James was thoroughly depressed. The soldier-adventurer had not only relinguished his dream, but his dearest love and friend.

In 1744, James found his heiress—a compatible woman of rank, with a pleasant house and acreage. His sister could now stay at Westbrook for the rest of her life, with a dry roof over her head.

Never one to write letters, James knew that a particular letter above all others had to be written. And so, at the polished mahogany desk belonging to his wife, he sat down, dipped his goose quill into the inkstand, and began.

"Dear Mary…"

She sat in the chair of the keeping room and held the letter to her breast, as she had done so many years before, when James had sent that first letter by Johnny.

Once again, she traced the design in the red sealing wax, putting off opening it. And when she could no longer resist, Mary carefully opened the letter and began to read.

Her smile turned into a frown. At letter's end, her hands were trembling with rage.

"Married!" she screamed, throwing the letter to the floor.

She stood and began to pace, her anger at the man filling her entire being.

"Married!" she screamed again, even louder, bringing Singing Rock from the kitchen to see what had caused her mistress such anguish.

"What's wrong, mistress? Can I help?"

Mary's dark blue eyes were filled with fury, her body shaking. "Go back into the kitchen, Singing Rock. I am the only one who can deal with this...this back-biting letter."

Uneasy at the woman's rage, Singing Rock quickly disappeared back into the kitchen.

An hour later, no trace of anger marred Mary's face. But her large, limpid eyes held a resolve that could not be disguised. She had been betrayed by James. To salvage her pride, only one avenue was left to her.

She dressed carefully—in blue silk, his favorite color. And then she rolled her hair in the English manner, pinning it at the nape of her neck.

The mirror recorded the regal set of her head, the fine features, high cheekbones, and firm chin, the still-youthful breasts that swelled under the tight bodice. With no sense of vanity, she examined her image as minutely as she would a deerskin for trade, searching for flaws, for imperfections. Finding none, she turned from the mirror and walked out of her house.

At that time of day the Reverend Thomas Bosomworth was in his parsonage garden, meditating. But as he opened his eyes he saw Mary Matthews walking past the hedge of red oleander. She hesitated, and then walked toward his front door stoop.

Hurriedly he left the garden and walked into the side entrance of the little house. And when his servant showed her into his study, Thomas was already seated.

"Good afternoon, Mary."

"And to you, Thomas."

"Come and have a seat," he urged, getting up to greet her. Turning immediately to his servant, he said, "Robert, leave us and see that no one disturbs us."

"Yes, Pastor."

Mary chose not to take the seat offered her. Instead she looked up at the young man dressed in his surplice. She wasted no time in small talk. "Thomas, do you still want to marry me?"

Thomas's heart skipped a beat. "You know I do. Have you come to me at last?"

"Yes, Thomas."

"My dear one," he said, wrapping her in his arms and almost suffocating her in his flowing surplice. "You have made me a supremely happy man."

# Chapter 33

Like any virile young man, Thomas claimed his conjugal rights often.

At times he felt obsessed with his wife, Mary, pushing everything else into the background. But when the thoughts of her kept intruding into his study and meditation, he became uneasy, recalling what people had whispered about the unfortunate episode with the lunatic Watson.

Yet had Watson been right? That she had the power to bewitch all men? The sweetness of her flesh, even the graceful movement of her hands, her quick mind, had bound him to her, as surely as any slave's chains.

But he was a newly married man. That was it. This period of self-indulgence would not last forever, he told himself. Still, it was not good for him to be swayed so often by the ways of the flesh.

Sitting in his garden on a sun-drenched afternoon in the middle of March, Thomas decided on his penance for Lent. He would give up sleeping with his wife on Tuesdays and Fridays. Yes. His abstinence would prove that he was not enslaved after all.

But today was Monday. And wasting no time, Thomas went inside to look for his wife.


Even after James Oglethorpe had left Georgia for good, Mary continued in her role as diplomat and interpreter for the Georgia colony. William Stephens would have preferred it otherwise, but he knew that neither Savannah nor any of the other settlements could hope to defend themselves against Indian hostilities. Mary was needed to keep the peace, perhaps even more now that France had declared war on England.

Soon after one of her long journeys to meet with some of the headmen of the Creeks, who were leaning toward the French, and with the possibility of another trip upon the horizon, a petulant Thomas, tired of his wife's absences, remonstrated. "Mary, a woman's place is beside her husband, not gallivanting over the countryside."

She tried to pacify him, but she was tired from the long day spent at the trading post. "Thomas, I am also Queen of the Creeks. This means that my people have just as much right to my time as you do."

"But it's unseemly...."

Her patience began to thin. "What's unseemly to you English, Thomas, makes perfectly good sense to me."

He had allowed her headstrong way much too long. He would have to put his foot down. "Then I suppose the only thing left to do is to forbid you to go."

Her eyes took on the look he dreaded, the look they had when she was crossed. "Forbid? You dare to use that word with me?"

"Yes. If it is the only way I can make you—"

"No one makes me do anything. I am the one who chooses to go. And I am the one who chooses to stay."

Thomas inwardly groaned. Why could not sweet, docile Purgia be standing before him now? She would never have dared to defy her husband.

"Then does this mean that you have chosen to go despite my own wishes in the matter?"

Mary showed her exasperation. From the moment she had married him, he had remained hidden behind his surplice, never seeing, never understanding what was going on in the world around him. These were disturbing times, and it was becoming increasingly hard to persuade her people to remain on the side of the English.

"Thomas, I don't want to argue with you again. But I must go. There's no other way."

"Then, Mary, don't look for me when you come back. I won't be here."

"And where will you go?"

"Back to England. For good."

"I'm sorry, Thomas. But you must choose your own destiny. And I mine," she added.

Thomas was true to his word. Upon her return, he was gone. Mary moved back into her own house. The parsonage had never been a home to her, as the

Cowpen had been, or even the smaller house that James had built for her on the square ten years before.

With Singing Rock, Charlie Bowlegs, and her other servants, Mary threw herself into her work as fur trader, carefully rebuilding what she had lost. When she thought of it, she wrote letters on her own behalf, still seeking the return of her land and the money promised to her more than ten years previously.

From James's house in Godalming, his sister Anne was busy relaying the secret Jacobite messages from her other sisters, who were so involved in the effort to return the Stuart line to the throne of England.

She had recently completed building the little houses, her forts guarding the approach from the river. They were now ready to receive her clandestine guests.

The bonnie prince had landed on Scottish soil, and the clans had gathered, sweeping down on Edinburgh and taking that city. Soon the Highlanders would be in England and the rightful king would be sitting upon the throne of England. Anne was confident of that, just as her mother, Eleanor, had wished before her death.

Yet, it was a great pity that her brother, James, was a commander in the armies against him.

General James Oglethorpe was also thinking of this as he waited in York for his orders. He remembered his Scottish Highlanders who had fought so bravely at Bloody Marsh, Fort Diego, and yes, at Moosa, where so many had lost their lives. He had worn the plaid with them and listened to their bagpipes—friends like Hugh Mackay at Frederica and John McIntosh Mohr of Darien, who had been taken prisoner by the Spanish.

He turned to the chaplain of his regiment, Thomas Bosomworth, and said, "I have grown tired of war. Almost as tired of it as this infernal waiting."

"There seems to be no end of it," Thomas agreed. "War and rumors of war—"

"My nephews, the Prince de Montauban and the Chevalier de Mézières are out there somewhere. Pray that I do not have to meet them on the battlefield."

"I will do so, General."

An hour later, James's troops were still waiting. And again James turned to his chaplain for conversation. "How is Mary?"

The question took Thomas by surprise. "She was well, the last I saw her."

"You are a lucky man, Bosomworth, to have her as a wife. I've never seen another woman in all of Europe who could compare with her. A brilliant woman, that's what she is."

Suddenly Thomas felt proud. The general actually sounded envious. He warmed to the discussion of his wife. "She is, of course, doing what she can to keep her people from going over to the French. In fact, on the day I left, she was planning a journey to meet with some of the hostile headmen."

A standard bearer rode at a fast pace toward James.

"Ah, here it is. The message we've been waiting for."

James urged his horse to a gallop and rode out to meet the rider. The intimate conversation between the general and his chaplain was over.

By October, the news for the Loyalists was grave. Few Englishmen had joined in the cause. And so, the Highlanders, greatly outnumbered, were fleeing northern England to return to Scotland. And the British armies were in pursuit.

The Yorkshire Light Horse, a new regiment commanded by James, had received orders to join the Hanoverian troops and engage them in battle. But if the opposing forces were too strong, then his orders were to post his army behind the Highlanders to cut off their retreat. They would then be surrounded, with the Duke of Cumberland's army advancing to cut them down.

But James's army was slow. He arrived in each small village and town only moments after the Highlanders had already fled.

"You have let the rebels escape," a furious Duke of Cumberland accused.

"Sir, I have not!"

"You will be struck off my staff, Oglethorpe, and a letter writ for an explanation of your conduct!"

With the Duke of Cumberland's action, both James Oglethorpe and Thomas Bosomworth were out of a job.

By 1746, when James was acquitted of all charges and reinstated, with a promotion, Thomas was back in Savannah. But he had lost his position in the colony to another minister, already living in the little parsonage.

"Mary," he said, standing at the open door of the Cowpen, "your husband has come home."

She stared at the man who had sworn never to return. But there was something different about him. "Where is your surplice?" she asked.

"I have taken it off for good. I am no longer engaged in the battle to save souls."

"Then mayhaps you can learn the fur trade," she said. "Come in, Thomas."

In the next few months he became her helper, eager to please, especially since she had grown much wealthier in the time he was away. Yes, Mary was a born merchant and an excellent administrator. It was to his advantage to cast his lot with her, totally. For in truth, he had no other choice.

But for him, Savannah did not have the best of memories. He had started out as a mere clerk, and the aristocratic Stephens would never let him forget it. But out of Savannah, he could become somebody.

"Mary, I was thinking," he said to his wife one evening as they sat by the fire.

"Yes, Thomas?"

"What would you say to opening up a second trading post, to take the place of the one that burned?"

"Would you be willing to help me with it?"

"Of course I would."

He had changed in so many ways since his stay in England. But would his industriousness continue? She wondered.

"I would not want it so far on the Altamaha again."

"No. It would be difficult traveling back and forth."

He could see that she was becoming excited about the idea. But he waited for her to speak again.

"Charlie Bowlegs tells me there is much traffic at the forks of the Ocmulgee and Oconee rivers."

"Then perhaps that would be a good place to look."

"Yes. We should go there soon and check out the possibilities."

Within a short time Mary had built the trading post with her husband, where the two rivers converged. And appropriately she had christened it "the Forks."

The land around the post was virgin territory, still unspoiled by the white man. Lush, green forests held great herds of white-tailed deer. Otters and beaver swam in the creeks and streams, their fur as beautiful and luxuriant as the water and the land.

The trading post was impressive, too. Much larger than the one at Yamacraw Bluff, it spoke of wealth and prosperity; for the news of its opening had spread rapidly, with the two rivers witness to the steady traffic of canoes and periaguas carrying deerskins to the post and leaving with traded store goods.

At times the periaguas also brought letters, such as the one from Thomas's brother, Abraham, who was representing Mary's claim with the trustees in England.

One evening, when Thomas returned from checking on the animals for the night, an indignant Mary held out the letter that had arrived that day. "We have finally heard from Abraham again. Look,

Thomas; the trustees have now questioned my royalty.

"Abraham says that unless I present an affidavit proving that I am queen, my petition will not be considered. It's another delaying tactic. They hope to drag out this affair until I am dead. Then there'll be no need to pay me or return my land."

Her words brought a chill to his heart. Thomas had not thought of that. Mary was some years older than he. If she died before the dispute was settled, then he would receive nothing.

"You cannot let this stalemate go on any longer. We must do something about it immediately. But who would you get to sign the affidavit?"

"My cousin Malatchee, King of the Cowetas. The trustees will have to recognize him, since his name is also on the treaties with the English."

By this time Thomas had the letter in his hands and was reading it by the meager light of the oil lamp. "But Abraham says that you will also have to have an official of the colony to vouch for you. I doubt that President Stephens—"

"I daresay if Stephens thought I had turned the Creeks against him and his little town, he would put his seal upon the paper quick enough. But no, under ordinary circumstances he would never sign it.

"Sometimes I wonder why I bother to keep the peace, since the English don't bother to keep their word. You would think that I would be accustomed to that by now."

"One should never become accustomed to wrong, Mary."

Mary became silent as she pondered her dilemma.

Thomas spoke up. "What about General Oglethorpe?"

"No, I will have no correspondence with James."

"Mayhaps you are right. I understand he has no friends left on the trust. If they will not recognize his own claims, then he certainly would have little influence concerning yours."

Suddenly Mary's eyes lit up. "Heron—the English commander at Frederica. He would be willing, I'm sure, since he was present at many of the meetings."

"Then we must act immediately."

There was another item that Thomas knew he could no longer put off discussing with his wife. Changing the subject, he said, "I bought something for you, Mary, when I was in Charlestown."

Mary sighed. "What is it this time, Thomas?"

"A herd of black cattle."

She reacted as he suspected she would. "Where are they now? Have you hidden them the way you did the six contraband slaves?"

A hurt expression marred his face. "No. I turned them loose on St. Catherines Island to graze. I thought the news would make you happy, Mary. Instead it seems to have put you further in the doldrums."

"Thomas, I know you mean well. But we can't afford any more expenses right now. All our money is tied up in the trading posts."

"Oh, that's all right. I didn't actually spend any money. I bought them on credit."

What was the use in getting angry with him? He would never change. But she tried once more to make him see. "You're going to have to stop buying everything that meets your eye, Thomas. I'm not a rich woman."

"But you will be, Mary," he assured her. "Once you get the legal titles to your land and the trust finally pays you for your services. We will just have to pursue the matter more diligently."

So they were back to where they had started.

"Let's go to bed," she suggested. "This has been a long day."

# Chapter 34

Abraham and Adam Bosomworth, brothers to Thomas, became more and more involved with Mary's legal situation. After Mary had gotten Heron, commander of Fort Frederica, to certify that Malatchee was, indeed, King of the Cowctas, and after Malatchee had sworn that Mary was Queen of the Creeks, with sovereign claim over the islands of Sapelo, Ossabaw, and St. Catherines, Abraham took the signed documents personally back to England to present to the trustees.

So, for a time, Mary's attention returned to the running of the trading posts and serving as interpreter and diplomat with the Indians for the Georgia colony.

Regularly she distributed gifts to the tribes; for it had become expected by the Indians, wooed as they were from all sides—the English, the French, the Spanish. Of course, their acceptance of the presents did not mean that they would choose allegiance to the gift giver.

Mary smiled as she remembered the great hoax the Spanish governor had played behind her back, sending word to the Lower Creek headmen that James Oglethorpe had returned from England and was in St. Augustine, waiting to greet them. They had gone, but then found that Oglethorpe was not there. The governor had lied, using the invitation as a ruse to try and persuade them to desert the English.

"We listened politely, Mary, to what the Spanish had to say," Chula, one of the headmen, had told her. "We feasted with them and drank with them in all merriment. But once they had given us the beautiful gifts, we disappeared that night."

Chula laughed as he told her, and she remembered laughing with him.

"Do you think they are still looking for you, Chula?" she had asked.

"If they are, it's too late. The gifts have been used up."

Three months later after Abraham left the Forks, Mary and Thomas huddled by the keeping-room fire, seeking to warm themselves. It had turned unseasonably cold, as it was wont to do that time of year, when the winds and the rains swept down from the north, following the pathways of the rivers.

"I am glad to be safe inside," Thomas said, rubbing his hands together and edging closer to the fire.

At that moment a bolt of lightning struck one of the tall sassafras trees directly outside, splitting it with thunderous action and sending splinters of wood, as sharp as arrows, in all directions.

They both jumped at the sudden burst of noise, but it was Mary who rushed to the window to see the amount of damage done.

"It's all right," she said. "The tree has fallen away from the porch."

"Well, I hope it isn't an omen—this storm—of worse things to come."

Mary remained at the window, watching. The acrid odor of sulfur permeated the entire compound, but so far, it looked as if there were little damage besides the fallen tree. The rain would, more than likely, keep down an unwanted forest fire, which happened often when lightning struck.

Thomas, finally turning his back to the hearth, said, "Were you in Savannah the day Oglethorpe left the colony?"

"No."

"Well, I remember William Stephens talking about the storm that day. It brought down the giant tree under which the general had pitched his tent that entire first year. To me, that didn't sound like a good omen for Savannah."

"I'd be more worried if I were Stephens himself," Mary countered, coming to rejoin her husband at the fire. "I remember that the day he came to Savannah, a buzzard lit on the sloop right beside him."

The two laughed together, the tension of the storm suddenly eased.

"I think I'll go and see how Singing Rock is coming along with the supper." Mary left the keeping room and walked toward the back of the large house. From there, it was a short distance to the separate little kitchen. She took the shawl hanging from the peg. And sheltering her head from the rain, she rushed across the small patch of ground, where small riverlets were already eroding the yard.

Singing Rock's movements were slow. She was growing old, and that was why Mary had seen to it that the woman did nothing but cook the meals. Doby, the young boy that Mary had taken in after he'd run away from the orphanage, was now her helper.

But as Mary looked around the kitchen, she saw no sign of the boy, "Where is Doby?" she inquired. "He's supposed to be helping you."

"He's here, mistress."

"Are my eyes growing dim? I don't see him."

Singing Rock laughed and pointed toward the large wooden cask that held the flour. "He's hiding from the storm."

"Doby, come out from behind that cask."

Slowly, the boy stood and began to walk toward her. "Yes, mistress?"

"Go and set the table," she instructed, ignoring the frightened look on his freckled face. "And put down an extra plate, as usual, in case Mr. Abraham should return in time to eat with us.

"And be sure to wipe your feet before you go into the house."

Once he had disappeared, Mary said, "You would think that a boy brave enough to run away to the wilderness would be equally brave when it came to facing storms."

"Edward Walking Stick was afraid of storms, too," Singing Rock reminded her.

"Yes. Maybe that's why I find it so hard to get angry with Doby."

A few minutes later, Doby splashed his way across the yard and ran into the kitchen. "He's come," the boy said in an excited voice. "I be settin' a place for him every night for the past three weeks. And he's here."

"Are you talking about Mr. Abraham?"

"Yes, mistress. He's as wet as an otter. Fell in the river, he did, when the boat hit a log floatin' downstream."

Mary grabbed her shawl, put it over her head, and ran toward the house. He was finally back. She had waited so long for the news of his meeting with the trustees.

"Abraham," she called out.

But it was Thomas, her husband, who answered. "Don't come in just yet, Mary. Abraham is taking off his wet clothes."

"Then I'll get some hot cider for him, Thomas, while you get a trade blanket from the store."

"I'd rather have a hot rum toddy, Mary," Abraham requested.

She retraced her steps down the narrow hall. She laughed as she noticed the muddy moccasin prints. Here she had reminded Doby to wipe his feet, but in the excitement of Abraham's return, she herself had forgotten.

By the time she got back from the keeping room, Abraham was already seated by the fire, with the red trading blanket wrapped around his body. His large feet were bare, but his face was covered in a two-week-old beard.

"Welcome back, Abraham," she said, handing him the hot mug of delicately spiced rum. She saw that he was still shaking from the cold.

"It's good to be back," he said. "Good to be anywhere," he added, "besides on the blasted water."

"Well, what happened, Abraham?"

He hesitated. But one look at Thomas's disappointed face told her that his brother had not brought good news.

"I'm afraid that the trustees did not approve your claim."

Mary became furious. "And what was their excuse this time?" she demanded.

Rather than answering, Abraham began to cough and sneeze. Thomas quickly spoke up. "Let the man get his breath, Mary. We have the rest of the evening for him to tell us what happened."

A disappointed Mary looked at her husband. He was right, of course. One of the few times. She nodded, indicating that she was willing to wait. After all, she already knew the outcome. The explanation would not change that.

"Find some dry clothes for him, Thomas. I'll go and help Singing Rock finish cooking the supper."

With Abraham dressed in Thomas's spare clothes, they sat down to eat. Singing Rock remained in the room while Doby dashed back and forth from the house to the kitchen for the platters of steaming, hot food.

For Mary, the succulent food that Singing Rock had been so careful to prepare had the taste of dried sea oats. It stuck in her throat, but she went through the motions of eating it and washing it down with the muscadine wine.

It was Abraham who appreciated the food. As Singing Rock served him another portion of venison and plum sauce, with a great wedge of tuckahoe bread, he looked up at her and said, "Singing Rock, it was thinking of your wonderful cooking that kept me going on that awful trip from Portsmouth to Charlestown."

A flicker of satisfaction appeared briefly across Singing Rock's weathered face, and then was gone. "I have a special dessert for you, too, Mr. Abraham."

Thomas glared at the old Indian woman and felt a stirring of jealousy. She had never taken the trouble to fix him anything special in all the time that he and Mary had been married. But then he became ashamed of his thoughts. After all, Abraham was like the prodigal son who had returned home. It was appropriate for him to enjoy the fatted calf. Yes, Thomas could afford to be generous, even to providing his brother with the dry clothes on his back.

It did not occur to Thomas that Abraham had never left his family in anger, as he had, to wander the world, or that the near-threadbare clothes loaned him bore little resemblance to the fine garments of the biblical parable.

"Will we be allowed a taste of this fine dessert, too, Singing Rock?"

She looked at the man seated at the end of the table from her mistress. She had never liked him, this fellow who could change skins quicker than a snake. But she disguised her dislike for her mistress's sake. "Yes, Mr. Thomas, there's enough for everybody."

Honey and wild cinnamon were mixed with the dried apples that had been cooked to perfection under the baked crust. And spread over the entire steaming dish were great globs of snowy cream, freshly made from the early-evening milking by Doby.

"Singing Rock, you have outdone yourself," Abraham said, finally pushing himself away from the table.

"Very good," Thomas agreed. "As usual."

"Doby, you may begin clearing off the table," Mary instructed. Looking at the two men, she said, "Shall we take our chairs back to the fire?"

They left the dining end of the long room, taking their comfortable chairs with them to arrange around the fire.

Mary was watchful, observing Doby going back and forth, until finally the table was clear except for the bowl of dried flowers in the center.

When they no longer had anyone to overhear the conversation, Mary said, "All right, Abraham. I have given you sufficient time to recover. Now tell me what happened in London."

He began to speak, filling her in on all the preliminary procedures, the hiring of a lawyer, his and his brother Adam's petition for an audience with the Board of Trade, who oversaw the business of the trust.

"In essence, Mary, the officials have referred the matter back to the Provincial Council in Savannah. To prove who you say you are, and that you have a real claim to the land, your petition has to go through William Stephens and his council."

Mary, who had kept her temper under control, now lashed out. "And who are these men across the ocean who have come up with such a position? Are they not aware that the original treaty between James and the Creeks, giving them permission to land their colonists at Yamacraw Bluff, acknowledges me as queen, with all sovereign rights? Why should I have to go through that pompous ass Stephens? He wasn't even here at the treaty signings."

"Now, calm down, Mary," Thomas urged. "I'm sure that it can all be resolved.

"Adam is already appealing the decision in London. But the lawyer suggests you show your good faith by going through the motions here that the trust has suggested."

"I'll do more than that," Mary said, her temper still at white heat. "If they want proof that I am queen, then I'll gather my warriors around me—Malatchee, too—and in a body, we will descend upon Savannah. Let the town get a taste of what it would be like—to have the Creeks and their allies as enemies, if I so chose."

"Do you think it would be wise, Mary, to—"

"Do not have the heart of a turkey, Thomas. If you don't want to go with me, then you can stay here."

She turned to Abraham, her brother-in-law. "Will you go with me, Abraham?"

He grinned. "I wouldn't miss your performance for any amount of money, Mary."

"Then, I, too, will go," Thomas said. "And although I will carry no weapon, I will dress for the occasion in the whole armor of God."

"I thought you had thrown out your surplice, Thomas."

He frowned at his wife. "No, I still have it."

"How many warriors are you talking about?" Abraham asked.

She paused, remembering Tomochichi's advice to James when the situation was so grave—to take only a small retinue to show that he was coming as a friend. That would be good advice for her, as well. She did not want to start a war—only to make Stephens see that she had waited long enough for what was rightfully hers.

"I could raise seven thousand—"

"Mary," Thomas cautioned, a look of alarm on his face.

"…but I will ask Malatchee for only a hundred." She smiled at both men. "I would not wish to give William Stephens an early death, before he had a chance to acknowledge my claims."

# Chapter 35

In July 1749, when the miasmas hovering over swamp and marsh seemed as impenetrable as the canebrakes along the rivers and the land suffered under an uncompromising sentence of heat, the Queen of the Creeks traveled toward Yamacraw Bluff.

With her were her cousin, King Malatchee, one hundred of his braves, and her husband, Thomas. In Abraham's place was the youngest brother, Adam; for Abraham had been summoned back to England.

The town of Savannah bore little resemblance to the earlier colony. Immigration was now at a standstill, and many of the original colonists had either moved to Carolina or gone back home in disgust. Continuing squabbles over land grants, rum, and slaves had divided the people. And although the laws had finally been changed that year to allow rum and slaves in the Georgia settlements, this right had little effect on the economy. Even with larger land grants, food crops were neglected in favor of mulberry trees and the production of silk.

Nearly every man seemed to be out for himself, pressing for a higher position, with entitlements suiting his more elevated station in life. And footing much of the bill for it all was Parliament; for private investors had seen little return for their money and had turned elsewhere to seek a profit.

This was the political climate of Savannah—as indifferent to the public good as the weather itself— with no hand, no leaf stirring...until the news of Mary's arrival reached the tavern on the town square.

"Indian Mary has come to town—and she's brought a band of howlin' warriors with her. Stephens has given orders to round up the volunteers. It looks like he's expectin' trouble."

The men quickly downed their rum, grabbed their muskets, and headed toward the powder magazine where the militia's ammunition was stored.

"I ain't never been in a massacre before," one young man named Corbin Larson confided to the older man beside him. "I hear it's a terrible painful thing, losin' your scalp."

The other man said, "I don't understand it. Must be a false alarm. Mary's always kept the peace before."

A voice behind him said, "I was ridin' in Noble's patrol boat the other day—"

"You mean his pleasure boat," another voice cut in.

"Well, whatever you want to call it. As I was sayin', he'd been warned that something like this might happen. The woman's powerful mad with President Stephens."

Henry Tutwiler, on the other side, laughed. "That's nothing new. So is half the colony."

As the horse guard and local militia patrolled the streets that night, and the women and children hovered behind closed doors, they all listened to the sounds coming from beyond the bluff, from the Old Town, the abandoned Yamacraw village that Tomochichi had deeded back to Mary.

The steady beat of the tomtoms, the singing and chanting of Indians celebrating around the campfire brought an uneasiness to those within the city. But one young Englishman, Adam Bosomworth, encamped with the Creeks, was enjoying every terrifying moment.

As a lad, he had been impressed with the sight of the Indian delegation sailing down the Thames. He had even memorized their names—Tomochichi, Toonahowie, Umpyche. He'd followed them throughout London. After that, when they had played their boyish games at school, Adam had always chosen to be an Indian from the colonies, with scraps of fur, secreted from his mother's sewing box, wrapped around his neck, like the otter skins in the portrait painted by Verelst.

But this was not a fantasy. He was living the real experience, because his brother had married an Indian queen.

By the next day, Adam was disappointed. Mary had chosen to leave the majority of the warriors behind as she, her husband, and King Malatchee went into Savannah to meet with Stephens. All day Adam waited, and into the night. Finally, the small group returned to camp.

"What happened?" Adam asked, cornering his brother.

Thomas was hesitant to speak until Mary was out of hearing. "Stephens said he could not listen to Mary's petition today. The council was not in session. So he entertained Malatchee, showering him with presents. But he didn't bother to give us any," he added.

"Does this mean we have to go back to the Forks and wait?" a disappointed Adam inquired.

"No. We'll remain here."

"But for how long?"

"The council meets tomorrow. Stephens promised to send for Mary when they were ready to hear her."

"Then why did she look so angry just now? It would seem that the news would make her happy."

"Mary has long ago given up believing what the man says. She told him so, not the most diplomatic way to go about it. Mary warned him that if he ignored her again and did not send for her so that her petition could be settled peaceably, then she would let loose an entire Creek army on Savannah and secure her rights by force."

The eagerness showed in Adam's young face. "Then we might march into Savannah after all."

"Yes."

The sun rose in the village that cried out with old ghosts. Few remnants of its earlier days remained. Yet, the wooden council house where Mary had first taken James to meet the mico Tomochichi, still stood. The structure had lost its roof, but the rounded clay seats were still in good condition.

Mary stood for a while at the entrance. Then she finally walked in, taking a seat at the far end, where she watched the motes of dust in the sunlight overhead dancing a shadow dance of memories.

There she remained alone, waiting for word that Stephens and the council were ready to receive her petition. All morning she waited, eating nothing. The sun ascended to its zenith and still no messenger had been sent.

When Adam finally appeared in the open doorway, Mary, hoping he carried good news, said, "Have you brought me the message from Stephens?"

"No, Mary. Only a pail of water from the spring. I knew you must be thirsty."

Much later in the afternoon, Mary realized that Stephens intended to ignore her. So she left the council house and gave the signal to get ready for the march into Savannah.

Mary dressed carefully, removing all vestiges of her English heritage. Her black hair was braided in two long plaits, held in place by the beaded red band about her waist, the color symbolizing the power of women in the matriarchal Indian culture. The deerskin dress was new, but the amulet about her neck recalled ancient powers.

Yet, the most striking aspect of her appearance was her face, half-hidden under the sacred pigments. Once again she had proclaimed her royal lineage to Emperor Brims, as she had done so many years before when Red Horse and his braves had come upriver to destroy her father's trading post and the entire settlement of Ponpon.

The jagged streak of lightning, the crescent upon her forehead, and the circles upon her cheek linked her to the most powerful clan of all—the Wind—with kinship traced from Sister Moon and Brother Sun, giving her rights unquestioned by all her subjects.

She was now ready to march into Savannah.

Thomas, dressed in his linen surplice, took up his position at the head of the procession, with Mary and Malatchee. Adam, determined to play some role in the drama, grabbed up one of the Indian drums from the encampment, for every military parade that he had ever watched had a drummer.

By the time they neared the gates of the city, Adam began to beat the drum in tempo to the marching of moccasined feet.

At the courthouse steps, an unhappy William Stephens waited to receive the Indian delegation, while the militia, stationed at strategic spots, held their muskets ready.

Stephens had gambled and lost—but only the first hand. Of course, he had hoped that Mary would not be so brazen as to challenge him, for it was not the best of times, with the garrison at Fort Frederica recently disbanded. Knowing he and his militia would have to handle the problem, he had already devised a plan.

He would continue using delaying tactics, trading on his knowledge of the Creeks' love for strong drink and presents. Finally, when Mary saw that nothing was going to come of this matter, she would leave peacefully. Yes, he would have to be pleasant, but firm.

With the sound of the drumbeat growing louder, the volunteers, called into action, tightened their hands around the stocks of their muskets.

"I don't see why we don't just shoot them all once they come through the gates and be done with it," young Corbin announced.

"No," Henry cautioned. "If we killed Mary, their queen, the entire Creek Confederacy would be down on us before we could turn around."

Corbin shook his head. "I'm confused by all this, Henry. If it's common knowledge that she's their queen, why doesn't Stephens go ahead and admit her claims?"

"The land, man! Two of the islands she was promised under the treaty with Oglethorpe have already been sold—to members of the council."

A third man spoke up. "And the only reason someone hasn't been given St. Catherines is because the Bosomworths rushed out and built a little house on it and stocked the island with cattle and horses."

In one of the newer houses built near William Stephens's town house, Annabelle Pettipoole Larson tightly held her baby in her arms and whispered to her neighbor, Hepsibah Grunewald, "I don't understand it. Before she died, Mama always spoke so highly of Mary."

"People change, Annabelle," Hepsibah answered. "Maybe this woman has lived among the savages so long that she's reverted to their ways, despite her English heritage."

"Yes, that could be true. I remember when she used to visit Mama. I was a little afraid of her, even then. Oh, how I wish Papa was here with Corbin."

The baby began to cry and Annabelle's attention returned to her baby. She began to rock her in her arms. "Hush, angel. You don't want the bad old Indians to hear you and steal you away from me."

"They're comin' through the gates, Mama. You got to come and see." Corby, her oldest, dashed into the house with the news.

In alarm, Annabelle said, "Did you see your papa anywhere? He hasn't been hurt, has he?"

"No, Mama. I mean I seen him, but the Indians don't have no weapons with them. Unless they're hidin' their tomahawks in their loincloths."

He pulled at his mother's dress. "Come with me, Mama. It's the most excitin' thing I ever seen."

"Saw, Corby."

"The most excitin' thing I ever did saw."

Annabelle looked at Hepsibah and shook her head. "Sometimes I wonder why I even bother."

But Hepsibah had become as eager as Corby. "You think it would be all right? I mean, if they have no weapons, don't you think we'd be safe to watch?"

Annabelle looked toward her disappearing son. "Corby, come back. You shouldn't be out in the streets alone."

Annabelle and Hepsibah followed after the child. He pushed his way through the crowd, and as he came to a stop at the edge of the main thoroughfare, they finally caught up with him. But then it was too late to do anything but remain where they were, for only a few yards beyond them, the terrifying procession was in progress.

As Mary came into view of the crowd her head was held in a regal manner, and her eyes had taken on a fierce look that few people were willing to suffer under for long.

Looking from Mary's tall husband, dressed in his long, flowing robe, to the woman beside him, Annabelle whispered, "I didn't realize that Mary was such a tiny woman."

"But how fierce she looks," Hepsibah countered. "And how handsome Malatchee looks."

Hepsibah's nervous laugh caused Megan Tutwiler, standing behind them, to scold her. "How can you even say such a thing?"

"Well, for an Indian, that is."

"You'd better not let your husband hear you talkin' that way about a half-naked heathen. I have a mind to tell the parson on you, Hepsibah Grunewald."

"Oh, please don't do that, Mrs. Tutwiler. I've already been denied Communion once this month."

"Have you thought that all of us may have taken Communion for the last time?" Annabelle said, with tears in her eyes. Shifting the baby to one hip, she reached out and took Corby's hand, as if to be linked with her family during the last moments of her life. "Oh, if Corbin were only beside us, I wouldn't be so afraid to die."

As the procession passed by, the women watched in utter silence. No one stirred, as if by remaining perfectly still, they could escape unwanted attention to themselves.

But it was not to be. Toward the end of the procession, as wave after wave of Indian braves had passed by, one of the older Indians at the end paused before Annabelle. He reached out and touched the blonde hair of her baby girl, as if he had never seen the color before. Annabelle stood frozen to the ground, praying that he would soon walk on. But then the gold necklace around her neck caught the sparkle of the late afternoon sun, and the old Indian's eyes were diverted from the baby. He pointed to the necklace. "Pretty," he said.

In terror, Annabelle smiled and said, "You like it? Then I'll give it to you." Quickly she removed the necklace and held it toward him.

"Me take?"

"Yes, you take."

In delight, he put it around his own neck and then rushed to catch up with the main body of the procession.

"Let's go home," Hepsibah whispered. "I don't think I can stand this another minute."

Annabelle was numb with fright as her friend led them from the crowd.

"Mama, why did you give that Indian the necklace Grandma Coreen left you?"

"Hush, Corby," Hepsibah admonished. "Can't you see your mama's had an awful experience?"

As Mary, Thomas, and Malatchee reached the courthouse, William Stephens, ignoring Mary, stepped down to greet the King of the Cowetas. Acting as if nothing untoward had happened the previous day, he said, "I am glad to see you again,

Malatchee. Come, the council and I have prepared another feast for you and your braves. And there is a goodly supply of spirits, as well."

Malatchee, like Tomochichi, had learned a favorite phrase to use with officials. In his halting English, he said, "I am happy to eat and drink with the mirthful men."

Stephens concealed his smile of satisfaction. Turning to Mary, he said, "And, of course, in your capacity as interpreter, you and your husband are also invited."

# Chapter 36

"Malatchee did not come to Savannah merely to eat and drink with you, William Stephens."

"Then let the fellow tell me himself what his business is. But the discussion will be much more pleasant over a tankard of rum."

Stephens, turning his back to Mary, put his arm around the Indian in a spirit of camaraderie. "Come with me, Malatchee, to my own house. My servants have been busy all day preparing a feast for you and your braves."

A ripple of pleasure spread through the ranks of the Indians at the promise of food and spirits. In no time Stephens had effectively lured the King of the Cowetas away from both Mary and Thomas.

The young king looked back for some sign of his kinswoman, but she had been lost in the crowd. With Malatchee's disappearance, there was nothing left for Mary to do but to follow.

Used to being entertained by the French, the Spanish, and the English, Malatchee, upon reaching Stephens's house, accepted the drinks that his host pressed upon him. And in a mellow mood induced by the spirits, he was quite willing to smoke the pipe of peace with the Savannah official.

Amid the aroma of the calf roasting in the pit permeating the open air and the rush back and forth from Stephens's house by his servants preparing the great spread of food, the Indian braves took their places in every available outdoor space. Sitting cross-legged, they waited in anticipation. Not far off were members of the militia with their guns poised.

Now was the appropriate moment for which Stephens had been waiting. In a confidential manner, he said, "Tell me, Malatchee, why have you brought your braves to Savannah?"

Having little command of the English language, Malatchee looked around for Mary. Only Thomas was visible at the edge of the crowd. So he motioned for Thomas to come to his side.

After talking briefly with Malatchee, Thomas served as interpreter for the young king's words. "To see that my kinswoman receives the title to her inheritance."

"Translate this for me, Thomas," Stephens said, his temper flaring. "Tell Malatchee that as far as the council is concerned, Mary has no claim to anything in this colony. And if he believes so, then Mary has duped him.

"Tell him, Thomas, that I consider the woman your half-breed wife, nothing more, and as such, a mere chattel with no legal existence under English law. And that if she thinks she can force us to ratify some wild scheme of hers, then I will send her to England in irons."

A red-faced Thomas did not have time to translate for Malatchee. Mary, walking through the crowd of braves, had overheard Stephens's words. In extreme anger, she came to face the man.

"You have no jurisdiction over me, William Stephens. I am queen and empress of both the Upper and Lower Creeks, and as such, I need not answer to you or anyone else here."

Stephens's temper began to slip further. "You have gotten out of hand, Mary, with your outrageous behavior—coming into our town and disturbing the peace. General Oglethorpe paid you off before he left for England. You deserve nothing else. By the treaties he made with the Creeks, we own all the land around us. You have no claim to any of it."

His words ignited her resentment against the entire colony, but especially against James. "You dare to talk of your white town, your general and his treaties? A fig for your general! You have not a foot of land in the colony. The very ground you're standing on belongs to me!"

"Mary, do you think you should—"

She brushed aside Thomas's hand on her arm. "Have you even read the treaties, William Stephens? I'm quite familiar with them, since I wrote them all. Yes, all! Not one gives any land away. You were allowed the use of my land, nothing more.

"And as for being reimbursed for my services by either Oglethorpe or the trustees—sir, I have not. And I still have other payments due, signed by the storekeeper Thomas Causton for all the food I supplied this colony for years."

"Causton is gone. There is no way that claim can be verified, since the figures in the books he left behind do not tally."

Malatchee, listening uneasily, but not understanding, looked from his kinswoman to the Savannah official. Stephens, seeing his concern, suddenly broke off the exchange. He smiled and said, "Enough of this arguing. Let us get on with the feast for our visitors."

But Malatchee, after a quick consultation with Mary, declined. He walked away, admonishing his braves to do the same. But like children promised food and presents, few followed their king that night.

By the next afternoon, when many of the braves were still sleeping off the effects of the strong drink, Adam began to think of the way his sister-in-law had been treated the previous evening. It would be good to remind Stephens that he had not yet won, that the Indians were still encamped at Old Town and not likely to go away until the matter had been settled. And so, rounding up a score of braves, he decided that another little parade through the streets of Savannah could do no harm. He had seen the terrified looks on the faces of many of the colonists at the sight of the Indians the day before.

Without telling either Mary or Thomas, Adam set out, with the drum under his arm and twenty of Malatchee's braves marching behind him.

Coming so soon after the first, the second march took the people by surprise. But mixed with the surprise was anger at this young upstart, beating the drum and leading a score of Indians.

"Noble, go out and arrest that young man," Stephens ordered.

"What about the braves with him?"

"Send them back to their camp. I want no trouble with them. But by God, no young Englishman is going to flaunt my authority."

By late afternoon, when Mary inquired as to Adam's whereabouts, one of the braves confessed. The Savannah official had thrown the young man in jail. Alarmed, Mary promptly went into the city to demand his release.

"Christ's blood, I've had enough of you and your family," Stephens bellowed. "Noble, put this woman in jail alongside her brother-in-law."

That evening, Thomas waited. And waited. But neither his brother nor his wife had appeared. "I fear something terrible has happened to them both," he said to Malatchee. "You stay here. I'll go into town to inquire." Dressed in his surplice, Thomas, too, set out for Savannah.

From the adjacent jail cell, Adam looked toward Mary, "I'm sorry," he said. "I thought I was helping, but I've just gotten you into deeper trouble, haven't I?"

"It's all right, Adam. When Thomas sobers up, he will miss us and eventually come looking for us."

She smiled. "I can hear him now, in his most pious voice, apologizing to Stephens for our errant behavior and assuring the man that it won't happen again."

"You know my brother well. Abraham says that Thomas has always been cowed by authority."

"But Adam, you know I'm determined to stay until this matter is resolved. And at least one good thing has come of your action today."

"What is that, Mary?"

"Thomas will have to appear before the council to get us out of jail. He can then hand over my petition officially, something that Stephens has tried to prevent. And with it in hand, they will be forced to act on it whether they want to do so or not."

Adam grinned. "I knew there was some reason I came into Savannah again."

"Oh, no!"

"What's wrong?"

"I've just thought of something," Mary answered. "What if Thomas forgets to bring the petition with him?"

"He wouldn't forget something that important, Mary."

"No, I suppose not."

The next morning, as Mary and Adam waited in their cells, an apologetic Thomas appeared before the council.

Stephens, from his position of president, glared at his former clerk, as if the man had just spilled ink on an important report. "Well, Thomas, what do you have to say?"

"I have come, sir, to request your indulgence. I understand that my wife and brother were put in jail yesterday."

"Yes, Thomas. They caused a disturbance again—something I will not tolerate."

"If it please the council, I have come to request their release."

"Why should we do that? They will only disturb the peace again. No, it's far better to let them remain where they are until they finally come to their senses."

A murmur of agreement spread through the council.

"But, sir, to remain in jail with murderers and thieves is a sentence far too strong...."

"Then, what do you suggest, Thomas? Would your wife be willing to suffer the ducking stool for her behavior?"

"You know as well as I that such humiliation for Mary would have dire consequences."

Stephens knew it, too, but it gave him great satisfaction to picture the proud Mary sentenced to public punishment for gossip and other misdemeanors.

"If I promised that she would not disturb the peace again, would you release her to me?"

"She's a mighty stubborn woman, Bosomworth. How do we know that she will obey you?"

"I'm certain that this experience in jail has been more than enough for her. I would be willing to wager—no, as a man of the cloth, I will make no bets. But I will be willing to pledge my utmost effort to see that she no longer does anything to upset the town."

Stephens looked around the council for confirmation. When each man nodded, Stephens said, "Well then, Reverend Bosomworth, I will place her in your hands. Your brother, too."

The president stood, by his action dismissing Thomas.

Thomas quickly bowed to William and to the men of the council. "Thank you all. You will not regret your decision this day."

As soon as he had left, William sat down. He shuffled the papers before him and said, "The next order of business is to acquire an affidavit of our own, signed by hostile chiefs, swearing that Mary is not their queen. All in favor…"

"Aye." The vote was unanimous.

"And in the meantime we will keep the Indians pacified. That means that we will have to appropriate additional money from the treasury to pay for the gifts. Is everyone in agreement?"

"Aye."

Once again the decision was unanimous.

The jailer came with the keys. First he unlocked Adam's cell, where the young man had spent the night with a pickpocket and a black man who had run away from his master.

"Adam Bosomworth, your brother's waitin' outside for ye."

"What about Mary? Is she being released, too?"

"Yes. The two of ye be good riddance."

The jailer walked over to the women's cell. And as Mary made her way to the door one of the women said, "Pray for me, Mary."

"I will."

But the jailer, overhearing the pregnant woman's plea, laughed and said, "It's too late for prayers for that one. As soon as her belly is empty of the child, she's goin' to be hanged, like the murderer she is."

"Mary, I came as soon as I heard...."

She looked at Thomas. "You went before the council?"

"Yes, I have just come from their chambers in the courthouse."

"And what did Stephens say?"

"Well, I had to apologize for your behavior, and promise him that—"

"No, Thomas. The petition. What did Stephens say when you handed over my petition?"

A look of chagrin covered her husband's face. "In truth, Mary, I was so worried over you and Adam that I completely forgot the petition."

# Chapter 37

Learning that the council had no plans to reconvene for the next several weeks, Mary was determined to wait.

In the meantime, William Stephens made a concerted effort to entertain Malatchee and his braves, who waited with her.

"It would do no harm, William," one of the leading citizens suggested, "during one of those periods of merry mirth, to get Malatchee's mark on a document, swearing that Mary is no queen. I understand that when he is full of drink, he is most amenable to any suggestion."

"He wouldn't even know what he was signing. Especially with all the presents dangled before him," another said with a laugh.

"Yes. We could tell him that he's signing for the presents."

Stephens smiled. "That appears a mite underhanded," he said. "But still, if we're not successful with the other document—I understand we have only one mark, that of an old Chehaw, and he's not an actual chief—then we might be forced into doing something like that to rid ourselves of Mary.

"In the meantime, we must make a public display of our affection for Malatchee."

Thus began the round of dinners and visits to the local taverns. On the Sabbath, Malatchee was even persuaded to attend divine services with Stephens so that the people would see that they had nothing to fear from this handsome young Indian who was a friend to the colony.

Mary's hands were tied during the few weeks of waiting. But hearing that the pregnant woman, Moira, had delivered her baby—a little boy—on the very night that Mary had been released and, learning that no one in the colony had even bothered to take a strip of linen or a shift for the child, she gathered what she could in a basket and visited the jail.

"Ho, I didn't expect to see ye back so soon," the jailer greeted her.

"I have not come as one of your charges, Mr. Pym. Instead I have brought a few things for the new baby in your midst."

"Don't know why you bothered. Nobody else in the town has. He's a sickly little chap—not apt to live much longer than the mother."

"When are you planning to hang her?"

"When the wee one is a month old, unless he dies before then."

The odor in the jail was sickening, despite the vinegar used to wash down the floors. August was not a benevolent time along the coast, with its sea winds stilled and the hot land breezes taking over. Even worse was the midsummer sun's effects upon the public buildings, for the incessant rays baked their walls from morn to night, making their unwilling occupants feel as if they had been shut up in ovens.

As Mary came to the closed cell door she saw the naked baby, hardly stirring on the filthy floor pallet.

"Moira?"

At first the woman, equally lethargic from the heat, did not answer to her name.

"Moira, it's me, Mary. I've brought some clothes for your baby."

A look of hope suddenly gave life to Moira's pale green eyes. "Mary?"

The young woman pushed herself from the floor and walked toward the opening. "You brought something for my little Clive?"

"Yes. And some food for you—some fresh fruit, bread, and cheese…"

"He's goin' to die soon. I have so little milk.…"

"Then I'll bring milk to you, Moira. For both you and the baby. Every day until—"

"Until we're both dead."

"Don't say that, Moira. If we see to the child, he at least will live."

As she waited for the council to reconvene, Mary found a new project to occupy her time—keeping the baby alive.

In Savannah, news of her endeavor was met with derision. As Annabelle and Hepsibah sat on the shaded porch of the Larson house and fanned themselves, Annabelle said, "Have you heard what Mary is doing now? Corbin told me he saw her going into the jail the other day with a basket loaded with goodies for that murderer and her bastard child."

"It seems that she could find something better to do with her time," Hepsibah agreed.

"Well, you know the adage about birds of a feather...."

Mary usually paid no attention to gossip. But late one afternoon as she was returning from her visit to Moira she happened to hear two members of the militia laughing and talking. She would not have stopped to listen if they had not mentioned her cousin Malatchee.

"They've got him over at the new tavern right now, gettin' him drunk enough to sign the paper."

She remained hidden and continued to listen.

"Stephens is a wily old bird," the other agreed. "Indian Mary can't put nothin' over on him."

Mary could make no sense of what they were saying. But a paper? What was Malatchee signing without her advice? Convinced that whatever it was could only be a detriment to both her and Malatchee, she began to rush toward the tavern.

At that time of early evening, just before sundown, when the wind shifted and a slight breeze began to stir, the new tavern was crowded and noisy. And that suited Muckross just fine.

Doing without whiskey and rum so long had made these Georgians a thirsty bunch. Yet, it had been a sound decision that day to open another tavern, leaving his son, Reuben, to run the one in Charlestown. It wasn't often that a former indentured servant could come so far as to be able to set up his son in business, too.

But few people knew about his past, not even his second wife, Hannah. It didn't seem so important, after all these years. For he had been a thriving tavern keeper when he had met her. That was one of the good things about being in a new country. Despite his lowly background, he was now a leading citizen, with acreage to build a plantation on and a thriving business in town. With a sense of pride, he looked around at the men in his tavern: President Stephens, the magistrate, the justice of the peace.

But at the sight of a woman bursting into his tavern, he lost his good mood. Muckross walked toward her to stop her. "Look here, woman. This is no place for you. Go home where you belong."

Mary stared at the man blocking her way. He was fat and had little hair on his head. What was left was completely white, matching the more robust set of side whiskers. His blue eyes were half hidden under folds of flesh, but still, there was something familiar about him.

"I'm looking for someone," she answered, undaunted by his manner.

"Then tell me who it is and I will send him outside."

"Muckross?"

"No. I'm Muckross. What is your husband's name, for I reckon that he's the one you're looking for."

"Don't you recognize me, Muckross?"

Just as there was something in his appearance that had caused her to remember her father's former servant, so there was in Mary's voice a quality that vaguely stirred the memory of the tavern keeper. He stared at her for a moment.

"Mary? Mary Musgrove?"

"Yes. But Musgrove no longer. I'm Mary Bosomworth now."

At the name, he became slightly ill. He took his apron and wiped the sweat forming on his brow. Here was someone who could ruin his standing in the community. "Please go, Mary. Don't make a scene for my sake. I've come up in the world...."

The chilling look that he remembered so well took over. "I'm not interested in you, Muckross. Only in rescuing Malatchee from William Stephens."

He watched as she searched the crowd, and then, spying him, Mary marched up to the small group gathered around the king.

"Malatchee, what have you done?" Her Muscogee words did not need to be translated.

"Too late, Mary," one of the men crowed. "Malatchee has just put his mark on this official paper, saying that you are not a Creek queen. Now you will have no need to stay in Savannah any longer. We have called your hand."

The full brunt of her fury landed on Stephens's shoulders. "You are responsible for this crime against me, William Stephens. You know he had no idea what he was signing."

With the witnessed document in his hands, Stephens had no need to be tolerant of Mary's behavior. "The crime is yours," he said, "for disturbing the peace again. I warned you, Mary. This time you are going to jail and your stay will be quite lengthy. Noble, call the guards and arrest this woman!"

Malatchee, too drunk to understand everything that was going on, nevertheless seemed to understand what Mary asked of him. But to make sure that her instructions would be carried out, she repeated the same message to the brave beside him. Both appeared distressed as Mary was carried away.

"Have another drink, Malatchee," someone urged, but he shook his head.

"Then, Corbin, escort the king and his braves to the gate. It's getting late and I expect they would like to return to their own camp."

Seeing Mary rough-handled by the two guards distressed Muckross, but he could not afford to intervene. As he served drinks to the men at one of the tables a curious voice said, "You acted as if you recognized the woman, Muckross."

He carefully wiped the spilled rum from the table. "Might have. Her husband, John Musgrove, used to come in sometimes to my tavern in Charlestown."

With a bland expression, he said, "Will there be anything else, gentlemen?"

"Yes," a voice at the next table answered. "One more round, to celebrate our victory tonight."

Muckross went behind the wooden bar and opened another cask, all the time hating himself for his cowardly behavior.

For her second incarceration, Mary arrived just in time to view the public whipping of the escaped

slave, Sam. His master, Badger Grice, had arrived to take him
back to the lowland plantation.

"Not too severe," Badger cautioned. "He's a valuable piece of property and I don't want 'im damaged. Just enough lashes to let 'im know I won't tolerate such behavior again. Then put 'im back in the jail cell, and I'll come for 'im first thing in the mornin'."

He threw an extra coin toward the man with the cattails.

"Thank ye, gov'nor. Can I do anything else for ye?"

"No. But if you have any trouble with Sam, you can reach me at the new tavern. I still have dust in my throat from the long journey."

"It saddens me to see ye back, Mary." Mr. Pym, the jail keeper, grinned as he locked her up for the second time. "Sounds like ye'll be spendin' quite a bit of time here, maybe even after the hangin'."

"That's not amusing, Mr. Pym."

"Didn't say it was."

He stared at the young woman feeding her child and winked. Ignoring him, Moira turned her back until he had gone. Then she looked at Mary, but said nothing.

Finally, Mary spoke. "It looks as if I'm back to stay awhile, Moira."

"I don't have much time left with my baby, do I?"

"No."

"How much longer? I lose track of the days, just sittin' here."

"A little less than two weeks."

"Oh, Mary. I never asked a livin' soul for anything but to be left alone. But I'm about to ask the biggest favor of you."

"What is it, Moira?"

"After I'm…" Moira swallowed and tried again. "After I'm gone, would you look after my little Clive? He don't have nobody else but me."

"Yes, Moira. I'll take care of him. When I get out of here, I'll take him back to my house on the Ogeechee. When he's old enough, I'll tell him about you, and what a loving mother you were to him."

"Oh, thank you, Mary. Somehow, knowin' he'll be took care of, it won't be so bad when…."

"Don't think of that now, Moira. You have almost two whole weeks to be with him."

"With him, and a friend. For the first time in my life, I have a friend." She reached out and shyly touched Mary's hand.

From the nearby cell, Mary heard a muffled moan. She knew it was Sam. Sitting in the hot jail cell, she could not feel sorry for herself. She would be getting out soon, with little damage done, if Malatchee followed her instructions.

That night Mary could only feel sorry for Sam and Moira.

# Chapter 38

By the next morning, Malatchee and his hundred braves had disappeared from the encampment at the edge of Savannah. They had quietly vanished, with no one realizing it until several days later, when Stephens finally sent one of his servants to spy out the camp.

"Not even a piece o' firewood left," the young boy said when he returned.

"What about the Bosomworth brothers—Thomas and that young firebrand Adam?"

"No sign of them either."

"Looks like you finally done it, William," the justice of the peace said. "Congratulations."

Stephens shook his head. "Don't congratulate me, yet. Mary's still in Savannah."

"But in jail, William. I hope you let 'er stay there till she rots."

"No, I don't dare keep her in there too long."

"Why not? She's been abandoned by her own people and that husband of her'n."

"That's what makes me so uneasy. No, knowing Mary, she's busy hatching up something. And when we least expect it, the Indians will descend on us again."

"Then it would be a good idea, wouldn't it, to tell Noble to double his patrols? So they can't ketch us off guard?"

Stephens nodded.

"And it wouldn't hurt none to send to Carolina fer some more rangers."

While Stephens and the justice of the peace talked, Mary waited expectantly for Thomas to appear. One day passed, and then two. Now, on the third day, she was really worried.

Perhaps Thomas and Adam had both gone with Malatchee. But if they had, without bringing her a change of clothes or money, she was in for a difficult time if she had to remain in jail until they returned.

She had some money with her, it was true, but it would not be nearly enough for her own needs, much less for Moira and the baby. She had seen the bargaining that had gone on with Mr. Pym. She could only do the same until her money ran out. And after that? Mary put that thought out of her mind.

"So ye'll be wantin' fresh milk and food every day, will ye?" he asked.

"Yes."

"It'll cost ye, Mary."

"I'm aware of that, Mr. Pym."

"Twice the price. I got to have my little stipend for goin' to the trouble."

Mary smiled. "Yes. Newgate prices," she said. Suddenly she inquired, "How long were you in?"

"Never. Who told ye such a lie?" he demanded, his face puffing up with anger.

"No one. But I notice that you run this place exactly like Newgate, so it stands to reason that you would be familiar with it."

"Had a relative who was once a warden there," he confessed. "But that don't tell me how you would know what went on."

"I once had a friend who visited the prison. He described it in detail."

Pym grinned. "Then he musta explained to ye how important it is to stay on the good side of the warden."

Mary smiled and nodded. "When you order the food, I'd also like a large bucket of water. It doesn't have to be springwater. But I want it fresh."

"Don't tell me ye're plannin' on takin' another bath."

"Then I won't."

"Waste o' money, I can assure ye, Mary. Two baths in one week. Why, I hardly take two baths in one year. You half-breeds must be a lot dirtier'n me."

"It's for the baby, too," she admitted.

The days in jail passed, alternately quick and slow. Despite the intense heat, each day ended much too soon for Moira, carefully marking off the days until she was forced to meet her Maker. But for the impatient Mary, the days dragged interminably. Yet she did not complain, for she was aware of time running out for her cellmate.

Mary's money also ran out, and when it was gone, the fresh milk and food stopped. Mr. Pym refused to extend her credit.

Where was Thomas? Why had he sent no message to her? And how much longer would she have to remain, illegally held and seemingly forgotten?

Mary looked at the baby on the pallet. He appeared sickly. Within a few days the progress he'd made was negated. Moira's milk was still not sufficient to nourish the child.

On the island of St. Catherines, Thomas remained hidden in the little house. He had fled from Savannah only an hour after he'd received word that his creditors from Carolina were planning to arrest him for his debts.

He was in dire straits now, because of all the cattle he'd bought on credit. And Mary could not help him. She had enough troubles of her own in Savannah.

Who would have thought that the affair would turn into such a stalemate? Mary should have watched over her cousin Malatchee more carefully. Yes, it was both their faults that he was in such a bad situation.

There was only one thing left to do—throw himself on the mercy of his former employer, William Stephens. If the man would not recognize Mary's claim, then at least he should give her her share of gifts allotted to the Indians by treaty.

Lighting the small oil lamp, Thomas sat down to pen his request to President Stephens.

Along the inland waterway linking Charlestown to Savannah, Abraham Bosomworth sat in the small boat and watched the Indian oarsmen. One short, one long—the strokes were unusual. But he could see how effective they were, for the boatmen did not seem to get weary as the boat skimmed over the water with such grace and speed.

It had been a long, tiring trip on the ocean, with a great storm advancing directly behind them. The waves had been high, even washing a man overboard. Abraham had been thankful to arrive safely on land. He was thankful now that he had been lucky enough to get a ride with the rangers so soon after landing in Charlestown.

He hoped that Mary would not be disappointed with the news he brought. Although the family lawyer had gained another audience with the trustees, they had promised nothing. But at least they were willing to listen if Mary presented her petition personally before them.

That would mean a trip to England for her and Thomas. Abraham knew that Mary did not have enough cash for the passage or living expenses in London while she waited to be heard. He wasn't sure whether she would be able to raise it.

Late that evening, as the boat drew up to the landing below the bluff, a scout turned to Abraham, who had spoken little on the way down the inland waterway. "Will you be stayin' long in Savannah?" he inquired.

"No. I'm headed farther south."

"Then, more than likely, you'll be missin' the uprising."

"What uprising? Are the slaves in revolt again?"

The man glanced at the Indian oarsman, who stood only a few feet from him. "No. It's some of the Indians. Their queen is stirring them up to go on the warpath."

"I don't believe that. She's always been friendly to the colony."

"Well, all I know is that President Stephens has her in jail, and he's expecting her warriors to come and try to get her out. The town's awful uneasy. That's why he sent for us—to shore up their militia and horseguard."

"Wouldn't it be simpler just to free her before anything happens to the city?"

"You don't know President Stephens. Stubborn as an ox. Even his own son writes letters against him to the trustees."

That evening Mr. Pym stopped before the women's cell in the jail. It was the last week in August, exactly one month after Moira had delivered her baby.

"Moira, the parson is outside, waitin' to hear your confession and repentance. You ready to see him?"

"No."

"Listen, girl. Your hangin' is tomorrow. This is the last chance ye'll get on this side to say ye're sorry."

"But I'm not sorry, Mr. Pym. I'd do it again if I had the chance."

"That's tellin' him, girlie."

Pym ignored the new cellmate, old Sally, who'd been locked up the evening before for causing a brawl. "Then the Lord ha' mercy on your soul." In disgust, Mr. Pym walked away.

"Mary, you understand, don't you?"

Privy to the sordid story of Moira's abuse and rape at the hands of the man she finally killed, Mary replied, "Yes, I understand, Moira."

"When...when it happens tomorrow, they promised me you could watch from the square. It'll mean a lot to me to see a friendly face in the crowd."

"Do you want me to bring little Clive?"

"No. It might mark him for life. He'll be all right by hisself for a little while."

That night Moira did not sleep. She sat on the pallet and held her child close to her breast. While Sally snored at the other end of the cell, Mary kept the vigil with Moira. The girl was only fifteen, the same age Mary had been when her own world had turned upside down.

Early the next morning, when the horizon looked particularly strange, with streaks of red vanishing into the ominous gray clouds, Mr. Pym jangled the keys as he walked to the cell to unlock it.

"Is it time already?" Moira asked, her face white and drawn.

"Not for you, girl. Ye got another few minutes. Mary's brother-in-law has come to fetch her."

"Abraham?"

"Mary, I tried to get you out last night. But I couldn't. I can't believe they did this to you."

"Well, go on, Mary," Mr. Pym urged. "Ye're free to go."

She hesitated, looking from Abraham to Moira.

"Mary!"

"Wait for me, Abraham. Near the public scaffold. I won't be long." Outside she could hear the crowd already gathering.

Down the river that Malatchee called the Sowanokee Hatchee Thlocka, he and his warriors came, rowing swiftly in convoy, two hundred strong. Seated behind Malatchee was Adam Bosomworth, exhausted but jubilant. They had done it—gone the breadth and width of the land, traveled by river and trace, to the peace towns and the war towns, to get the signatures of all seven kings of the Muscogees, or Creeks, swearing that Mary, Coosaponakeesa, was their queen and empress, with all sovereign rights to the islands of Ossabaw, Sapelo, and St. Catherines.

Now there was nothing to keep her claim from being recognized by President William Stephens and the trustees, not even the paper that Malatchee had been duped into signing.

They hid their canoes in the canebrakes and marched briefly to the bluff. There, they stopped to rest and to eat. In the distance, toward the city, a sound of drums, dismal and menacing, began.

Mary stood where Moira could see her. The green eyes, wide with fright, never moved from Mary's face.

Overhead, the storm clouds gathered, blotting out the sun. From seaward, a gust of wind came, flapping at Moira's dirty calico dress as she was led up the steps and positioned over the trapdoor.

"Murderer!" a voice from the crowd shouted.

Suddenly Moira's golden red hair took flight and lifted in flowing strands that turned and turned as the wind blew, as the raucous crow flew overhead, as Mary watched with eyes seeing beyond past and future, hope and despair, reality and dreams.

"Mary, are you ready to leave now?" Abraham's hand touched her arm. She looked around her. The crowd had gone.

"Yes. But I have to go back to the jail for Clive."

"No need for ye to bother yourself, Mary."

"But I promised Moira, Mr. Pym."

"That's what I mean. No need. The little fellow's dead."

"That's impossible."

"Look for yourself. Sally said it happened 'bout the time the rope was put about his mama's neck. He just made a gurglin' sound, he did, and then stopped breathin'."

Abraham, still at his sister-in-law's side as they reached the street, saw the pain in Mary's face. Feeling fiercely protective, he said, "Let's go back to the Forks, Mary. Today."

"I can't leave now. I have to wait for Malatchee to return with the signatures of all the kings."

Remembering what the ranger had said, Abraham felt a great need to get her out of the city. "These people are never going to recognize your claim, Mary, no matter if Malatchee brings back a hundred signatures. Savannah will only cause you more heartache."

"But can't you see, Abraham? Despite what they have done to me, I still love my father's people. They must be made to realize that the land is sacred. That the treaties are also sacred. If they are not made to honor the very first treaty with my mother's people, then they will have no reason to honor any other.

"No. As long as I live, I will continue the fight."

# Chapter 39

That day in Savannah, when Abraham came to get her out of jail, Mary did not realize how prophetic her words would become—that she would spend the rest of her life fighting for her heritage.

Abraham had been right about William Stephens. Despite the signatures that Malatchee had brought back, the man still would not recognize her claim. She couldn't blame Malatchee for what he did afterward—leaving Savannah in disgust and sending his warriors on a rampage through the countryside, killing the cattle and destroying the crops.

And she understood when he went over to the French, flying the fleur-de-lis beside his own royal flag from his village flagpole, as a symbol of his complete break with the English.

After the episode in Savannah, it had taken her ten more years of heartache, in that time managing to raise enough money to get to England. But that particular trip was no more productive then any of her other efforts. Even when the colony reverted to the crown, she kept on, working through the regimes of two royal governors, until in the end she finally received most of the money due her.

The voice of the royal governor was still strong in her ear: "We are reimbursing you, Mary, for the two islands that were sold. As to the third, St. Catherines, it will be recorded in our books as a gift to you, for your services rendered to the colony these past thirty years."

St. Catherines had been presented to her as a gift—her own land that had always been her Indian heritage.

Now, as she sat on the porch of the plantation house and gazed toward the long, narrow vista ahead, where the setting sun filtered its rays through the leaves of the great oak tree, the ill and weak Mary still clutched the black wolf pelt with her aging hands.

The she wolf had served her well, taking her on the hazardous trip through the past, where she had been forced to converse with ghosts.

Another voice, not of the past, but of the present, intruded, calling her name, each time a little more insistent.

"Mary, you must come inside now. You've been sitting out here all day. Let Sarah and me help you to your room."

Her hands stroked the old fur as she replied, "No, Thomas. I need a few minutes longer. It isn't finished yet."

"She's out of her head, Master Thomas," her bondservant Sarah whispered. "What do you think we should do?"

He had long ago given up trying to force Mary to do anything against her will. "Let her stay out here if she wants. After supper we'll come and check on her again."

At the end of the porch, the tame black crow hopped on one foot. Then he stopped and held his head to one side, as if listening to the conversation.

Noticing the bird, Sarah giggled. "Yes. Let's leave the two old crows out here together."

The man smiled at the buxom young servant. And when he was out of Mary's view, he said, "How would you like to eat in the dining room tonight?"

"Sittin' in her chair, at the other end of the table?"

"Why not? You might as well start getting used to your new place, once Mary's gone."

"But I want much more than her chair, Master Thomas."

"Then I'll give you all her personal items, Sarah."

"Includin' the diamond ring?"

Thomas hesitated. Not once during their married life had Mary removed the ring. It had always been a reminder to him that no matter how hard he tried, he could never displace the memory of the man who gave it to her.

He had planned to sell it once Mary died. But seeing his little Sarah with such a pleading look in her eyes, Thomas capitulated. "The ring, too."

Mary's face gave no indication that she was aware of their conversation. In the past week, Thomas and Sarah had often talked as if she couldn't hear them. But it didn't matter now. Their words, coming through the open window of the dining room, were no more significant than the high-pitched hum of the nearby mosquito.

She held out her hand to catch the light, the facets of the diamond attracting the old crow at the end of the porch. He hopped closer, eyeing the brilliance of the stone.

For twenty-three years Mary had worn the ring given to her by James that night at Frederica. And for twenty-two of those years she had loved and hated him with equal fervor.

He was the one who had driven her into Thomas's arms. And he was the one who had given her such dreams, and then caused her such despair.

For this reason, she had left James's ghost to deal with last. But before she made her reconciliation with him, there was another matter that she would have to take care of first.

She did not mind if Sarah wore her clothes, or slept in her bed, or sat in her place at the table. But the woman would not have James's ring. She would not be the heir to that part of Mary's past.

Mary reached down and twisted the ring, urging it, little by little, along the length of her finger, until it was finally off. She closed her hand around it, feeling the warmth of the gold, the coldness of the stone. And then she leaned over and laid the ring on the ledge of the porch banister. Sitting back, she waited for the glint of the sun to attract the robber bird.

The crow hopped along the ledge, but stopped a short distance away. He pecked at an insect on the silverlace vine and then flew to the nearby bush.

It was a game, played between the woman and the bird, each pretending not to notice the other.

But within a moment or two, the crow was back on the ledge. As the ring reflected the brilliance of the last vestige of sun, he suddenly swooped, picked up the ring with his strong yellow beak and flew toward the thicket at the edge of the marsh.

With a momentary regret, Mary looked down at her bare hand. Only once after James had placed it on her finger had she removed it. And that one time had taken place in London.

It was snowing that day, soon after her arrival to present her petition before the trustees.

As Mary closed her eyes she felt the snowflakes on her nose and smelled the aroma of hot chestnuts roasting over the meager fire farther down the street.

She had finished early at the dressmaker's and had stepped into the tiny tearoom next door to have a hot cup of tea while she waited for Adam to come back with the carriage. The scene came alive, as if it had taken place only yesterday....

All around Mary were the furs that she had spent her life trading. Men in hats of beaver, women in capes decorated with otter walked hurriedly past the window. And great deerskin lap robes, lined in silk, lay across the seats of the nearby carriages, while the footmen waited for their owners to finish their shopping and to return to the comfort of their carriages.

But the fur that she was wearing was the most elegant of all; for Mary had brought the cured skins herself to have them made into a cape for such cold weather. Charlie Bowlegs had done well, matching the furs—luxuriant red fox—which the dressmaker used to line the elegant damask cape and to decorate the cuffs and hood.

Her pride would not allow her to appear before these English trustees as her kinsman Tomochichi had done before her—a child of the forest in borrowed clothes. Instead, she would appear before them in clothes suitable to her station as queen, demanding her rights to be recognized.

As she took another sip of tea a horse-drawn carriage skidded recklessly across the slippery roadway and came to a stop before the tearoom. A curious Mary set down her cup and watched for its occupant to alight.

The door of the carriage finally opened. A woman, with her face shielded from view, hurried into the tearoom, while the carriage sped off, at a pace as reckless as had been its approach.

Quickly, the woman was ushered to an obscure table, out of sight of any passerby. As Mary took measure of her she saw that she was dressed differently from the English. By her actions it seemed that the woman did not wish to be noticed. Yet the uniqueness of her appearance assured that she would be.

When the young girl came back to Mary's table to replenish the tea, Mary said, "Who is the woman who just came in?"

"Oh, m'lady, I dare not say it aloud." She looked around her to see if others were listening. Then she whispered, "It's the Marquise de Mézières. I heard she crossed the Channel without a pass. And if the authorities find out, she'll be arrested for sure. But you mustn't tell anyone, m'lady. For I'd get into trouble for not reporting her."

At the mention of the name, Mary's heart quickened. So it was James's sister, the one who had lived at the Stuart court in France all these years. She had heard of nothing but the Elibank Plot ever since her arrival in England—how Frederick the Great of Prussia had taken up the Stuart cause, giving the Jacobites new hope, with messengers sent back and forth from France to England, carrying plans to capture the Tower of London and other strategic strongholds and even to kidnap the Hanoverian king, himself.

But for whom was this sister of James waiting?

Mary did not have long to wonder; for at that instant a tall man in tricorn hat, with faded red hair combed back into a military plait, walked slowly by. He was older and heavier, but Mary recognized James Oglethorpe.

He stood for a moment, looking up and down the street, and then, he, too, hurried inside the tearoom.

It was too late for Mary to make her escape. She bent over, as if searching for something in her purse as he passed by. She had no wish to speak to this man who had betrayed her. And looking down at the ring, she had no wish for him to know that she was still wearing it, that it had any more significance to her than some bauble she might have worn for a time and then stored in her linen press.

By the time she glanced up, he was seated at a table—not the one where his sister sat, but the one beside it. Mary watched as a clandestine conversation took place between sister and brother. The frown that had mirrored James's displeasure in the colonies now marred his face.

The frown gave way to a look of surprise as he glanced toward the table where Mary sat. So he had recognized her, too. Mary poured herself another cup of tea, this time with the hand that had worn the ring only moments before. She put off looking toward him again. Inevitably, their eyes met.

James stood suddenly, as if coming to her table. But then Adam's carriage pulled up in front and Mary, with nothing to say to James Edward Oglethorpe, placed her money on the table and fled....

Remembering that time so long ago, Mary cried out, "I should have waited to speak with you, James. I know I hurt you that day, almost as much as you had hurt me. It was in your face—that dear, stoical face that so seldom gave away your emotions."

Sanawa, her childhood nurse, had been right. People's lives were like two sticks, crossing for a while, and then moving farther and farther apart as each took a new journey of the soul alone. Now, with the years separating them, Mary realized that James had only played out the destiny that had been allotted to him, just as she had done.

She had not always understood her own destiny. Medicine Woman had told her that she would be Earth Mother of a great nation. But as each son was taken away from her she could not help but question the reason the Great Spirit had given her life.

Now she knew the reason. For she had understood the English. She had understood the

Creeks. As a daughter of both nations, she had finally brought them together in peace.

In the twilight, the gray mist, beginning its journey from the low-lying marshes, moved slowly toward the plantation house on St. Catherines Island. Beyond the palisade, the nickering of a marsh tacky echoed through the trees.

As Mary listened to the sounds around her she saw the great black vulture, the symbol that Emperor Brims had always carried with him to war. With a great flapping of wings, the bird came and took its place in the oak.

Mary wrapped the wolf pelt around her, and still, she kept her vigil of the darkening sky. Finally, she smiled as she saw the eagle gliding in winged splendor past the oak, past the roost of the vulture, and then soaring toward the sea.

"These are the feathers of the eagle, which is the swiftest of birds, and who flieth all round our nations. These feathers are a sign of peace in our land...."

The eagle had gone on ahead. By tomorrow she knew that the vulture would still be there, waiting for her. But she was not afraid.

In her heart she saw the welcoming faces—of her mother, Princess Rising Fawn; her father, Ian Yonahlongi Hatke; Johnny, Tomochichi, and Senauki, and her four sons, all smiling and beckoning to her.

"Thomas," she called out. "I'm ready to go inside now."

The reconciliation of Mary Musgrove Matthews Bosomworth, born the Princess Coosaponakeesa, was complete.

# Author's Note

For over two hundred and fifty years, the importance of Mary Musgrove to colonial America has been swept aside by many historians. Yet it was this most dynamic Native American queen and empress of the Creeks who saved the Southern colonies from disaster, time and again.

She was at James Edward Oglethorpe's side, as interpreter, diplomat, and liaison in his important dealings with the Creek Confederacy. She marshaled the Indian militia of thousands of warriors for England's war with Spain. And, despite adverse conditions, she remained true to her mission of keeping the peace in the Georgia colony for the twenty years following Oglethorpe's final return to England.

In one of the town squares in Savannah, a large statue of Oglethorpe, sculpted by Daniel Chester French in 1910, serves as a remembrance of his importance to the colony of Georgia. Not far away is a large rock in memory of Oglethorpe's friend, the aged Yamacraw mico Tomochichi. In contrast, Mary's historical significance has been diluted to a much-quoted tale portraying her as a "trouble maker" to the colony.

This fictionalized biography (formerly titled *Call the River Home)* is an attempt to remedy the misunderstandings concerning the woman who was born Princess Coosaponakeesa.

The trail to the truth was a tortuous one, sending me to England, to rare books and manuscripts, and to the various colonial records that encompassed the personal accounts of John Wesley, William Stephens, colonist Peter Gordon, and James Oglethorpe, as well as Spanish reports from St. Augustine.

Yet, there was something missing. I knew that I would have to find a new perspective, apart from the standard point of view. The breakthrough came in the library on the Creeks at Ocmulgee National Monument in Macon, Georgia, near the war town of Emperor Brims, with its ancient mounds a reminder of still earlier Indian cultures.

From then on, I immersed myself in all things Indian. And when I went back and reread the standard histories and diaries, I perceived the facts in a new light.

Whenever possible, I have used actual names. When they were lost, I have supplied names—such as Mary's mother, Princess Rising Fawn, and her English fur-trading father, Ian Yonahlongi Hatke. Sometimes I have embroidered one little-known event into several chapters. I have also disposed of Oglethorpe's legendary diamond which he gave to

Mary in a manner consistent with Mary's personality, although the ring's whereabouts still remain a mystery.

In recalling the image of one of the most remarkable women of the 1700s, I have tried to paint a true canvas. I hope her magnificent spirit will be pleased.

Frances Patton Statham
Hilton Head Island, South Carolina

# About the Author

Frances Patton Statham (pronounced Stay/tum) is a musician, artist, writer, and lecturer, with numerous awards in all four disciplines. She received her undergraduate degree, magna cum laude, from Winthrop University, her Master of Fine Arts degree from the University of Georgia, and an honorary doctorate from World University.

As a lyric-coloratura soprano, she has given concerts and lectures in such cities as Singapore, Madrid, Budapest, and Vancouver.

Chosen Georgia Author of the Year in Fiction on three occasions, she is listed in such biographical reference works as *International Authors and Writers Who's Who, World Who's Who of Women, Who's Who of Intellectuals,* and *Personalities of the South.*

She now resides in metro-Atlanta, Georgia.